The Tissue Veil

BRENDA BANNISTER

The Tissue Veil

What's a hundred years between friends?

Published by Silver Crow Books in association with Brown Dog Books and The Self-Publishing Partnership, 7 Green Park Station, Bath BA1 1JB

www.selfpublishingpartnership.co.uk

ISBN printed book: 978-1-78545-146-1
ISBN e-book: 978-1-78545-147-8

Cover design by Kevin Rylands
Internal design by Andrew Easton

Printed and bound by CPI Group (UK) Ltd, Croydon CR0 4YY

1
Emily

Saturday 2 February 1901
"It can't be good for you, Maria," Pa says, "to stand out in this weather."

"I *have* to go," my mother argues. "When will we see a day like this again? I have a slight cold, no more – what other chance will there be to pay our respects?"

The Queen is dead! Victoria, who ruled this country for over sixty years, has died at her home on the Isle of Wight. Ma reads the funeral plans aloud from *The Times* and, oh! what a complicated thing it is to bury a queen. Her coffin must be brought by boat and train to London, then put on a carriage and drawn through the streets – past the Palace, Hyde Park, Marble Arch and so to Paddington and another train to Windsor for her final rest.

Ma wanted us all to set out early to obtain a good place, but Pa expects a tobacco shipment today and can't desert his business. When he sees she is determined, he turns to me.

"Stay by your mother, Emily. There will be great crowds – be sure not to separate. And keep yourselves warm."

Ma thinks it will be best to go straight to Paddington and wait there for the cortège to arrive; that way, she says, we may be ahead of the crowd. But at nine-thirty, when we leave the station, the kerbs are already lined five deep. Ma squeezes through the throng, pulling me with her and ignoring complaints from those on either side. The roads are guarded by policemen and one tells us, "Watch your pockets, ladies. There are villains about who take advantage of a time like this."

We stamp our feet to keep them from turning numb and breathe into our gloves. Ma buys currant cake from a street seller, but is unwilling to give up our place to go in search of a coffee stall. The sky is a sombre grey and unbroken cloud presses down on us, threatening rain or snow. The cortège is expected before noon, but there is still no sign of it by twelve-thirty.

"She better 'urry up," says a joker, "or the train'll go without 'er!" A policeman gives him a disapproving look. At last we see the gun carriage with its sad burden, the new king on horseback and more crown princes than I can count or name. I see that Ma is caught up in the spectacle, despite the cold, but what I cannot credit is the sheer number of troops. Guards, cavalrymen, Scotsmen in kilts, men from the Indian army, sailors – all look polished, brushed and fed, the horses sleek and well-groomed. Yet how can so many be here, at home in London, while my brother Charlie and his comrades want for reinforcements and rations in the heat of South Africa?

The gun carriage enters the station and we watch until we can see it no more. The Queen's coffin now goes on to Windsor with all the kings and princes, leaving her people behind. The crowd seems reluctant to disperse and we cannot get back into the station. We try for an omnibus to King's Cross instead, but so do many others and it takes an hour before we reach the front of the queue. By the time we get back to Stepney, it is almost five o'clock and already growing dark. I feel cold and tired, but Ma is shivering violently and starting to cough.

Pa is not yet home, so I call for Daisy to stoke up the parlour fire and make us some tea. We have been looking into the faces of mourners all day and at first I don't notice the slump of Daisy's shoulders or the blank emptiness of her expression, but Ma follows her eye to the hall table where a long envelope with a War Office imprint lies waiting. It is addressed to Mr and Mrs Watts.

"Open it, Emmie," Ma whispers, "my fingers are too numb."

If only I could turn back time, fold up the page unseen, re-seal the envelope, make the postman take it back; but it's too late. I hold the letter outstretched for all three of us to read. Thousands have marked the passing of a woman who lived a long, long life and died in her bed, but not one of his family was at home to receive this terrible paper which tells us Charlie is dead.

Daisy's grief bursts through the air in a shrill wail, which I feel as much as hear. Ma utters a low moan. As for me, I stand helpless, like someone watching a play.

"Give me a hand, Dais," I say at last, "Ma's chilled to the bone. We must get her to bed."

There has been a certain coolness between Ma and Daisy ever since my brother ran away to war, leaving a letter for our maid but no word for our parents. When she learned that Daisy considered Charlie her sweetheart, Ma tried to argue her out of such a notion. His father would never allow it, she said; besides, Charlie was just a boy but would come back a man: his feelings were bound to change. Daisy had listened in sullen silence.

"It can't be," Ma whispers now. "They must be mistaken – he only turned seventeen last month."

Her eyes are wide and staring. She stretches out white hands and Daisy moves to clasp them, but Ma just slips through her grasp and falls to the floor. Somehow, between us, we haul her upright, drape her arms around our shoulders and guide her upstairs. I fill the stone hot water bottles to warm the bed and drag coals up the stairs to light a fire in her room, Daisy heats some broth and tries to coax her to eat.

All the while, my mind is pushing it back: *Charlie is dead!* No time to enquire or mourn: Ma's needs are too great. At one moment, her face is shining with sweat, the next, she's shivering again. She tosses her head from side to side, muttering to herself, flinging out an arm and kicking off the bedclothes.

"Should we call your Pa at the warehouse?" Daisy asks.

"I'll do it," I say.

Pa has only recently installed a telephone system and Daisy still regards it with terror, flinching every time it rings. Then I realise that Pa will have already left and call the exchange to ask for Dr Reynolds instead.

Dr Reynolds arrives within the half hour and Pa some ten minutes later. The doctor is already putting his stethoscope away, when Pa enters, grey faced, the War Office letter in his hand. In our haste to help Ma, we left it lying on the hall floor. I exchange a horrified look with Daisy, fearing his anger, but he just stands silently watching as Dr Reynolds takes Ma's pulse. The doctor finishes his examination, then takes Pa by the arm and draws him away from the bed.

"Maria has a fever and her lungs are congested, but that should clear with care. I am more concerned that this shock may end the remission in her *underlying* condition."

Pa nods dumbly and holds out the letter to him. "I thought

Charlie would get the restlessness out of his system – come home and settle to the business again. This enteric fever – what is it?"

"A name for typhoid and similar conditions. I am so sorry, Edward."

"His last letter talked of fever and pains in the gut."

"Those are symptoms. He would have grown progressively weaker. The disease is only too common in wartime."

Neither of them looks at Daisy or me. Ma is sleeping fitfully and I reach across the bed to grasp Daisy's hand. My poor brother!

" I don't think you should discuss this with Maria. It would be kinder to let her believe Charlie was killed outright," the doctor says.

"But she read the letter, surely?" Pa replies.

"She may forget the details. I have administered laudanum and you can repeat the dose – half a spoon, no more – in four hours. I'll call tomorrow, early."

Pa groans softly as he strokes Ma's brow. When Dr Reynolds rests a hand on his shoulder, he gives himself a little shake and bids us show the doctor out. I ask if we should make up the bed in Charlie's room so he need not disturb Ma, but Pa won't leave her side. Instead, he asks for an eiderdown, saying he will sleep on the bedroom chaise.

I know he still blames Daisy for not warning us of Charlie's plans. Pa wanted to dismiss her on the spot, but Daisy had always been Ma's special project. Perhaps he blames me too. I found the papers by accident – our own birth certificates and, with them, the birth and death records of a first born brother we never knew we had, an infant who lived only a few short weeks.

"What does it mean?" Charlie had asked, frowning at the dates.

"Ma must have had a baby before you," I said, "a little boy who died."

I feared Pa would catch us snooping and was anxious to put the papers away, but Charlie read them over and over, following the bundle with his eyes when I put it back in the bureau. My brother was tall for sixteen, strong and lean from the hours he spent cycling, the beginnings of a moustache furring his lip. Pa expected him to join his tobacco import business, just as *he* had joined his own grandfather, but Charlie grew restless when Pa and Baines, his warehouse manager, stood on the dockside, talking of exchange rates and margins. His eyes slid off sideways to the ships and the sailors and the promise of distant shores untroubled by arithmetic or a profit and loss account. He lacked only proof of age to pass as old enough to enlist – and I had put it into his hands.

A sudden spasm of coughing jolts Ma into wakefulness and she clutches my father's arm.

"Charlie?" she cries, as if imploring him to say this is all a bad dream.

Pa shakes his head and turns away. I used to envy my brother, who had been sent to college to continue his studies and was destined for a life in the world. All my parents' hopes were focussed on his future; now I wonder how any of us will endure his loss.

Tuesday 5 February 1901

Pa has received another letter, almost too painful to read, written by Charlie two weeks before he died. He was employed at one of the prison camps, where food was short, troops were scarcely better fed than those they guarded and fever ran riot. There was no proper sanitation, he wrote, and they were plagued with flies. *I wish I could see you all,* the letter ends. *If I could sit and read the newspaper to Ma I'd be sure to pick a cheerful story, nothing to do with the dirt and muddle here. Give my love to Emmie and, please Pa, be kind to my dear Dais.*

I think Daisy's feelings are more complicated than mine. Ma took her as a servant when Daisy's own mother died, but from the age of twelve she grew up beside Charlie and me. For most of that time she treated Charlie like a favourite brother, teasing him, spoiling him, letting him get his own way. In the six months before he enlisted, their friendship changed to something more. Perhaps Charlie looked at her with new eyes and saw a pretty, plump girl whose fair curls were forever escaping from her cap, and who, unlike me, never tried to put him down. And maybe Daisy saw the boy she'd always loved growing into a man – and the chance of a better life.

I like to think he would have kept his word, had he lived, and come home to marry her. For all his faults, Charlie was a simple soul – once set on a track he did not waver. If Pa had raised obstacles, he would have become all the more determined and Ma, who has always been fond of Daisy, might have been persuaded to smooth their path. I don't mean to detract from her real sorrow, but Daisy also mourns the chance of becoming a daughter to Ma and being raised from the position of maid.

Ma's weakness and fever have not improved and today, when Dr Reynolds was leaving, I took the opportunity to question him.

"Doctor, when you spoke to Pa the other day, you used the term *remission*. What does that mean?"

He looked at me sharply, apparently surprised that I remembered his words. Perhaps something in the earnestness of my face stopped him from brushing my enquiry aside.

"Remission, Emily, means that the symptoms of a disorder lessen or go away, usually for a time, occasionally permanently. Until recently, your mother has been experiencing just such an improvement in her condition."

"But this condition she has – what is it?"

"It is a disorder of the blood. An imbalance of the cells, the tiny units of living matter which make up our bodies. It's difficult to explain."

"And this is dangerous?"

"It leaves the body open to infection. It no longer fights disease as it should."

"Where does it come from? I know dirty water causes the fever that killed poor Charlie – how do you catch Ma's disease?"

"It is not something you catch, Emily, at least not from another person. *You* are in no danger. I've noticed similar conditions in people who worked in certain industries as children – factories where they use strong chemicals to make glue or paint."

"But that's not Ma's case."

"I know that. There is not always a reason; at least not one that we can discover."

"Is there no cure?" I asked.

"None that is reliable. Some doctors have tried a particular compound, but it contains arsenic, a poison, and your father does not want to risk its use."

"But then...?"

He stopped and seemed to recollect with surprise that he talked to a mere girl.

"Emily, I think a great deal of your mother, but I may only do what I can."

On Saturday morning, I walk to Fenton's store, in Watney Market, to buy black crepe for our hats. I hoped to see Sally, my best friend from school, whose father owns the tailor's shop, but Mr Fenton says she is visiting her grandmother.

Ma knew I missed my friends and would sometimes invite Sally when she finished her lessons, although her tales of my old school friends, or of putting on plays in the classroom, made me even more discontented than before. We had sat together at school, sharing a desk in the front row, our hands raised like flagpoles to answer a question or volunteer to read. The headmaster said he hoped *I* would continue for another year at least, even train as a teacher myself, but, while Pa always said *well done* when I received a merit for my composition or came second in arithmetic, he would rather have heard it from Charlie. He insisted I was needed at home and took me out of school once I reached fourteen. He doesn't see the purpose of extended education for girls. I thought perhaps I might be allowed to get a job instead, but with Ma so poorly it is out of the question.

"Miss Emily! I thought I heard your voice."

Pa's manager, William Baines, comes hurrying from the back of the shop where he is being fitted for a new waistcoat. He's a strongly-made young man of twenty-five or six perhaps, with black waving hair curling into long sideburns and a high complexion. I suppose some people might call him handsome, but his eyes are pale and watery and he peers at you too closely. I once told Ma that he made me feel uncomfortable, but she said I shouldn't condemn a man for his poor sight.

"You are shopping," he says. "Can I help?"

"I've finished my errand. I'd hoped to see my friend, Miss Fenton, but she's away."

"I am sorry for the loss of your brother, miss. Will you let me escort you home?"

"There's no need."

"All the same, let me walk a little way with you. We should be friends, you and I. Your brother's sad fate has left us both with a difficult situation to handle."

There's that same close, almost too familiar stare; I remember what Ma said and force myself to meet his gaze.

"I don't understand, Mr Baines. Losing Charlie is a sorrow we must bear, not a problem for solution."

"I speak of your parents. My job is to take your father's business affairs off his shoulders at this time, just as you support your mother. We should help each other, miss."

"*I* can't make my mother better. It's Charlie she wants."

I didn't mean to answer so sharply; he puts his hand to his brow and blinks his moist blue eyes.

"You blame me, miss. I blame myself. I couldn't help envying my cousin Fred and talking about the war at times. I'm afraid Charlie must have caught my enthusiasm."

I haven't thought about it before, but, yes, perhaps that was when it started. Ma and Pa held a dinner for our friends and neighbours when Mafeking was relieved and all the country was busy *mafficking* as they called the celebrations. Mr Baines told us how his cousin had been at the siege, declaring he would have joined up himself had his weak sight not made him unfit for action. It was the measles, he said, that had damaged his eyes.

"You do better here, Bill," Pa said, "supplying tobacco to our boys."

Dr Reynolds commented it was clean water they stood in

need of, not tobacco, but Charlie listened spellbound. He had always devoured stories of adventure and exploration in Africa and he never tired of hearing about Baines' cousin Fred's exploits.

"Miss Emily?"

Mr Baines holds out a square of perfectly laundered linen and I realise I am weeping. We bickered and fought and were, as people say, like as chalk and cheese, but Charlie was my companion for as long as I can remember.

"I am sorry to have distressed you. Believe me, I didn't know that your brother would be so foolhardy. I'll do all I can to support your father – we must talk again."

He raises his hat and leaves me clutching the soggy mess I've made of his handkerchief. I should feel grateful, I *do* feel grateful that he doesn't treat me as a child; at least he speaks to me as if I have a brain. He's told us he was an orphan, raised by his aunt for a few years, but obliged to fend for himself from the age of thirteen. Pa says Baines pulled himself up by his bootstraps, so I suppose he commands respect, but I don't fully trust him. The waistcoat he was trying in Fenton's was of deep purple brocade, worn beneath a grey wool jacket, and I wonder that he can afford such finery.

2
Aysha

December 2000

The moment Aysha gets off the bus, a blonde girl wearing a white puffa jacket over a football top and jeans jumps down from the wall and grabs her arm.

"Thought you weren't coming!"

"Sorry, Kas. First week of Ramadan – I didn't wake up in time to eat!"

"Here," Karen says, pushing a bag of crisps under her nose.

"Can't, can I?"

"Didn't think you were religious."

"I'm not really. Fasting's more of a family thing. Like you with Christmas."

"They won't know," Karen laughs and the bag of crisps makes a comeback.

Aysha glances at the other students milling outside college. "You reckon?" she says. Her mum would be disappointed if she cheated, and somehow she herself would be too.

"I thought we were going out next week – for the end of term?"

"We can go after college – the sun's down by then. Eid's

just after Christmas, so I can still come round and scoff all your chocolate!"

Karen raises her eyebrows. "Let's get a move on then – you know what Jo's like about latecomers."

"Yes, I happen to think Colin Firth's pretty hot as Darcy too."

Their English tutor, Jo Massey, is addressing her giggling literature group. "But I'd like to think that some of you at least have based your answer on Austen's original novel, not the TV adaptation."

The question is, when and why do Elizabeth's feelings towards Mr Darcy begin to change?

"Well, it's when she sees what a big... um... house he's got, miss," Karen snickers.

Some of the group, which is predominantly female, seem unhappy that romance should exhibit such a mercenary turn, but the Asian girls nod, seeing analogies between Darcy's stately home and income and a chain of restaurants or a British passport.

"What do you think, Aysha?"

"Well, she couldn't ignore it, could she – the house and money, I mean? Not when women couldn't work to support themselves. But it's like she can see he's got reason to be proud – that and hearing other people's good opinions of him."

Jo nods, pleased, and continues trying to coax from each student a response to the words on the page.

"That was all right," says Aysha to Karen when the session ends.

The girls clatter down the broad staircase to the canteen, where Karen selects a pack of sandwiches from the machine. The place is half empty. A few groups of lads are playing cards;

others rock back vertiginously on chairs to inconvenience passers-by. Karen swings her rucksack off her shoulder and manages to clout one on the head as they join a few of their tutor group at a neighbouring table.

"You off to the library?" she asks, when Aysha doesn't sit down.

"Later. I'm supposed to be seeing Andy Carstairs at one, but it shouldn't take long. I'll see you there."

A skinny black girl with wild spiralling curls looks up, slowly manoeuvres a wad of gum into her cheek and grins. "Watch yourself – heard he has a thing for Asian girls."

"Shut it, Billie." Karen says automatically.

The girl rolls her eyes.

"It's work, stupid," Aysha tells her. "I've got to run an idea for my history project past him."

"You thinking about that independent study already?" Karen queries. "I've no idea what to do."

"I thought about researching our house and the square. Like who used to live there, what the changes have been."

"Can you do that? I thought it would have to be more important – like the suffragettes or something."

"I don't know. That's what I want to ask."

"I like your enthusiasm," Andy says. "Yes, there are pitfalls, but I've got high hopes for you, Aysha. You're an able student, you could carry it off."

She is perched on a stool next to his desk in the humanities staffroom. Piles of books and folders barricade his computer, threatening to topple onto the keyboard, a coffee cup sits precariously on a ringbinder and a photo of a young boy is taped to the filing cabinet.

"What would I have to do?" Aysha asks.

"Find out names if you can, but don't get hung up on individuals, use them to relate to major themes and trends – changing industries, women and employment, migration. You'll have plenty of scope for primary sources – the census records, street directories, photographs. Remember, we're visiting the local history collection in Bancroft Road next week."

"So I can do it, then?"

"Write me your proposal first, but I don't see why not."

Aysha's mother has been cooking coconut samosas and her eldest brother, Mo, has brought sweets from the shops in Brick Lane. After the family have broken their fast, Aysha picks out a small selection and takes them to the old couple downstairs. She often sees the wife go out to the corner shop, but her husband rarely leaves the basement flat.

The old woman looks surprised, but asks her in and puts the kettle on.

"It's the young girl from upstairs, Bert. Brought us some... they're not spicy, are they?" she asks, eyeing the samosas suspiciously.

"No, this kind is sweet. And these are called jalebi," Aysha replies, indicating the shop bought offerings.

"Go down all right with a cup of tea." Bert picks up a syrupy coil and dips it in his brew.

"Can't take 'im anywhere," his wife complains.

"So, you all settled in?" the old man asks. "What is it – five, six months you've been 'ere now?"

Aysha nods. Her family moved to the square after Mo's baby

son was born and the council flat Dad bought in the eighties was just too small. The old couple's flat is separate from the rest of the house, but her family still has four whole bedrooms: enough for Mum and Dad, Mo with his wife and their son, her brothers Selim and Abdul, and a funny little space, tucked under the roof on the top floor for herself. It's an oddly proportioned room which must have been partitioned at some time to provide the shower room on the other side.

She gets to her ulterior motive for the visit and asks how long Bert and his wife Maud have lived there.

"Nineteen forty-six," Maud says, "after the war. I grew up across the square – where the flats are now – but our house got flattened in the Blitz. Mum and Dad and us kids moved in with my gran. Me and Bert thought we'd have to go further out when we got married, but then we heard about this place. It's not big, but it's home. Been here ever since."

"I'm doing a local history project at college. What was the house like then? It would have been all one once, wouldn't it?"

Perhaps they have photos, pictures of the square during the war.

Bert scratches his chin. "Well, the inside stairs to the ground floor were still there. When old man Donaldson – the landlord – died, back in the sixties, his son took them out and made space to put the bath in. There must have been a big kitchen, a scullery and a coal shed here once, but they'd already been knocked through when we came. They had maids when these houses were built, none of your machines to do the work." Bert reaches into the box and prises the last sticky morsel from the cardboard. "They're all right, love, these jelly whatsits of yours."

On the last day of term, Aysha gets up early to find her sister-in-law sitting in the kitchen nibbling biscuits and sipping mint tea. At first she thinks nothing of Reshna not fasting – she probably has her period – but then remembers the same scene last weekend, with Mum fussing over her and making her sit down to chop the vegetables.

"Is Reshna pregnant?" she asks, when the young woman hurriedly leaves the room.

Mum holds up both hands, fingers extended. "Ten week," she says. "Sick again – is good sign."

"Another baby?"

Ibrahim has only just had his first birthday. The house that seemed so spacious six months ago is beginning to feel overcrowded.

"Insh'Allah," Mum beams.

"Do me a favour?" she asks Karen on the bus home. "Come to the Local History Collection with me on Tuesday. I've told Mum it's something we've all got to do."

"Okay. But why? Won't she let you go alone?"

"Reshna's throwing up, so she can't help with the cooking, and Mum doesn't realise we've still got college work to do in the holidays. If I don't go soon the building will be closed until New Year."

"What're you looking for?"

"Well, I already found out our house was built in the 1820s and bought by someone called John Watts – a tobacco merchant. Another Watts was living there in 1891 according to the census, but that must've been his son or grandson. There were children, too, a boy and a girl. The next census isn't released until next year, but there are supposed to be street directories which show who lived where and what they did."

"I wonder what happened to them all?"

Aysha shrugs. "Maud and Bert mentioned some old guy they rented from when they first moved in. I've forgotten the name, but it wasn't Watts."

The doorbell sounds and Aysha calls, "I'll go!" She dusts her floury hands on her jeans and runs to open the front door to Karen. Her friend bounces in wearing a maroon tracksuit that Aysha hasn't seen before and a sparkling pair of Nike trainers. Her long blonde hair swings from a high pony tail, revealing twisted gold hoop earrings.

"Thought I'd check out the sales in Oxford Street," she says. "Can you come?"

"Karen!" Aysha's mum calls. "Eid Mubarak!"

"We're cooking," Aysha whispers. "You won't get away without at least tea and sweets."

"I thought Eid was the other day."

"It was, but we didn't see you then, so you're still our Eid guest."

The girls go into the living room and sit together on the long, squashy sofa. At its other end, Dad dozes beside the television, a glass of sweet tea cooling by his side. On screen, Barney the purple dinosaur is singing to no-one in particular, as Mo has just taken Abdul and Ibrahim to the park. Selim is listening to music on his earphones, nodding his head and mumbling lyrics; Aysha sees him shoot Karen the odd, covert glance. Mum hovers over them with a plate, her hands stained with turmeric.

"I've been stuffing myself silly, but I can always make room for one of your samosas, Mrs Khatun," Karen says.

Within seconds, a small wicker stool appears at her side and Mum gestures to Aysha to pour a glass of cola.

"You like the Christmas?" Mum asks.

Karen nods vigorously, her mouth full. She starts to rummage in her shoulder bag.

"What d'you get?" Aysha says. "Apart from what you're wearing, of course."

The only child of two working parents, Karen rarely wants for presents.

"The trackie? That's from Auntie Lou and Nan bought me the hoops. Mum and Dad got me this." Karen pulls a mobile phone from her bag. "It's the new Nokia. Look, it's really neat."

Aysha holds out her hand and cradles the miniature alien with its silver and black styling, ovoid buttons and backlit screen. Selim takes off his headphones and looks across, impressed. The red Peugeot he drives is a regular money pit and he can't afford to upgrade his phone.

"Aysha get Eid clothes," Mum interrupts, the English words pouring out in her anxiety to impress. "Son Mohammed buy. Put on, Aysha. Show friend!"

Aysha pulls a face, but Karen drags her upright. "Come on, Aysh, show me your gear."

"I haven't even tried it yet." Aysha says, closing her bedroom door behind them. "It's not like I'll wear it unless I go to a wedding or something." She holds up the hanger with its elaborately figured blue and gold tunic and blue harem pants tapering to a cuff of the same gold embroidery.

"On, on, on." Karen keeps up the chant until Aysha relents

and slips out of her top and jeans, hopping from one foot to the other to climb into the harem pants before pulling the kameez over her head.

"Zip me up, then."

Karen fiddles with the fastening on the back of the tunic then spins Aysha round to face her.

"Wow! You look like someone out of a fairy story. Like – what's her name in Aladdin? Princess Jasmine."

Aysha catches sight of herself in the mirror and scrunches her shoulder: the gold thread is scratchy. She twists her arm over her shoulder to tug at the zip, but Karen pulls her out of the room.

"You'd better show your mum."

Mum smiles approvingly and calls Reshna, who has been lying down. The young woman smiles shyly at Karen, but looks positively overjoyed to see Aysha in the outfit.

"You like?"

Aysha suddenly realises that it was her sister-in-law who selected the blue and gold.

"It's beautiful," she says. She turns to go back upstairs, but Mum lays a hand on her arm.

"Keep it on," she says, in Bangla. Aysha frowns, embarrassed at excluding Karen by the sudden switch of language, but her mother ploughs on. "Mo will be back with the children soon and Maryam is coming with the boys. Your friend understands," she adds as Aysha mouths a silent *sorry,* "this is still a family day. Maybe another time you can go shopping."

Abdul races in and snatches a samosa, while Mo unbuckles Ibrahim and lifts him from the buggy. He takes in Aysha's outfit and gives a short nod.

"Who was that just left the house?"

"Karen," Aysha says.

"I didn't recognise her. She's grown."

"Yeah, I noticed!" Selim grins. Mo clicks his tongue and frowns at him and Sel goes back to his music.

Aysha's sister Maryam arrives with her boys just as Mum lifts the last batch of samosas from the pan. Farhad, the elder, is only a year or two younger than Abdul, while Rahim is almost five. The three of them concoct some elaborate game which involves racing up and down both flights of stairs, screeching and diving behind the sofa, from where Dad looks on tolerantly, merely increasing the volume of the documentary he's now watching. Mum threatens Abdul with dire consequences if any of them go into the room where Reshna's resting and he constantly complains to his father that it's not his fault. No-one reprimands Maryam's boys.

Aysha's sister's marriage was arranged, but the family's choice of partner has been a lucky one. Maryam's husband Hassan runs a dry cleaning business with his father and, although they share a home with her in-laws, the house is large: an extended semi. At present, she's busy explaining her plans for turning the garage into a playroom for the boys.

"It's a pity you can't get the basement here, Mum. There's no way you can extend this house."

Maryam stretches out plump fingers and inspects her fuchsia nails before selecting a warm vegetable pakora.

"We've only been here a few months," Aysha comments, looking up. "Maud and Bert have been here years."

"Is plenty room," Mum adds.

Maryam waits until Mo has left the room to rescue his son from being trampled by the older boys. "I knew Ibrahim wouldn't be their last," she says, nodding towards the kitchen door. "Where will you put another one?"

Aysha stares. Suppose Mum expects her to give up her room? She'll never be able to study if she has to share with one of the children.

Mum shrugs and taps her nose at her elder daughter. They both switch to a rapid Bangla which Aysha can barely follow.

"These things tend to solve themselves," she hears her mother say. "In a couple of years there will be more room."

She doesn't understand. Mo and Reshna can't move out because Mo pays towards this house and Sel doesn't earn enough to live on his own. She still hasn't discussed university with her parents and hasn't decided whether to apply outside London or not, but, even if she does, she'll need her room in the holidays.

"You are not to worry," Maryam replies. "I'll talk to my husband. You can count on our help, when the time comes."

3
Emily

Thursday 14 March 1901

Ma's fever lessens by day, though she often wakes drenched with sweat at night. She keeps to her bed as the congestion does not shift; the troubling cough persists and her appetite stays poor.

"I'm sorry," she tells Daisy, when she sends back her food untouched, "but it all tastes the same. I *see* beef broth and apple pie, but I *taste* sawdust and tobacco leaf."

"Couldn't you just eat a bit of dust and tobacco then?" I ask. "To build up your strength?"

She smiles sadly. "Believe me, I try, but it just sticks. It won't go down."

If she complains of pain beneath her ribs and in her bones – pain which makes her clench her jaws and twist on the bed – Pa has left me instructions to administer laudanum. It frightens me because I know too large a dose can be deadly, but I cannot bear to see her in pain, so Daisy and I measure it together and check it again and again.

Today, when I go to her room, she is lying back exhausted but I can see she has been out of bed, because her jewellery box and its contents are strewn across the covers and she has her gold and pearl choker in her hand.

"It was my grandmother's," Ma says. "I want you to have it, Emmie."

"One day, perhaps. A long time yet."

"I want you to take it now. Then whatever happens, it's yours."

"What will Pa say?"

"It's mine to give. Do you have a safe place?"

I nod, thinking of the loose floorboard in my room, where I always hid my journal from Charlie, but my heart is breaking.

Friday 12 April 1901

I haven't seen Ma this morning. She was very weak yesterday and Pa says she's had a bad night. He has called the doctor and is staying home. She finds it hard to swallow, he says, and is struggling to breathe. He tells me to go to the market and to take Daisy with me. The blood oranges from Spain are still in season and she may be able to swallow a little juice if we squeeze them. Surely those spheres of concentrated sunshine cannot taste of dust?

When we have bought the oranges, Daisy goes in search of rhubarb and spring greens and I stop at the tailor's shop to speak to Mr Fenton.

"I was shocked to hear about your brother," he says. "Why don't you come and see us on Sunday? I expect you could do with cheering up and Sally will be glad to see you."

I start to tell him that Ma wouldn't want me to go out visiting while we're in mourning for Charlie, when the truth hits me. Pa has sent me out of the way! I run out of the shop and rush this way and that among the shoppers, frantically searching for Daisy.

"Whatever's wrong?" she asks as I spot her and grab her arm.

"Ma," I say. "We must run home, quick!"

We push through the crowds and people stare as we pick up our skirts and run through the streets, darting across Commercial Road, dodging the omnibus, horses, and bicycles and making the drivers shout. When we reach the square, the doctor's trap stands outside our house, with Ernie, our neighbour's son, minding the chestnut mare. But as we reach the steps our door opens and Dr Reynolds comes out. When I look at him, he slowly shakes his head.

"I'm sorry, Emily. There was nothing more I could do."

I hear a high pitched wail, the word *Ma!* screamed over and over, and finally realise that the voice is mine. Daisy has dropped her basket and the oranges tumble down the steps to the gutter.

"Here, boy!" The doctor beckons to young Ernie and tells him to call his mother. Mrs Black opens her door and I see the doctor talk to her. She comes straight over to usher us inside and shows Daisy and me into her parlour – like ours but somehow reversed — then goes off to make the hot, sweet tea the doctor has ordered. I think I must be shaking, because Daisy picks up a crocheted rug from a chair and wraps it around my shoulders. We just sit, stupefied, looking at a china rose bowl in the window, a painting of fruits over the hearth and a half-finished jigsaw puzzle of a battle at sea – Ernie's, presumably – on the floor.

"It's a nice house, ain't it?" says Daisy, then bursts into noisy tears.

Mrs Black returns with the tea and, as we sip the scalding liquid, the doctor returns.

"Do you have a spare room?" he asks her. "It would be better for Emily to stay here overnight. I'm going to give her father a sleeping draught – he badly needs rest – then I need to call upon a woman I know who can attend to poor Maria."

Now I cannot keep back the sobs – that she has become an object to be handled by a stranger.

Daisy looks up. "You mean laying out, sir? Because I'll do it. I was there when my own mum died and saw what was done. Don't give her to anyone else."

The doctor looks at her closely then nods. "Finish your tea and come."

I sit quietly crying, thinking myself alone, when I hear a small voice.

"She was a nice lady, your mum. She used to give me barley sugar."

I didn't see Ernie come in, but he's in the corner, cross-legged on the floor with his jigsaw.

"They'll let you see her, you know," he says, "kiss her goodbye."

I wonder at receiving such information from a child. Then I remember that our neighbour is the second Mrs Black: Ernie's own mother is dead.

"Do you remember your real ma then?" I ask.

"Of course," he says. "I was seven when she died."

"And when you saw her – afterwards – were you afraid?"

Ernie considers carefully. "I was afore I went in, but not when I saw her. They made her so nice." He returns to his jigsaw, then puts his head on one side. "You can help me with this if you want. It's all sea and sails and I can't find any pieces to fit."

I must have tossed and turned more than half the night and it is dawn before I finally fall asleep. I wake late, in a sunny room papered with a pretty pattern of birds and roses, and catch myself thinking how Ma would like it. Then I remember that she will never see Mrs Black's spare room and feel dull and hollow inside.

The next thing I remember is Daisy coming to tell me that Granny and Grandpa have arrived. Ma's parents are grieving too, but they are not helpless and together find the strength to organise what needs to be done. Granny closes all our curtains, covers the mirrors and hangs black ribbons on the door. Grandpa instructs the undertaker, meets with the vicar and deals with all those who call. They both travelled wearing their mourning clothes. I have no black outfit, but Granny goes through my wardrobe and tells Daisy to iron and sponge my grey flannel dress, then helps us to make armbands and veils for our hats. I am surprised that Pa does not take charge himself, but he seems in a such a stupor that I wonder if he has taken too much of Dr Reynold's sleeping draught. He speaks to no-one but shuts himself away in his little study, next to the dining room, where Ma's coffin lies.

Ma went to Harlow twice every year, sometimes taking Charlie and me, but I don't remember my grandparents ever coming to our house before. Even now, they don't sleep here; Grandpa has taken a room for them at a lodging house nearby. It seems strange that I never realised it before, but it is quite obvious that he and Pa don't get on. I don't understand why. Pa could be a severe father to Charlie and me – it was always to Ma that we went to be indulged – but no-one can doubt that he worshipped *her.* I visualise them now, retiring to their room as they did each night after dinner, Ma resting her head on his shoulder, Pa with his arm around her waist. Granny is less hostile, I think. *What's past is past, George*, she tells Grandpa, and *you cannot deny he loved poor Maria.* She arranges for meals to be sent to Pa's room and communicates the arrangements that my grandfather has made.

Tuesday 16 April 1901

I haven't been to a funeral before; poor Charlie is buried half a world away. On better days, Ma spoke of holding a memorial service for him, but she weakened so rapidly that nothing was done.

The hearse is drawn by four black horses with velvet coats and plumes of black feathers around their handsome heads. The coffin disappears beneath a sea of flowers. Grandpa has ordered a carriage to follow the hearse and Pa and I sit facing him and Granny. Nobody speaks. Pa sits rigid; he grasps his hands together and I hear his knuckles crack. I want to look back for Daisy, who is walking behind with some neighbours, but the carriage blinds are down.

In church I see Dr Reynolds, Mr and Mrs Black, and our other neighbours. I catch sight of Sally with her parents and am grateful to them for coming. The vicar describes Ma as an English matron who sacrificed her son for her country, but I don't recognise the mother I knew in his words. Ma loved pretty clothes, outings, and gossip and would have chained Charlie to her side if she could. Pa and I are at the front, on one side of the aisle, my grandparents sit on the other. At one point, as we sing *Abide with me,* Pa staggers and I think he will fall; then a tall dark figure steps from the pew behind us and William Baines takes his arm.

It's a beautiful spring day: birds are singing, the hawthorn trees in the churchyard are breaking into blossom. It's a day for holding hands and jumping on the patches of sunshine which dapple through the trees; a day for a walk in the park to throw bread to the ducks and to laugh at their upturned tails as they dive; a day for seeing the tall ships and the light sparkling on the river – so why are we laying her in the dark ground?

When all the mourners have left, Granny and Grandpa ask to speak to Pa and me in the parlour. Pa stands awkwardly, pulling the curtain aside to stare out of the window and avoiding my grandfather's gaze. I see a muscle in his cheek start to twitch.

"Edward," my grandmother begins, "we are all of us grieving, but we must consider Emily. You are in no state to care for your daughter at present – will you permit us to take her home with us for a while?"

At first Pa looks as if he would object, then I see him catch sight of his own exhausted face in the mirror. He sighs deeply.

"Emily?" he says hesitantly, looking at me.

Is the decision really mine? The father I know would never defer to his child: how he must be suffering! Yet I cannot bear the rawness of his grief, the wordless demand for pity, the constant need to guard my tongue. My grandmother stretches out an arm towards me and something in the movement reminds me of Ma. I'll go, I say, but just for a week or two. I wish I could take Daisy too, but someone needs to make sure Pa is fed.

Grandpa tells me to find a travelling bag and pack some clothes. I am to sleep at their lodgings tomorrow night, then go with them to Harlow.

Wednesday 17 April 1901

I still don't understand what happened this evening. I had sorted out books, clothes and sewing things to pack and sat with Pa in the parlour, waiting for my grandparents. I wished I could comfort him, but was afraid to speak. When I heard the cab draw up outside, I went upstairs to fetch my bag. The gas lamp in my room was turned low and the curtains were pulled back. I pushed the door open wide, then stopped. Across the room, beneath my window, a slight female figure sat reading at a small table.

"Ma?" I whispered.

The gas flared and I saw more clearly. It was not Ma. This person had long, straight hair, glossy-black, fanned out over narrow shoulders. She looked up and I saw a young girl, of perhaps my own age. Her features were fine and small and her skin a clear, honey brown. Her clothes were strange for a girl – coarse blue trousers and a sort of patterned tunic – but her face reminded me of the women English ladies employ in India as nursemaids to their children and who sometimes accompany them home. But why was she here, sitting in my room as if it were her own?

"Hello?" I ventured. But then I heard another voice, someone shouting.

Aysha! the voice called. It sounded like a young man. The girl raised her head and looked straight past me. Again the voice called, *Aysha!*

What now? she yelled.

I stepped back onto the landing, shocked both at hearing her speak and at the abruptness of her tone. I shouted for Pa.

"What is it, Emily?"

I turned back to my room. No girl, no desk, just my own armchair in front of the window, the moonlit trees swaying in the square outside and the wavering shadows from the gaslight. Was I deceived by a trick of the light?

"Emily?" Pa queried again.

"No matter," I called to cover my confusion, "just something I forgot."

I sit in a strange bed in the lodging house, writing my journal and listening to the sounds of wheels and hooves in the street outside, wondering how I can sleep. *Aysha*, I murmur; who can she be?

Thursday 16 May 1901

I have been with my grandparents a month. It is longer than I thought to stay, but it is peaceful here and life is orderly and quiet. Their house is a long timber-clad cottage and I sleep in a small, sloping attic, its plaster walls and ceiling whitewashed between crooked oak beams. There is a large garden where Granny grows the gooseberries and redcurrants that she uses to make jellies and jams and where hens scratch the soil between the bushes.

Sometimes I walk in the woods with Grandpa George and the collie, Pat, or along the river, to the mill. Grandpa is tall and thin, with a slight stoop from the years bent over his books. He doesn't talk much on our walks, but simply whistles to the dog or points out a bird or the glimpse of a deer with his cane. Since Ma died, he is greyer than I remember: I think sorrow has aged him.

Granny does not allow me to mope. I mend and sew and read. Although I have exhausted the books I brought with me, Grandpa was a teacher and there are a great many more here, so I have an ample supply. Some are too old-fashioned to hold my interest but, as Granny points out, many that do – such as stories by Jane Austen or Dickens – are older still.

My grandmother is a small, energetic woman in her early sixties. Her curly hair is mostly grey now, but still shows in places the same chestnut as mine. She is kind, although her manner is reserved. We didn't really know each other and for a time I lacked the courage to speak about what was bothering me, but my mind was troubled and eventually I did.

"Is it my fault, Gran? I found the birth certificate that helped

Charlie lie about his age? He'd still be alive if he hadn't seen it."

"Emily," she said firmly, "you mustn't think like that. If your brother was determined, he'd have found another way."

"Where was that baby born? Was it here?"

Granny was silent for a long time, looking faraway, as if into the past.

"Yes it was. He was a very tiny thing – born too soon."

"Was Ma ill too?"

"I thought she would go mad with grief. She was barely eighteen herself. We hadn't wanted her to marry so young but your mother could be headstrong."

"Yet you didn't stop her getting married?"

She looked at me strangely. "No, we did not."

A few days later, I asked, "Why did you and Grandpa never come to our house?"

My grandmother sighed. "We were wrong not to come. Men can be stubborn. Your father and grandfather quarrelled many years ago, after the baby, when your mother was ill and Edward felt we were keeping her from him. I don't blame him, Emmie. He always loved her. Too much perhaps." Ma had once told me that she was ill in the year following her marriage and had to return to her parents to be nursed. "Edward was a senior pupil at the school where your grandfather taught. If boys could not go home during the holidays, sometimes they boarded with us."

"They met here?" I said. "I thought Pa had always lived in London."

"Your father was raised by his grandfather, as you know. It was he who sent him here to school. Your father took over the tobacco trade when the old man grew incapable, then inherited both house and business when he died."

Another time, I brought out the pearl and gold necklace, which Ma said had been her own grandmother's. I had decided to bring it with me for safekeeping.

"Yes, it was my mother's," Granny said. "I'm happy that Maria gave it to you, but it's valuable, Emmie. You need to look after it well."

I treasure the necklace and hope to wear it when I'm older, but it's too grand for any dress I'm likely to wear now.

"Hasn't Grandpa a safe?" I asked. "Will he keep it for me here?"

I wondered if I should tell Granny about the young woman I saw in my room, but when she said how Ma went mad with grief after her baby died, I feared she would think I was losing my mind too. Even at home, there's no-one I can tell. Pa will blame my imagination, Dr Reynolds will have some perfectly sensible scientific explanation and as for Daisy, she is superstitious and sees ghosts in every shadow. Whoever, whatever Aysha is, I don't think she's anything to fear. But as days go by, my image of her starts to fade and I feel less and less convinced of what I saw.

I think about Sally, whose visits to her grandmother in Highgate are always filled with lively cousins, parties, expeditions and entertainments. She'd think me a complete country bumpkin now, with only Granny and Grandpa for company. And Daisy – I let myself abandon her so easily! I hope Pa is treating her well. He loved my mother too much, Granny says, but he has lost us all: baby Edward, Charlie, Ma. I've been away long enough: I come to a decision and tell my grandparents that I need to go home.

4
Aysha

February 2001

Mum announces that Aysha and Abdul are to spend the half-term week with Maryam in Romford. Abdul is eager to spend time with the boys and Sel's happy to have their shared bedroom to himself for a few days, but Aysha has no wish to spend a week playing nursemaid to her brother and nephews.

"I've got college, Mum," she says, "we don't get a holiday this term." It's a half-truth at least, as she's signed up for optional revision sessions on the Monday and Tuesday.

"Maryam need help with boys."

"I can't miss class."

"One week no matter. You not fail, Aysha. Get As and stars."

"It's harder now – A levels take more work. I need top grades so I... I just want to do well." Aysha trails off, torn between relief and regret. This could have been an opportunity to talk about uni, but she can't get the words out. Somehow the time is never quite right. Mum huffs a bit and goes off to phone Maryam.

"How come you're not off?" Sel asks.

Aysha shrugs. It's a risk, misleading her family: Sel knows

everyone and is bound to find out that students don't have to be in college next week.

After Jo Massey's revision class on Monday, the girls spent the afternoon in library, Aysha designing a questionnaire for psychology and Karen working on her business studies assignment. It was blissfully quiet since only the keen students were there. Today, they have individual tutorials with Andy Carstairs. Aysha's history project is really fleshing out. After repeat visits to the local history collection, she knows when each block of houses in the square was built and which ones were destroyed in the Blitz. She has made photocopies of early maps and photographs to compare with today and knows the names and occupations of many residents of the square in both the 1860s and 1900s. Now she's looking at the changes after the First World War, when women left domestic service for the factories.

"This is really promising," Andy tells her. "I understand your work in your other subjects is equally good. You should be thinking about your future."

"I do want to go to uni."

"I should hope so! And don't just choose the nearest one. You should be aiming high."

She should be pleased, she *is* pleased, warmed by his high opinion of her potential, but she can't see Mum agreeing to her living away.

"There's a special programme running for high flyers in August. It's intended to encourage students like you. I'd like to put your name forward – it's in London and won't cost you anything."

Aysha nods doubtfully, wishing there was some way of

leaping over the obstacles ahead. Nothing's been said, but in the last few months she's sensed a difference in her family's attitude to her education. There are subtle pressures, unspoken expectations. If only Dad would speak up – he's the educated one – rather than leave things to Mo or Mum. Once the revision sessions are over, she'll spend the rest of the week in the library or at Karen's; she doesn't like lying, but somehow it makes life easier.

The girls go out for lunch, as the canteen's vacation offer is limited. The air is too raw to linger outside so Karen suggests a trip to the expanding Docklands shopping mall. The whole area is a work in progress. Their walk takes them over the railway bridge, along makeshift footpaths, past building sites and across a pedestrian walkway to West India Dock. Aysha wonders if John Watts, the merchant who lived in her house, would have done business here. Andy's told them about a new museum planned for the quayside, which will be all about the river and the docks, but it won't be ready until after they finish their course.

Aysha stares across the water to an island of buildings which would not look out of place in Chicago or Manhattan. The iconic tower, topped with its pyramid of steel, flashes an aircraft warning light and is faintly wreathed in vapour, like a mountain hiding its peak in the clouds. The skyscraper is hedged in by other blocks and everywhere there is a scramble to build higher. She is both fascinated and repelled by the brutal beauty of the place.

Karen leads the way to the footbridge over the water and soon they are exploring the centre with its new shops and restaurants. Most are geared to the wants of office workers and bank employees with bonuses to spend: goods are expensive, but the mall is warm and dry and window shopping is cheap. They grab a coffee and a sandwich.

The Tissue Veil

Daylight fades early and the glittering eyes of the tall buildings already light up the deepening sky when the girls decide to take the train home from Canary Wharf station. Across the tracks, one of the red and blue trains moves jerkily away and Aysha notices a couple emerge from the escalator on the far platform. The young man's black puffa jacket with its red flashes catches her eye.

"Isn't that your brother?" Karen has spotted Selim too.

Sel lounges against a pillar, his arm lightly resting round the shoulders of a short blonde girl in a green parka who is looking up at him. Her hands are thrust into his jacket pockets. Aysha watches as the girl's right hand emerges from Sel's pocket holding a pack of cigarettes. Sel takes it from her and lights one, inhaling deeply. The girl reaches up and takes it from his lips, dragging on it herself.

Karen waves madly, trying to attract their attention.

"What are you doing? He's gonna know I'm not in college."

"Getting you a bargaining chip." Karen nods towards Sel and the blonde, who have definitely noticed them. "I'm guessing your folks wouldn't approve of that."

Sel arrives home at six-thirty to change for work and thrashes around the house looking for a clean shirt. One of the waiters is off sick, he says; he's filling in and needs to look smart.

"Good day at college?" he asks meaningfully, when Mum goes off to iron the shirt.

"Of course," she says, meeting his eye.

"What you playing at?"

"I'm not playing, I had revision classes this morning. What about you – who's your girlfriend?"

"Velna? She's not my girlfriend She does the bar at the

restaurant."

"Looked like a girlfriend to me."

"She's from Latvia," he says, as if that explains everything. Then, after a minute, "Don't tell anyone."

I won't if you won't, she thinks, but it's still not fair. Why should she feel guilty about attending a revision class?

April 2001

"I'm watching that!" Abdul objects as Aysha aims the remote to switch off the cartoon channel.

"No you're not," she says, picking her away between the toys which litter the kitchen floor. "You're playing with Buzz."

"I can do both," he scowls. "Mum lets me."

Ibrahim calls out hopefully, "Tubbies now?"

Aysha feels stale and twitchy through lack of exercise. Her unsatisfactory and frustrating spring break is already three-quarters over. Karen is soaking up the sun in Spain with her parents, but in cool, damp Stepney, Aysha's hardly been outside the house. Today, Mo is working day shift, Mum has gone with Reshna to her antenatal appointment and Sel has taken Dad to the hospital for his regular heart check-up. Abdul and Ibrahim have been left in her care.

Lack of sleep drags her down. For the last few nights she's stayed up late to draft both an English assignment and her local history study. She'd hoped to get to the library to type up her work on a computer; instead, she's cooked pizza for Abdul, fed rice and vegetables to Ibrahim and changed his nappy. Twice, hopefully, she's laid him in his cot, but the toddler has outgrown his afternoon nap and uses the mattress as a trampoline, jumping up and down and calling for *Aysh* and *Abu*. Picking at a slice of pizza and pouring another mug of coffee, she resigns herself to not getting to the library today.

The family all come home together.

"Sit," Mum tells Sel as he checks his phone for the sixth time. "Aysha make tea."

"Everything okay?" Aysha rests her hand on Dad's shoulder.

Dad looks sheepish. "More exercise, less calories. What they always say."

Mum snorts dismissively. Yes, he knows that already, Aysha thinks, watching her father sink back into the sofa, but it never translates into action. Why can't he find the willpower to do what he should? By contrast, her sister-in-law needs plenty of rest as she had high blood pressure in her first pregnancy.

"You be good for Aysha?" Ibrahim is perched on the platform of Reshna's swollen belly, playing peek-a-boo with the loose end of her headscarf. His mother lifts him high, then brings him down giggling for a kiss. "Clever auntie teach you speak English." She smiles at Aysha, peeping shyly through her dark sweep of lashes. "Is nice be with children, yes?" Reshna herself has learned a little English now.

Aysha's face burns and her eyes prickle.

"They just wanted the TV," she mutters. She'd itched to get back to her work and, grateful for the hypnotic power of the Teletubbies, had totally failed to see the day as an opportunity for bonding with the kids.

"Good practice," Mum says.

Aysha flushes and she rushes from the kitchen, torn between guilt and anger. No-one understands what's important to her – but how can they if she doesn't tell them?

She closes the bedroom door behind her and slumps in the

chair by the window, picking up a booklet without opening it. Suddenly, there is a draught of air, which is strange because both door and window are shut, and a swell of intense sadness washes over her. The sorrow is not hers: her own feelings of discontent are still there, but quite distinct from this. Someone, nearby, is desperately unhappy and she strains every sense to understand who it can be.

"Aysha!" Selim's shout breaks her concentration. "Aysh!" he repeats, flinging open her door, "You're wanted."

The emotion dispels in an instant, like a figure in a mist slipping out of sight. Something important has been lost and her irritation breaks through.

"What now?"

Sel reaches up to grasp the lintel, rising on his toes. "Why d'you run off? Mum's out of milk."

"You go. You're not due at work yet, are you?"

"I've been hanging around that hospital all day. I'm off out now."

Maybe it's the girlfriend. Sel attributes his increased demand for clean shirts to the fact that he's waiting at table, but that doesn't explain the excess of aftershave or the air fresheners in his car.

"I'll be down in a minute."

When Selim has gone, she picks up the booklet again. It's about the summer school Andy Carstairs wants her to attend. She's about to slide it back under her bed with her foot when her sock catches on a floorboard nail and she sees the short section of board next to the old fireplace lift slightly. The house has central heating and all the other fireplaces have been ripped out, but somehow her room was forgotten and retains the old grate and hearth. She has often thought that the original builders must have used all their offcuts of floorboards in here as there are so many joins. The nail which caught her sock is not quite raised enough to grip, but the board is definitely loose. Mum never knocks before barging into her room and there's no knowing when she'll decide on one of her periodic cleaning sprees. This would be a safer hiding place than under the bed.

The next day she lugs the cleaner upstairs to her room, saying that she's going to vacuum her room, but her real agenda is the space under the floor.

"Do stairs after," Mum calls.

Last night, she'd tentatively levered the loose board with a knife and confirmed there was a gap beneath. The space was thick with the dust of decades, lying in soft pillows like black cotton wool, and she'd shuddered at the thought of spiders lurking there. If she's to use the cavity as a hiding place, it has to be dirt and bug free.

Once or twice recently, she has smelt cigarettes and been convinced that Sel's been in her room. He doesn't smoke around Abdul or Reshna, but that doesn't mean he can contaminate *her* space. Sel can keep secrets, but she doesn't want *anyone* poking around there: the summer school stuff and some prospectuses are hidden under her bed.

The vacuum cleaner gulps down the dust balls with satisfying voracity. Aysha removes the nozzle and feeds the end of the flexible hose into the under floor space to complete the task. Suddenly the machine's noise changes as if something has blocked the tube. Carefully, she withdraws the hose, then reaches in to grasp a rectangular object, thickly encased in dust, but still recognisable as a book. Someone has used the hiding place before! She switches the vacuum power to the lowest setting to remove the dirt without damaging her find, then blows gently across it and finishes it off with tissues.

Now that it's cleaner, the cover looks like leather, dark green and finely grained. The contents seem to be some kind of diary. Flicking through, she sees page after page of a neat, looping script written in blue ink. There are a couple of entries from 1899, but most pages are headed by dates in 1900 and 1901. Aysha turns to the inside front cover and reads an inscription: *To dearest Emily from your mother, Christmas 1899.* On the opposite page a name: *Emily Watts.*

Emily Watts! It must be the girl in the census, who lived in this house!

"Aysha!" her mum calls. "You finish clean?"

Her first thoughts are that she can use this journal in her historical study of the square. Andy said not to get fixated with individuals, but surely this is a unique primary source? She can use Emily's narrative to illustrate generalities. Reading further, she's not sure. Whoever Emily Watts was, she wrote her story with such immediacy that Aysha almost believes the other girl is speaking directly to her. Submitting her words to the scrutiny of examiners would feel like a kind of betrayal. Perhaps she'll just *tell* Andy about the journal. For now, she replaces the book under the floorboard and finishes vacuuming.

Later that night she takes it out again to read in bed. If only she could reach out to this girl who had lost her brother and mother and was trapped unwillingly at home... How would she feel if something happened to Sel? Or Dad? But the sympathy she feels is useless, a burden that can't be delivered.

A few minutes later, shocked rigid, she sits upright in bed, frowning and staring at the page as she reads – her own name! She pushes the book away: this isn't right, someone's playing a trick on her. She looks again, but nothing's been inserted or altered; the words are embedded in the text. Surely no-one would forge a whole journal as a joke? It must have been some other girl. Emily couldn't have seen *her*, Aysha, back in 1901. Yet she has described her hair and clothes exactly: *she's wearing a sort of printed tunic over coarse blue trousers.* Aysha looks at the stonewashed jeans slung over her chair, then at the cotton top, patterned in blues and greens, hanging from the back of her door. And the words Emily reports hearing sound like the argument she had with Sel yesterday, when they'd all come back from the hospital. That feeling she'd experienced, of being aware of a sudden, overwhelming sadness – was that Emily; was the grief hers? If she hid her book here, this must have been her room too. Aysha's thoughts spiral and eddy like leaves caught in a whirlpool.

Now she definitely can't use the journal in her study, or let anyone see it. If Mum could read it, she'd think it was dangerous, like bad magic or something. She'd want to know where Aysha found it and that would be the end of her hiding place. But Emily had been a real person, a girl of her own age. Aysha doesn't understand yet, but she's sure the journal is important – she was *meant* to find it.

5
Emily

Monday 3 June 1901

Pa meets us at Liverpool Street station. He takes my bag and nods briefly to Grandpa, who shakes my hand and goes back by the next train. Pa looks tired and strained, his clothes in need of a brush; he doesn't talk much on the way home. Summer has arrived while I've been away. The trees are in full leaf and Ernie is sitting on the steps to his house, trailing a string for a half-grown ginger cat.

Daisy is so happy to see me that I feel guilty I've stayed away so long. She's made a sponge cake to welcome me home. Sally called a few days ago, she says, and has promised to come again soon.

"Pa looks ill," I say. "Has he been eating?"

She looks away at first, as if there's something she doesn't want to say.

"Daisy? What's the matter?"

"He's been drinking. Ever since you been gone. Started on that brandy your Ma put away at Christmas and soon sent out for more. It's a regular thing now, after dinner. I'm scared to go asleep in case he sets the house alight with his cigar. Perhaps now you're home..."

But dinner is stiff and uncomfortable when there's just the two of us. Pa has changed, become less confident, more querulous.

"It's good you're here again, Emily," he says at last. "I thought you might not want to come back."

"Why wouldn't I?"

"I was afraid they'd turn you against me. What did your grandparents tell you? What did they say about me?"

"Only that you and Grandpa quarrelled – a long time ago."

"They blame me for your mother's death."

"Not Granny," I reply. "She said you loved Ma too much, but how can that be?"

He doesn't answer but closes his eyes and holds his breath before releasing it in a long sigh. At last he gets up and says abruptly, "You've had a long day, Emmie. You should go to bed."

I don't tell Pa that, although my grandparents accepted my decision, they didn't want me to leave and had found excuses to keep me another two weeks. But this is my home; all my memories are here. How could I abandon Daisy or my father? All the same, I thought about my future while I was at Harlow and there's something I want to ask Pa. With only the two of us, there will be less housework for Daisy and less need of help from me.

"I'll stay home if you really need me to, Pa, but couldn't I get a job now? *I* could help you keep accounts at the warehouse – I used to get top marks in arithmetic. Or, I'm good at sewing – perhaps Mr Fenton would employ me?"

Pa frowns. "The docks are no place for girls, Emily. And why work for Fenton when I can support you? If you take up a manual post, even a skilled job, it will look like I'm struggling. I can't afford to lose the confidence of the market."

I hadn't considered that my working could affect Pa's business;

I'd thought his situation was too secure for that. "Couldn't I go back to school then and train as a teacher like Sally?"

"Fenton is booming and can indulge his daughter's fancies, but I don't see young Sally as a schoolmarm. Mark my words, she'll be married in a couple of years. I'll be surprised if she ever teaches at all."

"What am I to do then?"

"This house needs to be managed. Learn a woman's role. That girl Daisy cooks well enough, but she doesn't have a flair for what looks well. Your mother could transform a room with a few touches. Mrs Black is a young wife, I'm sure she will advise you."

It is a new century: must I really spend my days washing and dusting? I bid him goodnight and retreat upstairs. I shouldn't be surprised, but it's still a blow to have my suggestions dismissed in this way and I need to be alone. I turn the door handle, then stop. I have almost convinced myself that my mind played tricks when I thought I saw the girl called Aysha, but now I hear voices.

Do I have to? someone is saying. *I need to finish this.*

I push open the door and see her, framed in the window as before. She has a pile of books balanced on the desk and is biting her pen, just as I do when I'm trying to think. I can't see an inkwell, though, and her fingers are not stained, as mine usually are. The other speaker is male, but I cannot see him.

Come on, Aysh. They just want to see you.

I didn't ask them to come. I'm not being rude, Sel. I've got work to do.

The other voice sounds peevish and impatient and somehow I'm reminded of Charlie.

Don't take it out on me, he complains.

I watch as she snatches up a long purple coloured scarf and winds it round her head, covering most of her hair. She snaps her book shut and starts across the room. Uncertain, I step back onto our landing, out of her way, but when she reaches the threshold something strange happens. There is a kind of shimmer in the air, a wavering, and she's gone. I stand trembling. I don't understand who she is or what I heard, but I wonder if Aysha's unhappy too?

Thursday 6 June 1901

Sally called this morning. I'd hoped to see her alone, but she had her Highgate cousin Josh and one of his friends in tow. The young men were visiting and wanted a tour of the East End, she said. I longed for a walk, but saw little chance of conversation with Sally with her cousin there; besides, Pa would never approve such an outing while we are in mourning for Charlie and Ma.

Instead, I decided to please him by visiting Mrs Black and am received in her parlour, the room I was brought to when Ma died. Pa's right that she has a flair for homemaking: Elizabeth – as she bids me call her – is a skilled needlewoman and a careful manager and the house is pretty and neat. She has a woman who comes in to clean and wash, she says, but her husband's salary cannot stretch to a live-in maid, for there is no satisfying Ernie's appetite and he's forever growing out of boots! Her taste is good, but while Ma chose pictures and ornaments because she loved them, I think Elizabeth is more concerned with what is proper or pictured in the *Woman at Home* magazine she reads. She has a good many magazines, but I never see her with a book.

I would be bored in the house alone all day if I didn't have Daisy's company and a novel to read, but Elizabeth seems perfectly satisfied with her state. As her husband is fifteen years older than her, I ask how they met. She says her parents had a small hotel in Brighton, which her mother continued to run after her father died. Mr Black stayed there several times on railway business when he was sent to train new clerks.

"Later," she explains, "after the first Mrs Black, died, he brought Ernie to Brighton for a holiday, to take their minds from their loss."

"You're so lucky to have grown up by the sea," I say, "and meeting new people all the time, in the guests."

"Oh, no," Elizabeth tells me, "my mother was very strict about that. I was never allowed in the guests' lounge or to engage them in conversation. There were salesmen, and Mama always distrusted the travelling type of man."

"Then how...?"

"... did I meet Richard? Oh, I was very naughty! I used to spy on the guests from our parlour and listen to their talk. I knew what each person had for his breakfast and where he'd spent his day and I made up stories about them in my head. I knew Richard must be married, but I always thought him such a nice man. When we heard that his wife had died and he brought young Ernie to stay, I persuaded Mama to invite them to take tea in our parlour and to let me play cards with Ernie. Then one day, Richard asked Mama if I might walk with them along the front and a few months later, he came back on his own. Do you think that was shocking, so soon after his wife died?"

"No," I say, "for Ernie needed a mother." But I cannot imagine Pa, who is not much older than Mr Black, taking another wife.

" Richard says it was because he'd been so happy that he wanted to marry again. He says marriage suits him."

"And did you never want to work, perhaps run a business like your mother?"

"Good heavens, no!" she cries, straightening a cushion and looking round her parlour with satisfaction. "It's all right for Mama, I suppose, it's what she's used to, but it's not a settled thing, running a hotel, not like having a home of your own."

I ask how she finds being stepmother to Ernie: it must be difficult to take on a boy of his age who can recall his own mother so well; but it's not Elizabeth's way to look for problems.

"Oh, no," she says. "I believe he has quite forgotten. As long as you feed Ernie, he is happy."

"But when Ma died and I was alone in this room with him, he told me about his mother."

Elizabeth smiles tolerantly. "You must be mistaken, Emily," she says. "You'd had such a shock. Ernie never mentions his mother to me."

I like Elizabeth well enough, but she lacks both Sally's quick wit and Daisy's warm heart. I don't mind keeping her company from time to time, but if I must be at home I would rather be active. Already, Daisy and I have planned our schedule. We'll strip the beds and wash on Mondays, iron on Wednesdays and shop at the market on other days. There are no fires to clear or lay in summer so we can get away with dusting and polishing every other day, but even with just Pa and me, there seems to be no lack of employment in a house like ours.

What I really want is to be able to talk to someone about Ma, just as I imagine Ernie would like to talk of his mother, despite what Elizabeth says. I need to hold onto the facts of her, to remember that I had a mother and was loved. Daisy will speak about Ma and Charlie, but she gets so tearful that it upsets us both. I feel guilty, but I avoid talking to her, except for trivialities, just now. Pa is no use. He holds himself together by day, locking his grief away, but the brandy bottle loosens it by night and then he's quite unfit for conversation. I want to remember the Ma of my childhood; I want to recollect the stories she read to Charlie and me, recall the games we played on our little expeditions to the parks, and no-one can share these with me. There is only my journal. I wish Ma had shared my habit and left me her thoughts, but she always said she hadn't the patience for that.

Sometimes, when Pa is out, I go to their room, and take out her clothes, her jewellery and her combs. I lay the dresses against my cheek and bury my face in them, trying to find the merest waft of the perfume she wore or a long brown hair left behind. It was hard enough here when she was alive – Pa's masculine scents always overwhelmed hers – but now she is fading fast. This is *his* room now, not *theirs,* and I'm an intruder. There are glasses and a bottle on the bedside table, hair oil on the sheet.

Sometimes I wish I hadn't left her necklace with Grandpa in Harlow. When Granny told me the value of the gold and pearl band that had been her own mother's, I was frightened of losing it. But it was the last thing Ma gave me, something she wanted *me* to have, and it would be comforting to hold it now.

6
Aysha

June 2001

Aysha lowers herself onto a large beanbag in Karen's bedroom, wincing at the creaking of countless polystyrene beads. The girls finished college early today, so she's visiting her friend's new home. Mike and Janet, Karen's parents, recently bought a flat overlooking Limehouse basin.

This is the sort of place Sel had thought their family should move to – the walls smooth and right-angled, everything modern and windows like huge picture postcards. Karen even has her own shower room! But Mike is a plumber and Janet works in the city and they've only themselves and Karen to provide for; an apartment big enough to house Aysha's family would cost a fortune. This place is lovely, but not as comforting as her Stepney home, with its odd corners, half-landings and stray bits of moulding which have survived from Victorian times. And then there's Emily's journal – it would still lie hidden in dust if she hadn't found it.

"You still stressing about uni?" Karen says. "You said you told your family and they didn't say no. I don't know why you left it so long."

I wouldn't have, thinks Aysha, if my family was like yours, but there's no point saying this to Karen, who has only to mention a problem for her parents to wade in with sympathy or cheque book, as the occasion demands.

Mum and Mo hadn't commented at first, but Dad had said, *I can't stand in the way of all my children.* His words were well meant, but knowing he was thinking about Mo, Aysha couldn't look her brother in the eye. He'd been doing A levels nine years ago, when Dad had a heart attack, and he'd given up his university plans to get a job to support the family. She'd listened to the drip of the kitchen tap, until at last Mo broke the silence.

"University? What happened to being an assistant in a school or a library?"

"My teachers think I should aim higher."

"I see." Mo voice had held a tinge of bitterness. "Girls are lucky," he said at last, "financial responsibility doesn't fall on them. They don't have to choose between study and marriage. But I can see university graduate could be good."

"You know me," she tells Karen now, "no good at telling people things."

She wasn't born that way, but you learn caution when even to ask can put you in the wrong.

"Did you mention the summer school?"

"Sort of. Mum thinks it's something everyone applying to uni has to do."

"Surely they'll be pleased if you get a really good offer?"

"What?" Aysha jolts herself free of the reel re-running in her head. "Maybe."

"Probably think you're worth a few more camels with BA after your name!" Karen ducks the cushion Aysha throws at her.

"Seriously, by the time you've got your degree, you'll be twenty-one with a good job lined up and can do what you like."

Andy Carstairs had said something similar. *You need to be your own person, Aysha, spread your wings.* The advice is sensible enough and a persuasive metaphor – to soar like a bird on a current of air – until she remembers Ibrahim's sticky hugs, Abdul's unexpected confidences and Reshna's shy, sudden smiles. She's used to belonging to a family. Even Sel, who has teased and squabbled with her since her first wobbly steps, is an important part of her life. And then there's Dad: diminished by his illness so that she no longer feels she can rely on him, but still the father she loves. If only he hadn't got ill... it wasn't only Dad's life that changed all those years ago. His principles and tolerance once stood at the centre of the family; now there's a vacuum which Mo seems determined to fill.

Karen's mum taps on the door and passes cans of cola to the girls.

"You look a bit down, Aysha," she says. "Your dad still poorly?"

Aysha nods.

"D'you want to stay for dinner?" Janet persists. "I'm doing salmon. You can eat fish, can't you?"

Aysha smiles. Janet prides herself on her cultural sensitivity.

"Fish is fine, Mrs Carter, but I really can't stay. Mum's expecting me."

"What about Sel?" asks Karen, when Janet has closed the door behind her. "Is he still seeing that girl?"

She shakes her head. "They're sending him back home next year to visit our uncle."

There'd been a big bust-up between Mo and Sel because Mo

had seen him *fooling around with some Russian tart*. Sel was damaging the family reputation by his behaviour, Mo had said, injuring their prospects. *Aysha's* prospects, is what he'd meant. As if she had any intention of getting married! It was all a stupid game – plus points for being a graduate, minus points if your brother misbehaved.

"Well, at least it's not you going to Bangladesh," Karen says. They both know of girls who thought they were going on holiday and found themselves brides.

July 2001

Mo and Reshna have a daughter! Aysha can't credit that Safiya is only two weeks old: already she has the household in thrall. Mo is back working nights after his week's paternity leave, so the baby's crib is moved to the living room each day to allow him to sleep. Dad sits watching films, rocking the cradle with one hand and keeping an eye on Ibrahim, who has been banished from the kitchen because Mum keeps tripping over his toys. Reshna attends to each child in turn – changing, dressing, feeding – and Aysha is occupied in continually filling and emptying the washing machine. She has to remind her mum that the summer school she signed up for starts the next day.

"It's all arranged," she says, "I'll get in trouble if I don't go."

Mum is too hassled to argue.

"Yes, okay, go, Aysha, yes," Mum says, "but next week take Abdul Maryam house."

Aysha nods and Dad slips her ten pounds for her fares.

The event runs over four days at a central London college with a programme of talks, workshops and discussions.

"You should realise that you are valuable commodities," one

of the speakers tells the students on the first morning. "We all need to broaden our intake with bright students from inner city schools and colleges."

Aysha's not sure how she feels about being a commodity. She's painfully conscious of her ignorance; she has travelled little outside London. The tutors here are from places like Reading, York and Durham – what would it be like to live in these places?

"Why history?" a tall, angular woman from a Cambridge college asks her.

Aysha struggles to find the words. "Because sometimes I read something or see something and then suddenly I understand and it doesn't matter how long ago it was. It's all still here, in us."

The woman tilts her long face to one side and regards Aysha. "Don't you think that could be said to be romanticising the past?"

"No," she says, surprising herself, "because you have to work at it. Like when I did my local history research."

"Write that thought down and develop it. You're doing English, too, you say? Make yourself a schedule to include some background reading each day."

Perhaps the woman can see the panic in Aysha's eyes. It's all right for you, she thinks, imagining the tutor, with her long red hair and bony knees and elbows, cycling each day to a comfortable book-lined study.

"You have family responsibilities?"

Aysha mumbles something about the new baby in the house. She'd felt guilty this morning, skipping out to catch a bus when Safiya was crying, Ibrahim fretting and the breakfast dishes filled the sink.

"Of course there will be times when you can't keep to it. Shit happens." The woman waits for Aysha to suppress an embarrassed giggle. "Especially where there are babies, I imagine. But you'd be surprised how much time most people squander daily. Time you can use."

By the end of week, the task ahead seems just as daunting, but she does feel energised, ready to start. There are three other students from her college and a sense of solidarity has emerged. The last session finishes at midday and, as Karen has a vacation job in her mum's insurance office, not too far away, the girls share their lunch in a sunny square.

"So," Karen says, crumpling her sandwich carton, "is it Oxford or Cambridge then?"

"Neither. I liked the sound of the English and History course at York. But I don't know any of these places."

"To be honest, I've been to Spain more than to rest of England," Karen admits. "Except Cornwall. We used to go there for holidays. I've been to Liverpool, Manchester and Leeds with Dad, but only to the football grounds."

"How's work?" She knows Karen is tempted by the prospect of an immediate wage.

"Bit boring really – just filing and stuff. The people are nice, but I think I'll go to uni after all."

They walk back to the glass-plated entrance of the insurance company, where a young man in a striped suit holds the door open with exaggerated politeness. Karen flicks back her pony tail and flashes Aysha a grin.

7
Emily

Friday 9 August

Sally has come again at last, full of tales of her grandmother's house and her cousin Josh.

"Don't mock, Emmie," she whispers, "but I think I'm in love."

"Is this Miss Fenton?" I say. "Miss *Sally* Fenton, the *schoolteacher?*"

"I mustn't tell you the feelings I get when he looks at me with those melting brown eyes! Anyway, you can't preach – my father told me ages ago how you were pounced upon by a most eligible young man when you called at the shop."

"Oh, he means Mr Baines," I say, remembering. "He's my father's warehouse manager. I met him by accident."

"Your pa must pay him well! Dad said he was spending high on fancy waistcoats and that *you* were talking *very* earnestly – are you sure there's nothing I should know?"

"We were talking of Charlie," I say, angry that Mr Fenton had thought me capable of idle chatter when my brother was dead.

Sally looks contrite and squeezes my arm. "I'm so glad to see you, Emmie. I did call after your mother's funeral, but your grandparents had whisked you away. Now Mum and I are going to my other grandmother in Hastings for a month and I won't see you – or Josh – at all."

At this rate, August looks like being a dreary month, with Sally in Hastings and Elizabeth in Brighton visiting her mother. I long for the sea, but it's too much to hope that Pa will take a holiday.

Mr Baines calls on us after dinner. I haven't seen him since Ma's funeral, but he has brought a parcel of books and, while Pa fetches some business papers, he turns to me.

"I hope you don't mind, miss," he says, "but my landlady's a great reader and I thought you might like these stories she's finished with. It's a dull time for you, I know."

"That's kind," I say. After all, it *is* good of him to remember me like this.

"I don't like to think of you bored and lonely, miss. I know what a lively mind you have."

He blinks several times, then peers at me closely. My old grey dress has become tight and I feel somehow exposed.

"You've grown," he says. "It must be the country air."

I feel myself blushing. I'm sure it's not right for him to comment in this way.

"The air is healthy in Harlow, no doubt."

"Then it's good of you to come back to us here in the smoke."

"I couldn't stay away any longer; not with Pa all alone."

"Of course not, but I told you I'd keep watch over your father and take what burdens I could upon myself." He opens his parcel and places a book in my hands. "You see I have your family's interests at heart."

Pa and I are a sad remnant of a family now and I'm not sure what our *interests* are.

"Surely it's the business that concerns you?"

"I believe I see no difference," he says.

Pa returns with his papers and they spend perhaps half an hour in conference. The books Mr Baines brought are romances, lightweight and a little old-fashioned: not much to my taste, but he means well, I suppose.

Friday 23 August 1901

Pa has invited Dr Reynolds and Mr Baines to dinner. Just the usual mutton, he says; we're not ready for formal entertaining yet. The custom of prolonged mourning dress seems to have passed with the Queen, but it is still only a few months since Ma died and I hope my grey blouse and skirt are sober enough. I decide to ask Pa's advice. His manner is serious as he looks me over – I fear I remind him of her – but he approves my outfit. Daisy offers to put up my hair and at the last moment I let her add a green ribbon. It was one of a packet Mr Baines gave me last Christmas, when he brought brandy for Pa and lavender water for Ma. I fear Granny would think me too gaudy, but the ribbons do suit me and I don't wish to be ungrateful for all Mr Baines' gifts.

I am not called on to talk much to him – he and Pa are busy discussing the quality of tobacco in the latest consignment – yet whenever I look up from my dinner plate, I find his eyes upon me and feel sure that Pa and the doctor must notice.

I have not seen Dr Reynolds since the funeral either, though Daisy says he called on Pa while I was in Harlow. I answer his enquiries after my health and that of my grandparents, but then I fall silent, uncertain how to proceed. The doctor was Ma's friend as well as her physician; I need to find a way to talk about her without upsetting Pa.

"Tell me, doctor," I venture, "was it you who brought me into the world?"

I hold my breath, expecting Pa to reprove me, but he continues his conversation with Baines and the doctor smiles, delighted.

"Indeed it was! Such a bright little thing you were right from the start. A thick mop of chestnut hair even then. Your eyes were blue at first, of course, but you were still startlingly like your mother, and then they turned that marvellous deep brown! You don't realise what a pleasure it is for a doctor, Emily, to see the babies grow up."

Doctor Reynold is a bachelor and probably past marrying now.

"I often thought you were like sisters." William Baines has been listening and breaks into our conversation. "I believe you will be taller, Miss Emily, but you are your mother's double in every other way."

I blush and look down: there is nothing he could say said that could please me more and at least we are talking, mentioning her name.

"I hope that Emmie is not as wilful as Maria could be," says Pa, with a cough. "If only she had not insisted on that foolish expedition for the queen's funeral..." He falls silent, passing his hand over his eyes.

"But wasn't it her strong will that brought you together," I exclaim, "when you boarded with Grandpa as a young man?"

"That was different, Emily, and a time you know nothing about," Pa snaps. "What makes you say such things of your mother?"

I can feel my face redden. I am mortified to have goaded my father into rebuking me in public. William Baines watches him with interest as I mumble my reply.

"Only something Granny said when I was at Harlow. About how young and in love you both were when they agreed you could marry."

Dr Reynolds breaks in quickly. "Edward, Maria's underlying condition was the cause of her decline. She caught a chill, perhaps, but it was the shock of losing Charlie that made her illness return so strongly."

I can see that Pa would rather cut short this conversation but I may not have another opportunity. "Doctor," I ask, "how long do you think Ma had been ill?"

"It's hard to say. I first knew of her symptoms perhaps five or six years ago. There were good and bad periods, as you may recall. As I once told you, it is not an infection; no-one else in danger."

This time, Pa makes sure to bring my questions to an end by sending me to tell Daisy to serve coffee in the parlour. "Wait for us there," he says. "We'll join you directly."

The three men all stand up as I leave. Although I must obey Pa's orders, I am, it seems, the lady of the house. William Baines springs around the table to open the dining room door for me. He rests his hand on the door frame to detain me and for a moment I think he is going to touch the ribbon in my hair.

"Be patient with your father, miss," he murmurs. "He feels his loss strongly and you can't help but remind him of your mother."

Despite everything, I feel happier than I have for months. I am grateful to the doctor, who had great affection for Ma and who talks such good sense. It pleases me, too, that Mr Baines seems to understand my situation. I feel a little uneasy when he talks about Pa in such a familiar manner, but he has worked for us for some five years now and Pa values his business sense and treats him more like a colleague than an employee. He has such an energy about him and brings a breath of the outside world: I have to admit that I have begun to anticipate his visits with more interest.

8
Aysha

September 2001

"Good, you're here," Karen says, giving Aysha an unaccustomed hug when she gets off the bus. "I thought you mightn't come."

"Why?"

"Mum says most of the Wharf was evacuated yesterday and the trains are almost empty today." She looks at the sky. "Haven't you noticed?"

"What?"

"No planes. They've changed flight paths so they don't come over the city. D'you remember the explosion near South Quay four or five years ago. Dad was working in the tower when that happened."

"Wasn't that the IRA?"

"Yeah. This is different though, isn't it? Like, global?"

They'd been with Jo Massey's tutor group in the room next to the library yesterday, complaining at having to start drafting their personal statements already. Aysha had been glad of the preparation she'd put in at the summer school.

"Remember, be specific and be honest. Admission tutors can

spot bullshit a mile away –" Jo had broken off, noticing a couple of students not paying attention – "look, I don't know what's going on next door, but let's concentrate on what we're doing, please?"

Aysha looked up to see a crowd around a television on the other side of the glass wall of the computer room. A phone had rung in the room.

"Phones on silent. You know the rules," Jo said automatically.

A different ringtone had sounded, then another. Beyond the glass, a whole clutch of mobiles were being held to ears and the crowd around the television had increased, now including an IT technician and two of the library staff. Jenny Norris, the librarian, opened the connecting door and said, "You might want to see this."

At the back of the crowd, Aysha had no idea what she was watching. She saw a crowded city skyline with blue sea beyond and two tall buildings, one haemorrhaging grey smoke from a gaping wound near the top. Then, implausibly, a plane flew into the second tower and a huge explosion flared like a volcano. The television channel replayed the scene over and over, as if somehow the outcome might change, but then the walls of one of the skyscrapers bulged and crumpled like a tower of blocks built by a child. She heard the words *New York* and *World Trade Centre.*

Today, the college security guards are inspecting ID cards properly, not just waving students through. A number of small groups are standing around and there's an air of suppressed agitation. Jo Massey isn't in and her class is sent to the library. Aysha takes out her background reading, *Emma,* but the world of Jane Austen seems a universe away. Karen shrugs as she too gives up the piece she's working on, closes her file and goes back to her newspaper.

In history, Andy encourages them to talk.

"Aren't there always civilian casualties in war?" he challenges. "The Americans should know that, isn't that what people say? They even invented the name for it: collateral damage."

What's he doing? thinks Aysha, picking up on their teacher's deceptively light, satirical tone.

"But there isn't a war!" she says.

Wahida, a girl both she and Karen knew in primary school, looks up, eyes flashing above her niqab. "You don't think so? When US planes routinely bomb villages in Iraq?"

"That's no excuse for yesterday," Karen interrupts. "The people in those towers hadn't bombed anyone."

"I don't see how they could do that – kill themselves and all those other people." The speaker is a tall black boy called Derrick. "It's different if you're a soldier; you know, being heroic to save your mates, or if you're gonna die anyway – not saying I could do it, you understand – but to plan it in cold blood!"

"Every cause needs its martyrs," Andy says.

"Martyrs don't kill other people," Karen insists. "You can't call those guys martyrs. Mass murderers, yeah."

"They sacrificed themselves for their faith: that's what a martyr does," Wahida insists.

"All to be rewarded in Paradise," comments Andy.

"It's hard for an unbeliever to understand."

"In hell, more like!" Karen snaps.

"You're right," Andy says to Wahida, sounding uncharacteristically rattled, "you're looking at an out and out atheist here – but I don't believe your religion truly says that."

"It doesn't." Aysha's knowledge is pretty shaky, but she'd seen how Mum cried at the television last night, how Dad sadly shook his head and feared peaceable Muslims would be held responsible.

She sees Derrick look at her with interest, but Wahida turns from glaring at Karen to hiss in Bengali, "We all know where your sympathies lie!"

Even when they were little, the girl had resented Aysha and Karen's friendship. Wahida's mother came from the same village as Mum, and she'd expected Aysha to choose *her*.

"Wahida, we keep to comments we *all* can understand in this class," Andy says wearily. He looks as relieved as the rest when a messenger comes to inform them that college will again close early that day.

9
Emily

Saturday 12th October 1901

My sixteenth birthday seems likely to be a poor affair, though Daisy, bless her, has baked my favourite lemon sponge. Elizabeth is indisposed and Sally has been sent to practise teaching in a school in Hampstead, and is staying at her grandmother's house. I can't help thinking how different everything was a year ago, when Ma and I visited the Lyons tea shop in Piccadilly and bought chocolate to send to Charlie and pastries for my birthday. As it is Saturday, Pa is home but his spirits are too low for a celebration, though he shares my cake at tea.

At six o'clock, William Baines bursts in, out of breath.

"Mr Watts, sir, I've had a stroke of luck. Friend of mine had theatre tickets, but his wife's ill and he can't go. Isn't it Miss Emily's birthday? I thought you might care to take her."

I look up in amazement, surprised that he knows it's my birthday and that he doesn't use the tickets himself. But I cannot imagine that Pa will go.

"It's a kind thought, Baines," he answers, "but I'm not fit for entertainment at present."

"I understand, sir," says Baines, "but I was thinking of

Miss Emily. Is there no-one who could go with her? Surely she deserves a treat. Wait... I suppose *I* could even... but, no, I'm not related. It's hardly right."

"Nonsense!" cries Pa, brightening. "I'd trust you above any man to take care of Emmie and *you* should be the one to benefit from your friend's misfortune. Yes, she could do with an outing. Look what a shabby birthday she has if it's left to me! Emmie, go change your dress and get ready."

I fly upstairs, scarcely believing my luck. I have never been to the theatre, except once to the pantomime, and wonder what I should wear. Mr Baines says the performance is not until eight, so I have time to choose – but I've grown out of so many clothes! My grey dress is worn and faded; the yellow muslin too flimsy. At length, I decide to brighten my navy blue skirt with a cream lacy blouse of Ma's that she altered for me last winter and catch up my hair with two tortoiseshell combs. I look in my dressing table mirror and see a girl who is *going out.*

When I come down, Pa pours a brandy for himself and a whisky which William Baines quickly tosses back. Pa thrusts four half-crown coins at him and Mr Baines steps out into the square, calling a boy to go hail a cab for us. I am to take a house key, Pa says, so that Daisy need not be late abed. I don't ask if Pa will wait up; I fear he'll have drunk himself insensible long before we're back. After a few minutes, a hansom arrives and Baines helps me into the seat, then springs up himself. The driver fastens the wooden shutters over us and we go off at a brisk pace. Enclosed as we are within the confines of the carriage, with only the side lanterns for light, I feel obliged to speak.

"This is very kind, Mr Baines," I say. "I had settled for a quiet evening with my book. Just think that your friend's tickets were for tonight!"

"Call me *William*," he says, smiling, "or *Bill* if you please. And forgive me if I'm pleased your father wouldn't go, for it gives me the pleasure of your company."

I frown, wondering if my father was somehow duped, yet am too excited to regret the outcome. The cab jolts as the horse pulls up sharply to avoid another vehicle and I am thrown against him. The driver behind us cracks his long whip and Baines leans towards me. The carriage light sways and I cannot see his face.

"Don't be angry. This can be the first of many such outings – your life does not have to be so confined."

"I don't see Pa letting me run around the town as a regular thing, Mr Baines – I mean, William. Ma would never have allowed it."

"Possibly not. But there could be a way." He picks up my hand and traces the contours of my palm with his finger, the way Ma used to with Charlie. I should draw my hand back, but the sensation is just short of being tickled and strangely pleasant. "Forgive me for being forward, but I am determined to speak."

"I don't know what you mean."

"You are still young, and nothing need yet be said in public, but if your father agrees we might have an understanding."

"An understanding?"

He raises my hand and brushes it with his full dark lips. I feel a shiver travel down my spine. "Emily, Emily, so clever, so lovely, but locked up like a princess in a tower. If we were to enter an engagement, your situation would change."

I snatch back my hand. "An engagement? But I'm only sixteen." I'm truly shocked, yet suddenly his recent attentions make sense.

"I've always admired you and recently have flattered myself

that my attentions are not unwelcome – I couldn't help hoping when I saw my ribbons in your hair. I won't hurry you – it can be a long engagement, a year, more if you wish – just let me have your word." He takes out his handkerchief and dabs at his eyes.

"I'm not ready to be married," I say. "It's too soon after Charlie and..."

"Your mother can't have been much older than you when she wed," he says, capturing my hand again,"and you're a bright girl. Consider how your father depends on us both. This way you need never leave him – you secure his future too. But take your time! I won't press you more tonight. It's your birthday – you must enjoy the show!"

I cannot believe this is happening – have I really had a proposal of marriage from William Baines? I've felt so miserable, so bored and lonely these last few months, that perhaps I *did* welcome his visits and conversation, but I never saw him as a suitor. Yet, to be admired for my person and my mind – isn't that what I've always dreamed of?

I was expecting a play and perhaps the Strand or Drury Lane, but the driver stops in Commercial Street at the Royal Cambridge Music Hall, a huge place, recently rebuilt, William says, and capable of holding more than a thousand people! I am amazed at the elaborate decorations, the velvet drapes and new electric lights, and at finding myself part of such a colourful crowd, both on and off the stage. My companion is as good as his word: his only concern is for my entertainment. Our seats are at the front of the circle. In the stalls below us, a few well dressed young men in the audience – toffs, he calls them – shout comments and call out to the performers. They seem more rowdy than all the rest.

William must have been here before, because as each act comes on he passes me his opera glasses and says, *this chap is really funny*, or *look at the acrobats, Emily, have you ever seen such a thing?* The performers are wonderfully daring, though I'm sure Granny would not approve of their scanty dress, or of the female singer who dresses as a man. When I mention this to Mr Baines, he smiles and says he hopes *I* don't disapprove; but surely so many people would not come if it were wrong?

I'm glad of the interval, because the room is so hot. William gets me a soda, at the same time buying a large whisky and a cigar for himself. I shake my head when he offers me a sip; I'd rather he didn't drink so. Ma would take a small glass of wine at dinner and even allowed me a little diluted with water when I turned fourteen, but she always discouraged Pa from taking spirits. If only he would give them up now! William seems perfectly in command of himself, but I wish I could believe that a wife might persuade him to abstain.

The second half of the programme includes a group of boys dancing in clogs, all dressed in sailor suits and boater hats. They can't be more than eight or nine and I wonder at their confidence in going on stage before so many people. The crowd clap and cheer the boys, but when a woman singer is out of tune, I'm shocked to see her pelted with orange peel and pennies and to hear the young men in the stalls yowl at her like cats. How awful to be treated so unkindly!

The hour is late when we turn out onto Commercial Street, but I am too excited to be tired. I've never been out at such a time. There are crowds of people here, both men and women, but they are not the sort of people I see by day. The world seems livelier, more brilliant; I feel nervous yet exhilarated. William smiles and takes my arm.

"You're quite safe with me, Emily. If you can stand here a moment I'll get us a cab."

As he steps into the street to hail a hansom, two figures emerge from one of the arched doorways that front the theatre and a stout blonde woman calls out to him,

"Billy boy, it's never you? Ain't seen you in ages – been doing well for yerself? Here, Ruby, look who it ain't!"

"Take no notice, Emily," he says quickly. "You've heard me tell that I brought myself up the hard way. I've had to rub shoulders with some rough characters in my time."

I nod but as he goes to speak to the cab driver, the woman pursues him and I see him mouth, "Get lost, Gertie!" and pass her a couple of coins.

"Always knew you'd make a gent, Bill," she says. At the same time her companion steps forward and leans in to my face. She's short, ginger-haired, with pitted skin and unnaturally red cheeks. When I look into her eyes, I am shocked to realise she's hardly older than me.

"You'll be all right there, darlin'," she whispers, her breath sour in my face. "Billy likes 'em young and though 'is eyesight might be rubbish, you can it take from me the rest of 'im's in working order."

I get trembling into the cab and shrink to one side, trying to keep my skirts from touching him. Baines bites his lip in anger and we travel the short distance in silence, but when we reach the house and I take out my key, he puts his hand on my arm.

"You mustn't let those unfortunate women spoil our evening, Emily."

"Mustn't?" I say, my voice breaking. "Well, you needn't wait longer for my answer – it's no. No!"

I hope to escape, but he follows me into the hall and Pa calls from the parlour above.

"Is that you, Bill? Come up and have a nightcap! Where's Emily?"

I run to the second floor and the sanctuary of my room. I'm worn out, but my mind is exploding, fizzing with the noise, the music, the darkness, the women's faces – everything I've seen tonight. I need to clear my thoughts and write everything down.

It's silly, I know, but I still hide my journal under the loose floorboard: I can't bear to admit that Charlie will never spy on me again. My room is directly above the parlour and when I lift the board, I hear voices from the parlour below. Pa's speech is slow and slurred and I cannot catch every word.

"I wish you'd... me first, Bill... sorry if... won't push her. Emmie's... girl."

"I'm afraid... received the wrong impression... know... win her round."

"Don't... sure, Bill. Emmie's stubborn."

"... your permission to try?"

I can't hear Pa's answer, but Baines' voice is suddenly clear, as if he has moved closer.

"Let me fill your glass, sir. Thank you, I'll take a whisky myself. Forgive me for bringing up your late wife's name, but wasn't Mrs Watts very young when you married?"

"... seventeen, Bill. Ah... loved her!"

"Yet her parents allowed the match?"

Again, no answer, only the chink of the decanter. I fear Pa will suffer tomorrow. He makes a strange, strangled sound that starts as a hiccough and ends as a sob.

"You're tired, sir, done in. Why not stay in your chair? Here's your rug, the decanter's beside you. No need to stir. I can see myself out."

"G'night Bill."

I can hardly breathe as I lift out my journal and replace the floorboard. Why does he ask about Ma? After a few moments I hear heavy footsteps and the click of the parlour door. Then the same footsteps in the hall and the sound of the front door opening and closing. I peer cautiously from my window, tweaking the curtain back an inch, expecting to see Baines striding across the square; I lift the curtain further, but there's no-one out there. I wait, watching, because I want to go down and check on Pa, remove the brandy and place the guard around the fire. Perhaps he still stands on our steps, fastening his jacket or tying his shoe.

A sudden noise makes me turn – and he's there in my room, closing the door softly behind him.

"Hear me out," he says thickly. "I won't leave it like this."

Whereas drink deadens Pa's senses, it seems to inflame William Baines. A vein throbs at his temple, his eyes dart everywhere and he clenches his fists as if he would fight someone. I start to call out, but he's upon me in an instant, his mouth covers mine, one hand roughly clamps my chin, the other encloses my breast and I gag as his tongue is forced down my throat and I taste the whisky sourness of his mouth. I try to scream but no sound comes. I ought to fight but I'm as helpless as a mouse cornered by the cat. I cannot stir, even when he pushes me down and raises my skirt.

"You think... you're so... clever, Emily Watts," he pants, "so like your mother. Well, do you know how to make a baby? Because that's what we're going to do. You should listen to Ruby.

It's all in working order."

He holds me down easily with one hand as he shrugs off his jacket, then pulls at his trousers. At last I kick out and find a shin and he swears; something – my journal, perhaps – falls with a thud to the floor.

"Miss? Emily?"

Daisy opens the door and stands wide-eyed on the threshold, carrying a glass of milk and my stone foot warmer. As he turns, I grab his hand and sink my teeth into it. He yelps in pain and jumps back, snatching his coat.

"Here's another bitch!" he sneers. "I'll have you yet, miss." He thunders down the stairs and this time the front door slams.

I cannot stop shaking, cannot stop the choking sobs which rise. My throat still feels obstructed. Daisy says nothing but drags my chair in front of the door, gets into bed with me, and holds and shushes me all night long.

And this was my sixteenth birthday!

~

I stir in the morning when I hear St Dunstan's bells, feeling Daisy's arm still round me, but slide into sleep again and when next I wake it feels late. The day is bright and I am alone. I think I should get up, but my limbs won't work. I am lumpen and heavy, as if my bones were lead.

At times I think someone is in the room and call for Daisy, but then I see a figure seated at the desk in the window which is somehow mine, yet not mine, and I whisper to myself *Aysha*. Her back is to me and I cannot see clearly, but I do not think she is reading as before. She is gazing out of the window and rocking gently: she looks almost in a trance. When her long black hair falls forward, she lifts a hand to tuck it behind her ear. I am comforted to see her and allow my eyes to close once more.

When Daisy comes in with tea and the remains of my cake, it is already growing dark again.

"What time is it?"

"Past six," she says. She sits on my bed and begins feeding me as if I were a child, dipping the cake into tea and placing morsels in my mouth.

"Pa?"

"Slept till twelve. Got a mighty headache and gone to his bed again."

"I must speak to him, Dais."

She nods. "Not today, though. Rest."

10
Aysha

October 2001

Aysha arrives home early as afternoon classes are cancelled.

"Where is everyone?" Her mother is alone in the kitchen, rolling out pastry, and the air is fragrant with fried spices and garlic.

"Ibrahim fever. Is sleep with Mo. Selim take Dad eye test."

"Where's Reshna then?"

"Baby need... um... needle... " Mum gives up trying to find the English words and explains in Bengali: Reshna has taken Safiya to the clinic; Aysha's early, does she want to eat?

Aysha dumps her bag by the door and perches on the edge of a kitchen chair.

"I'm not hungry. I ate at college." She switches to Bangla herself and Mum beams.

"Have tea then. And sit properly. You always look like you're trying to run away. Talk to your mother for once."

Aysha shifts her weight onto the chair and takes a cup from Mum. "Reshna doesn't usually go on her own, does she?"

As far as she's aware, either Mo or Mum always accompanies her sister-in-law.

"She's been there before. It's not far; she has to start some time. Mo can't always be there."

"It must be hard, away from her family and home."

"At first, yes. But home is where your children are. Maryam is not so very far away, but she has a good home now with her husband and boys."

"Do you miss Maryam, Mum?"

Mum looks down and places a spoonful of filling in a pastry cone. "I can see her when I need to and now I have grandchildren under my roof. I am lucky."

"What would we do if Sel got married? We wouldn't have space."

"Sel won't marry yet," Mum shakes her head fondly, "he's not ready, but when he does, we'll work something out. When I was a girl, I shared with my sisters and my granny. None of us had our own room like you."

Aysha swallows hard, but she can't see any possible alternative to the current sleeping arrangements in the house.

"I'm not being selfish. It's just that I need to work for my exams and I can't help that I'm the only girl. Perhaps when I go to uni..."

"Ah, yes," Mum interrupts, "we must have a talk about that."

"Dad said it was..."

"Wait, Aysha, I'm not..." Mum breaks off suddenly as the doorbell rings. She holds up her floury hands and speaks in English. "Reshna back. You get."

Aysha's anxious to know what Mum had been about to say, but she slips off her chair and goes to the front door. Reshna stands trembling on the step, eyes full of puzzlement, clutching Safiya and pulling an unravelled headscarf across her mouth. Maud is struggling up the steps with Safiya's buggy. Aysha looks from one to the other in confusion.

"What happened?" she asks Maud, then repeats the question in Bengali to Reshna as the old woman is still trying to get her breath.

"Beetch. Boys say *go home, beetch.* What is beetch?" Reshna hurries past her into the hall.

"Maud?" she queries.

"Stupid louts at the bus stop," Maud mutters, "shouting at the little mother. Your sister-in-law, isn't she? Pulled her scarf off. Frightened the living daylights out of her, I should think." She waves her walking cane in the air. "I jabbed me stick at them and gave them a piece of my mind, picking on a young mum and a baby. Mind you, that probably scared her, too."

Aysha drags the buggy into the hall and thanks Maud. She lifts the old woman's shopping bag and starts to carry it down to the basement, but Maud stops her.

"No, ducks, I can manage. You go and see to that poor girl. And I'd rather my old man didn't know I've been clashing with the local yobbos. He's always telling me, don't get involved – he knows what I'm like. Come and see us soon, lovey, just don't mention this to Bert, eh?"

Aysha closes the door slowly and returns to the kitchen. Mum is holding Safiya awkwardly, trying to avoid covering her in flour; Reshna has run upstairs to her and Mo's room.

"Here," Mum says, almost dropping the baby into her arms, "you look after."

Mo stumbles downstairs not properly awake, tripping over Aysha's college bag and hastily knotting his lungi at his waist.

"The old woman from the basement," he asks Aysha, "what did she say?"

Aysha repeats Maud's words.

"White boys? Does she know them? Go down and ask."

She shakes her head. "Maud doesn't want her husband to worry. She chased them off and rescued Reshna – isn't that enough?"

Her brother looks ready to argue, but then sinks heavily onto the nearest chair. "I should have been there. Those animals spat at my wife and child!" His voice wavers and he bites his lip angrily. He is a small man, compact and muscled from hard work, but no match for a hostile gang. Mum puts her hand gently on his shoulder, looking at Aysha and tipping her head toward the kitchen door.

Aysha takes the hint and carries Safiya up to her own room, where she sits by the window, rocking her gently. She tries to control her own agitation, so as not to communicate it to the child, but after a time she realises that it's Safiya who is calming her. She's matched her own respiration to the rhythm of her niece's tiny lungs and emptied her mind of everything except the child's presence. Of course, she's held Safiya many times – she sees her every day – but Aysha can't remember being alone with her before. She strokes the baby's fine black hair and bows her head to catch the infant's breath.

Eventually the sound of a car door rouses her and she looks out to see Sel helping their father from the passenger seat of the Peugeot. She hears the front door's click, Dad's heavy step and a rising swell of voices from the kitchen below. Then Abdul comes from school and the television blares out. She wants to go down, to find out what's happening, but the sleeping Safiya exerts a stronger influence and she continues to sit, held in a profound trance.

A little later there is a quiet tap on her door and Mo, dressed now and fully self-controlled, comes in. He gazes around the small room, inspecting her bookshelves, the clothes pole across the alcove and the old fire place with its potted fern. Unlike Sel, who has always made himself at home, Mo hardly ever comes here.

"You've made your room nice, Aysha," he says. "I'll take Safiya now – she'll be needing a feed. It's good you made friends with the old couple – you're right, the woman was kind." He picks up one of Aysha's history text books, with its neon flags of Post-it notes marking pages. "You're studying hard, sister. Good."

Gently, she passes Safiya to him, her hand lingering on the child's head. "She's still sleeping."

"She's like Ibrahim, she behaves well for you." He frowns. "You know, this is just as I feared. First attacks on the mosque, now this. Ignorant people blame us all for what happened in New York. We need to stick together."

"Is Reshna okay?"

"She'll be fine; she's resting in bed now. But Ibrahim's still a bit feverish – it would be good if you could help Mum with dinner."

She's always looked up to her brother. When she was Abdul's age, he was the bright sixth-former, the would-be scientist, doctor or chemist: disturbing his studies was forbidden. A year later, Mum was pregnant, Dad was recovering from a major heart attack and Mo had taken a job. Sometimes she'd like to put her arm round him, tell him not to worry, everything will be all right, but her brother has always had his personal protective shell, a magnetic field repelling close contact. All she can do now is nod and follow him downstairs.

11
Emily

Monday 14 October 1901

I rise as soon as I wake, but Pa has already left for the warehouse. I'm relieved to find him gone; I dread telling him what happened. I spend all day rehearsing the words I must say and can scarcely swallow my dinner, but I don't need to start the conversation. As soon as Daisy has cleared away, he calls me into his study. He took only water with his meal and appears to have thrown off the lethargy of recent days.

"Sit down," Pa says, pulling out a chair for me. He fiddles with his collar – his neck is blotched with red – and clears his throat before going on. "Emily, I know I've been lacking in what a father should be. Your mother's loss had quite undone me, but I must do my duty by you now."

I hold my breath, not sure what's coming.

"William spoke to me today and told me what passed between you."

"Mr Baines? He admitted his conduct?"

"I know of his proposal and how you received it. He told me of it Saturday night, but it was too late then to consider it properly. He's concerned that he alarmed you that evening and begs your forgiveness."

"Alarmed me!"

"He knows he should not have embraced you, but when you came down to wish him goodnight, he felt hope and was carried away."

"Embraced me! When I came down? But..."

"Yes, Emily. You haven't been prepared for men's attention. If your mother had been here, she would have spoken of such things."

At any other time I would be treasuring this conversation to laugh over with Sally. Is Pa trying to teach me the facts of life?

"I am not ignorant," I say. "Miss Morgan instructed the girls."

"I know. I signed the consent for that instruction. But a spinster lady cannot teach feelings. That is a mother's role."

I drop my head and begin to weep; I can't help it. I want Ma, but she's beyond my calling.

"You should understand, Emmie, that for a young man like William, who must make his way in the world before he can think of marriage, ardent feelings can be difficult to manage. Especially for one who shuns promiscuity, who would preserve himself for his wife."

"He says what...?"

"He meant you no harm. No doubt his aunt brought him up him well. He's determined to honour his future wife by his conduct."

I cannot speak. I don't know what to say. I hear that woman's hiss in my ear, I feel his tongue choking me still. Oh, he was right! I *had* thought myself clever, but I'd had no idea what deviousness I faced.

"He was unwise to declare himself so soon, not yet six months since your mother passed away and you only just sixteen.

He wants refinement where women are concerned; he's lacked a father's guidance. We can be the making of him, Emily, you and I. He must be patient, but you can reward his patience and good faith. We've lost so much, but with William we can look forward to being a family again."

"But you don't understand, Pa. He was dunk and he tried to... to force himself on me!"

"He knows he may have been a little warm. An innocent young girl like you cannot judge the strength of men's feelings. It was wrong of me to push spirits upon him that night."

"But he doesn't tell the truth, Pa! I'm sure he lied about the tickets and he's lied to you again. I didn't come down – he followed me to my room! Let me call Daisy – she is my witness."

His face darkens and I know I've made a mistake. Pa never shared Ma's good opinion of Daisy and, ever since Charlie's desertion, has viewed her with distrust.

"That's enough, Emily. I'll hear no more. Daisy! I might have known. I'll not have a good man slandered by two hysterical girls. I should have sent that young woman packing six months ago, when she turned my poor son's head."

Tuesday 15 October 1901

Only when Pa goes out do I sit down and record the events of the past two days in my journal. Of course, as I write, I think of everything I should have done or said: shaken my father into consciousness on Saturday night, roused myself yesterday to speak to him before Baines got there first, pleaded with him this morning, begged him to hear me out. Even now, I could go after him and demand that he confront that man in my presence, but I just sit here helpless, unable to act.

To Pa, I'm an ignorant girl, shocked into hysteria by a grown man's ardour. He holds a grudge against Daisy, because Charlie confided his plans to her, and he dislikes our familiarity. He'll never take her word over Baines'. Besides, he commented recently that with just two of us to cater for now, he can hardly justify employing a full-time cook. I cannot risk provoking Pa further; I don't want him to dismiss her, both for her sake and mine.

I start to question myself, going back over everything that happened, however painful, because I need to know that I'm *not* that hysterical girl. William Baines drank a lot of whisky that night – before we left home, at the music hall and again, later, with Pa: perhaps it *was* the strong drink that caused his behaviour. But then I think how carefully he must have planned our evening to give himself opportunity to make his proposal. He behaved well enough throughout the evening – a little too familiarly perhaps – until those women spoke to us and made me reject him outright. He claims he just lost his head but, even if drink made him bold, there was cunning and forethought in everything he did. Leaving my father dead to the world in the parlour, pretending to leave by the front door, trapping me in my own room – surely no man who really cared for me would do that?

Another thought is nudging at the door of my mind, knocking and running away, like the boys do in the square, daring me to catch hold of its meaning. He asked Pa how old Ma had been when they married. I remember how strangely Granny looked at me when I questioned why she and Grandpa had not prevented Ma from marrying so young, and how evasive my mother could be when asked how old she was when wed. Is it possible... could she have been already expecting little Edward Charles?

I'm trembling at re-living that night, but I have to confront it, make myself remember everything that he said. I can still feel his greedy mouth, his rough grip, the insolent ease with which he pushed me down. I hear his words in my head: *do you know how to make a baby? Because that's what we're going to do.* My mind grasps at all the threads, trying to pull them together. And then I have it! He wants to push me into marriage, to force me to choose between him and disgrace! I look back over the year since Charlie ran away and, though it would have seemed ridiculous to think so at the time, I believe that even then he marked me out. I'm sure I'm right, yet it doesn't answer all my questions. Ma and Pa were young, in love and desperate to be together, but why would any man force a girl unwillingly into marriage or treat her so rudely, if he hoped to win her love? There must be something more.

I tell Daisy that Pa doesn't believe me, but I don't go into details. I don't want her to know her position is at stake.

"Don't worry, miss," she says, "he won't have the nerve to show 'is face in the house again. But if he does, I won't let you out of me sight."

I hope she's right. I consider asking Granny for advice, and even start a letter, but I cannot bring myself to write the words. I could go to Harlow, but I don't want to leave Pa again. With no-one left to moderate his drinking, I fear he will make himself seriously ill.

I try to tell myself that I'm blameless, but I can't deny that I enjoyed Baines' conversation and was flattered that he treated me as older than my years. My life seemed empty; I wanted to think that someone recognised my worth. I wore the ribbons he gave me and I was so quick to abandon Pa on my birthday for an evening's diversion. Perhaps I'm the sort of girl they call a tease and it's all my fault.

No, says a small, quiet voice in my head. Think of Sally: she flirts and jokes with Josh and his friends but she isn't treated like this. What William Baines did was unforgivable. I know that it's true, yet still I feel ashamed. When Daisy is kind to me, I blush to think she saw his hands upon me and I will *never* tell Sally. I can't let her know that, despite all her knowledge of the world, my experience is more terrible and true.

This time when I go to my room I fully expect to see that other girl who lives there: Aysha, my ghostly companion, whose presence is not scary but comforting. And she's there! Sitting by the window as before, gazing into space as if preoccupied. I see her pick up a book and start to read.

"Aysha!" I say, but she doesn't look up, though I can tell she's not concentrating. I wish I could talk to her. Whoever she is, she has her problems, too; I like to think she'd understand mine.

12
Aysha

October 2001

The whole community knows of Reshna's ordeal. The local Bangladeshi councillor telephones his sympathy to Mo, while a deputation of prayer-capped elderly men come to sit with Dad, demonstrating solidarity by chewing betel nut and drinking sweet tea. Mum is constantly phoning Maryam, spilling out torrents of rapid Bengali, happy for once for Aysha to keep out of her way. Sel and his car are called upon whenever Mum and Reshna need to shop. Sel doesn't complain, but he takes refuge with Aysha when the old men are downstairs.

"What's wrong with *your* room?" she asks as he lounges in her doorway. It's hard to concentrate on her essay with him standing there.

"Can't move for Star Wars figures."

She glances across the landing to the room where their younger brother has built what looks like an elaborate film set. Abdul is zooming a model space craft through a canyon of Lego blocks, throwing in cryptic references to the Force and the Dark Side. Aysha giggles.

"It's not funny," Sel complains, massaging a bare foot.

"Nearly crippled myself on that droid."

She can cope with her brother's presence as long as he just listens on his headphones and doesn't smoke, but he switches off his music and looks expectantly at her, as if he wants to talk. She lays down her pen.

"Was Mum still on the phone to Maryam?"

"Yeah, talking about you when I came up."

Aysha remembers that Mum wants her to take Abdul to Maryam's next week; she won't get out of going this time.

"What were they saying?"

"Didn't hear much. The old guys were chuntering on. Think Maryam's coming over tomorrow." Sel looks at his watch, "I gotta go soon."

She remembers something else she's been meaning to ask. "Mum and Dad said you might go to Bangladesh this year – is that still on?"

"Dunno. They said to go for Eid, but that's only two months away. I ain't even got a passport yet."

"D'you want to?"

"S'pose. Might as well." He seems oddly unconcerned.

"What about your friend Velna?" She wonders whether Mo's disapproval has had any effect on Sel. Presumably the girl is still employed at the restaurant.

"Velna's just a mate. I have to work with her, don't I? Anyway," Sel turns to go with a dismissive snort, "she's shagging the boss now."

He's putting on an act, she thinks, trying to scan his face for hurt feelings. But he's gone: across the landing to run the gamut of Abdul's film set, grab his shoes and leave.

Later that evening, Aysha turns back her rug and carefully levers the loose floorboard in her room, lifting out both Emily's journal and a small pile of university prospectuses. She still hasn't made her choices. The early deadline for Oxford and Cambridge has passed: a relief, as her teachers can no longer urge her to consider them. Her tutor, Jo Massey, hasn't had time to get on her case. Jo's brother was injured in the Twin Towers attack and she took time off to fly to see him.

"It's up to you, Aysha," she'd said, "but make sure it's *your* decision. Choose the right courses for you."

The glossy prospectuses are small miracles of design, brimming with promises of life and learning, as alluring as travel brochures or expensive magazines. Aysha shuffles them uncertainly, then fans them out, playing patience with UK cities – Cardiff, Durham, York, Southampton, plus a couple of London universities. Her family has no idea she's considering anywhere outside the capital.

She sweeps the pile to one side without coming to any resolution and picks up the journal, sniffing tentatively at the cover to inhale the leather scent. She hasn't re-read it recently – her course work has been too pressing – but she can't resist just holding the book whenever she stows her university papers under the floor. She knows many words and phrases by heart, having read and re-read them compulsively when she first discovered references to herself.

The journal seriously challenges all Aysha's rational beliefs, but to Emily her experience must have seemed more incredible still. Even if she'd seen Asian nursemaids or servants in London, what sense would she have made of a someone like Aysha living in the house? As far as she understands, it is only *her* that Emily saw, and only here – in the bedroom that must have been Emily's too – that this unfathomable link exists.

She didn't tell anyone. Not her father, nor her grandparents, not even the maid Daisy, who seems to have been much the same age as Emily herself. And nor has she. Aysha gives a little shiver at the thought of sharing a secret no-one else would believe with a girl who lived a hundred years ago.

She mustn't let the mystery prevent her from reading the journal objectively. Telling herself she's looking for strictly historical material, she makes notes of questions to ask Andy in history (1: causes of Boer War, 2: use of concentration camps), but her real preoccupation is Emily herself. How hard it must have been for such a bright girl to give up school, though it was probably a common enough story in 1900. And then to lose her brother and mother in a few short months – how brave she was!

The narrative had ended in the June of 1901 when Emily came home from her grandparents' house. It wasn't surprising she'd abandoned the journal, when everything she had to write about was sad. Perhaps it has lain under the floor ever since that time. Aysha flicks backwards from the end cover to see how many blank pages remain, then stops and stares, aware of a sudden heavy drubbing in her chest. There are entries she's sure she hasn't seen before! The last entry – very long – is written in an unruly, disordered script and carries a date in October 1901. There's no way she could have missed all this! Aysha drops the journal abruptly, as if it's too hot to hold. From the outside, the green leather book looks the same, but it's no longer an artefact, a historical document: it's a live channel to the past!

Three long minutes pass before she picks up the journal again, beginning to read after the last entry she remembers. She studies Emily's account of her conversation with Dr Reynolds and wonders if the illness was that killed her mother could have been leukaemia. Then she finds the entry for October 12th and begins to read: *My sixteenth birthday seems likely to be a poor affair.* Aysha smiles to herself: she always has problems explaining to her English friends that Muslim families don't celebrate birthdays as extravagantly as they do. But, as she reads on, smiles turn to frowns, interest to anger, and she reads and re-reads the words long into the night, unwilling to close the book on Emily's pain. Eventually, too exhausted to do anything other than reach to switch off her bedside light, she closes her eyes.

~

"Aysha! Is late now. You wake?"

She struggles into consciousness, uncertain what day it is. The clock reads 08.57. Mum puts her head round the door and Aysha quickly throws the corner of her duvet over the journal which has fallen on the floor. The prospectuses, thankfully, are under the bed.

"I had a headache and couldn't sleep – and then I did. Oh, I'm so late."

"Too much read," Mum says, looking round for a book to blame. "Need brain rest. Take day off."

"No, I'll go in late. I'll be down in a minute, Mum. I'm hungry."

As soon as she hears Mum's footsteps going downstairs, Aysha jumps out of bed to stow the journal and the prospectuses under the floorboard. She can hear Ibrahim calling for Reshna on the floor below and remembers that Emily could hear Baines and her father talking when she lifted the board.

The bedroom looks reassuringly familiar in the clear light of morning. This was Emily's retreat, the place she fled to after the trip to the music hall, a sanctuary that the man Baines had violated. He assaulted Emily, would probably have raped her but for her maid coming in. What was it Emily wrote? *I open my mouth to scream, but he is upon me in an instant!* She tries to visualise the struggle that must have taken place, wondering how the room was arranged in Emily's day. Now, there's scarcely room for her own bed, chest of drawers and desk, and the fireplace is oddly positioned in one corner of the room. Emily's room had been bigger than her own; the shower room on the other side of the wall wasn't there in 1901. Reaching out, she taps the wall which runs beside her bed and listens to the hollow, echoing sound.

1901. She'd checked the dates of Emily's last entries before replacing the journal – the attack had happened on Emily's birthday, October 12th, almost exactly a hundred years ago, and Emily had seen her in this room, the next day when she was lying in bed, drifting in and out of sleep. As when she first found the journal, she's frustrated by a powerful desire to reach out to the other girl; though it sounds like I did help, she thinks, just by being here.

But Emily died years ago. She must be going crazy!

She gets to college in time to join her history group during their mid-morning break, though not without arousing notice.

"What happened to you?" Karen asks.

Derrick looks at her closely, "You okay?"

Andy stops by her table as he comes back into the room. "We missed you, Aysha. You should phone if you have an appointment or something."

Embarrassed, Aysha mumbles an apology and something about a headache.

"Don't worry this time," Andy tells her, "it's not as if you make a habit of it. But Karen and Derrick could do with some help now."

She has passing thoughts about sharing the contents of the journal with Karen or even Andy, but puts them aside to concentrate on the task at hand. Her group is working on the effects of the First World War on women's lives. She and Karen have done the research, but Derrick is a wizard at PowerPoint, so they make a good team.

"We want to arrange to go ice skating," Karen whispers when Andy moves to another table. "The outdoor rinks open in November."

"It'll be Ramadan soon..." begins Aysha doubtfully.

"Not till the seventeenth of November," Derrick interrupts. Then, as Aysha looks surprised, he adds, "I checked on the internet when Wahida said she couldn't come."

"She wouldn't come anyway," Karen says, "but we're going before that – the week after half-term."

"You'll come, won't you?" Derrick asks Aysha.

"I can't skate."

"You'll get the hang of it."

"That's what you think," Karen laughs. "You haven't seen her in the gym – no sense of balance whatsoever!"

Aysha nods; despite her slight figure and plenty of enthusiasm, she's never excelled at sports.

"What's that got to do with it? We'll hold your hand. Just say you'll come, Aysha. It'll be fun." To her amazement, Derrick grabs her hand and glides it with his own across the table, mimicking a skating move. Karen catches her eye over his shoulder and raises a single, quizzical eyebrow.

In the afternoon, Aysha has a tutorial.

"Sit down," Jo says. "You look tired, Aysha. I know we all want you to keep up the hard work, but make sure you get your sleep too. Now, I'm hoping you're going to tell me you've settled on your UCAS choices."

"Yeah, I think so. I'm just not sure whether to put a couple of local ones in?"

"Because of the location or the courses on offer? Look, I'm not saying one place is better than another – I just think, for you, Aysha, to achieve your full potential, you need to get away. Surely that was the whole point of your summer school?"

It seems impossible that the summer school, with all the enthusiasm and the empowerment it generated, was only a couple of months ago. She feels like a piece of clay, taken away to be moulded, only to be squashed back into the larger clump at the end of the day.

"Did you do that when you were my age – move away?"

Jo considers this. "There wasn't really any other option – no higher education in my home town twenty years ago. My brother Paul and I were the first generation of our family at university."

"The one in New York? Is he all right?"

"Fine now. He was one of the lucky ones. Now, Aysha, just settle on your five choices as soon as possible. I'd rather not have to rush writing your reference, so be ready by Monday after half-term. Okay?"

I'll talk to Mum and Dad tonight, she thinks. Karen is applying for business studies and wants to stay in London; Derrick has surprised them all by opting for primary teacher training. So many choices: opportunities poor Emily would have jumped at.

She'd forgotten about Maryam coming. The house is chaotic, full of small boys dashing around and shouting confusing instructions to each other. Ibrahim, now nearly two, runs shrieking after Abdul and screeches loudly when told, *No, Ib'rim, you've got to stay on the Dark Side!* Reshna hovers anxiously on the landing, expecting disaster. The older boys play well together, but they delight in winding up the younger two.

Mum asks her to supervise the boys' tea while she and Mo talk to Maryam. She supposes they want to update her on Reshna's ordeal, though surely her sister has heard it all on the phone by now, but then Mo asks Reshna to watch the boys and tells Aysha they all want to talk to her in the living room.

Mum and Maryam are seated at one end of the sofa, Dad at the other, separated by Maryam's handbag and a Lego dinosaur. Aysha sees Mum push an envelope behind a cushion while Maryam fiddles with her bangles. Mo follows her into the room and stands in front of the television set.

"So, what d'you want to tell me?" she asks.

"Good news," Mo says.

Mum opens her mouth to speak, but – almost imperceptibly – Maryam shakes her head. Her sister scoops up her bag then reaches out to take Aysha's hand and pull her into the place beside her.

"Yes, sister. Good news for you, for your future."

For an instant, Dad's eyes meet hers, then he looks resolutely down.

She's sitting in the ground floor cafeteria, hunched over a polystyrene cup and shredding empty sugar sachets, when Karen arrives at college next morning.

"You're early. Making up for yesterday?" asks Karen, looking at her watch.

Aysha lifts her shoulders in a shrug and mumbles an indistinct reply.

"What's up?"

She briefly raises her head, then glares down at her coffee cup, whipping up a whirlpool with a plastic spoon.

"Well?" Karen flops down on the chair opposite, leaning forward to peer into Aysha's eyes and fix her with a level gaze. "Shit, Aysh, don't go all secretive on me."

Aysha blinks. Apart from a tremble of her upper lip, her only response is to tear open another sachet and sprinkle sugar patterns onto her coffee. Karen flicks back her hair and gets up. "Have it your own way. I'll see you in class."

"Kas." The voice is a thin, uneven quaver. "I don't know what to do."

Karen's back in an instant, gently removing the sugar-saturated coffee and covering Aysha's hands with her own.

"They've found me a husband."

"Your family? They can't! You can't, I mean – you're only seventeen. What about uni?"

'Oh, I can do both. Apparently. They've got it all worked out. Not that I listened."

"Want to come back to our place?" Karen asks at the end of a very long day.

Aysha has forced herself to show enthusiasm for Karen

and Derrick's efforts for their history presentation when all she wanted was to be alone. She shakes her head and turns towards the bus stop.

The family eats an early dinner in silence; even Abdul's usual exuberance seems stilled and he slides down from the table, taking Ibrahim with him to watch television in the living room with Dad. When Reshna starts to clear the table and Aysha moves to help, Mo puts a hand on her arm. "Just a minute, sister. I haven't got long before work and we need to talk."

"No run upstair," Mum adds.

Last night she'd stormed out, shut herself in her room and found herself reading Emily's words again. Nothing had changed, she thought: nothing mattered to them all except marriage and money. She scrapes her chair back and sits stiffly, ignoring her mother's frown.

"Listen, Aysha. We do want you to get your degree," Mo says. "I tried to tell you that last night."

"So why d'you want me to get married? Or is that just Maryam's idea?"

"Maryam wants the same as us, to secure your future. And it doesn't need to be an either or. Like I said, it's easier for girls – you don't have to be a breadwinner yourself."

She looks down, tracing patterns on the chequered tablecloth, rounding up stray grains of rice and corralling them into a blue square.

"Look what happened to Reshna. The world's gone crazy – it's no time for a young woman to be on her own. You need the security of a family."

"I thought I had that. Anyway, you can't compare me to... I'm not like Reshna. I mix with lots of people at college and I don't look different. It's not like that for me."

"You're a fool Aysha, if you think all this high street rubbish will protect you." Mo waves at her clothes – jeans and Topshop sweatshirt – with a dismissive hand.

She sees Mum nod encouragement at Mo. Oh, let him get on with it, say what he wants to say; he'll have to go to work soon. She has no desire to fight Mo, she's always looked up to him.

"I'm listening. All right?"

Mo draws a deep breath. "We've been told of a family..."

"Maryam husband cousin," Mum interrupts. "Very nice people, plenty money, one son only."

Aysha senses Mo waiting for their mother to pause.

"It's a good family," he says, "religious, but not over strict. The son is twenty-two, recently graduated. The family has a good business. They could afford to support you while you do your degree."

"Son nice looking. Very handsome!" Mum adds.

Aysha absorbs this in silence. Then, turning to Mo, she asks, "What about afterwards?"

"How – afterwards?"

"Will he let me work when I've got the degree? Because maybe I'll need to move to get a job. I'm not going to stay home all day – going to uni isn't a hobby, you know, it's my future!"

Mo shakes his head. "Of course you can work, but don't you want a family of your own?"

"I don't know; not for ages yet, and when *I* choose."

"Not rush," Mum says. "Exam, wedding, degree. One at time."

Aysha looks at her mother's face, searching for the slightest trace of irony. That's her next four years sewn up! "I can't see this guy wanting me to be away at uni half the year," she mutters.

"Away?" Mo says.

"Yeah –" assuming a confidence she doesn't feel – "away, like Durham or Cardiff or York – how's he going to like that?"

Mo combs his hair with his fingers and she notices a fleck of grey at his temple. What age is he now – twenty-seven, twenty-eight?

"There are plenty of universities in London. Why go somewhere you don't know anyone?"

It's hard to explain without seeming arrogant. She's picked courses which excite her, in universities and cities which look promising, but there could be local equivalents. It wasn't a conscious decision, there wasn't a specific moment, but somehow – incrementally – she has come to accept her teachers' evaluation, that she'll only fulfil her potential if she cuts herself free. There is a little hard seed growing in her, a pearl of ambition, which she can no longer ignore. She *can* do it; she shouldn't settle for second best. It's one thing to know this, another to say it: *how* to do it is something she cannot even envisage. Yet she will. Not today, not tomorrow, but when the time comes she'll find a way. What had Mum said, one step at a time? For the moment, she needs to avoid a fight.

"I suppose I could look at a couple more London unis."

"Have you filled in your application yet?" Mo asks. Of course he knows the timescale: he'd applied through UCAS himself,

"I have to do it next week. I will look at my choices, Mo, but I don't want to get married."

"Even studying in London, you'll be travelling more. A young girl mixing with strangers, meeting young men – it's easy to be led astray. Mum – and Dad – would feel better if you were settled."

"Is for best, Aysha," Mum says. "Baba health not good."

Aysha looks through the doorway to her father sitting in the lounge. Is this really what he wants her to do? He still has regular checks at the hospital, but he seems okay – unless there's something she doesn't know. If Dad is really unwell, perhaps she should stay in London, not to get married, but to be here, at home, with him.

"I'm too young," she says.

"Not now," Mo says. "We know you've got exams to think of. But next summer, after you've finished, when you're eighteen."

"No-one ready," Mum says, "learn after wedding. Reshna not ready first, she happy now, have children, husband." She beams at Mo, who turns his head, embarrassed.

"Times have moved on," he says. "You'll have a chance to meet this young man between now and the summer."

"What if I don't like him? Or if he doesn't like me?"

"Why make problem?" asks Mum. "Why he not like you? So beautiful! He good-looking boy. Clever. Nice car. Of course you like!"

"All we're asking," Mo says, "is that when his family calls, you treat them respectfully and give him a chance."

Is this is how Emily felt, trapped in her house by a man who wanted to marry her without any respect for her own hopes and needs? If Baines had acted differently that night, or if they hadn't met those women outside the music hall, Emily might have accepted him, not knowing the sort of man he really was: someone who got drunk and abused women! A sudden thought alarms her: how does she know Emily didn't marry Baines? Perhaps the pressure to please her father was too great. Will there be any more entries in the journal? She has to find out!

When Mo glances at his watch and stands up, she judges that she too can leave.

"So what's this amazing guy's name?" she says, her hand on the door knob.

Her brother picks up the sarcasm and throws her a disapproving glance, but Mum breaks in eagerly, "Name Jamil. Good name, mean handsome."

13
Emily

Friday 1 November 1901
Three weeks have now passed since my birthday and I have seen no more of Mr Baines. I hope Daisy is right and he will keep away. I've always done a share of the housework, but recently I've thrown myself into it – not for enjoyment but because keeping busy stops me from re-living that night in my head and I'm determined not to give Pa any cause for complaint. His temper is short lately and I'm afraid he frequently drinks himself to sleep at night.

Elizabeth has asked me to sit with her in the mornings, while Richard is working and Ernie is at school. She looks tired and pale and, remembering how Ma's illness affected her, I am concerned for Elizabeth's health. She laughs and asks if I can keep a secret: she is expecting a baby in the spring and has been suffering from morning sickness! Richard is delighted, she says, but they have not told Ernie yet. She spends the hours when he's at school in sewing baby clothes and teaching me how to smock. I do like to sew, but I prefer more active pursuits. I suggest a walk, thinking that fresh air would make Elizabeth feel better, but she seems to look upon her condition as an excuse for staying in her parlour all day.

"When will you tell Ernie?" I ask, thinking it strange that the boy who talked to me about his mother's death should be excluded from the beginnings of life.

"We're sending him to Richard's mother for the Easter holiday," Elizabeth says, "until after the baby is born. His grandmother will talk to him. I don't think it right that a young boy should be exposed to such things too soon."

"He knows all about kittens," I say. Ernie sometimes calls on Daisy after school for a slice of pie and to play with Mabel's latest litter.

"Emily," says Elizabeth, shaking out her needlework, "I hope you don't compare me to a cat."

Saturday 2 November 1901

We saw our first frost of the season this morning – just a crispness of white on the pavements, but it makes us feel winter is here. Daisy wants to cook Christmas cake and puddings. I cannot imagine Pa wanting to make merry – so much has changed and we have so little to celebrate – but he will want to keep to tradition. Elizabeth says we are too soon: *her* mother never made puddings until the end of November, but Daisy says this is when Ma always made ours.

I wish Pa and my grandfather were friends and it were possible for my grandparents to come here, or for us to go to Harlow. Granny writes to me regularly now and I know that *I* could go if I asked, but I can't leave Pa alone at Christmas.

"Shall we wish?" asks Daisy as we make breadcrumbs and chop the apples and raisins.

We always used to make wishes when we stirred the puddings or cake, but what could we wish for now that could possibly come true? Troops are coming home from South Africa; boats bring back the sick and injured, then fill up with reinforcements and return to the Cape. In the city, crowds cheer young men in uniform marching off to uncertain fates, but however closely I scan their faces, I'll never see Charlie there.

I don't know about Daisy, but I do make a wish all the same. Not for something to have, and not for anything now, but for one day in the future to be happy. Ma must have been heartbroken when baby Edward died, but she then she had Charlie and me. I'm sure she never forgot her loss, but she loved us and I believe she was happy. I hope one day I can be too.

We tie up three puddings in muslin ready to go in the boiler, but it's already late in the afternoon when they start to cook and we have to wait past bedtime for them to finish steaming. Daisy, who was up at six, is falling asleep, so I offer to watch them for the last hour.

"Mind you don't let 'em dry out, miss," she yawns. She doesn't trust me to keep awake, but she knows *she* won't either. I don't dare let myself sit down, so I occupy the hour lining up jars and packets in the pantry, writing lists of things we need and polishing the silver teapot. At last, I am able to turn off the boiler, remove the puddings and leave them to cool.

I'm not even thinking about Aysha, but when I go to my room I see her, slumped in a chair by the window. Her outfit is different and much grander than before: a blue tunic with matching pantaloons, embroidered in gold. They are clothes I imagine an Indian princess might wear, but she seems careless of them and looks as if, like me, she's exhausted.

"Aysha!" I say, but she doesn't know I exist. I study her face: she will not sleep well. Too much is written there.

She gets up, stretches, and begins to speak. Not to me or, it seems, to anyone else who's there; rather, I imagine, out of a troubled heart. At first I think I recognise the words, then I am confused.

It's a truth universally acknowledged that a young man in possession of a... a chain of fried chicken shops – she curls her lip – *must be in need of a wife.* Then her mouth twitches into a smile and she glides from side to side across the floor, swaying her arms as if she's dancing or skating. Then, suddenly, she's gone.

Miss Morgan showed the class a picture book of India once. There were paintings of forts and temples and elephants carrying maharajahs, and each of the illustrations was overlaid with a leaf of tissue paper. I would ask to see the book and try to remember the order in which each picture came, to guess what was underneath the overlays. The images were there, behind their tissue veils, but you couldn't quite see them until you turned the leaf. Sometimes I think that's how it is with Aysha: that she's here all the time if I could only see. But which of us is behind the tissue, I cannot tell.

14
Aysha

November 2001

"Hey!"

Derrick is sitting on the wall, apparently waiting for Aysha to get off the bus, since he immediately jumps down and follows her to the crossing.

"Good half-term?"

After that first Friday night, when Mo and Mum disclosed their plans, she'd been left alone all week. Mum herself took Ibrahim and Abdul to Maryam's, so Aysha just needed to look after Dad. Even Mo had been more relaxed than usual – *got his wife to himself*, Sel commented – though he'd asked to see her UCAS application at the end of the week.

"Yeah, not bad," she nods.

"I've done my UCAS," Derrick says as they cross the road and take the shortcut through the park. "Gonna hand it in to Andy today." He twists his white baseball cap into reverse and grins down at her. Her face is just about level with his biceps; his limbs seem to extend forever in the blue and white tracksuit and his feet in their pristine white trainers look enormous. He looks like he's grown a couple of inches in the last week.

"I've got to check a couple of things with Jo," she says, "but basically it's done." What she doesn't say is that she's completed two versions, one for college, one for public consumption at home.

"Skating's sorted. Friday afternoon, when we all finish early."

"Where?"

If it isn't far, she can get home in time to avoid questions, but she'd rather not admit that to Derrick; it sounds so childish.

"Broadgate, near Liverpool Street. Not all the rinks have opened yet. You are coming, aren't you?"

"I guess. I can't skate though."

"I'll look after you. I used to go to the Lee Valley indoor rink. Mum took me for my birthday once, then I got really keen. If you do fall over, get your hands off the ice – someone ran over mine when I was little. See?" he holds out his palm and Aysha sees a faint line, just below the thumb.

"Don't tell her that or she'll never go." Karen has caught up with them in front of college and wraps her arm around Aysha's shoulder. "Come on," she says, pulling Aysha aside, "you've got an audience. See you later, Del."

Surprised, Aysha notices a group of girls watching them. She glances back at Derrick, who is still grinning at her, and for the first time sees past the computer geek she helps with his essays. A couple of girls look positively hostile. Then, turning in the other direction, she sees dark eyes flash above a hijab and recognises Wahida.

"Shit, Aysh," Karen mutters as they wave their passes at security, "half of them want to scratch your eyes out and the other half are busting to tell tales on you. When did this happen?"

"Nothing's happened. He was just waiting at the bus stop."

"D'you like him?"

"Of course I like him. He's a friend."

Karen sighs. "I mean d'you fancy him? 'Cos he obviously does you."

Aysha stares then starts to giggle hysterically.

"What's funny?"

"Mo and Maryam say they've found me a husband, I'm lying to my family about UCAS – all I need now is for them to think I've got a boyfriend." She stops, leans back against the corridor wall and looks up at Karen. "I do like Derrick, but I can't get involved."

The form Aysha hands in to Jo Massey includes one London course, at King's College, but the others are scattered throughout England. Jo reads the list and nods.

"Good choices."

"It's not what my family wants. They expect me to stay local." She pauses, then holds Jo's gaze, hoping the tutor will take her meaning. "Do they have to sign anything?"

Jo gives her a long, level look. "Once you've got a place, you can apply for a loan in your own right. But if you're entitled to claim free tuition, you'll need evidence of parental income. Do you foresee problems?"

"I don't know."

Jo tucks Aysha's application form into her file. "Keep me posted," she says.

When the girls go down to lunch together, Derek waves them across to the table where he's seated.

"Don't you dare desert me!" Aysha hisses at Karen.

Derrick holds out two soft drink cans, offering them to the

girls. Aysha sits down and takes one, mumbling thanks.

"Cheers, Del," Karen grins, "but I've just remembered I've got a tutorial. See you later, Aysh!"

"Take it with you," Derrick says, tossing her the remaining can.

Aysha takes her sandwich from its cellophane and nibbles in silence; she can't believe Karen has gone. Derrick spreads his elbows wide across the table and studies her anxious face.

"If you don't like me, you've only got to say."

"I do like you," she begins, "but it's complicated right now."

"Try me." He pops the ring pull on her can and hands her back the drink.

"Look, I may not cover up like Wahida and some of the others, but I still can't... I mean my family still expect... oh, do you have a big family?"

"Just me and my mum. But I do know about expectations. She's worked her butt off for me all my life; I daren't let her down."

Aysha rests her chin on her hands, chewing her lip. "If I tell you something, please don't repeat it," she begins. Derrick mimes a zipping motion across his lips. "My brother and my mum have got it all planned. I'm supposed to get married next year, before I go to uni. Jo and Andy think I should apply to all these top places, but I've told Mum I'm only looking locally. I hate lying," her voice wavers, "but I don't know what to do. I can see you in a group, like skating and stuff, but I can't go out with you – if that's what you want. I'm too scared they'll find out."

She twists a length of her hair and drags it across her face. She wishes she hadn't told him; she's never felt so exposed. Derrick reaches out to touch her hand, talking to her through the veil of hair.

"You need friends, Aysha. I know you've got Karen, but you can count on me too."

~

As she takes her place in Jo Massey's Friday morning English class, Aysha can't help thinking that this has been the strangest week. It's like she's been transported to another universe where the normal rules don't apply, because whatever she's been doing – reading, chatting, typing an essay – on some level her mind has floated off towards Derrick.

She's not sure whether it's a nuisance or a pleasure, being aware that he is thinking about her, constantly watching her, trying to catch her eye. Since Karen pointed it out, she's noticed how other girls look at him. Tall, sporty, good-looking, *nice* – he could probably take his pick. *She* hasn't done anything to encourage him, just been herself. The whole situation is ridiculous, fraught with more obstacles and complications than she can handle: as if she doesn't have enough problems. So why does she feel like she's floating in a warm bath?

"It's all right, she's just in love," says Karen, when Jo has to ask Aysha a question twice. Jo's eyebrows rise as she looks over her glasses at Aysha, but she says nothing until there's a snigger from a couple of students across the room.

"I'm sure Aysha's feelings are nobody's business but her own. Do try to concentrate – *all* of you."

Aysha blushes and scowls at Karen, but her friend seems to find the whole business amusing, particularly Aysha's own stunned reaction. How naive she must seem. Karen was always changing boyfriends when they were at school – none of them lasted more than a few weeks – and she went out with one of the young men from her mum's office when she worked there in the summer. Her own inexperience is not just cultural – she knows plenty of Asian girls who have boyfriends – but she is used to living in her head, and this is not a rational matter at all.

"I'm not," she says to Karen after the class.

"Not what?"

"What you said. In love."

"Yeah, right."

"I hadn't even thought about him before he started following me around."

"And now?"

She feels the blood flow into her cheeks. "He's nice. *It's* nice, being liked. But like I said, it can't go anywhere. I've told him, too. It's only fair."

"Loosen up, Aysh. He's not asking you to marry him, he just wants to get to know you a bit. Why d'you think he was so keen to organise this skating trip?"

Aysha's eyes widen. "You mean...?"

"I mean we're meeting him and the others at the bus stop in fifteen minutes. Grab your coat and let's go."

Eight students – five girls, three lads, mostly from their history set – bundle onto the upper deck of the bus. Billie has brought her boyfriend Chris, from the photography course. Karen sits beside Aysha, while Derrick spreads himself across the double seat behind them, one hand gripping the rail in front so that when Aysha leans back his broad knuckles knead her shoulder blades. When the bus stops at the traffic lights, she catches sight of Mo amongst a group of white-capped men waiting to cross the road, presumably returning from Friday prayers. The upstairs window is grimy, but she still ducks her head.

"When do we have to be there?" she asks Derrick.

He unfolds a leaflet. "They close to re-do the surface after the midday session. We're in plenty of time for the three till five slot."

Across the aisle, Billie has slung her skinny legs across her boyfriend Chris's lap, while he is tracing the seam of the skin-tight jeans along her thigh. Billie reaches up and whispers something to him and they both glance in Aysha's direction and smirk.

"Reckon Del Boy's in luck."

"Shut your face, Billie!" Karen snaps.

Aysha leans forward and stares rigidly ahead; the other students in the party look embarrassed. As the bus swings around the corner towards Aldgate Station, Derrick gets up and gestures to the girls to go ahead of him. He stands as tall as the height of the bus allows, then turns to say something to Billie's boyfriend before following them downstairs. The three of them cross the road, then hurry down Houndsditch towards Broadgate, leaving the others to follow. They are first in the queue for skates when the ice reopens at three.

"Bit small, isn't it?" Karen comments. The rink is situated in a raised circular enclosure, approached by wide stone steps. An outer ring of shops and restaurants surround it at a lower level and the whole complex is overlooked by tall office blocks.

"Yeah, it's nothing like the Lee Valley one, " Derrick says. "The one at the Natural History Museum is bigger but it'd take too long to get there."

Had he chosen the nearest rink to make it easier for her to come? It seems plenty big enough to Aysha, who can't imagine doing anything except picking her way around the side, holding onto the barrier. Figuring out how to move seems to require part of her brain she hasn't used before. She tries a few shuffling steps, but then Karen and Derrick take one of her arms each and draw her forward.

"Keep your feet on the ice or we'll drag you over."

"Just glide."

She lets herself go and they pull her into the centre of the rink. The sun has come out and the ice sparkles. The other two change direction, but she doesn't understand how to do this. She feels her legs shoot forward, certain she's going to bring them all down, when an arm comes round her waist and holds her steady. Karen lets go her grip and Derrick alone guides her across the ice. Her cheek brushes against the cold zip of his hoodie and she catches a spicy waft of aftershave.

"Try to bend your knees," he says. "I won't let you fall."

He crosses the ice still holding her and deposits her safely at the edge. She watches as he skates back into the centre, performs a figure of eight, then picks up speed and goes into an extended spin. A few city workers, sauntering back from a liquid lunch, send up a ragged cheer and Karen mouths a *wow*. Billie's face shows grudging admiration and her boyfriend claps Derrick on the shoulder when he skates back to the edge.

"Where d'you learn to do that, mate?"

"I had lessons when I was a kid."

"Why did you stop?" Aysha asks.

"Took up football instead," he grins. "Got picked as goalie for the school team. Plus I knew there were plenty of skaters better than me. I haven't forgotten it all though, have I?"

He looks down at her, waiting for approval.

"No, you were really good out there."

He beams, and takes both her hands, gliding backwards on the ice. This time she trusts him, follows his directions, begins to learn how to shift her weight and move her feet. If he lets me go, I'll fall, she thinks, but I'm doing it, I'm skating! The cold air floods her lungs like a drug.

For some reason, the traffic both in and out of the city is gridlocked and the bus crawls along Commercial Road. Aysha stays on board until the stop past her square, then walks home in her usual direction. Maud is coming out of the basement flat as she reaches the house.

"Hello, love, you're late today. Reckon the Blackwall Tunnel must be closed with all this traffic." The old woman says she's going to the chemist for Bert's prescription. "Looks like you've got visitors –" she nods at a silver saloon parked in front of the railings – "unless your brother's got a new car?"

Aysha's not good on cars, but even she can see this one's out of Sel's league. As soon as she turns her key and steps into the hallway, Mum comes bustling from the living room, closing the door behind her.

"Is late, Aysha – where you go? Face red, hair messy."

"The traffic's bad, Mum. I've been walking."

"Have visitors. Go change – not jeans clothes, nice kameez."

"I've just got in. I'm tired." Aysha's legs are beginning to ache; skating has exercised muscles she didn't know she had and she just wants to rest. "Who is it, anyway?"

"Rahmans. Maryam husband friends. Mother, daughter, no son. Go – quick."

Relieved that Mum doesn't question her further, Aysha gives

in. She takes off her jeans and sweatshirt and slips on the shalwar kameez which Mo and Reshna gave her for Eid. Her feet are hot and sweaty from both skates and trainers, but there's no time for more than a quick spritz with body spray before she slips them into her sandals. She pauses in front of the mirror over the fireplace to brush her hair and wonders what Derrick would think of her in the embroidered blue suit.

Two visitors are installed on the far side of the living room. The sofa is meant to seat four, but Mrs Rahman is a large woman and seems to have flowed over at least half of it. Her daughter, a stolid-looking girl of about fourteen is slumped at the other end. Dad sits quietly in his usual chair and Mum has drawn her own seat close to Mrs Rahman. Reshna hovers with a tray. Aysha looks around for Mo, then catches sight of him with the boys in the back garden. Safiya is in her bouncing cradle and starts to gurgle on seeing Aysha.

"This daughter Aysha," Mum says, giving her a pointed sideways glance.

"Assalamu aleikum," murmurs Aysha, taking the hint and greeting the visitors. "Sorry," she says to Mum, "I didn't know we had guests. Something came up at college."

She takes the tray from Reshna and offers Mrs Rahman the spiced chai. The woman tastes the already sweetened drink and ladles in another heaped spoon of sugar. Aysha suppresses a smile: what was it Karen's mum used to say? *A moment on the lips, a lifetime on the hips!*

"You drive yourself, Mrs Rahman?" Mum switches to Bangla which, Aysha soon realises, allows her greater subtlety in verbal duelling. "I am so lucky, I can rely on my son Selim for chauffeur."

"My Jamil is also an excellent driver," the large woman replies, "but he was away at university until recently and I need my own transport. Jamil is busy working with his father now – helping him to expand the business. Five shops now, you know."

"Yes, indeed, it is good to keep business in the family," Mum nods. Then, "Is it just the one son and one daughter, Mrs Rahman? Safiya here is our son Mohammed's child. The first granddaughter – already three fine grandsons, alhamdulillah!"

The daughter is working her way through a plate of iced biscuits and only looks up when Reshna offers a glass of cola. Dad catches Aysha's eye and gives her a conspiratorial nod. Speaking in English, he announces, "Our daughter will be going to university too."

Both Mum and Mrs Rahman look surprised at the interruption.

"Husband make children to speak the English," Mum says, switching back herself.

"Jamil has business degree. First class honours. What are you studying at college?" Mrs Rahman shuffles round on the sofa, her heavy sari rustling, as she turns to address Aysha, giving scant acknowledgement to Dad.

"English, history and psychology," Aysha answers.

"Humph," Mrs Rahman snorts.

"Wants to be teacher," Mum adds.

"Actually, I'm not sure yet," Aysha begins.

Mum frowns and Mrs Rahman gives her a sharp look. Okay, she thinks, too much information. When Mo comes in with the boys, Mum asks her to help Abdul with his homework, presumably to show that her studies have their uses, and she's able to retreat to the table at the far end of the room.

"Is it yourself or Mr Rahman who's related to my sister

Maryam's husband?" Mo asks after being introduced. Aysha hopes the conversation is returning to safer ground.

"Your brother-in-law's mother is my second cousin. All our family are successful in business, you know. Your sister made a good match there."

Aysha looks up from Abdul's worksheet. Horrible, pompous woman! The son is sure to be equally repulsive: there's no way she'd want to live in that household.

~

Next day, Aysha finds Mo in the kitchen, giving the children breakfast.

"Do you want toast, Aysha?" he asks mildly.

"Why didn't you tell me she was coming?"

"Mrs Rahman?" He hands her a plate and a mug of tea. "I didn't know. It was just a courtesy call, but she wanted to see you of course."

Aysha gives a little shudder. Courtesy call? Probably trying to catch her out.

"Don't judge her by yesterday. You know what mothers are like about their sons. Maryam's mother-in-law was exactly the same at first, but they get on really well now."

"Mum wasn't like that with Reshna."

"That's because I got married back home. But you can be sure our aunts in Sylhet did the job." Mo sits at the table and spoons baby yoghurt into Safiya's waiting mouth. "I thought you looked really nice, Aysha. The blue outfit suits you – you should wear it more often. Sometimes you look a bit tired with all your studying, but yesterday you were glowing. I'm sure Mrs Rahman will give Jamil a good report."

"I don't see this Jamil being brought up for my inspection."

"Don't sulk, Aysha." Mo hands Safiya a rusk and pours milk for Ibrahim. "You don't need to know everything and you shouldn't be offended that his parents want to approve you. Maryam and I will be making discreet enquiries about Jamil's character as well as his prospects. Leave these things to us and concentrate on getting that London University place. If we are happy with what we find, we'll make sure you meet him. Perhaps next month, at Eid."

She tries to smile; he deserves that. He's a good man, her brother; he means well. But she can't see herself being given the time and space to study for a degree under Mrs Rahman's roof.

"You can always get your own flat," Mo says, as if reading her mind, "after you've graduated."

It's a positive charm offensive: Mo at his most domestic and reasonable. They are alike, the two of the family who most resemble their father; she understands his intentions.

"Her only son?" she says. "His mother won't let him go that easily." The daughter looks lazy, so Mrs Rahman's sure to expect her son's wife to help in the house.

"Not if you make it a battle," Mo says, lifting Safiya out of her chair, "but she will if it's what Jamil wants. A wife can be persuasive."

But that's just it: a *wife*. Perhaps this Jamil *is* ready for marriage, but she isn't. She can't wait for the weekend to pass so that she can see Derrick again. If she closes her eyes, she can still see him gliding backwards on the rink smiling at her, still hear the swish of blades and smell the cold air. Yet even if Derrick proposed to her tomorrow and by some miracle her family accepted a six-foot-six, black non-Muslim as her partner, she wouldn't be ready. There is so much she wants to learn, to see, to do, before committing to anyone. Even though they have been friends for years, it's hard to share her frustration with Karen. Her friend's parents have brought her up to expect to have it all and Aysha would rather avoid the criticism of her own family's attitudes which a direct comparison is bound to elicit.

There's one person who would understand this, but she lived a hundred years ago. Emily was shocked by William Baines' proposal, even before he assaulted her. She felt flattered, perhaps, and was tempted, just a little, because the marriage would help her father and give her the status of a grown woman, but she was restless to know the world; surely she too wanted all life's possibilities open to her?

Aysha has a sudden urge to go and raise the floorboard and take out Emily's journal – maybe there will be new entries she hasn't seen – but she doesn't dare do so during the day when one of the family may come into her room. She hid a copy of her UCAS entry there at half-term too, the real one, the one she handed in to Jo, and she cannot risk its being found.

When Sel slouches into the kitchen, Aysha realises she's hardly seen him for the last two weeks. Mum follows close behind.

"Need market shopping, Aysha. I tell you list. Selim drive."

She goes to find her shoes and jacket, glad of a chance to talk to Sel.

"So what was going on yesterday?" he asks as they pull out of the square and edge across the bus lane into a line of traffic. They are driving east and Sel reaches for the visor to shade against the low November sun.

"What have you heard?"

"Abdul said a fat woman came to look at Aysha. What's that all about?"

"Ask Mum. Or Mo. They've found me a husband."

"What does Dad say?"

Aysha considers. "Not much. He hardly ever says a word when Maryam's here. Why?"

"I thought I heard him and Mum arguing when I came home last night."

"What about?"

"Dunno. Couldn't hear properly." Sel grinds his teeth at the traffic ahead and executes a sudden left turn down a side street. The driver behind sounds the horn. "They're sending me back home in January," he says, when the way ahead is clear.

"On your own?" she asks. Like her, Sel was born in London; neither of them have been to Bangladesh since they were small.

" Na, some people Dad knows are going too – from the village next to our uncle's. Some land's been sold, belonging to Dad's family, and I'm s'posed to collect his share. Mo thinks he should go but he can't get the time off." He slows the car and edges down a side road. "Look out for a parking place."

Aysha points to a car pulling out of a space ahead and Sel manoeuvres the Peugeot into the gap. Neither of them moves to get out. The streets are crowded with Saturday morning shoppers, young mums pushing buggies and old ladies wheeling trolleys. Teenage girls finger the bright scarves and sweaters swinging from the stalls and fluttering in the breeze. Stately Somali women flow down the road in purple robes, past fashion wholesalers, jewellers, and convenience stores.

"Why does he need money now?"

"Probably this wedding of yours."

"There won't be a wedding if I can help it."

She hadn't even though about the expense. When Maryam married, Dad was still working and the wedding had been a lavish affair with a huge feast at the community centre near their previous home. Maryam had sat with Hassan on a platform looking glorious in her wedding finery, but still sobbed when she left her home.

"Whatever. I wanna get away for a bit anyway," Sel gets out of the car and lights a cigarette. "You got the list?"

Late that night, Aysha is in her room. She hears the radiator click as the central heating switches off and the house cools. On the other side of her bedroom wall, the toilet flushes, then the thin bar of yellow beneath her door disappears as the landing light is switched off. She waits another few minutes, then lowers her table lamp to the floor where it is screened by her bed. She pulls back the rug. She's practised now and levering the floorboard is the work of seconds.

A brown A4 envelope contains the photocopy of her UCAS application. She puts it to one side. Beneath, in the cavity between the floor joists, lies the green leather-bound journal that links Emily's life with her own.

She starts at the back and turns the unused pages one by one, until shadow traces of ink show through and the last blank sheet is replaced by one covered in handwriting. Despite having read her own name in the journal before, she still can't believe she's seeing the words – that flippant Jane Austen misquote – which she'd spoken alone in this room, just the other day.

Emily had been as puzzled as herself. She'd wondered if

Aysha, was there all the time and had tried to call to her: she wanted to make contact. But suppose the reverse is true. What if Emily is here, *now* in the room, as well as being present in the journal?

Can two people live a hundred years apart yet still somehow share the same space? Perhaps time isn't a one-way street. Emily described pictures in a book, partly hidden by tissue overlays – *veils* she called them. Could time be more like layers, like sheets of tissue piled together until they become opaque? She once watched a television programme about the excavation of Troy. Archaeologists had dug back through the centuries and found a series of cities, each built on the ruins of the others. But unlike rock, tissue is fragile; what if there are places where time tears and other layers show through?

"Emily," she whispers, "can you see me? It's Aysha, I'm here."

The digital display on her alarm clock flips forward to 00:30. This is crazy, she tells herself: if it's night in 1901, Emily will be asleep! She and Daisy got up early to start their chores.

She can't see Emily; she can't control when Emily sees her. All she has is the journal. Emily wrote about what happened to her and seeing Aysha was a part of that. But what if she writes to Emily – will it work that way round? Aysha tips the contents of her pencil case on the floor and picks out her favourite fine-tipped pen. She smooths the pages of the journal, admiring the flowing loops and curls of Emily's script. She must have used an old-fashioned nibbed pen, dipped into ink. The earlier pages have some smudges and blots, but the sixteen-year-old Emily has a neat hand. It would be sacrilege to write in her book with a modern ball point pen. Pencil perhaps? No, she can't bring herself to do it. Eventually, she takes a sheet of lined paper from her college binder. She'll write a letter and enclose it in the book. For a long time she sits thinking, then begins:

Dear Emily,

Don't be alarmed. My name is Aysha and I am the girl you sometimes see in your room.

I am seventeen years old and I live in the year 2001. I found your journal under the floorboard and have read it. I hope you don't mind. I use that space to hide things too.

I wish I could speak to you and I am sorry about your mother and brother.

Aysha

She folds the page and places it in the journal, at the place Emily stopped writing. At last, she returns both journal and her own brown envelope to their hiding place, puts out her light and climbs into bed.

Confused images crowd her brain: Abdul and Ibrahim play in Maud's flat in Daisy's basement kitchen, dragging a string for Ernie's ginger cat; she is in the park, watching Emily skate arm in arm with Karen across a frozen lake. Now it is night and the skaters are gone. A tall shape emerges from the shadow of the trees and the Dracula-like figure of William Baines in his evening cloak looms over her. Her mouth opens in a silent scream, but then the strong brown arms of Derrick lift her and she drifts into deepest sleep.

15
Emily

Monday 2 December 1901

I hoped to breakfast with Pa this morning, but at seven-thirty he is already wearing his Ulster and has his hand on the front door.

"You're starting early today, Pa?"

"Not soon enough, Emily. I've been too neglectful of business of late."

Daisy comes from the kitchen and touches my arm. "There's poached eggs warming and yesterday's muffins to toast. I'll bring some up."

"No, wait," I say. I've no desire to sit alone. "I'll eat with you in the kitchen."

The basement is warm and steamy, as Daisy has lit the range and already has the boiler heating for a wash. She opens the door to the furnace and hands me the toasting fork and a couple of muffins. The smell of toasting bread awakens my appetite and I'm glad to accept the two eggs, like blind white eyes, which she lifts from the poacher. I help myself to a slab of yellow butter and Daisy pours coffee for us both from the pot.

"It's as well I was up," she says, "or your Pa would've gone off hungry."

I'm glad he is showing more interest in his work again. He misses Ma, of course, but he needs to rouse himself – to look after his own interests, and mine.

As Daisy has the wash to begin, I clear Pa's breakfast things from the dining room. He didn't even stay to finish his meal: one egg is uneaten and his coffee cup half-full. I gather the dishes onto a tray, then stoop to pick up *The Times* from the floor. It lies open at a page with an unusual appearance: at the centre is a notice from a body called the Imperial Tobacco Company and all the surrounding space is filled with that company's name, printed over and over again. I suppose it must be some kind of advertisement. I read the notice carefully. As far as I can understand, some British cigarette manufacturers have banded together against the American companies who want to take their trade. If this is what sent Pa from the house so early, I wonder whether it bodes him well or ill. Pa rarely speaks of business at home and the one man who would once have explained it all to me has put himself beyond the pale.

I balance the paper on the tray and carry it down to the kitchen where Daisy is plunging towels and sheets into the boiler, forcing them down with the long wooden tongs.

"What's the news from the Cape?" she asks, waving a soapy hand at the newspaper.

Since Charlie died, Daisy has taken it upon herself to follow the fortunes of our troops. I'm not sure how to answer. We thought we understood when all the news was of the siege, but these reports are confusing, describing skirmishes rather than large battles, involving rebel groups called commandos. There is talk of a treaty, of the war coming to an end, but if people know they want peace, why don't they just stop killing each other?

The day is breezy and mild for December. Daisy cranks the handle while I feed the sheets through the mangle, then we hang them in the back yard and hope the weather will stay dry. She wants to marzipan the Christmas cake we made last month this afternoon and needs to shop for the ground almonds. We peer at the sky, mistrusting every cloud, but we can be to Watney Street and back within an hour so decide to take a chance.

Monday is a quiet day and we soon buy our ingredients. Afterwards, we stop to look at Sally's father's shop window, where there is a fine display of overcoats, but I am drawn rather to the large notice to one side.

Daniel Fenton Esq
Wishes To Advise
All Ladies And Gentlemen Of Distinction
That His New Oxford Street Store Now Offers
High-Class Tailoring For All Occasions.
Personal Attention Assured.

"That Sally Fenton's pa's coming up in the world, ain't he?" Daisy comments.

I haven't seen Sally since the summer. I'm sure she is busy with her studies, but what with her Highgate connections and her father doing so well, I rather feel she has left me behind. There is another, smaller notice beneath the announcement about the new store which reads,

Skilled seamstresses required
for expanding West End workshop.
Enquire within.

Mr Fenton is such a kind and indulgent father to Sally, that I feel sure he must be a fair and honest employer too. And Oxford Street is a modern, bustling place, full of grand new department stores. It must be wonderful to be part of it all!

"Your pa'd never hear of it," Daisy says, watching me curiously.

"No, of course not. I'm just interested."

But I tuck the words into a pocket in my brain.

"Emily, have you seen the *Times*?" Pa asks, after hunting through the dining room. He has been working on accounts since returning from the warehouse. I fetch the paper from the kitchen and hand it over, folded with the tobacco companies' advertisement uppermost. I'd like to ask what the notice means for his business, but he just takes the newspaper with a grunt and returns to the study.

Here is another puzzle. When I take my journal from under the floorboard this evening, I find a loose piece of paper inserted at the place I last wrote. It's a large sheet, not quite foolscap in size, already printed with lines and folded into four. At first, I feel sure there is writing inside, I can almost see it through the folds; yet when I undo it the paper is blank. How can this be? No-one knows of my hiding place. Who could have put it there – and why would anyone leave a blank sheet?

This paper is not like any other in the house. It's a single, loose leaf, but with all the edges smooth, not torn from a composition book. At school, we used rulers and pencils to mark out our margins and to draw lines for writing, but the ones on this sheet have been printed. I look at the lines again and then I remember: I *have* seen something like it before.

I take the paper to the window to examine it in the light. Aysha sat in this very spot, writing at her table on large sheets like this, that day when I lay in my bed – the day after my birthday, the day after the night when *he*, Baines... is the paper Aysha's? Could she have put it here?

She seems to belong to this house, but I cannot think her a ghost. Pa's grandfather bought the house when it was first built and Pa inherited it from him: only our family has ever lived here. She does not see me. I have looked directly at Aysha, even called her by name as I've heard the other voices do, without her knowing I'm there. Perhaps that's just as well. If she saw or heard me, she might think *I* was the ghost!

I re-fold the page and put it back in my journal beneath the floor. If Aysha *has* read my words, she may yet write perhaps.

16
Aysha

December 2001

Aysha assesses the fading light from the library window, checks her watch and starts to pack her bag. Ramadan has reached its fourth week now and it's time to break her fast.

As she walks through the library's security gate, Derrick appears from the computer room and joins her. They don't meet out of college, but he knows her timetable better than she does herself and is closer than a shadow.

"Thirsty?"

He passes her a bottle of water and she rummages in her bag for a small pack of dried fruit.

"Yeah. It gets hard to concentrate at the end of the day."

Derrick tried to go without food and drink himself on a couple of days, but it wasn't a success. Lately, he's taken to pestering her with weird questions she doesn't know the answers to, like what do Muslims who live in Scandinavia do when there's hardly any night? Or, can you have a quick snack if there's a total eclipse in the middle of a fast day? (She's pretty sure the answer's no to that one!) At least she's convinced him that the last thing she wants at sundown is a huge takeaway. Some sips of water, maybe a cup of tea and a few dates, are all she needs before the family meal later in the evening.

The lift is prohibited to able-bodied students, but it stands empty and Aysha lets herself be guided inside. Derrick rests his hands on her shoulders and picks up a strand of her hair. He bends his face towards her and she feels his breath warm on forehead, then the doors open on the first floor and Jo Massey gets in.

"Since when have you needed a lift pass? Or you, young man?"

"She's feeling faint with all that fasting, miss."

"Well, it seems she has a protector. As you're here, Aysha, I can tell you that all my tutor group's UCAS applications went off today. I've written you a blisteringly good reference, so let's hope you get some offers in the post in the new year."

Aysha looks down, gnawing her lip.

"If you have a problem, Aysha, I'm happy to talk," Jo says.

"What's that about?" Derrick asks, when they've all left the lift and Jo has moved away. "Am I a problem?"

"No, not unless you're distracting me." Aysha threads her fingers through his. "Jo knows my family aren't keen on me going away to study."

"Aren't keen?" he says. "Hardly covers it when they've got some bloke lined up to marry you."

"I told you, that's not going to happen. I just need to keep them sweet for a month or two."

They walk across the darkening park to Aysha's bus stop. The last leaves from the tall chestnut trees drift through the air and a late blackbird flies low out of the bushes, calling to its mate. A couple of boys of Abdul's age are playing by the swings. Derrick pauses, looking thoughtful.

"Are your family very religious?"

"Not especially," she says, "but my oldest brother is, I suppose. Why?"

"You won't dress like that one day, will you?" He gestures towards a woman pushing a child's buggy and wearing a long black dress beneath a duffel coat; her face is veiled except for the eyes.

"She's probably got jeans on underneath," Aysha laughs. She sits on a swing and kicks herself off, pushing herself higher, laughing as he tries to grab her feet. "I won't change how I dress. I told you, I'm like my dad and he's the one who made us all speak English at home."

"But now your brother's in charge? And if this bloke they want you to marry is strict, you'd have to change."

She lets the swing slow before jumping off in a wide arc. "I'm not marrying anyone," she says.

"Well, if your dad's so great, why doesn't he help?"

Sometimes she's thought Dad has been on the point of talking to her, asking her what she really wants, but Mum or Mo have always been around. And when Maryam comes, he invariably leaves her to talk to Mum alone. Life hasn't been easy for anyone since he had to give up work, but Dad couldn't help being ill. Why does he let Mum and Mo have their way all the time, as if he owes them something?

"I never knew mine," Derrick says. "Bastard dumped Mum before I was born. She's done everything for me; worked two, even three, jobs sometimes. But I'm gonna repay her one day."

Aysha smiles up at him. "What about your mum, then?" she asks. "Does she go to church?"

"Sometimes. She used to go to spiritualist meetings too."

"What's that about?"

"Getting messages. Contacting the dead. A load of crap."

Aysha feels uneasy, remembering the letter she wrote to Emily last month. Isn't that what she'd been trying to do, contact someone who died decades ago?

"Gives me the creeps," Derrick says. "I'm glad she doesn't go anymore."

Mum and Reshna are busy cooking when she arrives home. The warm scent of cardamom mingles with the sharp tang of coriander leaves, and the kitchen steams with the comfortable fragrance of rice. Aysha's empty stomach contracts as she sniffs the air.

"You break the fast, Aysha?"

"Just water and dates."

Mum pours her some tea and tells her to take Dad a cup while they wait for dinner. Her father is watching a property programme on the television, nodding as a middle-aged couple look out from the window of a vast, empty kitchen to admire cows grazing in a flat landscape. Aysha slides the usual jumble of pills, tumblers and newspapers across the side table to make room for his tea.

"Nice place, Aysha," he says, pointing to the screen. " Lincolnshire. I went there once. Big fields – like Bangladesh, so green."

"Would you like to go back, Dad – to Bangladesh, I mean? Sel said you're sending him soon."

"Selim? Yes, maybe he'll go. Unless Mo can take time."

"Have you really sold your family land, Dad? Wasn't it your home?"

"When you move across the world," Dad sighs, "you don't know where home is anymore." He taps a packet of pills. "I have to be where the doctors are."

Aysha perches on the arm of his chair and puts her hand on his shoulder. If only they could afford private treatment there, perhaps he could visit his home. Dad reaches up and covers her hand with his own. He used to read to her when she was still the youngest child. When he was helping to build the Docklands Light Railway and didn't have to work late, he'd come home and tell her about his day.

"I wish you could have held onto your land, Dad," she whispers. "I wish you could live somewhere green."

Mum opens the door to announce dinner, tuts at the television screen then moves across the room to switch it off. Abdul and Ibrahim are already seated at the kitchen table, Ibrahim in his high chair, while Safiya lies kicking at the toys strung across her bouncing cradle. Mo takes dishes from Reshna to place on the table.

"Lamb biryani," Mum says. "I teach you cook it, Aysha. Soon."

Aysha is about to comment, but Dad squeezes her hand. She pulls out a dining chair and helps him to his seat.

"When does your term end?" Mo asks.

"Next Wednesday. The nineteenth."

"Eid will most likely be Monday," he says, "You'll need to be home that day."

It's not a problem: the college lets Muslim students take the day as a holiday, but she wants to be sure she'll see Karen and Derrick before the end of term.

"I'll need to go to college Tuesday. I'll have work to hand in."

"Yes, okay," Mo says, "but get your work done early. There won't be time on Eid day."

Like everyone, they like to dress up, see friends and enjoy the end of fasting, but in the years since Dad's illness they haven't travelled far. Usually, neighbours drop by, Maryam comes with her husband and the boys and Aysha's on call all day, helping to make samosas and boil tea. Mo goes to the mosque in the morning and brings back sweets from the Brick Lane shops.

"We all go Maryam house Eid day," Mum tells her. "Hassan come with car. You, Abdul, Dad, me."

"Sel will drive Reshna and the children," Mo adds, "and I'll come on after mosque."

"It'll be a long day for Dad," Aysha objects, surprised. "The boys get noisy when they're all together."

"Maryam front room quiet," says Mum. "Nice armchair. Big TV. Boys have garage now."

Hass and Maryam have finished converting their garage into a playroom. Aysha hasn't been there since the summer so hasn't seen its completion.

"They have a downstairs toilet now too," Mo explains. "So no stairs for Dad."

Is that really why they're all going, to admire the home improvements? Aysha glances at Dad, wondering if he's been consulted over Mum and Mo's plans. Or Sel? He'd probably prefer to go out with his friends, but Mo assumes he'll do duty as family chauffeur.

"Maryam and Hass have invited the Rahmans to call," Mo says carefully, "with their son and daughter."

So that's the answer. Dad uprooted and all of them spending Eid in Romford so they can suck up to pompous Mrs Rahman and her spoilt daughter again. Only this time will be worse; there'll be her husband, the chicken shop king, and, of course, the heir to his empire, the oh-so-perfect Jamil.

"We're shopping for the children's clothes on Saturday," Mo says. "We'll get you a new outfit too. Come if you want, or Reshna can choose for you if you've too much homework. What colour would you like?"

"No need," she says firmly. She has no desire to waste his money impressing the Rahmans and, if she must dress up, her blue shalwar kameez will do fine.

In the first few weeks after writing her letter to Emily, Aysha checked the journal regularly, hoping for some acknowledgement of her message, but there were no more entries and her own A4 sheet remained inside. She has tried not to keep looking, knowing that Emily didn't write every day, but tonight, aware that it is over a week since she last examined the journal, she lifts the floorboard, still telling herself not to expect anything new. She turns the pages carefully: the A4 sheet isn't there! Holding her breath, Aysha checks the date on the last entry, realises with a thrill that she hasn't seen it before, and settles down to read.

She doesn't understand the references to the tobacco companies, but the expansion of shopping must have meant lots of new employment opportunities for women. And when were sewing machines invented? She ought to find out. Emily had mentioned sewing for Mr Fenton before, when she asked her father if she could get a job. Wondering if the girl ever plucked up the courage to ask him again, she reads on. Oh, my letter didn't work, she sighs at last: Emily found the paper, but the writing was gone.

She tries to get her head around this but can't find a logical explanation. But the paper did *something*: it made Emily stop and wonder where it came from: it made her wonder about *her*, Aysha, and her connection to the house.

She wakes in a panic. Daylight has already pierced the gaps in her curtains and is dancing patterns on the mirror over the fireplace. It's much too late to eat and she'll have to dash to reach college in time. Then the smell of toast from the kitchen below reminds her that it's Eid.

She leans out of bed and hauls her college bag towards her, taking out a brown envelope which Derrick had given her on Friday. He'd been designing something on a library computer that afternoon and wouldn't let her see. An intricate pattern borders the traditional Eid Mubarak greeting on a sheet of folded blue card; the signature inside is simply the initial D. Aysha gets up and stands the card on her desk, grateful for his restraint. The card could have come from any college friend.

"Aysha!"

Her mother hesitates only a second before entering, then goes to the window and hooks a coathanger carrying the embroidered blue kameez in a dry cleaner's bag over the curtain track. Mum herself is resplendent in emerald green and stops in front of Aysha's mirror to adjust the folds of her sari. Going to the window, she straightens a pile of papers on Aysha's desk, then picks up Derrick's card and replaces it without comment. Aysha remembers to breathe.

"Eid Mubarak! Clothes clean ready," she smiles. "Have breakfast. Do shower. Get dressed."

She puts on her dressing gown and follows Mum downstairs.

Abdul is capering around the kitchen, a cereal packet in one hand and new Game Boy in the other. Crispy clusters erupt from the open box and Ibrahim pounces on the stray fragments, cramming them into his mouth. Reshna wags her finger and says no when he picks them from the floor, but as she's smiling and laughing, Ibrahim takes no notice and laughs too. Mum catches Abdul by the arm and sits him at the table.

"All eat today," she says. "Be good boy."

"Eid Mubarak, Dad," says Aysha, crossing the room to give her father a hug. She kisses Reshna and attempts to pat Ibrahim's head before he runs away. "Where are Mo and Sel?"

"Mo went early to mosque," Dad says.

"Sel shower still," Mum adds. She looks at the clock. "Need hurry."

Dad dips toast into his wide breakfast cup and chews solemnly. He pops his tablets from their packs and washes them down with the last of his tea. "This is a good day for me," he says. "I needn't feel bad about not fasting anymore. Here, son!" He gets up when Sel comes into the kitchen, hair damp and spiky from the shower. "I'm done, you sit here."

Aysha and Sel eat quietly together, enjoying the luxury of breakfasting in daylight. The whole family is at ease; it's a shame that they have to put on their finery and traipse east to Romford. Not that they can't relax at Maryam's – at least they can after they've all expressed due admiration for the home improvements – but other people will call: neighbours, relatives and, worst of all, the Rahmans. She's been putting this day to the back of her mind: the day when she has to put a face to the name Jamil.

Mum is directing the family shower rota and shoos Aysha from the table the moment her plate is cleared. Reshna and the children are travelling with Sel, but Mum, Dad, Abdul and Aysha must be ready when Hassan comes at ten.

By the time Aysha has showered, dressed, and draped a long blue scarf loosely around her still damp hair, her brother-in-law is ensconced in the kitchen. Hassan is a big, affable man, with the capacity to make any room seem crowded. He accepts a cup of coffee, then drinks it standing, planted squarely in the space between the breakfast table and kitchen bench, so that Reshna is obliged to take a detour every time she needs to reach the fridge. Aysha flattens herself against the door frame.

"Well, there you are," he says, as if he's been waiting forever, though she heard the doorbell ring only a few moments ago.

Several further minutes of fussing are needed to determine whether Dad has his tablets with him and if he wants a rug for the car. Hassan ridicules this last suggestion, launching into an elaborate account of what he calls his car's superior climate control system – which appears to mean effective heating and air conditioning, rather than any concern for global warming. Eventually, she and Mum are seated in the back, either side of Abdul, who manages to put on his anorak, get into the car and fasten the seatbelt without once interrupting his Game Boy session. Dad sits in front, nodding intermittently, as Hassan expands on miles per gallon and acceleration.

The streets are dotted with little groups of Eid visitors: girls in bright shalwar kameezes, wives in new saris, boys in matching shirts and ties – splashes of rainbow colour daubed on the monochrome streets beneath dull December skies. Aysha makes out girls she knows from college; like her, they have abandoned their jeans and trainers for the colours of the subcontinent.

Hassan and Maryam's pebble-dashed semi has a paved front

garden with parking space in front of what used to be the garage.

"You'll see," Hassan tells Abdul as he parks, "the boys have got TV, computer games, football table. All their own space. You're going to have fun today."

"Make the most of it, son," Dad comments. "There's no room for that at home."

Aysha gets out of the car, making way for Abdul who slides across the back seat, Game Boy still in hand. She opens the passenger door for Dad and gives him her arm, while Mum gathers up the various Tupperware boxes she has brought and Maryam beckons from the doorway to hurry them inside. Aysha looks back at the tree-lined road, where a postman is cycling and a couple of women in Lycra are jogging past, then enters the house.

All the home improvements must be finished since Hass and Maryam feel ready to entertain. The house dates from the thirties, but little trace of that era remains: the floors are laminate throughout and the back of the house has been opened out to provide a large family dining room and kitchen, with a conservatory beyond. A separate front room remains, furnished with cream leather armchairs, a glass coffee table and huge television screen. Across the hallway, a door leads to the new playroom.

"Uncle! In here, quick!" Maryam's boys, Rahim and Farhad, pull Abdul inside.

Maryam is wearing a turquoise sari over a matching blouse and a succession of silver bangles clink together and slide down her arm as she empties the contents of Mum's Tupperware boxes into glass dishes.

"Where you apron?" Mum asks.

Maryam's mother-in-law emerges from the playroom and

meets them with a burst of Bengali. She takes the dishes from Maryam, then hands them back again on recognising Aysha, in order to greet her with a hug.

"Even more beautiful," she says, nodding at Mum and Maryam. A large striped tea towel is attached to her waist by two clothes pegs; she removes this and shakes it at Aysha, shooing her from the room.

"We've got plenty of hands," Maryam tells her. "No need for you to get messy. Let the boys show you their playroom, or go sit with Dad."

Dismissed, she wanders from the kitchen. She puts her head into the playroom where Abdul and Farhad, Maryam's elder son, bob up and down in front of a television screen showing a racing car track, game controls in hand. Rahim, the younger boy, screeches at them both, urging on first one then the other. The boys' bottoms hover over three beanbags, never quite sitting down. An actual electric racing car track lies abandoned. Coloured plastic crates sit on the metal shelving units which line one wall and at the far end of the room, in front of a large window overlooking the back garden, Hassan has installed a wooden bench and two stools, perhaps in the hope of promoting more studious pursuits. Aysha backs out, closing the door quietly.

Dad is in the front room with Hassan and his father, who are discussing a recently opened branch of their dry cleaning business. Hassan's granny, a tiny old woman wearing an enormous fluffy pink cardigan over her sari, addresses odd, disconnected remarks to Dad.

"You want the TV on, Aysha?" Hassan asks. She shakes her head and looks around in search of a book or newspaper, wishing she'd brought something of her own to read. A magazine rack yields the local paper, a toy catalogue and a copy of *Laundry and Cleaning News*. She hopes Sel will bring Reshna and the children soon.

It would be churlish not to admit that her sister has a very good life: Hassan is a generous, easy-going husband, Maryam is on good terms with her in-laws, the extended house has space for everyone and they are all conspicuously satisfied with a life she has no desire to share.

When Sel's car draws up, bringing the rest of the family, Abdul and Farhad begin a pre-emptive whine that Ibrahim will spoil their game. Hassan tells Farhad that his younger cousin is his Eid guest and he must entertain him, yet when Rahim also protests that he isn't going to play with the babies, his dad just shrugs and tells them to *talk to your mother*. The boys are still remonstrating with Maryam when the doorbell rings.

"I'll go in the playroom and keep an eye on them," Aysha offers.

"Yes, yes, go with Aysha," Maryam urges Rahim, "but don't jump all over her, she needs to stay smart."

Rahim wants her to play Scalextric with him. Aysha predicts – correctly – that she won't be any good at this. It doesn't help that Ibrahim is wriggling on her knee and trying to grab the control, but Rahim seems happy that he's winning for once and doesn't tire of retrieving her wayward car. Sel would be better at this, she thinks. She'd hoped he would play with the boys, but after dropping Reshna and the children, he stayed only long enough to wish a perfunctory *Eid Mubarak* to Maryam and Hass. Another thought occurs to her: Derrick would enjoy the game. She smiles, imagining his long legs sprawled across the floor and his broad thumbs dancing over the buttons.

She makes up for her lack of driving skills by constructing multicoloured Lego bridges to span the car track and Rahim dives all over the room rounding up stray bricks for her when the plastic bucket is exhausted. She's putting the finishing touches to an ambitious structure when the playroom door swings open. Hassan stands on the threshold, pointing out his DIY handiwork to a stocky, heavily-jowled man of about fifty.

"See, no radiators," Hassan is boasting. "Underfloor heating, all done with wires. Conservatory's the same. Easy when you start from scratch."

The jowly man nods then says something quietly in Bengali to Hassan. Aysha doesn't catch the words but, from the way Hassan nods and they both look in her direction, she feels the man has spoken about her. She glimpses a flash of fuchsia pink shalwar trousers and gold sandals behind the two men, then hears the rustle of heavy fabric. A woman's voice rasps, *pick up your feet, Dolly, don't slouch.* The Rahmans have arrived.

Aysha turns back to the boys. Rahim's car has jumped the track and collided with her bridge; Ibrahim grabs at it and the whole edifice collapses.

"I know that feeling." The light voice is unfamiliar. "My sister Dolly was always treading on my models."

The speaker is a slight young man of medium height, wearing black trousers and a grey shirt. He's clean-shaven with short wavy hair and wears an expression of mingled boredom and amusement. If this is Jamil, she has to admit he looks the best of the family. Maryam bustles past him, clearly annoyed at the casual nature of their meeting. She rounds up the boys with the promise of snacks, pointedly thanks Aysha for watching Ibrahim and Rahim and tells her to *come and meet our friends.*

The conservatory table has been piled with food. Reshna sits in the corner sipping squash, Safiya in her lap, while Hassan's mother fusses over them both and feeds the baby puréed vegetables. Despite the verbal sparring of their previous meeting, Mum and Mrs Rahman greet each other as old friends and set to gossiping enthusiastically, while Mr Rahman and Hass's father talk business. Reshna keeps Ibrahim at her side, but the three older boys are busy piling their plates with samosas and pakoras. The Rahman girl – Dolly? – has positioned herself strategically beside a dish of sticky golden gulab jamun.

Aysha moves to join her but Maryam puts a detaining hand on her shoulder, adjusting the blue scarf which Aysha has draped loosely around her neck and wrapping it over her hair.

"Patience, sister," she says, as Aysha shrugs her off. Mum beckons her over.

"Aysha, Mrs Rahman – you remember?"

As if she could forget! Mrs Rahman's voluminous chin rests on her chest, but she raises her eyebrows and surveys Aysha quizzically until the girl realises that a formal greeting is required.

"Eid Mubarak, Mrs Rahman. Assalamu aleikum."

The woman waves her hand at her daughter. "Dilwara," she says, "Dolly. She is like me. Eats too much."

The daughter shoots her mother a poisonous look and shuffles uneasily on her golden shoes.

"It's nice to see you again, Dolly," Aysha says. "That's a wonderful shade of pink you're wearing!"

Mrs Rahman snorts. "She insisted on having it."

Aysha feels sorry for the girl, but doesn't know how to help. She excuses herself in order to take a plate of food to Dad, who must have been abandoned in the front room. To her surprise, he's not alone. The aged granny has fallen asleep in the corner, but Dad is engaged in animated conversation with the young man who had spoken to her.

The newcomer turns towards her.

"I'm Jamil," he says, offering to shake her hand. "You must be Aysha."

The handshake is a considered gesture, she thinks. A strict Muslim, Mo, for instance, wouldn't take an unrelated female's hand. Jamil's telling her he's a relaxed, modern guy. She hesitates, but as Dad seems unconcerned she puts out her own hand.

"So you're the historian?" He smiles at her frown. "Your father told me. Which uni are you going to?"

Caught off guard and unwilling to mislead Dad, she mumbles, "I'm not sure. I haven't had offers yet. Where did you go?"

"Birmingham. I've been talking to your father. I wish I'd done engineering too."

"You have to be prepared to get your hands dirty," Dad says bluntly, his eyes resting on the expensive watch which peeps from beneath the young man's immaculate cuffs.

What stopped him then? she wonders; then remembers the force of nature that is his mother and changes tack. "Did you like it – Birmingham, I mean?"

"Yeah, it's great – I go back quite often, but I'm home for Eid and I'll be helping my father to expand in the New Year." There's a vague, faraway look in his eyes as if his heart is elsewhere.

"You must be pleased to have a position waiting," Dad suggests.

Jamil gazes out of the window; a thin, sleety rain has started to fall.

"Yes," he says, "of course." The same uncertain expression

crosses his face. "Well, so long as we can manage to agree over the future of the business. Dad wants to turn us into a halal version of McDonald's. I have to say that's not my vision."

Aysha would like to ask how he would do things differently, but Dad lays a cautioning hand on her arm, as if to say that these father-son disagreements are not their business. He takes time to select a tit-bit from the plate by his side, then tells Jamil, "Get yourself some food, young man. My daughter Maryam will expect you to do justice to her cooking."

Jamil smiles awkwardly, "Of course."

"Good-looking young man," Dad comments when he's gone.

She senses he disapproves of Jamil for speaking too freely about his own father. There's complicated family stuff going with the Rahmans, but she's in no position to judge.

"So, is he your cup of tea?" Dad asks, smiling.

"I can't tell," she says. "I've hardly met him."

Mo comes directly from the mosque, or as directly as public transport allows. He stands on the threshold of the front room, blowing on his fingertips and shaking the sleet from his prayer cap.

"You okay, Dad? Comfortable here?"

The aged granny wakes with a start and asks, "Did you buy the fish?"

Dad nods in her direction. "You see I have company," he says, "and just now Aysha was talking to an interesting young man."

Mo takes off his cap and twists it in his hand. "Aysha? Was Mum or Maryam present?"

Dad finishes the samosa he is eating before gently putting down his plate. "No need, son, her father was here."

"I expected them to stay longer. I wanted to talk to Jamil

Rahman myself," Mo tells Maryam. "Even Mum says she barely spoke to him."

Mrs Rahman had suddenly risen with her familiar crackle of fabric and gathered her troops: they were expected at two more relatives' homes, she'd said: no peace for the Rahmans on Eid day.

"His mother kept us both talking," Maryam explains. "It would have been rude to break away."

"All the same," Mo says, "this could have been managed better."

In Aysha's opinion managing Mrs Rahman is never an option and the family's departure is a general relief: even Maryam's in-laws, whose connections they are, relax. The day wears on, punctuated by sporadic visits from other friends and neighbours, a constant stream of refreshments and the back-to-back showing of old Indian movies on DVD. Mum and Hassan's mother argue amicably over the identities of a past Bollywood generation and the granny joins in the songs from the films, mumbling the lyrics with her toothless, red-stained gums. Reshna creeps in to join them, leaving Mo and Hass to supervise the children in the playroom.

Aysha picks up used plates and cups and takes them to the kitchen, where her sister is loading the dishwasher.

"We must wait now to see if they make a proposal," Maryam says. "Mrs Rahman seems quite taken with you, Aysha."

"What about Jamil, doesn't he have a say?"

"Of course, but marriage is family business. Especially when he will be working so closely with his father."

"And where do my feelings come in?"

"Aysha, we've already told you that the final choice is yours. But surely it's better to start university knowing you are provided for? No need to decide yet – if a proposal does come, we'll arrange another meeting."

And that's it, she thinks? I'm supposed to make up my mind on the strength of a few short conversations? Jamil looks decent enough, but even if it wasn't for uni, even if I didn't know Derrick, I couldn't do that.

Sel returns at five. Whoever is riding with him needs to come now, he says, as he's working tonight. *Around,* he says when Maryam asks where he's spent the day. Mum and Reshna are watching a film, so Aysha says she'll go back with Dad and Abdul. Hass will bring the others later. Abdul is in the middle of a game and looks mutinous until Aysha promises to play with him when they get home. For once, she hardly notices the smell of cigarettes when she settles into the back of Sel's car. It's been a very long day.

17
Emily

Wednesday 25 December 1901

Christmas Day is mild and damp. Pa and I walk to the early service at St Dunstan's, taking a wreath of starry Christmas roses to place on Ma's grave. Pa glances up at the clock, high on the tower.

"Go into church, Emily, please. I'll find you."

I keep a place for him in the pews, but a good ten minutes pass before he joins me and I can see he's been weeping. Somehow the familiar words and music take over, but when I listen to the story of Mary's child, who came healthy into a stable, I can't help thinking of little Edward Charles, born too early to survive. It's foolish, I know, but somehow I miss him, this older brother I never knew. We slip away quickly at the end of the service, both anxious to avoid neighbourly concern.

Pa tells us to set the lunch table for six. Elizabeth and Richard come bringing Ernie and I suppose Dr Reynolds to be expected, as he is often late if called to some emergency. At one o'clock, Pa tells Daisy to go ahead and serve.

We try our best to be jolly and, as if by mutual agreement, do not mention Charlie, Ma or even the war. Elizabeth has taken Ernie to a play of Gulliver's Travels as a Christmas treat and tells us about the show.

"I should like to be on stage, like Master Smith!" cries Ernie, referring to one of the child performers who played the Lilliputians. I begin to question Ernie about the young actor, but Elizabeth raises her eyebrows and shakes her head as if to warn me not to encourage him.

"How is Timmy?" I ask, referring instead to a kitten from one of Mabel's litters, now living next door.

Ernie says Timmy is a great mouser and is about to describe his exploits, when the door opens and Daisy shows William Baines into the dining room. As always, he is fastidiously dressed. A scarlet waistcoat peeps from beneath his jacket, his dark hair and thick sideburns are neatly trimmed, his complexion glows ruddy and fresh. Daisy's face is thundercloud black as she catches my eye. I grasp my knife and fork so tightly that my nails dig into my palms and my knees clench together. He can do me no harm in company, yet I feel his presence at our table on Christmas Day is an insult I should not have to bear. It strikes me, too, that Pa is not entirely comfortable; he gestures to the empty seat next to Richard and, as the goose is already carved, instructs Baines to help himself.

William Baines appears quite at home, grasping Richard's hand and wishing him a Merry Christmas, complimenting Elizabeth on her new hairstyle, and teasing Ernie, now demolishing a pile of roast potatoes, about his appetite. Finally he turns in my direction with a brief 'Miss Emily' and a nod. His real purpose must be to talk business, because once he has acknowledged the rest of us he turns to my father,

"I know you are wary of the Imperial Tobacco Company's power, Edward, but it was the only way forward for our British trade."

"Perhaps," Pa replies awkwardly. Surely Baines used to defer to him more?

"Amalgamation's the future. Otherwise the Americans will destroy us."

"But we're middle-men, not producers, Bill," my father says. "All the separate deals we've negotiated with our customers may be void now and, if there's a price war, our profits will be cut to nought."

If Ma were here she would know how to steer them away from business talk at the table and turn the discussion to matters of interest to all our guests, but I soon run out of ideas for conversation with Elizabeth and am reduced to plying Richard and Ernie with food.

Ernie has brought his new *Snakes and Ladders* board so when Daisy has cleared the dishes away I offer to play with him. The game is very easy to learn: if, as I suppose, it is meant to reflect life's ups and downs, I can't help thinking that this has been a very snaky year. Pa and Baines include Richard in their conversation for a bit, but then Pa excuses himself, pleading urgent business and goes with Baines to the study. I am worried that this must seem a slight to our neighbours on Christmas Day. Richard makes no comment but comes to watch Ernie and me play, then persuades Elizabeth that they should both join in the next game.

I know that Elizabeth likes to rest in the afternoon now that her pregnancy is advancing, so ask Daisy not to delay bringing the mince pies and coffee.

"If Mr and Mrs Black leave before *'im*," she tells me, "you come down to the kitchen directly."

But a few minutes later, Pa and Baines emerge from the study. Pa mops his face and appears flustered; Baines looks relaxed as he folds a document into four and places it in his coat.

"The same agreement as before?" he says to Pa, who hesitates then nods.

"I am sorry to leave so soon," Baines says, surveying the room, "but I do wish you all the compliments of the season."

Richard rises to shake his hand, but Elizabeth glances from Pa to me, wondering, I think, if she has missed something. Pa makes no comment when Baines has gone. He joins us for coffee, but the Blacks leave shortly after. I survey the abandoned cups and wait for Pa to say something. The party has broken up early. We have little to celebrate and I'm an inexperienced hostess, but it *is* Christmas and I hope he knows I tried my best. When he does speak, it's about another matter entirely.

"Emily, your mother gave you her gold and pearl necklace, I believe?"

"Yes, Pa."

"Will you fetch it, please?"

"I don't have it," I say.

"Emily, don't play games with me. I have need of the necklace – just for a while – as security. You shall have it back." He sounds weary. In the last six months his hair has greyed and he looks older than his forty years.

"You need money, Pa?" I know we are not rich, but he has never mentioned a lack of funds before. I wish I'd listened more carefully to his conversation with Baines.

"A temporary measure until the New Year. There is an account – an obligation – I would rather settle now. Don't question me further, Emily, just bring the necklace to me."

"But I don't have it here, Pa." I don't know whether to feel relieved or sorry. "I took it to Harlow and Grandpa said he would keep it for me in his safe."

Pa grasps his head in his hands and his half-laugh turns into a groan.

"Shall I write to Grandpa?"

He rests his hand on my shoulder and shakes his head.

"No, Emily, it would take too long," he says. No doubt the thought of Grandpa knowing he needs money is unwelcome too.

A thought strikes me; I remember that odd little scene after lunch.

"Whom are you obliged to, Pa?"

Pa looks up, starts to speak, then walks to the fire and stares into the mantle glass. The pale winter daylight has faded; I ought to light the lamps but fear to disturb him.

"Margins are so small now, no room for the little man, not for the specialist anymore." He is addressing himself as much as me, I think. "If you can't pay the shipping company, they impound your cargo. But I shouldn't have taken his money, not on those terms."

"You have borrowed money from Mr Baines, Pa?"

He looks down at the fire. A piece of coal hisses, flares a vivid sulphurous yellow and sends sparks skittering across the hearth.

"What are the terms you spoke of?"

"A percentage of the business," he mutters finally.

"And today you sold more?"

He says nothing, which I take to mean yes.

"How can this man have money to lend out of the wage you pay him?"

"Bill's always had dealings on his own account," Pa replies. "Buying and selling surplus cargo, dabbling in stocks and shares, lending at interest to those who have an urgent need. I admire that in him, his enterprise."

"And swindling people out of their businesses?"

"No, Emily, it's nothing like that. I accepted his money; he has every right to lay down his terms. I am the one at fault. You have grounds for complaint against *me* if your expectations are reduced."

"My expectations?"

"You're my only heir. I hoped to buy everything back, but I thought it mattered little – if he were to marry you – how much was his or mine. If only you could have returned his affection..."

I am sorry for Pa, and I'm shocked to see how defeated he seems, but above all I am angry. I don't believe I was ever the object of William Baines' love. Profit was always his aim.

"I'm sorry, Pa, but I cannot marry that man. Not to save your business or your conscience!"

I flee upstairs to the solitude of my room, guilty at not going to help Daisy, but much too agitated to be of use. As I fling open the door, I hear voices: Aysha is talking to the one she calls Sel, whom I sometimes hear, though have never seen.

Don't smoke in here, Sel. It gives me a headache.

Can't smoke in my room, 'cos of Abdul. Can't smoke downstairs 'cos of the baby. Where can I smoke? It's freezing outside, if you haven't noticed.

I thought you were giving up. You know the risks, Sel. It does what it says on the tin.

Oi!

She makes a sudden, snatching movement and a small packet appears in her hand. She holds it up, as if out of his reach, and I see in large black letters the words DAMAGES HEALTH. Then – as if an unseen hand has grabbed it back – the packet disappears.

I back out of the room, close the door and lean against the landing wall, thinking hard. For some time an idea has been taking root in my brain: what if Aysha is from the future? Perhaps I just delude myself to bolster my courage, for while I should be afraid of a ghost, however young and pretty, how can I fear someone who is not yet born? Ah, but if she lives in this house far in the future, Pa and I and Daisy will all be gone. Is that what *I* am when I see her, an invisible ghost haunting the house where I lived, unable to make my voice heard? But if I am right, perhaps Aysha knows things that we do not. Why did she speak about risks? Did the packet contain cigarettes and if so, what did the words on the packet mean? Tobacco is just a leaf, a natural product; but then... so are many poisons. Ma lived with Pa's cigars all her married life. She slept with a man who had tobacco in every fibre of his clothing and every pore of his skin – could that have harmed her? The smoke made her cough and she opened their bedroom window even in winter; Daisy used to hang Pa's clothes outside to lessen the smell.

Yet it doesn't make sense: Pa is not ill, or does not seem to be; nor Baines, who is a regular smoker too. I give up the puzzle and go down to help wash up.

18
Aysha

December 2001

"Aysha!" Mum calls. "Karen. Phone."

Aysha takes the receiver and sits on the bottom of the stairs. The phone is corded, the fixed line situated in the hall where Mum stands waiting, watching her expectantly.

"Hi Karen, Happy Christmas! What've you been doing?"

"Oh, you know, the usual. Eating, drinking, opening presents, watching telly. Dad's put his new exercise bike together. Mum's totally out of it – been at the G&Ts all day."

"Say the Happy Christmas to Karen." Mum retreats a little way down the hall.

"Mum's here," Aysha says cautiously. "She says Happy Christmas."

"O*kay*. Just listen," Karen says. "Mum and Dad have this buffet lunch thing organised for tomorrow. Our next door neighbours and some relatives, nothing major. But they've said I can invite a couple of friends too. Can you come? About midday?"

"Mum," she says loudly, knowing her mother hasn't strayed far, "can I go to Karen's tomorrow?" She turns to the wall and whispers, "I'll ring you back. Who's coming – of our friends, I mean?"

Karen laughs, "Wait and see!"

"Finish dinner, Aysha," Mum says when she returns to the kitchen. Only her parents are there. Sel's working, Mo has volunteered for the Christmas night shift and Reshna is putting the boys to bed.

"Mrs Carter's asked me to lunch tomorrow," she says, "and I want to take Karen her present too."

"Maybe go," Mum says. "If Sel drive you."

"I need to tell them tonight," she says. "It's not far. I can walk."

Any proposal has to be inspected, walked around, viewed from every angle. What about the weather? Mum asks. Will she wear her kameez, what if there's nothing she can eat, who else will be there? Just Karen's family, she tells Mum; it's a buffet so it will be easy to avoid any meat; and no, her black trousers and the blue top she bought on the market will be more suitable. She'll wear a headscarf, she adds, as a concession to both modesty and the weather.

Dad lays a hand on Mum's arm; his eyes twinkle. "What about the pakoras you made earlier, wife? Could Aysha take some as a gift?"

Mum beams. "Take biryani too! Say proper food. Not like restaurant."

Aysha's eyes meet Dad's. At times he seems more like his old self, more outgoing and assertive. She hopes it's a sign of better health, but she's not sure. When they came home in Sel's car, on the evening of Eid day, he'd spoken of wanting to see them all settled, but only if the decisions were right. Sel should go to Bangladesh in January with a cousin's family; it would do him good to get away. The money from the land sale would be for all his children, for whatever purpose. Aysha had hoped to speak to him further when they got home, on his own, but Abdul claimed her promise to play *Guess Who?* and somehow it hadn't happened. The thought that Dad might have reason to be putting his affairs in order flutters like a wounded bird inside her.

Now he gives her the barest of nods, a gentle encouraging lowering of his eyes. Stay well for me, Dad, she thinks as she goes to make her return call.

Later that evening, she's in her bedroom wrapping gifts, when there's a tap at her door. She shoves the packages under the bed: dangly earrings – turquoise coloured seahorses on silver hooks – for Karen, and a keyring in the shape of a pair of football boots for Derrick. She's pretty sure that Karen has invited him too.

"Can I come in?" Sel asks.

"Not if you're going to smoke," she says, eyeing the pack in his hand. "Please, Sel, you know it gives me a headache."

Where is he supposed to go? he grumbles. He can't smoke in his room because of Abdul, nor downstairs because of baby Safiya. It's too cold to stand outside or sit in his car.

"Just pack it in then," she says.

Dad used to smoke; it probably contributed to his heart attack. People didn't know any better when he was young, but Sel learned the facts at school just as she did. It's useless lecturing him, but she can't help it; they grew up together, used to be so close. Seeing him playing with the cigarette pack, flipping it over in his palm, passing it from one hand to the other like a deck of cards, she makes a sudden snatch.

"Oi, Aysh!"

"Can't you read?" she snaps, waving the health warning in his face. "It does what it says on the tin."

He grabs her wrist and wrests them back. "Yeah, well, maybe I don't care."

"Oh, Sel, what's wrong?"

He sits down on her chair and stares out of the window.

"I saw Velna the other day."

"The girl from the restaurant? Is she okay?"

Sel makes a strange little snorting noise. "She *was* pregnant. But after our big brother warned me off, he had a word with Raj, the boss, and he, like, thought he'd do me a favour and take her off my hands. Raj gave her money for the clinic and reckons I owe him now. She's says she's going home now. I should care!"

"You obviously do."

"Fat lot of good it does me." He puts an unlit cigarette in his mouth. "That could've been my kid."

"I thought you said..."

"Yeah, well. Listen, Aysh, maybe you're planning to marry Mr Smart Arse with the chicken shops, but if not, don't leave it too late. You can't make yourself into someone else just to please Mum and Mo. Sometimes you have to fight."

She blinks away the tears. She shouldn't have got into the habit of disregarding Sel: he knows her far better than she does him.

"I'll sort this land money out for Dad," he says, "but then I'm outta here."

~

Aysha hesitates outside the third-floor apartment. The front door is ajar and the throaty strains of Rod Stewart pulse from the hall.

She taps softly and pushes the door open further.

"Good. You're here!" Karen pulls her inside. "Welcome to the madhouse."

"What do you mean?"

"Remember my Auntie Lou?" Karen whispers. "Flirting with anything in trousers."

"Not taking my name in vain, are you, Kas?"

The woman at the far end of the hall is squeezed into black leggings and a clingy silver sweater and bears a certain resemblance to Janet, Karen's mum. She sashays towards them in time to the music.

"You're never little Aysha! Remember me taking you two and my Julie to the zoo when Kas was eight?"

Memories of a hot September day, penguins and ice cream slowly surface.

"Aunt Louise?"

"It's Lou, darling. Let's have a look at you – still a pretty little thing. Mind you, quite grown-up now, I understand." She lurches forward and exhales unfamiliar fumes in Aysha's face. "There's a gorgeous young man in there – six foot plus of melted chocolate – and this niece of mine tells me hands off – he's Aysha's! Good luck to you, girl. They say it's always the quiet ones."

"Sorry!" Karen mouths, taking Aysha into her bedroom. "She and Uncle Jim got divorced last year and there's been no stopping her since. Don't look so worried, Del's perfectly safe – he's talking football with my dad."

"I wasn't..."

"Who d'you think you're kidding, Aysh? You know you're a rotten liar." She pulls off Aysha's jacket and inspects her outfit. "Nice top. Leave your coat in here – what's all this in the bag?"

"Mum sent some food."

"Cool. I'll take it through. There's loads of stuff to eat, but ours all comes straight from the freezer at Sainsbury's, except for the turkey. I did make sure there's some veggie stuff for you."

"I've got you a present. It's only little."

Karen tears open the tiny package. "They're really lovely!" She immediately swaps the earrings she's wearing for the seahorse ones. "This is yours," she says, taking a box from her bedroom drawer. "Take it with you and go see Derrick while I sort the food. Otherwise Dad'll turn Sky Sports on and Mum'll go mental. She made him promise no football while we've got guests."

A drinks table has been set up in the living room, near the entrance to the kitchen, and about half a dozen people are clustered there. Lou is engaged in animated conversation with two men in their thirties, though the animation appears one-sided. Aysha sees a well-dressed couple snatch glances at Lou and raise their eyebrows. In the middle of the room, two women of about her mum's age shuffle and tap their feet to the music. A blonde girl, who could be Lou's daughter, Karen's cousin Julie, is perched on the lap of a beefy young man and is feeding him from a shared plate. The youth looks up, notices Aysha and stares at her with frank appraisal.

She finds she can't move; she doesn't belong here. The route to the window where Derrick and Mike are sharing a sofa looks hideously exposed. Still eyeing her, the young man sucks the sauce from a chocolate éclair off the blonde girl's fingers.

Someone comes up behind her and she turns to see Karen's mum.

"Kas said you were here," Janet says, resting her hand lightly beneath Aysha's elbow. "Thank your mum for the whatsits, won't you? And don't believe anything my daughter tells you, I'm as sober as a judge today. Got to be with this lot. Neighbours and family, dangerous mixture! Now, do me a favour and go and talk to your young man. I need Mike to rescue Hugh and Gary from Lou." She steers Aysha across the room whispering, "The boys next door. I've told her they're gay, but she takes it as a challenge."

The whole manoeuvre is accomplished as smoothly as skating across a rink: Janet deposits her beside Derrick and collects her husband. Aysha tries to thank her but can only smile. She stands awkwardly, clutching her present from Karen, until Derrick takes her hand and pulls her into the place vacated by Mike.

"I didn't think I'd see you till term starts," he says.

"I wanted to see you."

"Shall I get us some food?"

"Don't go. I feel like I'm on display here." She must sound pathetic, but she's really not comfortable alone. She's known Karen's parents for years and thought she was used to slipping between her world and theirs, but today it feels like she's drowning.

"Shove up, Del." Karen hands a plate of food to Aysha and sits beside them. "Trust me, you can eat it. Help yourself to grub, Derrick, and get Aysha a Coke while you're there. You okay, Aysh?" she asks when he's gone. "Mum thought you looked a bit lost."

Aysha hopes Janet doesn't think her ungrateful. She and Karen have taken pains to set up this meeting for her.

"I don't know what came over me. Your family parties are a bit different from mine."

"One extreme to the other, eh? When Del comes back, I'll open the doors to the balcony. It might be a bit chilly, but you two can sit out there in the quiet. Remember Paul, the guy from

Mum's work I went out with in the summer? He's coming soon. Called me up out of the blue the other day. What d'you reckon, Derrick," she says as he returns with a loaded plate, "wanna admire our view?"

The balcony overlooks Limehouse marina where tarpaulined boats pack close in winter hibernation and a thicket of masts rocks gently in the breeze. The vertical blinds in the lounge are partially closed, so that the small metal table and chairs on the balcony are secluded, as well as sheltered from the weather. Derrick rests their plates on the table and moves the chairs together.

"You heard anything more from what's 'is name?"

Aysha shakes her head. She regrets telling Derrick about meeting Jamil on Eid day; he's obviously spent Christmas stressing.

"Probably nothing'll come of it. I think he was just humouring his parents. I reckon he's got his own plans."

The pale sun hides behind a cloud and she shivers.

"I just don't want you to be part of them." He draws his chair even closer and rests his arm round the back of hers. "You cold?"

She leans into his shoulder and feels his warm breath on her hair, recognising the familiar mingled scent of aftershave and Derrick himself. Down below, clustered on a walkway across the water, some Bangladeshi girls loiter, taking photographs of each other beside the yachts and launches. The weak light triggers the automatic flash on their cameras. One figure looks familiar and Aysha leans forward for a better view; but then Derrick puts his arm around her shoulder and she turns her face to his.

19
Emily

Friday 27 December 1901

I wonder if Pa has parted with an even larger share of the company than he has acknowledged. His mind has been so troubled since Ma died, his judgement so often clouded by strong drink, that I fear he may have lost count of the papers he has signed. I won't let myself be in that man's debt! Surely Pa's objection to my working can no longer stand? If his need for credit is so great, nothing *I* do will affect it. I have decided to trust to my own judgement and visit Mr Fenton.

Sally is home and glad to see me. She is working for her Preliminary Certificate and must decide whether to enter a training college next year, or go as a pupil-teacher to a local school.

"The headmaster thinks I should do it properly and go to college," she says.

"What about Josh?"

"He has taken a position as an articled clerk in a law firm. My grandmother, who holds the purse strings, thought he was becoming too distracted by yours truly, so we are both under orders to be sensible."

"Sally, what do you know of your father's employees? Those

who sew for the West End store?"

"Not much," she says. "There are homeworkers, here in the East End, the ones people call sweated labour. That's a hard life, though Dad pays as much as any other owner, I think. The girls at the store do the fancy work and they're paid more and seem glad of their posts. Why do you ask?"

"I want to work. If your dad still needs seamstresses at the store, I'd like a job."

"I'll talk to him," she says. "But the hours are long, Emmie. Are you sure?"

I tell Daisy my plans, since they will affect her most closely. Not only will she be alone in the house all day, she will have to manage the cooking and cleaning on her own.

"If you can sit and sew all day, I'm sure I can keep house," says Daisy, "but it'll be mighty quiet without you!"

I don't say this to Daisy, but I hope that by working I can safeguard her position, since Pa will need her here in the house. This is her only home. I think she would have worked for Ma for nothing except her keep, but she cooks, cleans and looks after us and she deserves her pay. This time, Pa doesn't put up a fight when I tell him what I want to do.

"Don't think you can solve my problems with what you'll earn, Emmie, but if you really must, then give it a try."

Mr Fenton has said I can start on the sixth of January. He says some of the girls at the store live in rooms nearby, but I intend to get up early and catch the underground train from Bank. I am to learn the hand sewing of ladies' garments and train on the machines, too.

Monday 6 January 1902

Oxford Street is a booming place where new shops are opening all the time. Mr Fenton's shop is not a department store like Fraser and Sons, but a specialist tailors providing made to measure clothes for both ladies and gentlemen. It stands on a corner, at the junction with another thoroughfare. I walk up to the main entrance but am soon put in my place by a doorman who tells me that sewing room girls must not use the front door, but turn down the side street, enter an enclosed yard and climb the outside metal stairway to the top floor. Clearly the paying customers are not meant to meet the hands who toil behind the scenes.

There is a long narrow table in the middle of the workroom, covered by a white cloth, and some dozen girls sit at it, working on machines. Their skirts, like the floor around them, are covered with threads and snippets of cloth, Several smaller tables are for those doing hand sewing.

A man called Arthur Smythe is in charge of the room, allocating the work and checking its quality. He sets me sewing samples of different stitches and asks if I have used a sewing machine.

"No, sir," I reply, "I have only worked by hand."

"You're neat enough, but you'll need to speed up," he says. "You know the boss, I hear?"

"Mr Fenton? I went to school with his daughter."

"Well, there's no favouritism here – or not till you've earned it. The wage is seven and sixpence for nine to seven, Monday to Friday, with an hour for dinner. Saturdays nine till two at a shilling when there's enough work on. I'll put you with Lottie. There's an order for two blouses, same pattern, you can follow what she does."

I had not even asked about the wage before. There is a tuppenny fare each way on the train, which leaves five shillings and tenpence, from which I must buy my tea and keep myself in stockings.

Lottie is sharp-faced blonde of about nineteen. She and a girl called Kathleen work at a table which has the advantage of a window and the thick grey London light. Lottie gives me the pattern pieces for a blouse and shows me where the tucks must be and how to insert the lace trim before the garment can be assembled. She is a strict supervisor and checks my stitching every few inches. Lace is expensive, she says, and if I spoil it, Arthur will dock money from her wages. That doesn't seem fair, I say.

"Arthur's all right," she tells me, "though you must remember to be on time and that it's always Mr Smythe to his face. Oh, and don't spend all day in the you-know-what, the lav. He looks after us in the workshop pretty well, better than that la-di-da lot downstairs that measure up the customers and do the fittings. Watch out for Miss McPherson, who fits the ladies, she's a real tartar."

Our room is immediately above the fitting area and there is a twisting inside staircase ending in a half-glazed door which opens onto the floor below. Orders, fabrics and patterns arrive by that route, but the girls are forbidden to use it without permission.

"Sure and keep away from Mr Sutcliffe, who measures the gentlemen," adds Kathleen. "If he asks you to work late, mind you remember an appointment and excuse yourself, or he'll have you measuring his inside leg."

"'E ain't got anything worth measuring, if you ask me," says a spotty, lank-haired girl, who turns round from her machine at the central table.

"No-one is asking you, is they, Doris?" snaps Lottie. "Keep your mouth clean and your eyes on your work or your seams will wander."

The machinists are mostly engaged in sewing linings for jackets and skirts, which are then stitched in by hand.

After four hours of work, when my fingers are numb and my back rigid with bending over my needle, Arthur blows a whistle and announces the break.

"One hour, sharp, ladies."

"Did you bring anything, Emily?" Lottie asks. I nod, because Daisy has packed up some bread and cheese with a slice of cold beef.

"When it's warm enough to sit out," she says, "we usually walk to a garden square, but today we'd best eat over there in the corner, where you can take a drink of water, then we'll go and window-shop all the stores."

Lottie produces a hard-boiled egg and a dry-looking bun, which she finishes in no time; Kathleen has a bit of bread and a slice of cold bacon. I am obliged to bolt my food if I am to go out with them. I have my long wool coat with a fur collar, which Ma had made two years ago. It's short for me now, but still warm. Kathleen eyes it curiously as she and Lottie wrap woollen shawls around their shoulders and we go down to the street.

"What are you doing here, Emily?" she wonders. "You don't look as if you need to earn a crust."

"My Pa's in business," I say, "but he's not been doing well since Ma died last year. I'd rather support myself, if I can."

"Well, you won't make your fortune," Lottie says, "but it's a wage. Do you live at home?"

"Yes. Don't you?"

"Some of us board a few streets away, towards Covent Garden. There's a woman, Mrs Pegg, rents out rooms to dressmakers and shop girls. I share with Kathy. She's from Ireland so she doesn't have family here."

"I don't like to leave my Pa just now."

"Fair enough. But if it you change your mind or it gets too much to travel, I can put in a word, you know."

We walk to Regent Street and stare at the windows of Hamleys, the famous toy shop. There are dolls, tin soldiers, clockwork toys and kits for tennis and croquet. Kathleen gazes in longing at the dolls with their lace bonnets and porcelain smiles.

"Would you look at those?" she whispers. "If only I could send one for my sisters Bridget and Maeve."

"They're just dolls," I say. "You could make a rag one and dress it nicely for them."

"You'll have had a doll," Lottie snaps. "Books and toys and the like – you can tell that by looking at you. Kathy's sisters've never had anything bought from a shop. You don't know what that's like."

I bite my tongue; I have a lot to learn.

The afternoon passes slowly. The sun sets about four, but darkness comes earlier here, where the tall grey buildings cast long shadows, and the gas lamps are lit by three-thirty. Electric lighting has been installed in the showroom downstairs but it hasn't climbed our staircase. Somewhere in the building there must be a boiler, because an iron radiator stands on one wall and a pipe runs around the room. Around four-thirty, we are allowed to use the small gas ring in the corner to make a cup of tea.

When I reach home it is past eight and I am almost too tired to eat. Daisy has warmed my bed and brings me hot water to wash. Pa seems almost cheerful when he bids me goodnight: I'm sure he only agreed to let me try the job because he thinks I will soon give up.

Wednesday 8 January 1902

Mr Smythe tells me that my work is promising and I can stay. I hadn't realised I was only on trial! I know the names of most of the girls now; they are friendly enough, but treat me like a child, even though one or two are younger than me.

This morning, Lily, one of the buttonholers, was called downstairs to the fitting room with some finished garments and came back with a tale.

"Girls, d'you remember Sir Roger what's 'is name, the one who's a Member of Parliament and whose suit we made last month?"

"What of him?"

"He's brought his wife. She's being measured up for a riding suit, nothing but the best, he says."

"Wife?" says Bella. "I've seen 'er in the street before and the 'orse ain't bin bred that can carry *that* ladyship. What was this one's figure?"

"She goes in and out like me mother's egg timer."

"Let's 'ave a look at 'er."

Mr Smythe is out of the workshop at present so Bella and Lottie creep down the narrow stairs and spy through the glass panel of the fitting room door. They come back ready to burst with silent laughter.

"That, my angels," says Lottie, "is no ladyship. *That* is Miss Celia Witherspoon, star of the London Pavilion and all the other music halls between here and Timbuctoo. Dirty old bugger! Close your ears, Emmie."

Friday 10 January 1902

At last the longest week of my life is over! Mr Smythe takes me aside and says I've done well for a new girl, but I'm to come back Monday, not tomorrow.

"It takes time to get used to the hours," he says, "what with taking the tube and all. I'll need you next Saturday, mind."

I force myself to eat a good meal when I get home. Part of me wonders why on earth I'm doing this. I have laboured all week and earned not much more than my fares and a hot meal each day. The little that is left will never make good Pa's debts, but at least I needn't feel indebted to William Baines for my bread. For Lottie and the others, this is their life, the only respectable choice they have. If they can do it, I can too.

Pa asked about the underground journey. I believe he is anxious because there was a bad accident recently when a train caught fire in a tunnel, but he has not enquired about my work at the store; he is still waiting for my resolve to weaken.

Monday 13 January 1902

It was barely light when I left home and a dull and chilly morning. Doris, the machinist, is ahead of me on the stairs.

"Oh, *you're* back," she says. "Thought you might 'ave 'ad enough."

Mr Smythe nods to me as we enter the workshop.

"We'll start to train you on these today," he says, indicating the row of Singer and Jones machines with his hand. "I think you'll be most useful as a hand stitcher, but it's best if you have the skill to use them."

"Mary's still poorly with the mumps," says Doris. "She can use 'er machine, I s'pose."

"Thank you, Doris. Perhaps you'll show Emily how to load a bobbin and thread her machine. She can use some of that striped cotton to practise."

Doris screws up her nose and makes a face. The cold has made the cluster of pimples on her forehead stand out angrily.

"It ain't startin' time yet. I got the bellyache and 'ave to pay a visit."

The other girls arrive and when Lottie comes up I tell her that I'm put with Doris this morning.

"She's a bit rough, Doris, but she's a good machinist. Come out with Kathy and me at dinner time – we thought we'd walk to Grosvenor Square."

When Doris reappears, wiping her hands on her skirt, she bids me watch carefully while she threads her machine. She shows me how to raise and lower the foot, catch up the bobbin thread and position the fabric to sew a seam. It looks easy enough to turn the handle to work the machine, but each of my hands has a separate role to learn and if I don't keep the wheel turning smoothly, it spins backwards and breaks the thread. It takes a lot of practice and a good few false starts before I feel able to show a line of stitching to Arthur Smythe. Still, sewing straight seams by hand is a tedious job, so it's good that machines can free us for more interesting work.

At one o'clock we set out to walk to Grosvenor Square. We sit on a bench and eat bread, cheese and onions. I parcelled up the remains of our Christmas cake this morning – the fruits are still moist, though the marzipan and icing are turning brittle – and share it with Lottie and Kathleen. There are hungry pigeons waiting by our feet but the girls lick their fingers and dab up all the crumbs.

"Well, Emily," says Lottie, "and how did you spend your weekend?"

I admit to having been so tired that I did little except eat, read and sleep.

"You must've done your laundry," says Lottie, looking at my clean collar and I don't like to admit it was done for me by Daisy.

Kathleen is a Roman Catholic and attends St James's church twice for mass on Sundays, she says. I ask her why she left her family to come to London.

"Me dad went to America back in '96," she says. "Promised to send for us all when he'd saved the money for our passage. He was working on the building sites and he wrote to me mam quite regular until two years ago, but then the letters stopped. She don't know if he's dead or if he's got himself a New York woman. There's six of us still at home. I send her whatever money I can."

She looks tearful and Lottie squeezes her hand.

"Don't upset yourself, Kathy, you do your best. Aren't you going ask me what I've been doing, girls?"

"Well, what did you do, Lottie?" I ask.

"Saturday afternoon I spent my sixpence on a lovely soak in the Endell Street baths – warm water, soap, two towels, nothing but the best! And on Sunday I went walking with a certain Jimmy Tomkins!"

"The doorman?"

"The very same. He's been asking for the last month, but I was sure to make him wait."

"Where d'you go?"

"Hyde Park. And he hired a boat and rowed me round the Serpentine!"

"He's a handsome lad, but was he a gentleman, Lot?" Kathy asks.

"Well he did put his arm around me, but only to help me out the boat."

"You'd be married for less back in Ireland!" Kathy declares. "And has he asked you for next week?"

Lottie nods, smiling, and wraps her shawl round her tightly as she turns to me.

"You're a pretty girl, Emmie. You walking out with someone, or don't your pa allow it?"

I hesitate, wanting to return their confidence but not sure what to say. "There's no-one I like, but I think Pa wants to see me married."

"To someone you don't like?" asks Kathy.

"Someone who wants to marry me for reasons of his own and has tried to take advantage of me."

"There are plenty who'd take advantage but they don't usually want to marry you," Lottie laughs. "What happened?"

I never intended it, but I find myself telling them all about Ma and Charlie, about William Baines and the events of my sixteenth birthday, and my fears that Baines will somehow gain control of Pa's business.

Kathy lets out a long, low whistle.

"You need to know how to look after yourself," says Lottie. "You should've used your knee, like this, hard between his legs."

"Why don't your dad believe you?" Kathleen wonders.

"He's not been himself since Ma died and Mr Baines has always been there, telling him what to do and lending money when Pa was short. Now he can't afford to break with him."

"Sounds like a cunning divil, sure enough," Kathleen says, "and you're right to stay clear of him."

Lottie says it's time we walked back. They take my arms and

walk either side of me and for the first time in months I don't feel alone.

20
Aysha

January 2002

"It's all right for you, you're up to date with everything," Karen complains.

Andy's history students sit stunned by the quantity of work being thrown at them. It's the same in English, Aysha tells Derrick. Timed essays, practice papers, unseen criticisms all stretch before them for the next half-term. One of the boys has a university interview the following Thursday and has to miss a test.

"We'll fix another time for you to do the paper," Andy assures him. "Can't have you losing out." He offers to rehearse interview questions in the next tutorials and asks if the others have heard from any of their choices. No-one else in this group has had a response, though someone in Karen's business studies set has a provisional offer and a boy in Derrick's geography class has already been turned down twice.

Wahida follows them out at the end of the session. All week, Aysha's had the uneasy feeling that the other girl is watching her, especially when she's with Derrick.

"You haven't heard from Greenwich, have you – I thought you applied there too?" Wahida asks.

"No, she hasn't..." Karen begins, but Aysha, quicker on the uptake for once, digs her in the ribs. Greenwich *was* on the UCAS form she showed Mo and her parents, but not on the one Jo sent off. The post usually arrives before eight and it's Aysha who picks it up, even on college days. At that hour, Mo is either working or sleeping and Mum is busy with the boys. She's almost relieved no letters have come yet. If one of the unis calls her for interview, she'll need to account for a day's absence, and find the money for the train fare, though Jo has mentioned that the college has a hardship fund that can help.

"I've already said I haven't had any replies," she says sharply, "and who said I've applied to Greenwich?"

Wahida looks hurt. "I don't remember – does it matter? Maybe Andy. I expect we've chosen different courses, but it would be nice to know someone there. We sisters should stick together." She's slight, like Aysha, and similar in height; now she stands gazing levelly at her, ignoring Karen and Derrick.

"That's not the point of uni, is it?" Karen says, linking arms with Aysha. "Sticking to what you know? Aysha's my best friend, but I don't expect her to choose places to suit me."

"I only wondered... "

"Don't worry, Wahida," Derrick says, kindly, "you're bound to hear soon."

The girl gives him a contemptuous look and turns away.

"What is it with her?" he asks.

"Just jealous," says Karen. "She doesn't think Aysh should mix with infidels like you and me. Mind you," she adds, lowering her voice, "from what I hear, her choices are all over the place. Different subjects for each uni – politics, South Asian studies, history. Jo said not to do that. It looks like you don't know what you want."

Aysha is silent, trying to locate the source of her unease. History is the only class she shares with Wahida and she's sure Andy has never mentioned her choices in class. What made her think Aysha had applied to Greenwich? Wahida's always been the odd one out in the history set. She has strong opinions, and likes to air her views. Andy's always patient, and even seems to enjoy debating with her, but many of the class resent the time she takes up. They've never been close – does Wahida really imagine they could be best friends at uni?

Aysha parts from Derrick and Karen outside college. Derrick has started an evening and weekend job at the local supermarket and Karen's keen to get home and finish her course work before going out with Paul. At four-thirty on a drizzly evening as the light is fading, Aysha crosses the road to walk down the narrow street which skirts a local school. As always, it is lined with parked cars. When a window glides down and someone calls, she backs away from the kerb towards the grass verge on her left. Then a voice says her name and she looks back.

"Jamil?"

The driver who leans from the window of a small silver car is more casually dressed than when she last saw him. "Yes, it's me, Aysha. Can I talk to you?"

She stands undecided, conscious of the rain penetrating her headscarf and dripping down her neck. "Mum's expecting me home."

"I'll drive you. Or we could go for a coffee."

"They'd go mental," she says, shaking her head.

No way can she go home in his car, even if he is her family's choice of husband. A café would be just as bad and it's too wet and dark to sit in the park. What can he want?

"Just sit here in the car then. Ten minutes – please. Look, you're getting wet. We won't go anywhere – you can hold the keys if you don't trust me."

"It's not that," she says, glancing over her shoulder.

He opens the door. "Then get in."

She sits on the edge of the passenger seat, trying not to shed rain onto the grey leather. A perfumed car freshener in the shape of a footballer hangs in the windscreen, though, unlike in Sel's car, there's no trace of cigarette or food odour. He said he wanted to speak to her, but he seems unable to start.

"Families, eh?" he sighs, eventually. "Complicate life, don't they?" She raises an eyebrow, unable to dispute this. "I'm not vain enough to think I made much of an impression on you at Eid, Aysha, but our families have certain expectations. I'd like to know how you feel. Be honest with me."

She looks up and sees troubled eyes. "Honestly? Well, I've nothing against *you,* but I'm in no hurry to get married. I want to concentrate on uni first."

He breathes out: a long, relieved exhalation. She has a nervous urge to laugh but suppresses it as inappropriate.

"You mean you don't want to either? Then why don't you tell your family." Surely it's easier for a man?

"It's not that simple." He looks down and a faint blush tinges his cheek. She waits for him to go on, but again he hesitates. Perhaps he feels obliged to please his parents if they're giving him a job. Then again, he's been away in Birmingham for the last three years and says he still goes back – maybe he's met someone there and thinks his family won't approve. She watches as raindrops play chase down the windscreen, refracting the headlights of cars passing in the road.

"I need your help," he says at last. "Working for Dad's not my dream job. I want something with prospects, not pushing cheap chicken to local kids. I've applied for loads of posts in the Midlands, been shortlisted too, but Dad will cut my allowance and take the car back if he finds out – he's always planned for me to join him. I can't get married at the moment – I have to concentrate on finding work. I just need us both to go along with their plans until I know I can support myself. It won't take long with my degree and references. I'll break it to Dad once I'm earning, so nothing will reflect on you."

"I don't know," she wonders. "Why do I have to get involved?"

"I wouldn't have asked if I thought you were keen to get married," Jamil says, fixing her with an expression of perfect sincerity, "but your dad said you're applying to uni. It will take the pressure off you too, won't it?" He leans closer. "I really like you, Aysha. We can still be friends and who knows what might happen a few years from now."

It sounds like he's really thought this through, but she's still unsure. He doesn't care about his parents and maybe he's spinning her a line too, with his hints about the future; but she'd been prepared to mislead him: she'd hardly even considered that. And he's right: it will make life easier for her too if Mo thinks she's cooperating.

"What do you want me to do?"

"Forget we ever had this conversation. When my parents make a proposal, just go along with it for now. They know you have to finish your A levels; they won't expect a wedding yet and I only need a month or two. There was talk of us meeting, getting to know each other. We can still do that – officially I mean. Will you do it? Promise?"

Aysha nods, relieved that the prospect of marriage has receded, yet feeling life has just become even more confused, with new secrets to keep. Still, it can't hurt if she does as Jamil wants and buys herself some time.

21
Emily

Saturday 18 January 1902

Arthur Smythe tells me I am needed this Saturday, so I report for work. About half the machinists are in, plus most of the hand stitchers. The mood in the room is lighter than usual, in anticipation of an early finish; we do not take a meal break, but are allowed a cup of tea at eleven. The talk is all of how we will spend Sunday: Lottie says that Jimmy Tomkins has offered to take her to the zoo.

At one o'clock, Mr Smythe calls me and says I am needed downstairs. I brush the threads from my clothes and start towards the outside door, but he calls me back and tells me to take the internal stairs. I can feel the girls' eyes upon me and wonder why I am wanted and by whom. Has Pa spoken to Mr Fenton and made him change his mind about giving me the job?

But when I go through the forbidden door into the fitting area, I see Sally sitting on the dark red chaise which is there for customers to rest. She is wearing a green jacket, long but fitted tightly at the waist, over a full plaid skirt and a cream lace blouse similar to the ones I helped to make on my first day. A broad-brimmed hat matches her jacket and is decorated with ribbons and feathers in a lighter green. She looks like an advertisement from one of Elizabeth's magazines and I feel positively dowdy in my work skirt and apron, with my hair tied back from my face. She jumps up to meet me, but then appears to lose her balance and uses her long umbrella for support. There is something different about her, a change in her figure, not just the new, stylish clothes.

"I am in agony!" she hisses. "Grandmama had me fitted with my corset and I can hardly move."

I try not to laugh. It must be one of the new models, the type which pushes the bosom forward like a pigeon's and tilts the hips back, so that the wearer is for ever in danger of toppling over!

"You look wonderful!" I say. "That green really suits you."

"It is the new me, my dear, as ordained by Grandmama. I am her pet and she wants to make a lady of fashion out of me. But I need some sensible company – say you will come with me to lunch!"

When I explain that I have another hour to work, she pouts and offers to ask her dad to let me off early. I won't let her do that, so she takes up a pattern book and agrees to wait.

"Meet me outside at two," I say, not sure if I'll be allowed to use the inside stairs again. When I go back to my work, Lottie and Kathleen want to know why I was called and several other heads turn to hear my answer.

"A friend came to see me."

"Must be an important friend for Arthur to call you off work and send you down the inside way," muses Lottie. "Is your friend a customer?"

"It was Miss Fenton," I admit, "Mr Fenton's daughter. I went to school with her." I see Lottie's eyes narrow; Bella and Doris exchange glances.

"Better watch yer tongues, girls," Bella mutters. "Boss has got himself a spy in our camp."

"I'm not a spy!" I cry angrily. "Sally's an old friend." I make sure to carry on working until Arthur blows his whistle at two o'clock, then I splash my face with a little water, comb my hair and go downstairs with the girls, wishing them all a good weekend. Sally stands waiting at the front of the store; she seems to have perfected the art of leaning on her umbrella. A moment later, Mr Fenton himself appears.

"Emily," he says, "I have been hearing good things of you, but Sally here is unhappy that I've stolen her friend, so you'll do me a favour if you'll take tea with her." He turns to Sally, "Here, treat yourselves to some fancy cakes." He gives Sally two half-crowns and beams with pleasure when she leans over to kiss him on the nose. I have always liked Mr Fenton, but I can't help thinking how long I've worked and how many stitches I've sewn to earn as much as he's carelessly handed over and wonder if he has any idea how his seamstresses live.

We decide to walk down Regent Street to Piccadilly, where there is a Lyons tea shop. Sally stops at all the shop windows, which are displaying the new spring fashions. I find it hard to reconcile this sophisticated young woman, who attracts many admiring glances, with either my school friend or the teacher she is training to become.

"I called at your house this morning," she says, when we are settled at our table and the waitress has brought tea and éclairs. "I had no idea you would be working Saturday too."

"I do what the job requires," I reply. "When you start to teach, you'll do the same. Do you remember how Miss Morris used to take our composition books home in the basket of her bicycle and was always in school by eight o'clock?"

Sally dabs cream from her lips with a napkin and pulls a face. "I'm not sure how long I will teach, Emmie. The store is really doing well and Dad and my Grandmother regard college just as something to keep me occupied until I am old enough to marry Josh. Oh, yes," she adds, seeing my surprise, "they are in favour of it. It keeps money in the family, you know. We must wait until he qualifies and I am eighteen."

"I don't think I could train for something I knew I would never do."

"Well, perhaps I'm not such a swot as you would be. I do what's necessary and it fills up the day. When I'm married and have children, we need not hire a governess. Who knows what the future will bring?"

"And are you sure – about Josh, I mean? Of course you are fond of your cousin..."

I'd always regretted that Ma and Pa had no siblings to provide cousins for me.

"Emmie, I didn't see Josh from the time I was eight until we met at my grandmother's two years ago – he had been away to school and we never met. Yet the moment I saw him, I knew."

"And Josh too?" I persevere. "Are you sure he's not just going along with your grandmother's wishes?"

"Really, Emmie," she says haughtily, "don't you think me worthy of love? I can't think what has made you such a cynic."

I apologise quickly, saying I only wanted to be sure of her happiness. She is right: I am becoming cynical. Baines, Pa, even Elizabeth, and now the workroom talk, have made me so.

Friday 24 January 1902
I have been working at hand sewing again this week, learning new techniques all the time: today, adding pintucks to a bodice. I am becoming used to the hours and am not so tired as at first.

The girls who work here can never afford the price of the garments they sew. Most of them make over used clothing that they buy from market stalls, where the goods are not even second, but third or fourth hand, yet they still feel pride in seeing their work on the mannequins or on a more fortunate customer's back. Mostly they are decent girls, like Lottie and Kathleen, obliged to earn a living and hoping to marry in a year or so. One or two, like Lily the buttonholer, are saving to buy their own machines and set up as dressmakers in their own right. Susan, another of the hand stitchers, wants to train as a nurse when she's eighteen, because, like Charlie, her brother died in South Africa, in his case of an infected wound. I haven't considered nursing before, but too many young men die of dirt and poor care: learning to improve their chances of survival seems a worthy aim.

Doris, her friend Bella and a few others are rougher types whose conversation is coarse, with tales of the public houses they frequent on a Friday or Saturday night and the men they meet there. Yet I begin to see that there is no fixed line that determines who is respectable and who is not – we are all young women making our way in the world as best we can.

Life at home has fallen into a pattern too. From Monday to Friday, Daisy serves dinner to Pa and me when I get home around eight. Pa still doesn't ask about my work, but he is clearly impressed by Mr Fenton's success and says he is doing roaringly.

We have had no visitors since Christmas; there is no talk of entertaining friends or neighbours or spending money on fancy meals. Elizabeth is growing larger by the day and does not go out in the evening; we see nothing of Richard or the doctor, nor for that matter of Baines himself. The anniversary of Victoria's funeral will soon be here, of that bitter day when we learned of Charlie's death. All of us – Pa, me, Daisy – must deal with it in our own way.

After we've drunk our coffee, I spend an hour in the kitchen, drying the dishes and ironing my blouse for the next day. Daisy likes to hear about the girls at Fenton's store, identifying especially with Kathleen, alone in London without her family, but she's scandalised when I repeat some of Doris' and Bella's stories.

"Your poor Ma would've 'ad a fit if she knew you'd heard all that!"

I find it harder to talk to her about our own shared history. Somehow, we've never recovered the closeness we shared when we were both nursing Ma and when she rescued me from William Baines: too much knowledge stands between us. Daisy is still outraged that Pa invited him on Christmas Day, but I say I wish to put the man from my mind. I have not told her that I've spoken about him to Lottie and Kathleen.

22
Aysha

January 2002

The clock reads one-thirty; Aysha still can't sleep. At first, knowing Jamil's secret had been a source of satisfaction; now she feels guilt at deceiving her parents. Mum will be overjoyed if the Rahmans send a proposal and all the time Aysha will know it's just a sham. The temporary sense of empowerment was an illusion: she's dependent on the success of Jamil's job search.

What's worse, she's quarrelled with Derrick. She bites her lip in frustration as she remembers his anger when she told him about meeting Jamil.

"Shit, Aysha!" he'd shouted at her. "What were you thinking? You've met this guy just once and you get in his car? Anything could have happened to you!"

She'd made it worse by laughing. She didn't see the problem; she didn't know Jamil well, but she could tell he was harmless.

"Tell that to his parents," Derrick said. "Sounds like he lies to them about everything."

"That's different."

"Why – because he's Bengali?"

"No, course not."

"Come home with me then," he said. "Come to my house. My mum'll be there. If you can get in that geezer's car, you can do that."

She'd stared. He was jealous.

"We're not all prejudiced. Just 'cos I can't meet your family, it doesn't mean you can't meet mine."

Her hand had stretched out to him, but he looked away, drawing the back of his wrist across his eyes. A moment later he had disappeared across the park.

Did she dream the tap on her door? A second knock jerks her awake. She reaches for her dressing gown and stumbles to her bedroom door. Sel stands on the landing, dressed in his suit and black puffa jacket. Aysha frowns and shivers; it's still dark and the central heating hasn't yet kicked in.

"What's the time?" she yawns.

"Six-fifteen. I knew you'd forgotten – it's today, innit? I'm going to Bangladesh."

"What, now?"

"Na, not yet. Dad's cousins are picking me up at eight. Mum 'n Dad are up – writing even more lists of instructions."

"Give me a minute," she says. "I'll come down."

Sel reaches into his jacket and thrusts his mobile phone into her hand.

"Thought you could use this." He extracts a charger and top-up card from another pocket. "It's pay-as-you-go, but there might be a few quid left on it. I've cleaned my stuff off and the number's on the card. I bought a new one that works over there."

Her eyes speak her gratitude; she's humbled by his unexpected thoughtfulness. How is it that the brother who's teased and squabbled with her for the past seventeen years can turn into a friend just as he's going away? Once or twice recently, she's been tempted to confide in him about Derrick, but he's still an older brother and she can't be sure that he'll apply the same standards to her friendships as to his own.

"Well, d'you want it or not? You don't have to mention it to Mum, like."

She takes the phone and throws her arms around her brother.

"Keep safe, Sel."

"I ain't gone yet." He reaches out and tousles her hair. "Come and have some breakfast."

Mum and Dad fuss and fidget their way through the next hour and a half. Dad has written letters in both English and Bengali detailing his wishes regarding his share of the family land. Mum has packed presents for the women of the family in Sel's luggage: Marks & Spencer cardigans, face cream, packs of paracetamol, English soap. She wants to make sure Sel knows who gets what. Reshna is sending photographs of Ibrahim and Safiya for her mother in the next village.

Mo looks preoccupied. Aysha guesses he thinks it should be his place to go and carry out Dad's business, but even if he takes leave he can't go without Reshna and the children, or afford the airfares to take them with him. Abdul eats his breakfast in silence and casts sideways glances through his eyelashes at them all. Sel winks at Aysha and adopts a stern expression.

"Just 'cos you've got the room to yourself for a month, don't go wrecking my stuff, right Ab? I don't want to find your Lego in my bed when I get back."

Abdul nods solemnly.

"Yeah, well, be good, bro. Look after the littl'uns, eh?"

The letter box on the front door clatters. Mum looks at the clock and comments, "Uncle is early."

Sel goes to the door but reports that it was only the post, Aysha looks up in alarm: this is the first morning she's forgotten to pick up the mail herself.

"Just junk stuff," Sel says, throwing a clutch of supermarket leaflets on the table, but when Aysha goes upstairs, he follows and pushes an official-looking envelope into her hands.

"It says *Personal*, so I thought..."

This time, the knocking is unmistakeable and is immediately followed by several blasts of a horn. Aysha goes to the window and spots a large estate car, already crammed with passengers and luggage. Mo is carrying Sel's suitcase to the kerb.

"That's me, then," Sel says, his expression poised somewhere between eagerness and regret. "See you in a month, Aysh!" He takes the stairs two at a time, shoulders his flight bag and is gone.

"A month," she murmurs. "Insh'Allah."

Aysha pauses briefly to answer Maud, who is on the stairs from the basement flat and wants to know what all the hooting's about, but she hardly notices which number bus she boards and doesn't respond when Karen catches up with her outside college.

"Good weekend?" Karen asks. Then, inspecting her face, "What's up with you?"

"My brother's just left for Bangladesh. I'd forgotten it was today."

"Sel, you mean?"

Aysha nods.

"Well, it's not as if you're particularly close, is it?"

She opens the gloved hand which still cradles a shiny red handset and stretches it towards Karen. "He just gave me his phone."

"Let me see. Cool! Can I put my number in for you?"

"He's not been there since we were little and now he's got to sort all this money stuff out for Dad."

What if he gets into trouble? There've been stories about people from the UK being swindled, driven away, or worse, by unscrupulous relatives.

"Your dad must think he can look after himself," Karen says, dismissing Aysha's sibling anxiety with the carefree ease of an only child.

"And I quarrelled with Derrick." She glances round quickly to see who might be listening. "On Friday. Before we went home."

"What about?"

"It's complicated." She hasn't told Karen about meeting Jamil last week.

"Suit yourself." Karen flicks back her pony tail. "Don't you want to hear my news?"

"Of course."

"Ta-da!" Karen conjures a letter from her bag with a theatrical flourish. "Offer from Westminster. Business Studies." Then she grimaces: "Two Bs."

"You'll do that easily. Will you live at home?" She bites her lip, her eyes widening as she suddenly recalls the long, cream envelope which lies unopened in her pocket. "I nearly forgot. This came this morning. Sel picked it up and slipped it to me before he left."

"I don't believe you," Karen says. "All this time we've been waiting and you haven't opened it, not even on the bus. Is that a

Cardiff postmark? It looks thick – that's a good sign. It only takes a page to say no."

They sit on the wall outside college. Aysha removes her glove and slips her little finger into the corner of the envelope; the paper yields, revealing a thick wad of folded sheets.

"There's a map and directions," she says doubtfully. "I suppose that means they want to interview me."

Karen has snatched the next sheet. "No, look – what's this? AAB. It's an offer all right."

"I need to get the grades first."

"They wouldn't offer if they didn't think you could do it. Jo thinks you can. I bet you'll get lots of offers – they'll be fighting over you."

Aysha is still reading. The letter invites her to an open day, either during half-term or later, in April. She can't delay talking to her parents much longer.

"There's Del," Karen says. "Are you two talking?"

"I guess."

"I'll leave you to it then. See you in class."

Karen skips off and Derrick settles on the wall beside her. His eyes shout defiance as he pulls off a woollen hat to reveal a really short crop, with a lightning bolt razored onto his scalp.

"Oh!" Aysha puts up her hand and traces the line tentatively.

"Don't you tell me I look like Harry Potter. I had enough at the checkout yesterday."

"No," she says, " I like it. It suits you." Their glances meet, then dart away, like playground children unwilling to be caught.

"I'm sorry," they both say together.

"I shouldn't tell you what to do."

"I know you're just looking out for me."

"Yeah, well..."

"What you said – about meeting your mum? I'd like to."

He beams. "Really? I'll sort it."

She shows him her letter and Sel's mobile phone. They are still circling around each other, wary; but they've survived their first row. They're still friends.

23
Emily

Saturday 25 January 1902

Daisy has told me that she's recently had news of her eldest sister Ethel, the one who lives in Bethnal Green. Ethel already had a family of four, but has recently been delivered of twins and Daisy, who has not seen her for some years, wants to visit. Daisy's sisters have done little for her, but they are still her family and she is due a day off. I tell her to go as soon as Pa has breakfasted; I am working a half day, so can be home early to make his tea.

The workroom is quiet as only four machinists are in. Kathleen is here, but Lottie is visiting her mother in Kentish Town. Bella and another girl turn up shivering and feverish, their eyes and noses red and raw. Arthur Smythe sends them home when he sees them, despite Bella's plea that they don't want to lose their pay.

"Look at the state of you," he tells them. "Dripping snot all over the place and by Monday everyone else will be sniffling too."

I am afraid he will ask the rest of us to work longer to make up for their absence, but Arthur wants his half day too and sends us away at the usual hour. The train is quiet and I have space to sit and read my book. Fewer workers travel into the City and the

West End on Saturday and it is too cold to encourage day trippers. I remember that Daisy will be out all day and plan to stay in the warmth of the kitchen and perhaps try my hand at a cake.

I don't see Pa's coat in the hall so go straight upstairs, meaning to change my clothes and sit and write for a while before starting to bake. I lift the floorboard in my bedroom to retrieve my journal and immediately catch the familiar smell of cigar smoke. My bedroom is directly above our parlour; Pa must be home after all.

I go down and tap at the parlour door: no answer. I think I must be mistaken and that, as it is cold and the windows have not been opened, tobacco fumes from the previous night still linger. Daisy normally empties Pa's ash trays and airs all the rooms, but she has not had time to do so today. As I push the door, the smell becomes overpowering; I need to open windows and clear the air. Then the door swings fully open and I jump back with a gasp. William Baines is sitting beside the empty hearth, reading and annotating papers, pen in one hand and cigar in the other. The stub of another cigar lies in Pa's ashtray on the fender. My first thought is that I am alone with him in the house and I imagine the fear shows on my face; my second thought is that he too looks uncomfortable.

"Where's my father?"

"He'll be home directly. He asked me to look over some accounts. Come and sit down, Emily. I'm not going to bite you, though I still feel the impression of *your* teeth."

"How did you get in?" How dare he make free of the house, inviting *me* to sit in our own parlour!

"By the key your father gave me, of course. Do you think me a housebreaker?"

"There is little I would not believe of you, Mr Baines," I say, still standing and holding onto the door.

"Would you believe me if told you I regret how I acted on the night of your birthday?"

I glare at him as fiercely as I can, not trusting the contrite expression he wears.

"I was afraid I'd lost all chance of you and allowed the drink to lead me astray."

"You seemed to act with intention to me."

"Then my intentions were misdirected," he said. "I have always been impatient."

"Is that what you call it – impatience? You lied to my father afterwards. You... you misrepresented yourself and me. To talk to Pa of keeping yourself for your wife!"

"Your father had the good fortune to marry the woman he loved when he was scarcely a man. His grandfather handed over this business and made that marriage possible. Life doesn't run so easily for all of us. I've missed talking to you, Emily. Tell me, how is working for Fenton?"

"I manage," I say, conscious of my pricked fingers and old skirt.

"Harder than you thought, I imagine. I congratulate you for sticking at it, though I don't approve of women working when they don't have to. But then I have always admired your spirit."

I am still nervous, but he seems intent only on talk and there are things I want to know.

"What are you doing to Pa? Are you out to ruin him?"

"Why would I ruin him when we are partners?"

"Partners?"

"Your father needed both my business head and financial support, so we came to an agreement. You must know that when your mother died he didn't think clearly or manage well."

"You encouraged his drinking!"

"It eased his sorrow. Was that so bad?"

"Yes, if you took advantage of it. I think you always had this planned – it was you who encouraged my poor brother to enlist."

Baines puts down the papers and draws deeply on the cigar; he locks his eyes with mine.

"I encouraged him to think of the army, yes. I liked Charlie – he was a lively boy and it was obvious his heart wasn't in business. I regret his loss sincerely, but I didn't know he would falsify his age. As I understand, it was *you* who found that birth certificate he used."

"You envied Charlie. You coveted his place."

"And if I did? I've no family, Emily. No mother, no sister; no father to promote my employment. My aunt gave me a home for a few years, but she still made a distinction between cousin Fred and me. Everything I have I've struggled for. Why shouldn't I be envious? Why shouldn't I want what Charlie valued so little? Don't condemn envy – without it there is no motivation to succeed."

He speaks with such passion that I find it hard to answer him. Don't Lottie, Kathleen and the others envy the women whose clothes they sew? Do they not constantly contrive to improve their lives, whether through work or marriage? Yet there is a world of difference between their honest ambition and his devious scheming.

When he stands and walks towards me, I instantly back away.

"Emily," he says softly, "can't we start again? I have answered you truly. My feelings for you were the only cause of my offence. You are concerned for your father – marry me and be mistress of your own house. Help me to look after him as a son would."

His cheeks are flushed and his black hair is dishevelled where he has been grasping it. He gazes at me earnestly; for once his eyes do not water and I am struck by how handsome he is. He is near six feet tall and broad-chested; there is a keen intelligence in his look. Does he truly love me or is it the business he wants? My knees tremble and I can hardly stand. How can I reconcile this rational, persuasive man with the brute who tried to force himself upon me that night?

"You shouldn't be afraid," he says. "I *am* a passionate man – but a girl like you will come to appreciate that."

I had felt I had him on the defence, but somehow he has twisted everything and regained the upper hand. I hear the front door open and my father's step in the hall.

"Pa!"

"Ah, Emily," he says, coming in. "I'd forgotten you would be home early. I meant to speak to you." He turns to Baines, "I have asked the carrier to collect your box, Bill. You can take the room that was Charlie's, on the top floor at the back. Give us a few minutes, please."

Baines nods and leaves and I hear him walk upstairs.

"What's happening, Pa?"

"We are partners, Emily. Bill has invested heavily to tide us over a difficult patch. It was my own fault – I let matters slide. I could not have survived without his help and it's only fair that I help him to defray his expenses by offering him lodging."

"You mean he is to live in this house?"

Pa nods.

"In Charlie's room?"

"Yes, and I expect you to treat him with courtesy, Emily."

How can I live under the same roof as that man, my room

just across the landing from the one which is to be his? Is it decent, even with my father's protection? Pa's judgement must be blinded by his desperate need. If I continue to hate and despise Baines I will be worn away by bitterness, but if I do not I will be lost completely. More than anything, I fear the weakening of my own resolve.

Daisy comes home in time to produce a meal of cold meat and potatoes, and Pa, Baines and I eat together with every appearance of civility. Now that this partnership has been established, Pa *does* seems more settled, even cheerful. I really hope Baines spoke truly when he identified Pa's interests with his own.

When Daisy learns he is to sleep here, she offers to bring her mattress into my room, but I tell her I will push the desk in front of the door. I am not afraid of Baines, I say; I do not tell her that I'm more afraid of myself.

Sunday 26 January 1902

I cannot face being civil to William Baines over the breakfast table. As Pa often sleeps late on Sundays, my plan is to rise early and take Daisy with me to church before either of them comes down, but when I go into the dining room I find Baines already there, devouring eggs and coffee. He jumps up at once to pull out my chair. I'm obliged to thank him for his courtesy, but do not intend to invite further conversation, turning instead to Daisy, who is bringing my toast.

"I thought we could go to the service at nine."

She looks surprised – we've been irregular churchgoers of late – but she nods and says she'll get ready.

"Will you pray for me?" Baines asks, looking up and smiling.

"For an impatient, envious man?"

"It is a year since Charlie died," I answer. "We have matter enough for our prayers."

"Of course," he says gravely. "Forgive me."

We find a clump of snowdrops growing in a pot outside the kitchen and Daisy and I take them with us to place on Ma's grave. Help me, I beg her silently, tell me what I should do. It troubles me that Charlie has no memorial: I try to visualise the cemetery in South Africa, where he must lie, but cannot. Pa should have his name carved here, on the headstone, beneath Ma's. In the church, I catch sight of friends and neighbours I've not seen for some time. Richard and Elizabeth are there, with Ernie, hair plastered down and mutinous in his Sunday best, and two or three girls I remember from school. When we walk home, Daisy tells me about her sister's family – a tribe of riotous boys plus the new twin girls all contained within the thin walls of a two-bedroom house.

"I'm glad I don't live with Ethel," she muses, "there's never a minute's peace in her place. It's not the same, without your ma, but I wouldn't want to leave."

"Well, now I'm working, Pa can't do without you," I say, hoping I'm right.

"What're you going to do about *'im*?"

"I can't do anything except keep out of his way. I don't like the idea of him as my father's partner, but Pa does seem to be more himself now. I'm sure Mr Baines has a talent for business; I wish I could believe it was only the drink that caused him to treat me as he did."

Daisy gives me a funny look and walks on.

I pass a quiet afternoon, making ready my clothes for the next day, writing up my journal and reading a novel, before helping Daisy with dinner. I steeled myself to suffer Baines' presence during the meal, but afterwards he joins Pa and me in the parlour and I badly feel the lack of a table between us. I am determined he won't drive me away.

"Where is your embroidery, Emmie?" asks Pa. "It always soothes me to see you at work."

"Perhaps Miss Emily doesn't sew for pleasure now that she does it for a wage," Baines suggests, glancing at Pa as he speaks.

"There may be truth in that," I admit.

"It seems a pity not to use your skills in the home."

"I wish you would reconsider, Emily," says Pa. "I appreciate you are trying to help, but with Bill's contribution the business is sound and I can afford to give you an allowance for the bit of spending money girls require. You don't need to earn."

Bill's contribution! I know what I earn makes no difference to Pa, but I will not be beholden to that man.

"It's a good thing, Bill," adds Pa, taking up his box and offering Baines a cigar, "that *we* don't tire of the products of our trade."

For some reason, I am reminded of that scene with Aysha, when she rebuked her brother for smoking.

"Have you ever wondered, Pa," I ask, "if smoking is good for your health?"

They both look at me in genuine surprise.

"Why, the benefits are well known," Baines says. "Even Reynolds will tell you it clears impurities from the lungs. I beg your pardon, Edward, but it is a pity your wife never had a taste for tobacco."

"Wherever do you get such ideas?" asks Pa.

I say I have forgotten: in the newspaper perhaps.

"I have smoked from ten years old," Baines says, "and I assure you, I feel no ill effects. It invigorates," he adds, drawing deep on his cigar then blowing smoke upwards through his dark lips.

"Well, I share Ma's dislike," I tell Pa, ignoring Baines.

"Your mother's illness made her more sensitive to smoke," Pa says, "but when we were younger she enjoyed the scent of tobacco. She still shared a cigar with me... on certain occasions."

"It's an acquired taste," adds Baines, turning to me, "like so many things."

I have an early start in the morning and need my rest. I leave them them to their cigars, whether healthy or not, and kiss Pa goodnight. Baines stands and opens the parlour door with exaggerated politeness, bending his head slightly towards me, an amused look in his eyes as he bids me sleep well.

Once in my room, I move my chair against the door then undress to my chemise and drawers. I rest my hands on my head and look in the mirror. I see the chestnut down in my armpits, the gentle rise of my breasts and the inward curve of my uncorseted waist, and I think: *this* is what he sees. This, the imagined me, is the source of his private entertainment. Later, I hear him moving around in the room across the landing; I hear the noise of a heavy box being moved, the drag of drawers opened and shut, the sudden creak as he springs into bed.

The girls at work are full of talk of their young men: talk to which I listen but do not contribute. Lottie and Jimmy were walking out today; she has already planned exactly what liberties she will allow him and when. Doris who sits behind us and is always eavesdropping on conversations – *earwigging*, as Lottie calls it – tells her she's a cold-hearted cow, whereupon Lottie retorts that spreading her favours around hasn't done Doris much good, as far as she can see, and Arthur Smythe has to intervene with, *keep your cat fights for the alley, girls.*

Kathleen has had a letter from a boy from her home town who is coming to London to work next month and continually takes it from her pocket to re-read it. Lily is engaged to an ironmonger's son, who will share his father's business when they marry; she gives urgent, whispered accounts to Susan of the time they spend together. There is a whole scale of incremental intimacies, I've learned, depending on length of courtship and seriousness of intent.

With Baines, there would be no holding hands or clumsy kisses from a shy young man. To yield an inch would be to surrender completely. *I am a passionate man*, he said. Ma once commented that for men with strong feelings, it's not a bad thing to be married young. She would lean on Pa's shoulder as they retired to their room after dinner each night. Was that passion, what they had, still after nearly twenty years? Was it then they shared a cigar? And what would my life be if I did not fight Baines, if I gave up my job, acquired his tastes, became a wife?

An image from one of Charlie's adventure books comes into my mind. It is of a snake which mesmerises its victims, small animals, a rabbit perhaps, before it strikes.

24
Aysha

January 2002

Sel's old phone beeps from beneath her pillow and her hand moves on reflex to retrieve it. *Wake up,* the text reads. *Lunch mine 2day? Mum's day off.*

She has no classes on Friday afternoons, but her habit of working in the library until four-thirty means she won't be expected home. She presses a few buttons and sends *okay*. Pulling back her curtains, she watches the postman's unhurried progress along the adjacent side of the square. When he turns and passes her house without stopping, she grabs her dressing gown and heads for the shower. The water is warm, but she shivers as it splashes over her skin. Derrick's close to his mum. He says she works for a care agency and that she brought him up alone. A strong woman, probably; critical too, perhaps.

Downstairs, Reshna is feeding puréed banana to Safiya and Mum seems to be engaged on an inventory of the kitchen cupboards.

"Any news? Has Sel phoned?" Aysha asks.

"Not Sel yet," Mum says. "Karim Ali speak Dad from Sylhet. Is fine, arrive safe. What time you home, Aysha?" she adds.

Aysha turns away, collecting a mug from the drainer before answering.

"Usual time. Why?"

"Need go supermarket," Mum says, "but tomorrow okay."

Aysha breathes out and sits down. Without Sel to drive her, of course Mum will need help with shopping. When Abdul and Ibrahim tumble in, each demanding the remaining serving of Cheerios for breakfast, she makes a mental note to add cereal to Mum's list.

Mo arrives home from his night shift as she leaves for college, passing her on the doorstep.

"Ah, Aysha," he begins and appears about to start a conversation, but then Ibrahim runs shrieking *Baba!* down the hall, Safiya lets out a wail and Mum calls to Abdul in a warning tone. Mo sighs and says, "We'll talk soon, sister."

She has psychology first, then joins Karen for English at eleven. Karen has already told Jo Massey about their uni offers and Jo keeps them back at the end of the session to arrange tutorials for next week. Aysha leaves Karen talking to Jo and skips down the stairs to meet Derrick in the canteen.

"Want to join us, Aysha," Wahida looks up from a group of girls eating lunch as she and Derrick pass by, "or are you skating again?"

They hurry across the deserted park, then Derrick takes her hand as they thread through the shoppers in the market. The grey January drizzle swells to rain and stallholders spread plastic sheets over their wares.

"Not far," Derrick says, pulling up the hood on her jacket with his free hand. His home is a maisonette in a low-rise block with the entrance on an open walkway on the second floor, up two flights of dingy stone steps. Aysha looks around dubiously but then he turns the key and colour rushes to meet them as vibrant blues, warm apricots and splashes of jade spill from the walls, rugs and pictures in the small hallway.

"Wow!"

"Mum likes her colours," he grins.

Aysha smells spices and grilling fish and feels suddenly hungry. A tall woman emerges from the kitchen to greet them. Derrick's mother is wearing a long blue skirt and bright green sweater and her hair is gathered on top of her head in a colourful scarf. She's younger than Aysha expected and moves with an athletic ease which reminds her of Derrick.

"Welcome, Aysha," the woman says simply. "Lunch is ready. I am Grace."

Derrick hangs their coats in the hall cupboard, then leads her to a small table at one end of the living room, set for three people. Aysha is surprised at this formality and smiles nervously, then watches entranced as Grace serves them the beautifully grilled fish and vegetables. She's fascinated by the woman, but scared of her too.

"I hope you like fish," Grace says. "I love to cook but we don't often have a guest."

Aysha's mouth is full, but she smiles and nods.

"Derrick's always been popular," the woman says, with a fond glance at her son, "but he's not brought a girl home before. So, tell me about yourself, Aysha. What are your aims in life?"

"Mum!"

Derrick frowns in embarrassment and Aysha is momentarily tongue-tied by this frank interrogation.

"What's wrong?" Grace arches her perfectly plucked eyebrows. "How will I know if I don't ask?"

Aysha can't help laughing, but then finds herself taking the question seriously and answering in full about her plans to study English and history, articulating ideas she's not shared before, even with her tutors. "I suppose history's more important to me," she says, "but I love literature too because it's like a route into the past." This is like being interviewed for uni, she thinks; each time she pauses, Grace nods encouragingly and waits, clearly expecting more.

"I don't know what it will lead to," Aysha admits at last. "I s'pose I might want to teach, share it with others."

She can't think what else there is to tell, but Grace pours her a fruit juice and says, "Go on."

"Well, I'm not boasting," she says, "but the teachers say I'm good at my subjects. I want to see how far I can go."

"It's good to know what you want, girl," the woman says, "to admit it to yourself." Then finally she changes direction and lets her go. "Derrick has applied for teacher training," she says. "He will be good in primary school, I think. These boys of ten, eleven, need a male role model."

"Derrick didn't..." Aysha stops.

"... have one?" finishes Grace, not taking offence. "Actually, he saw my father and brothers every day when he was small."

"But I didn't need a bloke with Mum around," Derrick laughs. He gets up to clear the plates and Aysha starts to follow him to the kitchen; Grace lays a hand on her arm.

"He's saying I'm a pushy mother. It is not easy, raising a boy alone, but Derrick is a good son. I want him to do well."

Aysha bites her lip. "I won't stop him. We're just mates, you know."

"No," Grace says, "I think you'll do him good. Provided you don't hurt him."

Aysha wonders what Derrick's said to his mother. Does she realise Aysha can't tell her family about him? Has he mentioned Jamil? He returns with coffee and Grace gets up to fetch a pineapple cake. She asks about Aysha's parents, her brothers and sister, her nephews and niece, then tells Aysha about growing up on Saint Lucia and her grandmother's family there. It's a different sort of pressure, Aysha thinks, being Derrick: he's the focus of all his mother's hopes. Karen's an only child too, but her parents have each other and are more relaxed about what Karen does.

She is attending to Derrick, who's calculating if they have enough time to watch a DVD before she leaves, but senses Grace staring at her. When she looks up, the woman's eyes are fixed on a point somewhere above her left shoulder.

"I wonder who it is who's watching over you?"

"What?" she asks, confused.

"Mum, don't do this. You'll freak her out."

Aysha remembers him saying his mum was psychic or a medium or something. Spiritualism, was that what he'd said?

"I sense a – presence. Behind your shoulder."

"A ghost?" she laughs. "I don't think Muslims are meant to believe in those."

"Not exactly; as I said, a presence. She is a guardian perhaps."

"She?"

"Definitely female. Young, I think."

A camera flash flares in her brain and jolts her from bemusement to urgency: could it be Emily? "Can you speak to her?"

"No, Mum," Derrick says firmly, before Grace can answer.

"Don't involve Aysha in all your spirit crap."

Grace shrugs. Aysha would like to question her, but doesn't want to start an argument between mother and son. Derrick wants her to choose between DVDs of *X-Men* and *Chicken Run* and, though she hasn't an overwhelming desire to see either, the novelty of sitting next to him on a sofa, watching a film on a wet Friday afternoon, holds a certain attraction.

~

Mo delays a scant three seconds between tapping on Aysha's bedroom door and entering. She senses his impatience to say something, the way his habitual modesty is tempered by self-importance.

"Not working then, sister?"

It's a chilly Sunday afternoon and she's sprawled on her bed, a fleece round her shoulders, library book in hand. She finishes the paragraph she's reading before looking up; Dickens is not part of her A level syllabus, but Mo doesn't know that. Jo gave her a list of wider reading and she's chosen *David Copperfield.*

"You have to read the text before you can write about it," she says tartly. "Course I'm working."

The words on the page are calling her back, like the dreams of a sleeper who's been roused too soon. Mo tuts as he does when Abdul is cheeky. He looks down at her lounging figure and folds his arms.

"Mum needs your help. Mr Rahman and his brother are calling on us after dinner. This is important, Aysha – your marriage offer."

And studying isn't? Aysha rolls her eyes upwards and closes

the book with a resounding clap. Something snaps in her; she doesn't care if her irritation shows.

"They're coming to speak to Dad and me," Mo continues, "but they'll want to see you too. Get dressed properly and serve them tea."

It's not going to happen, don't waste your time! She wants to shout it aloud, but she's given Jamil her word. Not for the first time, she wonders if she should have promised to play along with his deception.

"The son isn't coming then?"

"Jamil Rahman? No, he has to go to Birmingham this weekend. Poor chap has a toothache and his dentist is there."

Poor chap indeed! She swings her legs off the bed and sits up.

"You can't settle anything yet," she says. "You promised I'd have time to get to know him first. No point finding out I can't stand the guy if you and Maryam have already made up your minds."

"I wish you'd be more positive," Mo grumbles, lifting his chin and gazing past her to the leafless trees in the square. "The Rahmans can give you a comfortable home. There'll be no need for a student loan while you do your degree. They've even offered to pay your fees!"

She can't understand why the Rahmans are so keen on her. The family is obviously richer than hers. Perhaps Jamil's parents realise he's not that keen to join the business. Mr Rahman must fear losing his son's involvement and want to tie him to home.

"I don't think I need to pay fees. Not on what Dad gets."

"But once you marry, it's your husband's income that will count."

"Huh! Better not get married yet then!"

"Don't try to be clever. Mum and Dad are getting older; they need to see their children settled. It's been bad enough keeping track of Sel; I don't want them worrying about you too. You should be happy that Maryam and Hass have such good connections."

All weekend she's been warming herself at a little inner fire, fuelled by the hours spent at Derrick's house on Friday: the experience of sharing food and a movie, of just being yourself in the company of someone you really like. Grace helped her to articulate what she wants in life, but it's about what you don't want too.

"I don't want to owe my degree to their fast food empire."

Mo stares. "What on earth's got into you, Aysha? You're acting like a child of Abdul's age."

"I don't like the Rahmans and I don't want to live with them."

For a moment, she sees anger flare in Mo's dark eyes; then, visibly, he changes tack and opts for a more conciliatory approach.

"These things work out. Once you've got your degree and you're both earning, you can get a place of your own. It's more than Reshna and I can hope for." He pauses. "I thought you liked Jamil when you met him."

"Half an hour with all the kids running round – how can I tell? If I must get married, I need time to get it right."

She watches his forehead twitch, the outward sign of an inner conflict; Mo's not used to insubordinate women.

"I always thought you were the sensible one," he says at last. "Please, just do as I ask for now and respect our guests. Maryam and Mrs Rahman will arrange some sort of meeting when Jamil gets back."

She's almost forgotten she's supposed to be going along with his plans, but a little defiance won't hurt. What she wants to know is how long this pretence must be kept up: whether Jamil's job search has made any progress. Perhaps, even in company, she could give him a hint to meet her after college again; next time, she'll tell Derrick what's happening in advance.

"What time do you expect them?"

Now that she's co-operating, Mo is already halfway out of her door.

"Eight o'clock. Mum's getting early dinner for six."

That's an hour before she needs to help in the kitchen. She retrieves *David Copperfield*, but her head is too full for reading. People marry the wrong person even when they have free choice: look at Dickens' characters – at David's poor mother, bullied by Murdstone and his ghastly sister, and then David himself, falling for that silly Dora. Dickens' own marriage was disastrous, according to Jo, and in those days you couldn't get out of it.

She's worried about Emily, too. Ridiculous, she knows. Whatever happened to the other girl was over and done with years ago; nothing she can do can change that. Yet the journal continues to grow; she read a new entry even today. Emily's story is still unfolding and it feels like it's happening now – it's like watching a film and knowing what's going to happen and wanting, *really* wanting, to tell the hero. She wishes she could warn Emily about Baines; she can't help thinking he still holds a fascination for her, despite his appalling behaviour. She's like me, she thinks: she's growing up, she wants to know about life, about what it's like to be loved. What Baines wants is not love; it's possession, control, conformity. It's like he's grooming her. Every time she opens the journal, she's afraid of reading that Emily has agreed to marry him. Don't be fooled, she thinks; he's dangerous!

I'm not being stupid, she argues, because I've influenced Emily already. Hearing me and Sel made her ask her father about smoking. Aysha still hasn't shown the journal to anyone; she's scared people will think she's forged the whole thing. Karen wouldn't, but she'd want to tell everybody; she'd like to show Derrick but he's freaked out by his mum's psychic stuff, so she's not sure. She wishes she could speak to Grace on her own.

A quiet tap at the door rouses her. Reshna holds out a shalwar kameez on a pink plastic coathanger.

"Please take. You keep," she says.

Aysha looks at the rich greens and purples; Reshna had worn the outfit a year ago, for Eid. "But it's yours," she objects. "It really suited you."

"I'm too fat now," Reshna says, switching to Bangla. "The top has been tight on me since Safiya was born." Aysha's not sure this is true, but her sister-in-law thrusts the outfit into her arms. "You try," she insists, her eyes radiating a generous enthusiasm which Aysha can't bring herself to reject.

"All right," she says. "Can you help me?"

Reshna giggles like a schoolgirl as Aysha undresses. She lifts the kameez over Aysha's head, tugs the heavy fabric into place and zips it up. There's a dupatta – a long matching scarf – Reshna says, and rushes off to find it. The tunic fits perfectly. Aysha can't help admiring herself in the mirror, then remembers the reason for her transformation and thinks that if Emily was watching now, she'd be worried about *her*.

Later, she helps Mum make the traditional sweet, spiced tea, boiled on the stove. The Rahman men hardly look up when she enters. She hears mention of wedding gold, of caterers and dates in July, and Dad catches her eye with his fond, anxious smile. The sort of event they expect would cost a fortune.

"When is the girl eighteen?" Mr Rahman asks. As if she's not there.

"Next month," she says firmly, determined to be acknowledged, adding, "I hope your family are all well, Mr Rahman." Mo looks up sharply, but he can hardly complain at her politeness.

Mr Rahman stirs extra sugar into his cup and turns towards her. "My wife is quite well, thank you. Jamil has the toothache. Dolly is looking forward to having a sister."

Aysha dismisses a fleeting pang of guilt at disappointing Dolly and takes the tray from the room, content with this one, small instance of asserting that *she* has a right to be involved in all this.

~

It hasn't been a bad week at home. Mo, relieved presumably that she cooperated last Sunday, has dropped the subject of her marriage, except to say that Hass plans to collect her and Mum on Saturday, so they can meet Jamil and Mrs Rahman at the Romford house. Her friends give conflicting advice: Karen sees advantages in playing for time, and even sympathises with Jamil for having to deal with his overbearing parents; Derrick is unhappy that she's been drawn into his plans.

"You ought to be honest – about uni at least," he insists. "The longer you leave it, the harder it's going to be."

Now, this morning, when she intercepts the post as usual, there is a letter with a York postmark. She's already decided against attending the February open day at Cardiff; she can hold onto the offer until the later date offered. The York letter feels satisfyingly thick. You don't have to prioritise choices, but she's always had an irrational bias in favour of the north, of living in a great medieval city, and, if they'll have her, this is where she'll choose to go. She tucks the letter in her bag, intending to open it on the bus.

Her first class is not until eleven o'clock today and Mum asks her to stay with Safiya while she and Reshna take Ibrahim to the health centre. It should only take half an hour, she says. Dad has already been collected by community transport for his weekly day centre visit. Mo is sleeping after his night shift, but he's easily disturbed and she resists the urge to get the letter out, just in case.

When ten o'clock comes without Mum and Reshna returning, she grows anxious. At last, Reshna bundles a shivering Ibrahim into the hall; Mum follows with the buggy.

"Sorry late."

"Did you have to wait?" Aysha asks.

"No, I talk," Mum says. "See Monwara Begum at health centre. You go now Aysha. Very sorry late."

Aysha tosses her head, annoyed she's been kept waiting by Mum's gossiping.

"Mum say Monwara Begum, wedding soon. Aysha make good match. Very nice family. Plenty money." Reshna blushes with pleasure at stringing so many English words together, but it's all Aysha can do not to snap.

"Nothing's fixed, Mum. You shouldn't say anything."

But Mum laughs and taps her nose. "Monwara old friend. No need secret. All good."

She has to stand on a crowded bus, so opens the letter in Jo's tutorial. It invites her to an interview on February 21st, or rather two interviews, since she's applied for joint honours.

"Three weeks today," comments Jo. "You're up to date on your coursework, so you've plenty of time to prepare. Get Andy to rehearse the history interview with you – it's where he did his degree."

"How long does it take to get there? Could I get a coach?" And how much will it cost, Aysha thinks.

"Not unless you mean to stay overnight," Jo says. "The train's quicker. It takes about two hours from King's Cross, but allow another hour to get to the campus and find the right place. And don't book to come back too early – take the opportunity to look around."

Then, without any warning, panic strikes. The months of hard work, the secrecy, the impossibility of sharing her hopes with anyone at home, have all taken their toll. The interview times are 1.30 and 3.00 pm, so there's no way she can be home before late evening. Aysha's lower lip trembles; she twists and pulls the tassels of the scarf she's wearing.

"The college has funds to help with fares if money's a problem."

Everything's a problem! Somehow she's always pushed difficulties into the future, trusting that things will work out, ignoring the widening gap between the path she intends and the one she admits to. Ridiculous! Her eyes stings from shame and her voice becomes an incoherent sob. What's the point of all her efforts? She'll never do it. Jo passes her a box of tissues.

"I think you'd better start at the beginning."

"I don't see that you owe this young man anything," Jo says at last.

"Let him deal with his own family problems. You have enough of your own." She opens her file, "But you're almost an adult, Aysha, eighteen next month. You need to decide what *you* want. I understand you don't want to alienate yourself from your family, and it's not my place to influence you, but it'll be a crying shame if you waste your talents."

Aysha blows her nose and rubs her eyelids. "I know."

"I'll refer you to the student adviser for help with the fare, but you have to do your bit too."

"I just need to see Jamil this weekend first."

"As long as it's not another excuse to procrastinate. For someone who's never late with her work, you've a tendency to put everything else off."

I'm a coward, she thinks, as she walks blindly down the corridor. I've never been good at telling people things they won't want to hear, but let me just get this weekend over and I'll tell them the truth.

25
Emily

Wednesday 29 January 1902

The girls can tell I am preoccupied this week, because I have made mistakes in my sewing. They say I've not answered when spoken to, and that there is a little frown which doesn't leave my brow.

"Come on, Emmie," Lottie urges, "what's up?"

"You remember the man I told you of – Mr Baines? He has become my father's business partner and is living in our house."

"And you're still there? What are you thinking of, Em?"

"It's my home. And there's Pa to think of. Mr Baines' behaviour has been correct towards me so far, though he *is* too particular in his speech."

"He's still after marrying you?" Kathleen asks.

I nod. "They both – he and Pa – want me to stop working."

"What about you?" says Lottie. "What do *you* want? You ain't thinking of marrying him, Em?"

"No, of course not, but sometimes I can't help thinking it would make life simpler. I wish I did not provoke such feelings in him."

Maisy, an older woman who comes in to sew occasionally

when we are busy, is sitting at the next table and has been listening.

"You want an 'appy life, not an easy one, girl," she says, "but you marry 'im and you won't 'ave either. There's chaps as always want what they don't 'ave, but soon as they get it they looks elsewhere."

"Come away, "Lottie says. "One of the girls at Mrs Pegg's is leaving next week – you could have her bed. Kathy 'n me'll ask tonight."

I'm not sure. I'm not going to marry William Baines, but I don't want to leave Pa and Daisy, or give up my home. I was born in that house and all my memories of Ma and Charlie are there, within its walls. *Here,* I sat and read my lesson to her; *there,* we chalked our hopscotch games in the yard. There's something else, too: Aysha. I have seen her five or six times at most, and always in my room. I don't understand how this happens, but I know that it's special, given to me; I want to see more of her, understand who she is. I don't want to spend my precious earnings on lodgings, but I suppose it can't hurt for Lottie to talk to her landlady. I'll feel happier knowing that if things get too uncomfortable at home, there is somewhere I can go.

Friday 31 January 1902

The early post this morning brought a letter from Granny. We have corresponded regularly since I returned from Harlow last summer, but now that I work at Fenton's, I'm often too tired to write. Her news is worrying: my grandfather has had a seizure which has affected his speech and movement. *He has not been the same since your mother died*, she writes. *It is a cruel thing to bury one's child.*

Whenever I think of Grandpa, I picture him striding along the riverbank, cane in hand, whistling Pat to his side as he comes to a stile. I don't think I ever saw him express emotion; perhaps he didn't want to show his feelings in front of me, but more likely this reserve was usual. Ma's death struck him hard. Grandpa had disapproved of her marriage and quarrelled with Pa, but he had never stopped loving his only child.

Granny writes that he is out of danger, but I want to see for myself and discover for the first time the restrictions of being employed. I am working tomorrow and all next week, but if I speak to Mr Smythe, I may take the following Saturday and go to Harlow for the weekend – not long enough to be much help, but unless I am to give up work, there is no other choice.

Arthur Smythe agrees to me taking next Saturday off, so I tell Pa what I propose to do. I wait until he is alone: I don't want to feel that I'm asking for William Baines' approval. However, the atmosphere between them seems strained this evening and Baines goes out after dinner.

"I'm sorry to hear about your grandfather," Pa says, raising his glass of port so that the firelight is reflected in its golden depths. "George and I never saw eye to eye, but he was a fine teacher. It's Ada I pity. He'll be a poor patient."

"You don't mind if I go next weekend, Pa?"

"Mind, Emmie? What do I mind anymore? I thought I minded you working, but you do. I minded giving up half my business, but it's done now. My idea is to finish with minding. But... you will come back?"

"It's only for a night, Pa. I have work on the Monday."

He feels sorry for himself. It is a year this weekend – a year since the old queen's funeral, the War Office letter and Ma's relapse – but he guards his sorrow jealously and forgets I have my own.

Monday 3 February 1902

The moment I arrive at work, Lottie and Kathy are bursting to tell me that a place at their boarding house will come vacant next week, as the present occupant, Florrie, a shop assistant at Frasers, gets married on Friday. They want to take me to see the house and meet the famous Mrs Pegg.

"But I haven't said I want the room!"

"Just come and visit," Kathleen urges. "Then if things get difficult at home..."

"What is the cost each week?"

"Four shillings for your own room, with breakfast and dinner all in, three bob if you share," Lottie says, "but you can walk to Fenton's and save the cost of your fares."

I realise that for all my newfound independence I don't support myself in the way Lottie and Kathleen do. Pa still supplies the roof above my head and pays for the food I eat at home. Daisy's labour provides me with hot water and clean laundry and often a lunch pack too. After paying my fares on the tuppenny tube, I buy tea, stockings, pen and ink for my journal and any other small items I need. I am able to save the rest, which is why I have enough for the train fare to Harlow, but there will be little left over if I pay my own rent.

"Don't make up your mind now," Kathleen says. "It's a big step, leaving your father, and you only sixteen. Just come for a visit."

"But I'm going to Harlow this weekend and cannot expect your landlady to keep the place for me. There will be other girls wanting it, surely?"

Lottie tells me they can sweet-talk Mrs Pegg and in the end I agree to walk home with her and Kathy one night this week. I rather think they intend to sweet-talk *me.*

Wednesday 5 February 1902

At dinner, Pa wants to know the time of my train to Harlow on Saturday and I tell him ten-thirty. I wonder if he will ask me to reclaim Ma's necklace, but he does not, offering instead the money for my fare.

"There's no need, Pa," I say. "I have enough."

"No, Emily," he insists, putting two florins on the table. "You must not be so independent. Keep your earnings for pin money. I don't want you visiting your grandparents in old clothes. You must tell me if your boots are worn or too small."

"My boots *are* wearing thin, but there's a good pair of Ma's I can take on – that is if you've no objection, Pa?

Pa gazes into his soup for a moment then shakes his head. I am wondering where this sudden concern for my feet has come from, when he answers me himself.

"I called on our neighbours yesterday as we hadn't seen Elizabeth or Richard since Christmas."

Elizabeth's baby is due in March and she does not get out much. I must find time to call on her too.

"She had those ladies' magazines and catalogues around her and asked me where *you* shop for boots and shoes. Maria used to do all that, I said, and I noted her expression. She thinks I neglect your needs and that is the reason you are working. Should I buy you some cloth for a dress, Emmie, now that you know how to make your own?"

I can't help smiling at the thought of Pa discomfited by Elizabeth's implied disapproval.

"I haven't time to make a dress before Saturday, Pa, but I promise I'll choose some cloth when I get back. Granny has more concerns than my wardrobe just now."

"Now you're mocking me, Emmie. I'm only trying to help. Take the money, please."

All this time, William Baines, who has dined with us, says nothing. He holds the newspaper close to his eyes, but I am sure he is listening with his usual close attention. He excuses himself and leaves the room before I do, but I find him waiting, standing above me at the turn of the stair.

"So, you're going to Harlow this weekend. Your grandparents do not like me, I think."

"Why do you say that, Mr Baines? They hardly know you – they only met you once, at my mother's funeral."

"You correspond with your grandmother. Perhaps you write ill of me."

He fears that I have reported his behaviour to Granny!

"I don't write about you at all except to say that you are living here. I believe she is uneasy about that."

I step up to the next stair meaning to pass him, but he keeps his hand on the banister.

"Is she concerned for your reputation?" His upper lip curls with amusement and his moist eyes glint. "She need not fear – I'll make an honest woman of you."

"Don't tease me!" My eyes smart; he amuses himself at my expense.

Baines comes down one stair and grasps my arm. I try to pull away, but he will not let me pass.

"Don't be afraid, you're perfectly safe – you can call for your father at any time."

"And if I did, you would claim another misunderstanding. *I* understand you too well."

"You think so?" He bends, places both hands on my shoulders

and peers into my eyes, then lifts his right hand and runs his forefinger gently down the side of my cheek until it comes to rest in the corner of my mouth. I had steeled myself to expect a kiss, but the intimacy of this touch is far more disturbing. My teeth are clenched rigid.

"There, I knew you wouldn't bite, Emily. I have to go into the city on Saturday – I'll come with you to Liverpool Street station."

I want to object, to say that I travel into the city alone each day now, but he turns and goes up to his room. I go to mine and fasten the door with the small bolt I bought at the market, which Daisy helped me to fit. I wonder how he dares to speak to me this way. Even now, after four whole months, I could sit down with my father, make him listen to me and expose Baines for the liar he is. Yet I do not: I am afraid that Pa is so dependent on both Baines' money and his energy that to break with the man might ruin him. And with every day that passes, my tormentor grows more secure.

Would Pa believe me? He *is* better now: he drinks less and attends to his business; but only Daisy knows the truth of that night and he has already discounted her word. Even she does not know the whole story. I never told her that Baines proposed to me, or about the two street women who spoke to us outside the music hall. Everything about that night fills me with shame: Ma was just six months dead, and I'd always mistrusted Baines, yet I was so flattered by his conversation and so blinded by the chance of a night out on my birthday that I left my father alone and put myself in that man's power.

I need my mother. I cannot imagine confiding in my grandmother, or in Elizabeth, and Sally has become a young lady of fashion who left me behind even before I became one of her father's employees. The only people I've told my story to are Lottie and Kathleen – girls I've only known a few weeks; somehow it was easier to talk to them.

What frightens me is that Baines won't give up, will not accept a simple refusal. Why should he when Pa has brought him into this house and treats him like a son? Will it be possible to continue to reject the man, yet still live comfortably under the same roof?

I cannot think anymore; my head aches; I need to sleep.

26
Aysha

February 2002

Only a few more days and Aysha can forget about Jamil Rahman and his problems. There's not likely to be a chance for a private conversation today, but she'll find a way to communicate somehow. He'll just have to accept that she's changed her mind; there's no way she can keep up the delaying tactics now that York has called her for interview: she *has* to tell her parents. Maybe once they know *he* doesn't want to get married yet either, they'll stop trying to organise her life.

"Good. Look nice." Mum beams when she comes downstairs in the outfit Reshna gave her. She can't let herself think about her mother's disappointment when she learns there's no wedding to plan. A pity that she'd had to boast about it to someone – Monwara, wasn't it? – the other day, but it sounded like she hadn't seen this person for ages, so perhaps it will be just as long before they meet again.

Hass arrives at ten wearing a red and white tracksuit.

"I've got a football match today," he says, hustling her and Mum towards the car. "Have to just drop you at the house, but I'll bring you back later."

Aysha quickly slides into the back seat, shoving a large sports bag to the far side. Mum sits in front.

"Very kind, arrange meeting," Mum says. She switches to Bangla and tries to engage Hass in conversation, but there's a sports programme on the car radio and he keeps turning it up to catch some snippet. Mum gives up and addresses Aysha instead, but with the speakers crackling in her ears, she can say quite truthfully that she can't hear. Both Derrick and Karen took her in hand on Friday, making her rehearse the conversation she needs to have with Jamil and practise breaking the news to her mother and Mo. She puts her hand in her bag and cradles her mobile phone, switched to silent, but holding encouraging texts from each of them.

As promised, Hass deposits them at the front door and drives swiftly off. Mum takes a few minutes to recover her dignity, smoothing down her sari and making little harrumphs to herself, grudgingly accepting Maryam's apology as she takes their coats. The Rahmans are expected shortly and coffee cups and pastries are already laid out in the conservatory. The atmosphere there is balmy, warmed by Hass's vaunted underfloor heating and the morning sun.

"You serve," Maryam tells her. "You look sweet today, Aysha. I know Mrs Rahman seems hard to please, but she really likes you. She thinks you'll be good for that daughter of hers."

"I'm not marrying the daughter." Or the son.

"No, but it's nice to be friends." Maryam puts her arm around her and drops her voice to a whisper. "Hass's parents are out. My husband's such a kid – he's persuaded them to drop by the park to watch him play." She smiles fondly. "Jamil seems a pleasant young man. I don't think you'll have any problems there."

It was her sister who put Jamil's name forward: Maryam wants Aysha to have what she has. She'll be disappointed too. Maryam's been lucky: she and Hass are a proper couple, comfortable together, but surely she knows it's not always the case?

When their visitors arrive, Mrs Rahman shoulders her way down the hall with the familiar crackle of embroidered sari; Jamil is tight-lipped, and Aysha can't help thinking that they've had words.

There follow the usual ritual polite enquiries – husbands, children, health – involving Mrs Rahman, Mum and Maryam. Aysha serves the coffee and cakes and smothers a giggle when Jamil's pastry disintegrates and he makes a clumsy attempt to brush the crumbs from his shirt onto his plate. If this was for real, she thinks, this might be my only chance to get to know him and I'd never know what secrets he was hiding. Their mothers' conversation stalls and she decides to jump in.

"I hope the dentist sorted your tooth out."

"Thank you," he mutters, "it's much better. I have another appointment next Friday."

"Must be good dentist. Go all way Birmingham," Mum says.

Jamil shrugs and avoids Aysha's gaze. She supposes he's having job interviews there.

"Waste of time!" His mother shakes her head impatiently. "Plenty of good dentists round here. Half an hour and back at work, no need for a weekend trip." Was this the cause of their disagreement? "Still," Mrs Rahman continues, recovering herself, "no matter; treatment finished soon."

"Are you enjoying working for your father?" Aysha asks.

Jamil frowns. "I'm finding ways of saving him money," he says.

The door from the playroom slams and the two boys burst into the conservatory.

"Rahim broke the controls," Farhad complains.

"Didn't." Rahim starts to cry. "I only dropped them."

"It'll just be the batteries come out," Maryam tells them, "but you mustn't throw them, or Dad will take the game away."

"I'll go," Aysha says, getting up and taking the boys by the hand. Sure enough, the handset is missing both cover and batteries.

"Here's one," says a voice. She's not surprised to see Jamil behind her. Rahim pounces on the other battery and she snaps them back into place.

"I really am having dental treatment," he says, as she presses buttons to check everything is working.

"Whatever," she says briskly, "but we need to talk. Monday, after college?"

"What about? I can't take more time off."

"Was it the batteries?" Maryam asks from the doorway. "I've made more coffee," she adds, then calls the boys to come and see their Nani.

Clearly they are not going to be left alone to talk. Aysha throws Jamil a pleading look and he mumbles, "Okay. Four-thirty."

"All go well?" Hass asks as he drives Aysha and Mum back home. He'd arrived home in high spirits, asking the boys to guess whose daddy scored the winning goal.

"Fine," she says. The difficult admissions have still to be made, but at least this meeting is over.

~

"Hello, love. This yours?"

The morning is grey and raw. Bert, wearing a purple plaid dressing gown and standing huddled at the entrance to the basement flat, provides an unlikely gash of colour.

"Postie put it in ours by mistake," he says, waving an envelope. "Maud's having a lie in. I'd 'ave brought it up myself, if it weren't for my knees."

Aysha glances round quickly before descending the half dozen steps to the entry but none of her family is looking out the window.

"Thanks. Yes, it's for me."

Suppose Bert had handed it to Mum or Mo? She stuffs the envelope unopened in her bag. Despite the cold, the old man wants to talk.

"I said to Maud, it's from one of them universities – young Aysha must be going away to college soon. Your mum and dad'll miss you, love. What's happened to your brother? We used to see him come in and out all day in that red car of his, but it hasn't shifted for ages."

"Sel's away, visiting family." She makes a show of fiddling with her glove in order to peek at her watch. "Look, I've got to get to college just now, Bert, but thanks for keeping my letter. I'll come in and see you and Maud soon."

There had been further news of Sel this morning. Another of Dad's cousins – a connection of the family Sel travelled with – telephoned to say he'd heard Sel had been sick.

"Nothing to worry about," the cousin told them, "probably some stomach bug or the heat."

Mum wanted to know how they could be sure it wasn't more

serious and who – if anyone – was looking after her son.

"There's a girl in Uncle's house," Mo said. He'd visited Dad's brother when fetching Reshna from Bangladesh a few years ago. "She does the washing and housework. They'll get her to care for him." This young woman was a poor relation of his uncle's eldest son's wife, he explained, slightly lame so without marriage prospects. They all have to trust that Sel will be okay.

Thankfully, traffic is light and she arrives at college early. The smokers are still loitering outside the entrance and Andy Carstairs is among them, discussing football with one of the librarians and a security guard.

"Aysha! Jo told me about your interview. Let's make a time to run through possible questions. After class tomorrow afternoon?" He stubs his cigarette carefully and bins the butt before going inside.

"You've had an offer?"

Aysha turns to see Wahida at her elbow. Aysha flushes; she knows the girl's had a string of rejections and tries to avoid the topic whenever she's around.

"I had one from Cardiff a few weeks ago and I've got an interview at York," she admits. Then, feeling she may as well come clean, "I had another in the post this morning. From Southampton."

Wahida swallows and nods. For a moment Aysha thinks the other girl has conquered her jealousy and is about to offer congratulations, then two hands cover her own face from behind and Derrick's voice says, "Told you they'd be fighting over you soon."

The uneasy smile is withdrawn and Wahida's eyes contract to arrow slits. She glares at them both and turns on her heels muttering, "I suppose *she* can do three degrees *and* get married all at the same time."

Aysha shakes free of Derrick and follows her.

"What're you talking about? Who said anything about getting married? Derrick and I are good friends, that's all."

"*Derrick?*" the girl sneers, her raised eyebrows disappearing beneath her headdress. "Oh, I know *that*."

"Forget it," Derrick says.

"What did I ever do to her?" Aysha is trembling.

They separate to their different classes. Aysha is still upset by Wahida's remarks and wishes she knew the reason for her attitude, but she's more concerned that Jamil will keep his word and meet her today. In English, Jo Massey looks at her questioningly, clearly expecting an update after their recent heart to heart, but Aysha keeps her head down and leaves quickly at the end of the session, avoiding her tutor's eye.

She can't avoid questions from Derrick and Karen at lunchtime. Derrick's frown deepens as she recounts meeting the Rahmans at her sister's house; when she admits that she's meeting Jamil after college, he crushes the empty cola can in his grip.

"You wait for me tonight," he says. "If you're meeting this guy, I'm hanging around."

Her last class finishes at three-thirty and she waits in the library for an hour, flicking through magazines with Karen, until Derrick comes from his maths class and they all go down together. The staircase is crowded and he wraps his arm round her protectively.

Outside, it is nearly sunset. Screeches and whirring wings of starlings fill the air; on the ground, gangling boys jostle and joke, confidential girls erupt into shrieks of laughter and couples briefly entwine, sharing a few moments before going their separate ways. When she pushes through the crush to the pavement edge, a car in the side street flashes its headlights.

"That him?"

"Think so."

"Don't let him talk you into anything," Karen says.

"I'm not leaving until you're out of the car," Derrick adds.

"He's harmless."

She walks steadily down the street and opens Jamil's car door, aware that Derrick and Karen have taken up position in the doorway of a shop opposite.

"Thanks for coming," she tells Jamil, getting in.

"What's this about?" There's a hint of impatience in his voice. "Dad's keeping track of all my hours this week."

That makes sense; Jamil's father's no fool.

"Have you sorted a job yet? I've got uni offers and I have to talk to my parents."

"Give me a chance. It's only a couple of weeks since I saw you. Things don't happen that fast."

"I got the impression you had interviews coming up."

Jamil looks irritated. "I just missed out on one. Made the shortlist but got pipped at the post. Swear the bastard who got it knew someone in the firm. But I've got more applications in and another first round selection on Friday. You promised. It won't be long now."

"Why don't you just tell your dad?" she asks. "He won't be happy whenever it is, but you can't keep disappearing off for interviews – how much dental treatment can you need?"

"I told you, I haven't any money of my own," he says. "Mum and Dad don't know, but I've kept on my flat in Birmingham. I need an income."

"Just go then. Do shop work or be a waiter or anything until the right post turns up. Show your family you're serious about this."

"I can't do that!" He seems genuinely shocked. "I've applied for retail management positions – how will it look if I'm working on the tills or stocking shelves? And I'd still have to take time off."

It would look like you're keen to work for them, she thinks, angry that he's both lied to his own parents and made use of hers for his own convenience. She can see him clearly for the first time: he's spoilt and selfish. Jo's right, this isn't her problem.

"But you don't mind cheating time off your dad? Look, I know I promised, but I've changed my mind. You'll have to sort your own life out."

"What do you mean?"

"I'm sorry, but I need to tell my parents this marriage won't happen."

There's more to it, she thinks. Why keep paying for a flat in Birmingham when he's short of money and doesn't know where he'll end up working?

"It's not just the job, is it? You've got someone there – a girlfriend?"

For an awful moment she thinks he's going to cry, but that if he does it will be from anger and frustration. He takes a deep breath, exhales, then reaches inside his sweatshirt and pulls out a wedding band on a gold chain.

"You're *married*?"

"Her name's Jyoti. She's Sikh. We met at uni. She doesn't finish till this summer."

"When were you going to tell me?"

"You said you didn't want to get married, so I didn't think

it mattered."

"You've got a nerve! Does her family know?"

"Yeah. They haven't quite cast her off, but they've made it clear she's my responsibility now. Don't drop me in it, Aysha. Give me a couple of weeks. That's all I'm asking." His voice is low and desperate.

She shakes her head: two weeks aren't going to make a difference to his situation and she needs to act now.

"You can't expect me to keep my word after this. I'm telling Mum tonight." She reaches across to open the door but he flicks a switch to activate central locking. She tugs at the handle. "Hey! Let me out, Jamil!"

He grabs her wrist and twists it back painfully. "I thought you were on my side. I didn't have to tell you. I could have just stood you up."

Let her think he intended to marry her and involve her family in all that expense? The shock might have given Dad another heart attack and Sel's already risked his health on a needless trip to raise money. She wrests her arm free and her elbow nudges the horn.

Derrick speeds across the road and charges the door. The car rocks.

"Let her out, you fucker, or I'll wreck this heap for you." He has the windscreen wipers in one hand, the other is preparing to wrench the wing mirror.

"Get the bully boy off!" Jamil spits.

"Then open the door," Aysha says quietly.

Pale and sweating, he unlocks the doors, then slumps over his steering wheel. Aysha escapes quickly and falls into Derrick's arms, while Karen dodges traffic to run across the road. The silver car's engine roars as Jamil suddenly swings out of his parking space and speeds away.

"Sorry about that," Derrick grins. "I wouldn't really have hit him, you know."

"You didn't need to," she says, shaking and laughing all at once. "He's just a coward. Besides, look at the size of you!"

"We've got an audience," Karen says and Aysha turns to see a bunch of lads laughing and, a few yards apart, a shocked group of veiled girls, who turn quickly away. One of the college guards comes across to see if there's a problem.

"It's okay, mate," Derrick says, "all under control."

But it isn't, Aysha thinks, still shaking and rubbing her wrist, and I'm not.

~

All next morning Aysha is aware of being judged: covert comments in the classroom, quick whispers and nudges on the stairs and, everywhere, sneaky sideways looks. When Derrick joins her at lunchtime, Billie and her crowd make a detour to saunter past their table.

"Oh, *Der*-rick," Billie drawls, "there's this bloke what's bothering me. Can you chase him away?" The gang dissolves into exaggerated giggles and goes on its way.

"Were you very late for work?" Aysha asks. Derrick had rushed off after the confrontation with Jamil to do his evening supermarket shift.

"A bit, but it was okay. Supervisor owed me a favour. What about you – d'you speak to your family?"

She looks down. She'd still been in shock when Derrick left

and Karen had taken her for a coffee, insisting she shouldn't put herself through anything more that night. But that hadn't been the reason for her delay. The cousin who'd phoned about Sel had visited and he and her father were holed up in the lounge for most of the evening. She could have spoken to Mum or Mo, but she'd hoped for Dad's moderating influence.

"It wasn't a good time," she says, "but I'll do it tonight."

They both have history after lunch, together with Karen, Billie, Wahida and the others. As usual, Billie takes time to settle, sighing loudly when Andy tells her to remove her headphones, taking out a mirror to check her make-up, then fussing through her bag for several minutes before finally producing a pen.

"That one's quiet today," Karen remarks, nodding towards Wahida. The girl hardly looks in their direction today, not even when Andy reminds Aysha to wait at the end of class.

"I have to go; I said I'd be in early today," Derrick says. "Text me later." He leaves with Karen and Aysha waits for the rest of the class to disperse.

"How do you feel about this interview?" Andy asks. "Jo tells me you still have some family issues."

She smiles weakly. "To be honest, the interview's the least of my worries, but I don't want to mess it up, or sorting all the other things will be for nothing."

"You've had some other offers too, haven't you?"

Aysha nods. "Cardiff and Southampton, but I always wanted to go to York, after the summer school. It just fixed in my brain."

"Well, you've got to choose somewhere and I think the course would suit you. You know it's my old uni?"

"Yes. Jo told me." She'd also advised her not to bother mentioning Andy's name.

"I wasn't always the model student," Andy admits. "Didn't do a stroke until my third year, but I do know what they expect. If you're up for it, we'll do a bit of role play." He straightens his chair and leans forward earnestly, "You've expressed a desire to study medieval history, Miss Khatun. It's not part of your A level syllabus – can you explain your interest?"

She hesitates outside the front door, rooting in her pocket for her key. There's no sound from inside as she turns it in the lock, yet she has the strangest feeling that someone is behind the door. But the hall is empty and she stops to take off her shoes and hang up her coat. Then she looks round and Mum is there.

"Dirty slut girl!"

For a moment she doesn't know what has happened. It feels like the floor has come up and hit her; like she's a small child who has smacked into the pavement and is frozen in that moment of shock before seeing blood and starting to bawl. Pain floods her face. She sinks to the bottom stair in disbelief. Mum has never struck her before.

Abdul stands staring in the doorway, but Reshna drags him away, holding up her scarf so that Aysha cannot see her face. Mum mutters Bengali words she has never heard before. Then,

"How you do this to me?"

"What, Mum?" she sobs. "What have I done?"

"Ride in cars. Make fights. Go with black mans."

"Mum, I can explain... has Jamil's family said something? Has Mrs Rahman called you?"

"No Jamil. No Rahman. What I tell them?"

Mum's face convulses with rage and she snatches a leather trainer from the shoe rack in the hall and brings it down hard on

Aysha's shoulder.

"No." Mo comes from the kitchen and lays his hand on Mum's arm. Aysha raises her face in gratitude but his eyes are frozen. "Bring Aysha into the kitchen. We'll talk there."

Stunned, she follows them. Mo pulls out a chair and she sinks onto it, trembling, unable to control the convulsive sobs which threaten to choke her. She needs a drink – tea, water, anything – but the table is bare.

"Mo? Mum? What's this... about? If... Jamil's telling lies about me, I need to know."

"Jamil? Why you keep say Jamil? Monwara Begum come. Say how you go with boys, not tell family. No-one say lies. Monwara daughter see you – tell mother."

When the name comes into her mind, she pushes it away; but then she knows she's right.

"Wahida?"

"She good girl. Monwara say her you get married. How you get married now?"

"There was never going to be a wedding."

"No," Mo snaps, "you were deceiving us all along."

"I never said I wanted to get married –" Aysha's voice is barely a whisper – "but I'm not talking about me. Jamil Rahman can't marry me – and he's looking for jobs in Birmingham."

"That rubbish talk."

"No, Mum, it's true. The only car I've been in is his. He came looking for me and made me promise not to tell."

"I find that hard to believe," Mo frowns. "Why would he deceive his parents?"

"Because they're always pushing him into doing things he doesn't want, but he's spoilt like the rest of the family and doesn't want to give up his daddy's money!" She forces herself to stand and face Mo. "Jamil was your choice – see what you got me into!"

Mum is throttling a tea towel in her hands.

"If he tell you, why you not say?"

"I told you – he made me promise. When we were at Maryam's on Saturday I asked him to meet me again. I wanted to tell him I couldn't keep his secret any longer. Then I found out he's married!" She looks at the closed kitchen door. Where's Dad? She needs him to hear her.

"He not married."

"It's true, Mum. He's got a wife and flat in Birmingham."

Aysha nurses her throbbing cheek. The unfairness of it all chokes her. Jamil might lose his allowance, but once he gets a job, he can lead the life he wants with Jyoti, away from his overbearing parents. Mum is temporarily silenced; Mo's brows knit together as he turns to the window, now dark with rain. In the square, the tall lime trees thrash in the wind and somewhere a car alarm has been set off. He closes the curtains before speaking.

"I think we're forgetting something. What about the fighting? The black boy?"

"My friends at college were worried about me. And they were right – when I said I'd tell you, Jamil got mad and wouldn't let me out of his car. Derrick came and scared him off. There was some shouting, but it wasn't a fight."

"Who is this Derrick?"

"Just a friend. Like Karen. Another student."

She can see Mo struggling to accept what he's been told. He knits his brows, massages his chin and appears to be chewing on air. Mum opens her mouth several times, but closes it without utterance; she keeps looking at her son, waiting for him to speak.

"I need to make enquiries," Mo says. "If what you say is true, we made a mistake about Jamil. We'll be more thorough next time."

"There won't be a next time. I'm not going to get married."

"That's enough, Aysha. Go to your room. There's more to discuss but I need to phone your sister first."

I'm almost eighteen, she wants to shout, I can do what I like, but she picks up her bag from the hall and trails upstairs in silence.

27
Emily

Thursday 6 February 1902

Did I cry out? I dreamed that Ma was brushing my hair. *You must not cry so, Emily*, she said, *you'll spoil your gown.* I cannot have slept long. At first I thought I was actually weeping, but I am awake now and the sobs I hear are not my own. My eyes slowly adjust to the night. I focus on a patch of grey, where the window frames the starlight from the square outside, and make out a dim silhouette. It is Aysha who weeps.

My door is bolted, but there are people in the room. I hear a man's voice: not the brother she calls Sel, but someone I haven't heard before. He speaks softly, like one who is used to others listening and has no need to raise his voice. The words become clearer...

I've spoken to Maryam. You're going to spend some time with your sister. They'll collect you Saturday.

She turns from the window with a low groan. What has happened? What are they doing to her?

What about college?

Ask your teachers to set you some work.

I've got an interview.

There is a pause, as if the other is considering.

Maryam can take you.

What, to York?

I hear a change in her voice, a flash of defiance.

York? You said you'd applied in London.

It's up to me where I go. I'm eighteen next week.

Another voice comes, an older woman's, muffled, in a language I cannot understand.

Too far, that's where, the man replies. *It's out of the question. If you get into trouble here, you can't be trusted away from home.*

But none of this was my fault!

No? Not lying to your family and going with unsuitable boys?

He must have passed her something because now there is a piece of card in her hand, something glossy. A photograph.

Where did you get this?

That doesn't concern you. You're in the habit of going to this person's home.

No, that's not true. It's not... you don't understand!

You've got till Saturday – make sure you break with the boy.

The voices fade and I see her more clearly, head in hands, slumped over her desk by the window. I don't understand what she's meant to have done, but the other voices don't believe her and I know how that feels. She's being punished for something that isn't her fault. Suddenly, she acts, snatching up a bag and stuffing it with books and papers, rolling up clothes and forcing those inside too. I sit up in bed transfixed as she takes a small knife, levers up the loose floorboard I know so well and takes out a brown envelope. Then I see a small green book in her hands and know it is my journal.

She holds my book to her cheek, before placing it back

beneath the floor.

I mustn't take it, Emily. You might not find it again.

"Aysha," I cry, "I'm here! Don't go."

And I'm sobbing now, because I know she has read my story and because Aysha is leaving home.

28
Aysha

February 2002

Once again, Aysha's problems are the main story at college.

"You know you can stay with Mum and me," Derrick says for what must be the sixth or seventh time.

She's spent most of the morning relating the events of the previous night to him and Karen. She hasn't mentioned being hit; she doesn't need to: a dull red weal beside her eye is turning purple. When Derrick touches it enquiringly with his finger, she turns her head away. It's not something she can talk about: the shock of Mum's violence is still too raw.

"Karen's already asked her mum," she tells Derrick. "She says it's fine to go there."

Much as she'd like to spend time with Derrick, and to see Grace again, she can't stay with them. If Mo and Mum ever do relent about university, it will be better if it's Karen's family she's been with. Until Mo produced the photograph, she'd hoped she could win them round; she'd told them about Jamil, she was in the right: they just needed time to come to terms with the facts. Then she'd been blasted by Mo's pent-up rage and contempt.

"But how did your brother get a photo of us?"

"It must have been taken after Christmas. When we were on Karen's balcony." She hasn't stopped replaying the Boxing Day party in her head since recognising the image of herself in Derrick's arms.

"You think that was her too?" he wonders. They have already commented on Wahida's absence; she's never normally misses class, but she hasn't shown up for college today.

"I remember girls taking pictures of the marina, but they were across the water and they all had coats and scarves. I couldn't tell who they were."

"Didn't you see them, Del?" Karen asks.

Derrick looks sheepish, "I was too busy looking at Aysha, but from where she says these girls were, you'd need a really decent camera to get an image good enough to identify us."

"Wahida can't afford anything like that," Karen says. "She's always complaining how hard up she is."

"Perhaps it wasn't her then. But who else would do it?"

They stare at each other wordlessly, trying to think. Andy Carstairs has left them working on an essay while going to fetch some handouts, but neither Aysha, Karen nor Derrick has picked up a pen. Billie, who has actually covered a page of A4, looks across from the next table.

"Know what I think?"

"It's nothing to do with you, Billie," Karen snaps. "Since when did you care about Aysha and Del?"

"Suit yerself." Billie pops a stick of gum into her mouth and manoeuvres it from cheek to cheek. "But don't forget, I do photography A level, don't I?"

"So what? You think you can tell whose camera it was when we don't even have the photograph?"

Billie leans back on her chair and blows a gum bubble, enjoying their attention.

"I might. See, the college bought these new Olympus digitals for our course and two of 'em got signed out over Christmas. Jamie borrowed one, Runa had the other one. And if I'm not mistaken –" she rocks back on her chair, pausing for effect – "Runa and Wahida are big buddies."

"Go on, Billie," Aysha breathes.

"Well, these cameras have got real powerful zoom. Like the ones the news guys have, you know, them paparazzi. They might not have even known it was you until they brought the pictures up on a computer screen. Hey! You lot gonna sort Wahida out – when she gets up the nerve to come back?"

"No point," Aysha says. "It would only cause more trouble."

Billie shrugs and grins, like one who's never seen a problem with trouble.

"This goes a long way back," Karen adds. "Wahida thought Aysha should be friends with her, but you have to choose your friends. We were always mates, weren't we, Aysh, right from reception class?"

Their plan is for Karen to take home the books and clothes that Aysha smuggled out today, with more to follow tomorrow. On Friday, Aysha will go home with Karen. Sunday – 10th February – is her birthday: she'll be eighteen. Simple enough, though she'll spend her last two evenings at home in a state of terror in case Mo packs her off to Romford early. As it is, she will have to rely on a very limited wardrobe at Karen's.

"No worries," Karen says, "Mum'll put your stuff in the washer-dryer over night."

Aysha knows Janet won't mind, but hates the idea of causing extra work or expense. She can't afford to pay Janet for her keep, but she can walk to college from Karen's home so her weekly maintenance allowance from the council will be enough to cover lunches and personal articles. She's used to her family barging into her room at home, but sharing with her friend will mean even less privacy. Karen is still seeing Paul, her boyfriend from her mum's office and Aysha has the impression there are regular weeknight phone calls, made from Karen's bedroom. What will she do with herself – sit in the lounge with Janet and Mike, doing her homework? There'll be no Abdul or Ibrahim to read to, no Safiya to play peek-a-boo with, no Bert and Maud. No-one will tell her if there is news of Sel or or if Dad is unwell.

Derrick and Karen are thinking about her birthday.

"We ought to go out. Del could come round to dinner and me and Mum would make a cake, but it's not much of a party."

"I wouldn't've done anything anyway," she says. "We never celebrate birthdays much."

"But it's your eighteenth!" objects Derrick. "You've got to do something. Oh, shit, the essay," he adds, as Andy comes back into the room. "We haven't even started..."

~

Aysha nudges her bulging college bag out of sight under the kitchen table; after two days of smuggling out clothes and books, there are still too many things she'll have to leave behind.

"I'm going to see Bert and Maud this morning," she says, addressing the cornflakes packet and, behind it, Dad, who has his pill boxes spread before him and is nursing a cup of tea. "I have to return their old photos before I go to Maryam's."

Her mother stands at the sink, muttering to herself in Bengali. She and Aysha have not spoken directly to each other since Tuesday evening; the yellowing bruise on Aysha's cheek is hidden by her hair but is *there* – a visible affront and evidence of dissension. Aysha catches the words *home early* and *pack clothes.* Dad looks up and smiles benignly. Mum hasn't left Aysha alone with him this week and she wonders what he's been told.

"Why's Aysha going to Maryam's?" Abdul demands. "Can't I go?"

"Another time," Aysha tells him, ruffling his hair. She drops a kiss on her father's bald head, squeezes his hand and retrieves her bag while Mum is busy at the sink.

At first she hesitates on the basement threshold, then allows Maud to draw her into the little front room. A small table is laid before the gas fire where Bert is seated in his dressing gown, carefully peeling shell from the top of a boiled egg. Maud sets down a brown tea pot and encases it in a knitted cosy.

"I expect you're in a rush, love, but step inside a minute. Don't let all the warm out."

Bert looks up from his egg and winks. "Off to meet a young man, I reckon. Oh, to be young again!"

Aysha bursts into sobs.

"Now see what you've done!" Maud scrunches up her forehead and glares at him. "Take no notice, Aysha, love, he doesn't mean to tease."

The old man's contrite face is just another wrench.

"It's not your fault, Bert. It's just... well, things are difficult at home."

Maud looks at her shrewdly. "I don't say anything against your mum and that brother of yours. They keep to their ways, me and Bert keep to ours, but you're different. Now when you first moved in, I had a good conversation with your dad and Bert enjoyed talking to him about being in India in the war, but I s'pose he's like us and don't get out much now."

"He doesn't go far in winter," Aysha says. She delves into her backpack for the envelope containing the old couple's photographs and a crumpled roll of sweaters and nightclothes unravels, depositing her toothbrush on the floor. Aysha hastily bundles up her clothing and passes the envelope to Maud.

"Not coming home tonight, love?" The old woman doesn't miss much.

She hesitates, uncertain. "I'm staying with a friend, just for a while. Please don't say anything upstairs."

"Your mum'll worry if you haven't told her. I would if you were a daughter of mine. You hear such things these days."

"I'll phone them, I promise. In a day or two." She looks pleadingly at Maud and the words come in a rush. "They won't let me go away to uni. I'll get packed off to my sister's if I don't leave today."

Bert plants his two gnarled hands on the table, the branching purple veins protuberant on their backs. He pushes down heavily to raise himself upright then hobbles over to stand beside Aysha.

"She's a good girl, Maud, and a clever one. If she needs to get away for a bit, it's none of our business. How old are you, love?"

"I'm eighteen on Sunday."

"Well, there you are then. In 'thirty-nine, I was packed off to France at eighteen and Maud here went down to Kent to work on a farm. You'll be all right – just look after yourself."

Maud nods. "He's right, you know. I forget all the things we had to do. But take our phone number, love, just in case you need anything."

Karen has visibly simmered with expectation all day. Her dad has set up the camp bed in her bedroom, she says. It'll be great: they can watch late films on cable TV together when they've finished their work, or lie in bed gossiping until they fall asleep. But we're not kids anymore, Aysha thinks; this isn't some glorified sleepover. Derrick wants to know what's happening on her birthday – should he come round, or will they go out? – whereas the only questions occupying Aysha's mind are at what point will *being late* become *not coming home*, and what will her family do when it does?

The birthday issue has not been resolved by the time they leave college. Derrick has a Friday night shift at the supermarket, so they agree he'll phone her in the morning.

"Ready?" Karen asks. Perhaps sensing her friend's hesitation, she links arms to direct their joint steps towards Limehouse. Passing her usual bus stop, populated with its familiar, jostling queue, Aysha feels an almost visceral tug.

"See you Monday, girls," Andy Carstairs calls, and they both nod and wave. They stop at the local newsagent to avoid drawing attention to the fact Aysha's not heading home. Wahida still hasn't returned to college – she's phoned to say she has the flu – but she's not the only one with sharp eyes. "Do you think they'll call the police?" she asks Karen. "I don't want Dad to worry."

"Shouldn't think so," Karen shrugs. "Well, not yet, anyway."

Karen's home is empty when they arrive. The flat reminds Aysha of the pictures in lifestyle magazines, where homes are unnaturally clutter-free and a few chosen accessories are artfully arranged.

"It's so tidy."

"Mum never leaves home without straightening the cushions and wiping the loo seat," Karen says. She dumps her coat and bag in the middle of the floor, switches on the television, then goes to the kitchen and throws open the fridge door. "Dad says it's our job to make her feel needed."

It's all Aysha can do not to clear up after her – pick up the coat or place the Coke can in the bin – but she contents herself with tucking her own things out of sight and hanging her jacket on one of the hooks in the hall. Sipping from the can Karen has given her, she goes to the big picture window and looks out at the balcony where she and Derrick were snapped in that fateful photograph. Wads of charcoal cloud spread low on the horizon, illumined with the last red flares of the sun, and little blocks of yellow light from the flats across the water stud the darkening sky. Lamps sway gently on the boats in the marina below and everywhere seems deserted. The evening stretches before her; she wonders what to do next.

"Mum'll be in soon," Karen says. "She said she'd order takeaway tonight." She tosses Aysha the TV remote, "Here, you choose. Chill out a bit."

"Actually, I thought I'd start that English essay. Where did you put the things I gave you yesterday?"

Eyebrows raised, Karen hauls herself from the depths of the sofa and goes to her bedroom. Aysha follows. "I've put your clothes in these two drawers. You can hang stuff in my wardrobe too – I've made space. Your college stuff is inside that plastic crate. Mum thought you could use it as a bedside table. Sorry about the soppy bedding; I didn't know we still had it."

The low bed has been made up with a Disney-themed duvet

cover. A stack of fluffy pink towels and three padded coat hangers are piled at its foot and a lidded pink crate is next to its head. The rest of the room is decorated in shades of plum and lilac: Karen has moved on from pink.

"I remember you had all the dolls, when we were little." Aysha sinks onto the bed and smooths the cover to examine at the images. "You used to play Ariel and I would be Belle. I always wanted to be allowed to sleep over, but –"

"– but your brother Mo used to come and collect you. He scared me. Mum would ask him in, but he'd just stand on the doorstep till you came out."

"You never said."

"I didn't want to stop you coming. He was always so serious and everyone said he was clever. I couldn't imagine him having a joke."

Footsteps sound in the hall. Karen clutches her arm in mock alarm and they both collapse on the bed, laughing, but what would they do if Mo came to the door now? She hasn't realised till now what a big deal it is for Karen, having her here.

There's a tap on the bedroom door and Mrs Carter looks in.

"All right, Kas? Hello, Aysha, it's lovely to see you."

Aysha gets to her feet to thank Karen's mum for letting her stay.

"Don't mention it, love. You know you're welcome. Make yourself at home and let me know if there's anything I can do. Here, I got you some bits. I wasn't sure if you'd be able to bring much." The bag she gives Aysha contains a collection of toiletries.

"That's really kind, Mrs Carter."

"It's Janet, love. You've known me since you were a little girl. Now listen, Kas has told me how things stand, and while I don't like the thought of upsetting your mum and dad, I do think you should be allowed to finish your A levels and get on. Do you think they had any idea that you weren't coming home today?"

Aysha shakes her head sadly.

"Well, I suppose that's for the best. Otherwise you probably wouldn't be here."

"She doesn't want her dad to worry," Karen says. "He's got a bad heart."

"I don't want them calling the police, but I don't know what to do."

"I've had an idea," Janet says. "Will your brother be home – the one who's been hassling you?"

"You're not going to tell him she's here, Mum?"

"Give your mother credit for a bit of sense." Janet kicks off her high heels, picks up a house phone and dials 141 to withhold caller ID. "Now what's your home number, Aysha."

Aysha recites the digits, wondering what she intends to do. Janet puts a finger to her lips, then Aysha hears her voice transform as she asks, "To whom am I speaking?"

"That's her insurance office voice," Karen whispers.

Aysha tries to reconstruct the unheard half of the conversation.

"I have a message for you from a young woman who has come to us for help. I believe you're her brother?" There is a short pause before Janet continues, "I wouldn't normally advise contacting relatives at this stage, but she is anxious that her parents should not worry about her safety. Please inform them that she is perfectly well."

There is a longer delay this time while Janet nods, shakes her head and pulls a whole catalogue of comical faces. Aysha imagines Mo's outraged response and his demands for information.

"I'm afraid that won't be possible, sir," says Janet smoothly, "and I'm not at liberty to divulge this address or telephone number. The young lady will contact you herself when she is ready to do so. Do I have your assurance that you will pass her message to your parents? Thank you." She switches off the phone before he can reply.

"Wow, that's brilliant, Mum!" Karen grins. "He'll think Aysh has gone to some women's refuge or something."

"That's the general idea, Kas." Janet has reverted to her normal voice.

"But they're bound to find out where I am," Aysha says. "I can't stay here all the time – someone will see me when I go to college."

"I'm just buying you some time, Aysha, There's no point walking out if you're going crawl straight back." She puts the phone back into its cradle and turns to her daughter.

"Stick the kettle on, Kas. I could do with a cup of tea."

When Karen's dad texts to say he'll be home in twenty minutes, Janet picks up the phone again to call the local takeaway. "We normally have a curry on Friday night," she tells Aysha. "I know your mum'd cook it from scratch, but I don't work all week for nothing. It's my treat."

The dishes are nothing like home cooking, but they're tasty and Aysha is hungry. They eat at the kitchen table and Karen's parents open a bottle of wine, topping up their glasses and taking them to the sofa together when they finish eating. She and Karen pile the cartons and remnants into a bin bag and stack the dishwasher. Aysha glances curiously into the lounge; she's never seen her own parents with their arms round each other – nor even Mo and Reshna for that matter.

"Leave them to it," Karen says. "I thought you had an essay to start."

They go back to the bedroom. After an hour or so, Karen closes her business studies textbook with a decisive snap and announces she's going to take a shower. Aysha sprawls on the camp bed, notes spread in an arc around her and a paperback copy of Browning's poems propped open. She'd like to get the essay written in rough over the weekend, ready to type up at college on Monday, but her mind keeps straying to the charming – and embarrassing – image of the couple snuggling together on the sofa, and trying to work out what she is reminded of. Then she remembers Emily describing her parents retiring to their room after their evening meal. No doubt they weren't as demonstrative in public as Karen's parents, but the words suggest a real, perhaps passionate, relationship. Emily's father's neglect of her needs and of his business previously puzzled Aysha. Her own father has more or less given up as head of the family, but *he's* old and has a weak heart – Emily's pa was still in his prime. It was as if nothing mattered to him anymore. She remembers a discussion in her psychology class: the deaths of his wife and son must have triggered a severe depression and it was this the man Baines had been able to exploit.

Karen returns, swathed in a plum fleece dressing gown, a striped towel turbanning her hair. "What do you usually do late at night?" she asks. "I mean, I know you don't have TV in your room, but do you listen to music or read or what?"

"I usually just go to sleep," Aysha admits, "but if I can't, sometimes I read Emily's journal. You remember, I told you how I found it under my floor."

Karen perches on her bed, shakes out her damp hair and picks up a brush. "You're still reading it? You must know it back to front by now. Anyway, how come I've never seen this journal

– weren't you going to bring it in to class?"

"It's complicated," Aysha says slowly. She genuinely wants to share the journal's secrets, but she's afraid she won't be believed. "It's not like a normal diary."

"How d'you mean?"

Aysha gathers up her notes and stashes them in a file before turning to Karen. "Well, it's still happening. Growing. There are entries now that weren't there when I first found it. It's like I'm reading it as it happens, only all those years ago."

"No way!" Karen leans forward eagerly. "Did you bring it with you?"

Aysha shakes her head and her friend pulls a face. "It belongs in the room – *our* room. If I take it away I don't know if Emily can get it back."

Twice Karen opens her mouth to speak, then closes it again. "That's just weird," she says at last. "You're talking about someone who lived a hundred years ago."

"I know."

"You don't think it's a trick – that someone's playing a joke on you?"

"No-one in my house writes English well enough to do that. Well, perhaps Mo or Dad do, but it couldn't be them. Besides, I always put the journal back under the floorboard with my UCAS forms. No-one knows it's there."

If she can't explain it to herself, how can she expect someone else to understand? But having got so far, she can't hold back. Karen is sitting cross-legged, elbows on knees, chin on hands, blue eyes staring and wide.

"There's something else. Sometimes Emily writes about seeing a girl in her room – sort of there, but not there – like a ghost, I suppose. She describes what this girl's wearing, what she does and says. She even hears people calling the girl's name. You won't believe it, I mean *I* wouldn't, but it's me!"

She sits rocking herself on the camp bed, arms wrapped around her body like a life-preserver. Karen watches her, frowning furiously.

"Have you told anyone else – does Del know?"

"No. I wanted to tell you both, but I didn't want you to think I'm crazy. I'm not making it up, Kas. I've got enough problems as it is, but so has she – Emily, I mean."

She lifts her chin and offers an uncertain, lopsided smile. Karen reaches out and grasps her hand.

"I read a book when I was younger – can't remember the title – but there was a girl who kept going back to Tudor times. She opened a door or went round a corner, and sometimes it was the present, sometimes the past."

"But I'm not doing that; *I* don't see anything."

"But perhaps *she* does, only not the past. Maybe Emily sees the future instead."

To hear someone else discussing ideas that have occupied her for months is both bizarre and liberating, like finally taking off a tight garment she's been wearing.

"Tell me about her, then. What does she write about?"

"Things that happen to her. A lot of it's sad, but exciting too, because I feel like I'm in her head."

"That's settled, then. The shower's all yours, so go and get ready for bed. I'll make us a drink, then you can tell me all you remember from the journal. This is going to be better than a late-night movie."

The alarm clock registers one-thirty before Aysha stops talking. Across the room, in the darkness, Karen breathes out in a loud sigh.

"Poor girl," she says. "God, that Baines was a bastard. What a creep! So do you think she left home?"

"She doesn't want to leave her father," Aysha replies, "but I think she'll have to."

"The way you talk about it – like it's now or still in the future!"

"That's because of the journal. It's how it seems to me."

"Funny, isn't it, that you've had to leave as well," Karen says thoughtfully. "She must have really needed someone to talk to. That Sally wasn't much of a mate, swanning off with her posh relatives, and, well, maybe you did too. So, what's a hundred years between friends?"

The idea of being Emily's friend adds to the warmth that Karen's support already supplies. Aysha stretches her toes towards the foot of the camp bed, hoists the duvet round her shoulders and when Karen says goodnight, she's already asleep.

29
Emily

Saturday 8 February 1902

I am ready to leave for the station soon after nine. Daisy hugs me and hopes I will find my grandfather improved; Pa simply bids me take care. William Baines must have risen early too, for he has already breakfasted and is dressed for business. He is freshly shaved, his cheeks ruddy, and seems in high spirits. Daisy, as ever, gives him a black stare, but he makes a point of addressing her.

"I will be out all day and it threatens to be a cold one. A good reason for one of your excellent marmalade puddings tonight I think, young Daisy." I see her flush; she distrusts Baines for my sake, but I know she finds praise of her cooking hard to resist.

The bag I have with me is small, just enough for an overnight stay, but Baines insists on carrying it and, as soon as we step into the street, he offers me his arm too. I cannot restrain a shiver at his touch, but he laughs and cries, "There, I said it was cold!" We pass the Blacks' house and I see Elizabeth pull back her curtains with one hand as she rubs her back with the other. How large she has grown! William Baines smiles broadly, draws my arm closer and raises his hat to her.

We walk along Commercial Road until we get to Sally's

father's original shop on the corner of Watney Market. Sally's mother is outside, signalling instructions to a young man who is dressing a tailor's dummy in the window. Mr Fenton now spends all his time at the Oxford Street store.

"Good morning, Emily!" Sally's mother calls. "You're not working today?"

"My grandfather's been ill," I say. "I'm going to Harlow to visit him and Granny. Mr Baines is accompanying me to the station."

I am annoyed that I feel the need to explain myself and that half my acquaintance is around to see Baines take my arm in public – something I suspect causes him much satisfaction. He says nothing but bows to Mrs Fenton and hums softly to himself as we continue our walk. The pavements are almost empty, the day too cold to encourage anyone to linger; horses waiting outside shops while their carts are unloaded snort and stamp their feet, eager to be moving again.

"You're quiet today, Emily," he says at last.

"I am thinking of my grandfather – wondering how changed I'll find him."

This is true, but my mind has also been occupied with Aysha and questioning why the man whose voice I heard seemed so angry with her, wondering if she is indeed leaving home and if I will ever see her in my room again.

"Your grandparents will be glad to see *you*."

"I cannot stay long enough to help."

"I am sorry for the old man and for the burden on your grandmother, but your father and I must be grateful to that job of yours if it brings you home."

"Everything's changed. I don't feel it is my home anymore."

"Ah, don't say that!" He puts down my bag, seizes my other hand and twists me towards him.

"How else should I feel with my mother and Charlie gone?" I free my hands, grab my bag and start walking, conscious that we are becoming a spectacle and thankful for the relative quietness of the street.

"Be grateful that *you* are alive," he says.

"What do you mean?"

"You can't bring your mother and brother back, or turn back the years for your grandparents, but you can make a good life for yourself and a home for your father. If you're willing."

"To marry you, you mean?"

"Yes, if you will. I know we got off to a bad start, that I allowed my feelings to run away with me, but I promise to be a most devoted husband."

He grasps my arm and my bag again and we cross the road at the junction with Commercial Street, dodging the omnibus and a couple of carts. "Come now, Emily, don't think I don't admire your independence," he says as we regain the pavement, "not many girls could do what you've done – find a respectable living for themselves."

"You're wrong," I say. "There are many of us – and there'll be more."

"But for most it is temporary, driven by need. It is not like men's work. Which of them would not give it up for marriage and a home and family of her own? Look at Elizabeth. She's magnificent!"

He admires her, I know; celebrates her pregnant form.

"I am only sixteen, as you are well aware. I don't want to be anyone's wife or mother yet."

"You have grown up this year, Emily with all that has passed. I see your mother's daughter; a woman, with a woman's feelings."

"Feelings which do not lead me to marriage, sir. I wish you would give me my bag; it's only a few yards to the station now."

Already we are jostled by a throng of travellers and the smells of oil, coal and steam mingle in the air, but he keeps my luggage firmly in his grip until I have bought my ticket and boarded the train, saying he'd promised my father he would see me on my way.

At last the guard blows his whistle and, one after another, the carriage doors close in a fusillade of slams. Baines raises his hat ceremoniously and turns to leave the platform, his mission complete: for whatever reason, accompanying me here has been a source of satisfaction to him.

My compartment is empty. I rest my bag on the rack, sink onto the long seat, fling out my arms, stretch my legs as far as they will go and let the air drain from my lungs. For the first time for days, I breathe easily. Although my grandfather's illness is the reason for my journey, and an occasion for concern, I am so relieved at finding myself alone, without Baines or Pa to observe me, or Arthur Smythe to check my stitches, that my head spins with happiness. The engine too seems to take a deep breath, then to puff and gasp it out again as we pass beneath the station's high metal arches and inch our way between the tenement buildings and factories that line the track.

Gradually, we leave the city behind and I catch a glimpse of a brown river, which must be the Lea, cutting through low marshes. The water is crowded with laden barges, but I see swans and moorhens too. To my right, the wintry sun hangs low in the sky; to the left, beyond the marshland, church spires mark out higher ground. Two spaniels race along the towpath disturbing a grey heron, which flaps slowly over the water.

I feel sure we are already in the countryside, but very soon I see streets again, row upon row of little houses, newly built, which huddle close to the several small stations at which we stop. They must be homes for the workers who travel into London each day. Further on, we pass huge circular metal structures – the gas holders for the lighting companies. At last, there are proper ploughed fields and orchards and the railway runs close to the path of the river again. If only I could forget the reason for my journey and just lose myself in watching the trees and hedges rush by, but I can't help wondering what I will find when I reach my destination.

I wrote to tell my grandmother of my visit, but I do not expect to be met, as she cannot leave Grandpa alone. A cold blast buffets me when I step onto the platform at Harlow and I turn up my collar in readiness for the mile's walk to the house. However, just outside the station, I am hailed by a red-faced youth leading a piebald horse shackled to an open cart.

"Beg pardon, but are you the Miss Emily what's going to Hawthorne Cottage?"

When I say that I am, he takes my bag and helps me onto the seat beside him. Clean sacking lines the cart and the young man himself looks freshly scrubbed, but there is a tell-tale scent of meat, which makes me think they must both be in the butcher's service. I wonder that all the local cats and dogs do not form a trail! The driver seems a bashful youth: several times, I feel sure he is about to start a conversation, but then see him think better of it and stare at the reins in his reddened hands instead. The horse proceeds at a leisurely pace, pausing beside every gate or drive we pass, until the young man clicks his tongue to direct it on.

"That's a very steady horse," I say. "What is his name."

"It's an 'er," he says, the red of his cheeks spreading earwards. "Bessie's a good 'orse," he adds, but then falls silent. I'm sure we are both relieved when the mare pulls up before the clapboarded walls of Hawthorne Cottage and my grandmother waves from the porch.

"Thank your father for the use of his cart, Wilf," she calls to the youth. "Miss Emily is catching the five-fifteen tomorrow. If you can return her to the station, there will be a shilling for you."

"There's no need, Gran," I say as Wilf drives off. "I don't mind walking."

"Nonsense. It pains your grandfather that he cannot drive you; he wouldn't have you walk."

"How is he?"

"Recovered enough to be frustrated by his weakness. He can't grip a cup, or a pen to write and his words are not always clear."

"He's not able to walk?"

She shakes her head and takes my arm, saying "You can judge for yourself. He'll be glad to see you."

At my grandmother's instruction, I carry my bag to the room I stayed in last summer. There is water in the jug so I splash the train dirt from my face and hands before going down to the study. Grandpa is sitting in his high backed armchair, a rug over his knees; an unopened book lies on the small table by his side, but his spectacles are nowhere in sight. His mouth turns down on the left side and is working as if he is trying to discharge a word.

"Mria," he says, "Mria."

"No, George," Granny says gently, " not Maria. It's Emily – remember?"

I crouch beside my grandfather and take his hand. Pat, the

dog comes from behind the chair and lays his head on my knee.

"What can I do for you, Grandpa?" I ask. He turns slowly and seems to see me properly for the first time. A tear hovers at the corner of his eye.

"Why don't you read to him while I prepare lunch?" Granny says. "No, not the essays –" she substitutes the book on the table with one from the shelf – "I've been reading him *A Tale of Two Cities* – see, I've marked the place."

It must be hard for her, having a house to run but needed as a carer and companion too. A local woman, Pamela, comes twice a week to clean and wash, and a man helps with the garden, but otherwise she and Grandpa have always managed alone. I pull up a chair beside him and start to read.

After some forty minutes, Granny announces lunch. She helps Grandpa into a kind of wicker chair on wheels and draws him up to the dining table. There is a chicken broth and as he cannot manage a spoon, my grandmother feeds him. I can see that this dependency distresses him; I can also see how much of *her* time is used up.

"He will improve," she tells me. "Even now he's so much better than last week."

Grandpa falls asleep after lunch; the effort has been so great. I start to clear the dishes away, but Granny says,

"If you want to help, take that dog for a walk. I haven't the time and Pat hardly leaves his side, but the poor thing needs a break too."

The dog looks confused when I call him from the study; he keeps running back to see if his master is coming. But when he sees the leash taken down, he starts to yip and turn circles around me, and so we set off along the lanes and through the woods nearby, where I let him run free. I'm pleased to see the loyal creature leave his cares in the study and follow his nose through the undergrowth, doubling back to communicate his pleasure in a series of short excited barks.

"I wish I could stay longer to help you," I tell Granny, when we return.

"Emily, we're just pleased you could come at all. Your grandfather has me to care for him; you have to think of your father, I know."

"But there is so much for you to do!"

"Pamela has agreed to work more hours. But how *is* your father, Emily?"

"Better than when I returned from here last year," I say, cautiously. I have never written to her about Pa's drinking. "Working hard again."

"And that young man Baines is living at your father's house?"

"Yes," I reply, looking away, "Pa can't manage without him."

"It seems rather irregular, but then so does your working. I suppose with your father and your maid there it will be all right. Just be sure you do not become too familiar, Emily."

For a moment I think I will tell her what has passed between us, and how I choose to work so as not to owe Baines my bread. But Granny has cares enough and I don't have the words to tell her the truth.

"I hope you aren't too fond of this young man," she says, mistaking my silence for embarrassment.

"No, not at all, Granny. Quite the opposite."

We do not keep late hours in the country. There is no gas in the house, only paraffin oil and candle light. I build up the fire and am relieved to find a large store of logs in the outhouse – cut by my grandfather before he fell ill.

In the morning, I take the mending basket and sit with Grandpa while I darn and sew. Granny says the best help I can give is to keep him company while she cooks. She worries that she has not attended church for several weeks and hopes God credits good intentions.

Pat looks at me expectantly after lunch, so I take another walk with him while Grandpa sleeps. Poor dog! There won't be any outing tomorrow. All too soon, we hear the creak of the butcher's cart and Wilf appears at the door. I hug my grandfather and feel his eyes follow me to the door. When he is fully wakeful, he knows who I am, but at other times his mind wanders out of reach and I am sure that it is Maria, my mother, whom he believes he sees.

"I'll come again when I can, Gran."

"You will always be welcome, Emily," she says.

I am glad that Bessie knows the road well, as it is growing dark when we drive to the station. Wilf is as tongue-tied as before, but when I thank him for his assistance, he does manage to mumble,

"Safe journey, miss."

I half expect to find William Baines at Liverpool Street, but there is no sign of him. A sleety rain has started to fall, so I decide to spend one of Pa's florins on a cab ride home. Lottie and Kathleen would think I throw money away, but tomorrow is a work day and time enough for the tuppenny tube.

Pa has already dined. He calls Daisy to bring me a meal, but I convince them that a sandwich in the kitchen is all I need. I don't enquire after Baines, but when we are in the kitchen, Daisy tells me he went out before dinner, dressed for a night on the town.

"I've put clean linen in your room," she says, "and there's a pork pie if you want to take a slice tomorrow."

I don't know what I should do without her. I eat cold beef and bread and recount my cart rides with the bashful Wilf and we both have a heartless giggle at the poor lad's expense.

30
Aysha

February 10 2002

Derrick wouldn't take no for an answer. "I'm taking you out to lunch. Karen too, if she's free."

By the time he'd phoned on Saturday morning, he had everything planned and all her objections covered. Yes, he could afford it, he'd saved his earnings; no, they wouldn't bump into her family because they were going to south of the river to Lewisham; and getting there wouldn't be a problem because his mum would drive them.

Was Grace joining them, she'd asked?

"That's up to you," he said. "She says it's your party."

Ever since meeting Derrick's mother, she'd wanted to see her again. She'd liked Grace, but most of all she wanted to tell her about Emily and ask more about the protective presence she claimed to have sensed. Anyway, Karen would feel more comfortable with a fourth person present.

"She can't drive us and not eat," she'd told Derrick. "Tell her to come."

She gives her long dark hair a shake in front of the wardrobe mirror and unplugs Karen's dryer. Apart from spare jeans and sweatshirts, the only other clothes she has with her are the black trousers and blue print shirt destined as her interview outfit, but this morning Janet and Karen presented her with the floaty maroon top she's now wearing. With long loose sleeves and draped cowl neckline, the new garment definitely covers her body, but the fabric is transparent and she's borrowed a black silk vest of Karen's to wear underneath. The overall effect pleases her and the bracelet Derrick gave her for Christmas is a perfect finishing touch. She's always felt she looks younger than her age but, inspecting herself in the mirror now, it's the body of a young woman she sees.

Yesterday had felt most peculiar. After Derrick's phone call, she'd been alone in the flat for most of the day. Mr Carter left early to join a West Ham supporters' coach to Bolton, while Karen announced she needed to go shopping with her mum. To buy a present for *her*, she realised later, though they also came back loaded with food. Janet had refused to accept any money from Aysha's maintenance allowance towards her keep, but she'd hoped to shop for some things herself – fruit and vegetables, perhaps. Now the large fridge and kitchen cupboards were bursting with produce and Karen insisted it wasn't safe for her to be seen at the market. So, she finished her essay draft, started reading 'Persuasion', watched a DVD of 'Billy Elliot', made a tuna sandwich, read some more... and tried not to worry about what might be happening at home. When the phone rang, she panicked that her family had traced her, then realised the handset had a caller identity function and the display clearly said 'Paul', the name of Karen's boyfriend.

She'd never considered herself in danger of forced marriage: her family wasn't like that, or at least that's what she'd always believed. But the shock of Mum's slap and harsh words still reverberated through every nerve. In truth, Jamil's secret marriage had been a lucky break; theoretically, she had the power of veto, but, if he'd been free, how many times would she have been allowed to say no? Until recently, she'd been concerned for her education; now, Mo's reaction to her friendship with Derrick bothers her too. Her feelings have developed at a slower pace than his but, once taken root, they've grown strong; admitting her love for him arms her against giving in to her family.

Mr Carter's coach wasn't due back until ten and Karen was out with Paul, so Aysha had the surreal experience of joining Janet on the sofa for pizza and the final of Pop Idol. Janet telephone-voted several times and made Aysha promise faithfully not to tell Karen the result as she was recording the programme for her.

"Let's see the birthday girl then." Janet directs her towards the window, where the daylight is streaming off the marina. "Look, Mike, she's a real picture, eh?"

"Don't embarrass her, Mum," Karen objects, but her dad merely grunts, scarcely raising his eyes from the match reports in his Sunday paper. The equanimity with which both parents had met Karen's eleven-thirty return last night still amazes Aysha. When asked about her evening, Karen had just pulled a face and said Paul was getting too serious.

"They're here," Aysha says when her phone pings. She peers out of the window to see Grace's small blue car pull into the parking bay below. She and Karen grab their jackets and head for the door.

"Have a good time, girls," Janet calls, winking at Aysha. "No need to hurry back."

The Turkish restaurant looks quite modest from the street, but the interior opens into a vast dining area arranged around a central grill where chefs are busily turning meat on skewers and shaping large flat breads.

"Smells good," comments Karen, sniffing the air appreciatively. "Been here before, Del?"

"No, but Mum came for a work do," Derrick says.

A slim-hipped young man in black trousers and red shirt beckons them forward and leads them to a vacant table. The restaurant is busy with several large family groups enjoying Sunday lunch.

"You're not supposed to be eyeing up the staff," Karen whispers as Aysha's eyes follow the retreating waiter.

"He reminds me of Sel," she says. Then, to Derrick and his mother, 'My brother, I mean.'

"The one who's been causing you so much trouble?" Grace asks.

Aysha wonders what Derrick has told her. "No, Selim, the middle one. He's in Bangladesh and we heard he was sick. I hope he's okay."

"Probably just a tummy bug," Karen says.

"I'm sure there's no need to worry," Grace adds. "I understand medical facilities are good there now."

"Are you a nurse?" Karen asks diffidently.

Aysha senses that she's trying to fathom Grace. Derrick's mother has her own distinctive style, which today involves a long flared skirt in deepest pink, black boots and sweater, and a length of lace fabric, also black, wound around her head. Karen was uncommonly subdued in the car, as if her usual practice of teasing Aysha and Derrick hadn't seemed fitting in the presence of his glamorous mum.

"Just a humble care worker. I call on my old folk in the morning to get them up, wash, dress and feed them, then in the evening I do it all in reverse. I'm obliged to wear a white uniform, so when I'm off duty I... express myself." Grace tips her head to one side as she looks Karen in the eye. She has an uncanny instinct to read unspoken thoughts and, in this case, to answer them. "Well, aren't we a good-looking party?" she continues. "No wonder we're attracting attention."

"Are we?" asks Derrick.

"Do you see any other table with a colourful black woman, her handsome son, a perfect English rose," she touches Karen's hand then smiles at Aysha, "and a delicate Asian beauty?"

Aysha sees Derrick's embarrassment and is relieved when the waiter returns.

"I hope the food is all right for you, Aysha," Grace says. "It's meant to be halal here, but if you're worried, the veggie dishes are wonderful."

Aysha is touched by her thoughtfulness. She has decided she'll do her best to follow a halal diet at Karen's house, but won't be rigid or make life difficult for others. She orders apple and melon juice and a Turkish pide topped with minced lamb and onions. When the others have ordered too, Grace excuses herself and goes to the ladies'. Derrick leans forward and takes Aysha's hand.

"Sorry about Mum – she can be a bit OTT at times."

"Don't be silly," she says, "you know I like her. It was really nice of Grace to drive us."

"Yeah," Karen adds, "she must be brave to come out with us three!"

Aysha doesn't really see Grace feeling nervous, but maybe there's some truth in Karen's comment. Derrick and his mum are close and it can't be easy seeing him attached to somebody else. Grace deals with it in her own special way.

"She'll miss you when you go to uni," she says, thinking aloud. Derrick has a couple of offers for education courses, one from Leeds and one from somewhere in the south east.

"Maybe she'll get herself a fella," Karen suggests.

Derrick frowns. "She should do something for herself. I wouldn't mind so long as whoever it was treated her properly," he says. "They say my dad was a real bastard. It's taken Mum a long time to get her confidence back."

"Shh," Aysha warns, seeing both Grace returning and a waiter bearing down on them with loaded plates.

The table is piled high with the pide, couscous salad, spiced aubergine dip with warm pitta breads, plus kebabs for Karen and Derrick. For the next fifteen minutes, no–one speaks, except to make appreciative noises, but when the man returns to refill their glasses, Derrick beckons him aside and whispers something. Aysha sees Karen catch Derrick's eye.

"Come to the loo with me," Karen says, grabbing Aysha's arm.

They're probably plotting something and it will be simpler if she plays along. Karen takes time sampling the liquid soap and hand cream provided and admiring the trendy stone basins.

"I expect you'd have liked to stay at Del's place," she says, "but you're better off with Mum and me. Grace is nice, but I reckon she could be a bit possessive."

"I wouldn't have gone there unless there wasn't a choice," Aysha replies carefully, "but it's nothing to do with Grace. I still hope my family will come round, but it won't ever happen if I move in with Del. I'm just grateful to your parents for having me."

"Your mum'll want you back, surely?" Karen moves to the hand-dryer and their voices are drowned by its sudden roar. Aysha shrugs; she's felt her mum's outrage and she's not sure.

As soon as they're at their table again, a beaming waiter appears carrying an enormous cream cake, topped with eighteen candles which dart and flicker as they hurriedly move dishes to make space. The man coughs self-consciously and then launches into a rather tuneless version of *Happy Birthday*, nodding hopefully at Derrick, Karen and Grace until they take pity and join in. Several of the large parties on other tables turn to wave and cheer and even start to sing. A little boy runs over shouting *Blow candles, blow candles* and, laughing, Aysha lets him help. With the whole restaurant's gaze upon her, she hardly knows where to look, but she does raise her eyes to meet Derrick's and rests her hand on his. Eighteen! She's an adult; she can make her own family now.

"Enjoy!" the waiter says. "I bring coffee on the house."

Derrick grins. "I hope you like cake with your cream."

The cake is sponge, filled with fresh fruit, but by far the greater part of it is whipped cream. Aysha dips a finger into the topping and licks to show her approval, then sits back as the waiter passes plates.

"I haven't had a birthday cake before."

"What, never?" Karen asks.

"Not like this. Dad would buy sweets like halva and barfi for our birthdays, but I never had a cake made specially for me." She turns to Derrick with a happy smile, "Thank you."

A muffled ring sounds somewhere and Grace opens her bag to check her phone.

"I thought I had a call," she says.

"I heard it too," Karen adds, "but it's not my ringtone. You got yours, Aysh?"

"Yes," Aysha says, "but no–one knows my number except you two." Yet when she delves in the jacket pocket and fishes out the phone, it shows a missed call.

"Are you sure your parents don't know about the phone?" Derrick asks. "Could your brother have told them?"

"No, I'm sure he didn't." She puts the mobile down on the table, reluctant to hold it. "He said to keep it to myself."

"Suppose he phoned home?" Karen says. "He might have told them if they said you were missing."

Grace reaches over and picks up the phone. "It's a mobile number," she comments, after pressing a key. "Only one way to find out."

Aysha is already eyeing the phone as if it were a creature that might bite, when it rings again. "You answer it, Grace," she begs. "Please."

Grace moves away from the table and finds a quieter corner. They all watch as she presses a button and puts the phone to her ear. "Hold on a minute, young man," they hear her say, "who exactly are you?" Then, "Yes, I think I can do that. Aysha, it's your brother." When Aysha shakes her head urgently, she adds, "Your brother *Selim*."

"Perhaps he's calling for your birthday," Derrick suggests.

"I doubt it," she says, reaching out slowly to take the phone from Grace. “Sel never remembers things like that. Something must be wrong.”

31
Emily

Monday 10 February 1902

I have to remember to concentrate on my stitches today, for between thoughts of my grandparents, my own situation and Aysha's, my mind is apt to stray.

Lottie and Kathleen want to know my opinion of their lodgings, which I visited in the lunch hour. The street is only fifteen minutes' walk from Fenton's and the bustle of Oxford Street, but it seems a whole world away. I imagine the houses were good once, but now they are partitioned into meagre little rooms, where only the high ceilings remind you of their former grand dimensions. The landlady, Mrs Pegg, is a stout blonde person of about forty-five years who calls herself a widow, though Lottie whispers to me that she is still married to a sailor who jumped ship in the South Seas fifteen years ago and never came home. Whichever is true, she definitely doesn't trust in men and will not allow male callers. Even the cats must be female and, when Lottie walks out with Jimmy, she has to meet him at the end of the street.

The vacant room is just big enough to hold a bed and chest of drawers; a few hooks and nails on the door serve as wardrobe.

A little, dingy window overlooks a courtyard that is criss–crossed by a cat's cradle of laundry lines, but the linen is clean and the room is across a landing from a larger one shared by Lottie and Kathleen. The girls also have a small gas ring which they use to boil water – hauled two flights of stairs from the kitchen below – and to make toast.

"Will you be wanting your meals, dearie?" Mrs Pegg asks.

"If I take the room, then, yes," I say, "but I haven't yet decided."

Mrs Pegg gives an exaggerated sniff. "You must suit yourself, I suppose, but don't take too long. I said I'd keep the offer open, as a favour to Lot and Kathy here, but Friday's me limit."

My eyes drift to the faded paper curling from the walls and to Lottie and Kathleen's stockings, drying on the line of string hung above the gas ring. My own room at home is papered with a chrysanthemum design; there's a Turkish rug beside my bedstead and a blue basin and jug, which Daisy fills with hot water for me.

The girls' faces are happy and eager.

"Go on, Em, take it. It'll be such fun!"

I suppose Mrs Pegg sees I'm still undecided because she repeats her deadline. "I must know by Friday if you want the room. And it'll be one week's rent in advance."

One moment I cannot credit I'm even thinking of leaving Pa and the house I grew up in; the next, I'm calculating how much money will be left after paying my rent. No wonder Mr Smythe reminds me that the jacket I'm working on is needed today.

I hurry home tonight. I'm tired and speculating about my fellow travellers on the daily journey has lost its fascination. As soon as I enter the house, Pa calls my name. I find him in the parlour with our neighbour Richard, who is pacing up and down before the hearth.

"Thank God, Emily!" he cries. "My wife has need of you. I have telephoned Dr Reynolds, but he is out on a call and Elizabeth won't hear of my going to fetch him until she has a woman to sit with her."

"Elizabeth thinks the baby is coming early," Pa explains. His own face looks stricken and I wonder if he's remembering when Ma gave birth to their first little boy.

"Your father has sent your housemaid, but she's only a girl," Richard says.

"But Daisy's older than me – and I know nothing about babies!"

"Really? I always thought you older. But Elizabeth wants *you*. She knows *you*, Emily, not your maid. Please, just keep her company until the doctor comes."

I am worn out by indecision and bone weary from being jostled and shaken on the tube; I'm hungry and eager for my bed, but I cannot refuse. Richard sends Daisy back and she whispers to me in the Blacks' hall,

"False alarm, if you ask me. I was there when my sister birthed 'er eldest. If *she*," nodding in the direction of Elizabeth's parlour, "was 'aving proper labour pains, you'd hear 'er across the square. Send poor Ernie back to me and I'll feed 'im. He'll get no supper else tonight."

Elizabeth spoke of sending Ernie to his grandmother for the Easter holidays, when her confinement was expected; tomorrow is Shrove Tuesday, so if she *is* in labour, it is six full weeks before time.

I sit beside her and she grips my arm so tightly it hurts.

"I'm scared, Emily. I've had such cramps in my stomach – do you think it can be happening? I thought my Mama would be here when the baby was born, but she's not planned to come for over a month yet – oh, what if the child's too small?"

"Elizabeth," I say, taking her hand, "you know I've no experience of such things. We must wait for the doctor."

She has been so absorbed by her pregnancy, making things for the child with her knitting and sewing and nursery decorations, that I know Daisy believes she has neglected young Ernie, as he often sneaks round to our scullery door for a slice of cake or pie. Yet now she seems in a panic and totally unprepared. I try to distract her.

"Keep calm and wait and see what Dr Reynolds thinks. Why don't you show me the baby clothes you've made?"

Elizabeth rummages behind a cushion and brings out her work basket. I admire a sweetly embroidered infant gown and ask about the pattern for a knitted bonnet. Soon she's chatting happily with only an occasional pause to massage her swollen belly. I do not think her pain can be so very great, yet I would not be in her shoes. Then it suddenly occurs to me that if Daisy had not rescued me from Baines five months ago, I could soon have been in that very same state.

When Dr Reynolds arrives, Elizabeth admits her pangs have lessened. "I knew Emily would do me good," she tells him. "God willing, if I and my child are safe, I can do the same for her in a year or two."

Dr Reynolds, who has already greeted me fondly, turns with an enquiring glance. He wishes to examine Elizabeth, so Richard offers to walk me home and collect Ernie.

"What does Elizabeth mean, do the same for me?" I ask him.

Richard looks embarrassed. "Well, you know, marriage is usually closely followed by motherhood," he explains, "at least when the wife is young and fit."

"But I am not getting married," I say.

Richard taps his nose. "Of course you are wise to keep it close, but your fiancé is too eager to be discreet. We'd wondered that your father permitted him to live under the same roof, but Mr Baines explained that you are waiting until a year has passed since your poor mother left us before making your engagement public. He seems sensitive to your situation and talks of you with the greatest respect."

"Who else knows this?" I cry, turning my head so that he cannot see my anguish.

"Well, my wife entertained old Mrs Robin yesterday – she may have mentioned your plans to her."

May have? There is not a chance that she did not; and if Mrs Robin knows, so does the whole square. No wonder Dr Reynolds regarded me so strangely. William Baines has played me false again and drawn all our neighbours to his cause. How can I not marry him now without losing my good name?

After half an hour, Dr Reynolds stops by. He lets Daisy show him into the parlour, but will not take off his overcoat or relinquish his hat and bag.

"Thank you, Edward, but I cannot stay. I am on foot and have another call to make," he explains, when my father invites him to stop for a nightcap. "I just wish to deliver a message to Emily."

Pa nods to me and I step from the parlour, pulling the door shut behind me.

"Richard asked me to thank you, Emily, and to let you know that Elizabeth is well. The body starts practising for labour some weeks before the child is due. There will be plenty of time yet for her mother to come to her aid."

"I'm glad to hear it," I reply, taking care to speak softly so that my voice does not carry to Pa in the room behind me, "for *I* may not be here to help."

"So I understand. I've been concerned to hear rumours," he says, looking at me keenly, "concerning a wedding. Elizabeth is a healthy young woman of twenty-four, a good age to give birth. You may be tall and strong, but you are still a young girl. I wouldn't want you to repeat the history of your mother's first pregnancy."

"That's not what I meant," I whisper. "I have no intention of marrying, Doctor, and I hope you will contradict such rumours wherever they occur."

"I shall be very glad to do so, my dear."

Dr Reynolds brought me into the world and was fond of my mother; he is the nearest I have to a protector.

"You know that I work for Fenton's?" I begin. "I am thinking of taking lodgings closer to the store."

"I'm sure the journey must be arduous."

"It can be, but that is not the reason. I do not feel... just lately, I no longer feel comfortable here. If I send you my address, Doctor, will you let me know how my father does? I mean, if he should fall ill? There's no–one else I can trust."

Dr Reynolds places his hands on my shoulders, then bends and gently kisses my forehead.

"My dear girl, of course I will. Excuse me, but Edward is a fool." Shaking his head, he turns and goes out of the door.

All night my eyes strain to see her. I catch myself turning quickly to the window, trying to glimpse her world from the corner of my eye. But nothing; nothing at all. I am sure she has left. If take up my floorboard, will my journal still be there or has Aysha changed her mind and taken me with her, wherever she has gone? But no, it is here, in my hand, and though I should sleep, I re-read everything I have written over the past two years. I see now that Mr Baines' behaviour was all of a piece, how he first singled me out for attention when I was fourteen, flattering me with his conversation and treating me as older than my years. I have blamed myself, but how could I be expected to withstand a man like that? I wish I knew why Aysha's family are so angry with her, but everything I hear of her life puzzles me. There must be some misunderstanding, for I am sure she is good. I wish I could talk to her! I know that she has made a decision to leave and that it is as hard for her as it is for me. But if she can do it, so can I. I will tell Mrs Pegg and speak to Pa tomorrow.

32
Aysha

Monday 11 February 2002

Aysha is still mentally replaying her conversation with Sel next morning, as Derrick waits outside the apartment block to walk with her and Karen to college. He won't accept that there's little risk of her family snatching her off the street, and that no-one is lying in wait, ready to bundle her into a car.

"Mo doesn't drive," she explains. "There's only my sister's husband and I can't see Hass getting involved."

"Your brother might know other people who would," he says. "It doesn't hurt being careful. Unless you don't want me here?"

Aysha smiles and slips her arm in his as they thread through the back streets, between the flats. The early morning sunshine is already fading and clouds are massing towards the river. When they reach Westferry, Derrick glances around cautiously, scrutinising the car drivers dropping commuters at the station.

"Do you think Sel will phone your parents?" asks Karen.

"He has to let Dad know about the land," she replies, "so he might as well tell them the whole story while there's five thousand miles between them."

"Your dad's gonna be upset about the money, especially if his own brother swindled him," Derrick muses. "Sounds like he was expecting a fair bit of cash."

At first she'd wondered if Sel could have misunderstood the situation. He'd been ill, after all, though he sounded okay yesterday. He'd said that the land, half of which was their father's, had been gradually sold off by Dad's brother and the money used to pay medical and school fees, for repairs and extensions to the family home, and for investment in a disastrous fish farming enterprise.

"Sel said they hadn't really seen it as cheating," she says. "Uncle knew he should have told Dad at the time, but he expected to make enough money from the fish farm to repay him. People in Bangladesh have crazy ideas that everyone in the UK has pots of money. They thought we didn't need it."

Aysha couldn't quite grasp what had gone wrong with the fish farm: something about a flood washing the bamboo cages away. She's ashamed to admit to feeling almost relieved the money is gone. What with the fiasco over Jamil and now no money for a wedding, surely her family will realise she's not meant to get married? But it doesn't just affect her. As Sel pointed out, Dad could have used the money for other things; as it is, he's spent a considerable sum on an airfare to Bangladesh and on all the presents taken for the extended family there.

The main reason for his call was to check Dad's state of health before breaking this, and other, news. Where was she, he'd asked, and who was the woman who answered the phone? Long story, she'd said, and told him the basics. She didn't know how Dad was; best talk to Mum first. Trouble was, he'd said, that was only the beginning.

"I don't know how they'll take it," she tells her friends. "First me and now Sel."

"So he's not coming home," Karen wonders, "because of some girl he's met?"

"He wants to marry her."

"Impulsive, your brother?" Derrick asks.

"He messed around at school and I suppose he can be irresponsible, but that's not how he sounded yesterday."

"He's only been there three weeks," Karen says. "You can't get to know someone that quickly."

Aysha nods. Sel had told her that he'd become ill and was looked after by the girl Mo had mentioned. She was a distant relative of their uncle, poor cousin to his eldest son's wife, born with a club foot, given house room but treated like a skivvy by the rest. The family hadn't known what to do with Sel when he got sick just two days after his arrival. He was an embarrassment, this young nephew who'd come to ask for money they didn't have and was now unpleasantly ill. The young woman had washed and cleaned Sel, spoon fed dhal to him and given him cooled boiled water to drink. They'd talked and talked, about his life and hers, and by the time he was better, he was determined to rescue her from the drudgery of her existence and to raise enough money for an operation on her foot. It helped, Aysha imagined, that he said she had a beautiful face.

His uncle had tried to dissuade him. If he couldn't repay his brother, he said, the least he could do was prevent this nephew from acting like a fool. But then Sel lost his temper with his female cousins when they ordered Shilpi – that was the young woman's name – to fetch and carry for them. How was it, he'd asked, that a girl with a twisted foot worked harder than all the other women in the house? Did they think Allah had given them straight legs just so that they could sit on their fat arses all day? At this, their uncle became angry. Sel and Shilpi were both ungrateful wretches who deserved each other, he said. As a nephew, Sel was owed hospitality, but he wouldn't waste his advice on him anymore. Let his brother, Mohammed Abdullah, get on a plane from England and sort out his own offspring. Sel and Shilpi had gone to the neighbouring village, where her mother lived. *She* was more than happy for her daughter to marry this young man from England.

"But as far as I understand it," Derrick says, "he can't bring her back here, not yet anyway, and not unless he has a decent job."

"That's just it. He says he wants to stay there." Sel had started to expand on some hare-brained scheme of teaching British driving skills to Bangladeshis planning to come to the UK, when the credit on his phone ran out. As she'd thought, Sel had no idea it was a special day when he phoned, yet it had been wonderful to hear his voice; she hadn't realised how much she missed him. But this will be a heavy blow for her parents: she can't decide if Sel's news will take the heat off her, or make them all the more determined to bring at least one rebellious child into line.

She turns to Derrick. "I'm sorry the call took up so much time yesterday. I really loved the restaurant – especially the cake."

"HAPPY BIRTHDAY TO YOU!" sings Karen in a deep flat voice like the Turkish waiter's.

Derrick shrugs. "I think I might like this brother. At least he seems to follow his heart."

"You meant to talk to Del's mum about Emily's journal too," Karen adds.

"What's that?" Derrick asks.

"Aysha's got this diary she found, written by a girl who used to live in her house, and there's some really weird stuff going on.

Like this girl – Emily – writes about what's happening to her and each time Aysh looks there's more added. She says your mum's a bit psychic and she was going to tell her about it."

Derrick frowns. "She used to be. She still comes out with some strange stuff at times, but she doesn't really get involved nowadays – she knows I'm not keen." Then, when Karen objects that she doesn't think you can just give up being psychic, he adds, "She'd be interested, though, I'm sure."

They reach college early and hang around in the foyer looking at a display by the photography students. Karen points out some views over Limehouse Basin and across the Thames on what looks like a wintry afternoon. The name underneath is Runa Begum, Wahida's friend.

"Looks like Billie was right," she says. "There's some of her stuff here too. I'd no idea she was so good."

Billie's pictures are of building sites, graffitied shop shutters and subway walls, black and white studies of kids hanging out in the park. Billie has never really shone at academic subjects, but it strikes Aysha that in these powerful images the girl has found her voice.

She arranges to meet Derrick at mid-morning break, but Jo Massey detains her after their English lesson and leads her into one of the small interview pods next to the staffroom.

"Sit down, Aysha," she says. "I had a phone call from your mother early this morning."

Aysha perches on the frayed edge of a blue office chair. She's not surprised that someone has called, only that it's her mother. Mum usually leaves phone conversations in English to Mo.

"If I understood her correctly, you haven't been home since Friday," Jo continues, "so I'm guessing there's been some kind of argument with your family." She listens in silence as Aysha explains why her confession hadn't gone to plan.

"I knew they'd be disappointed about Jamil," she says, "but the real problem was that... someone... told them about me and Derrick. My brother thought there'd been an actual fight between him and Jamil. And then Wa... the same person gave Mum a photo of us together and they wanted to send me away to my sister's." She does her best to sound matter of fact, but the catch in her throat betrays her.

"And what were you meant to do about college?"

"They said Maryam – that's my sister – would drive me every day, but she's got two boys to look after, and a really old granny. She'd never keep it up. And Mo won't hear of me going to York."

Jo tosses her head and mutters, "Well, really!"

Aysha looks away. In the staffroom outside the pod, an engineer is taking the photocopier apart and a student posting an assignment in one of the tutors' pigeon holes glances curiously through the partition at her. She turns back to face Jo, feeling she ought to defend her family.

"It's not that they're racist or anything, not really. I mean my brother works at the hospital and he mixes with staff from everywhere. It's just that they think people should marry within their own cultures. And no boyfriends."

"Hmm," says Jo.

"What did you tell my mum?" Aysha asks.

"That you're an adult now and I'm not allowed to give out information without your permission – happy birthday, Aysha, by the way – but that I believed you to be perfectly safe. I hope you *do* have somewhere to stay?"

"Yes, with Karen."

"And is that a long-term arrangement?"

"Her parents say I can stay till I go to uni, but I hope it won't be that long. I really hope I can go back home."

Jo chews on her biro and runs a hand through her hair. Aysha notices a few traces of grey flecking the wiry brown curls.

"I think I advise you to stay put for a while. Notify UCAS of your change of address and concentrate on your interviews and exams. Yes, you'll have to go back at some point and you'll need evidence of parental income if you think you're eligible for course fees remission. If you need help, come to me. The student adviser's expecting you today – she's sorted your train fare to York. And we'd better go through interview questions this week too."

Aysha texts an apology to Derrick and heads for her next lesson. The months stretch ahead of her like an unfinished sentence. She has her studies, and friends who care, but there's still a hollow place inside her: a dull hunger that never quite goes away. It will be strange for Abdul, having the bedroom to himself, if Sel doesn't come back. Perhaps little Ibrahim will share with him now: they'd both like that. Sel said he needed to travel out of the village to make a call and he didn't know when he'd be able to speak to her again. There's so much she didn't have time to ask him yesterday and no easy way to ask now.

The house will reshape itself without her and Sel, as it must have done so many times in its past; yet her top-floor room overlooking the square is different: special to her and to Emily. She needs it to remain empty; she has to be able to retrieve the journal again.

33
Emily

Wednesday 12 February 1902

I tell Lottie and Kathleen that I will take the room, but ask them not to inform Mrs Pegg until I have spoken to Pa. They promise to say nothing, but this does not stop them interrupting my work every few minutes to share some snippet of life at the boarding house – the idiosyncrasies of the plumbing or last night's menu – and eventually even I begin to catch their enthusiasm.

I have the remainder of the money Pa gave me when I visited my grandparents so, with this week's wages, I will have just enough to pay one week's rent in advance. I can't take many clothes with me, just work wear and an outfit for best. I can fetch more when needed. There won't be space for many possessions: just a few books, my journal and writing things. I am glad Ma's necklace is kept safe in Harlow.

I cannot help worrying about Pa. He's mostly sober now, but his mood is subdued. A year has passed since we learned of Charlie's death; I wonder how he will cope with the even more painful anniversary to come? When we were growing up, Pa always maintained a reserve with Charlie and me, keeping his innermost feelings for Ma alone. He rarely thought to ask *our* opinions, but expected us to conform to his, so it was to *her* we went with our confidences, to be loved and indulged. Neither of us has fulfilled his expectations; I have failed him, just as Charlie did.

If my brother had shown interest in the tobacco trade, perhaps one day Pa would have admitted him as an equal; but now that can never be. I think this is how William Baines has gained such influence: he appears to defer to Pa even as he schemes to win advantage. Pa took over a thriving business from his grandfather and cannot help but admire a man who appears entirely self-made. But my father is still young; he could marry again. I wonder if Baines feared losing his influence to a new wife and hoped to secure his place through marrying me?

On reaching home, I take time to change my clothes before dinner, being sooty and dirty from the smuts and smoke of the trains. William Baines is already at the table, but I give him only the briefest of nods and avoid being drawn into conversation during the meal. When Daisy clears the dishes away, I give a little cough.

"Pa, I need to speak to you."

My father frowns slightly, then makes a little flourish with his hand as if to tell me to go on. Baines drains his coffee cup and leans back in his chair, pointedly turning away from us to watch Daisy edge her way awkwardly out of the room, balancing the tray on her hip as she twists the doorknob.

"Alone, Pa. I need to speak in private."

Pa opens his mouth then closes it again when he sees I am in earnest. He looks like a startled fish. William Baines picks up his newspaper and gets to his feet.

"I've no wish to trespass on your secrets, Miss Emily."

His eyes are watchful and uncertain, his gaze drawn back to

me as he slowly crosses the room.

"Well, Emily," Pa says, when we are alone, "what is it?"

I take a deep breath to stop my voice from breaking.

"I want to tell you, Pa, that I will be renting a room to be near to my workplace. It is a respectable house, where some of the other girls live."

Pa sets down his coffee cup and stares at me. He picks up his used napkin, crumpling then flattening it over and over again.

"I can see the daily journey must be taxing, Emily," he says at last, "but I did not believe you so stubborn that you would choose to sacrifice your home and your father rather than this wretched job. If the travel tires you, give the work up. You can't make a difference with the little you earn and I've said I will pay you an allowance."

"If it were just the journey, I wouldn't do this, Pa. I don't want to leave you."

"Why then?"

"I told you once before, Pa, that... that man... insulted me and you chose to accept his word over mine. The other night I discovered that Richard and Elizabeth – even Dr Reynolds – believed me secretly engaged to him. He had told them as much! Can't you see how compromised I am by his being here?"

Pa stirs the half-empty cup. "I know Bill still cherishes hopes of you, but that's his misfortune. Perhaps Elizabeth has fathomed his feelings and misunderstood yours."

Even now he makes excuses for him.

"Not just Elizabeth," I say. "Richard even told me the date. I am to marry when Ma is one year dead! I'd give up my job and stay at home, if you would send that man away."

His face is a battleground for conflicting emotions, where

love and hope are conquered by fear and despair.

"I can't do it," he whispers. "It would be the ruin of me."

I have respected him, loved him, feared him, but never before now despised him. I rise to my feet and glare angrily down as he continues to crumple the creased linen.

"You blame me for choosing work before my home, but you have chosen your business over me. I would happily be poor with you, but I won't owe my keep to that man's money, or stay to be the object of his ambitions and lusts!"

"Lusts?" he queries. "What do you know of lusts?"

"Ask Mr Baines."

I shoot the bolt on my bedroom door and begin to pack a few items of clothes in the carpet bag I took with me to Harlow. When I lift up the floorboard to reach my journal, I can hear Pa stomping about in the parlour below. There is an irritable shout of *not now, Bill*, then, *where the deuce did Daisy put the brandy?* I fear for Pa, but it's not in my power to save him.

"You've decided then, miss – about that room?" Daisy asks when she brings the stone bottle to warm my bed. "Your ma would 'ave a fit to think of you living in a place like that."

Of course she'd prefer me not to go, but *she* need not contend with the attentions of William Baines or struggle each day with the crowded underground train.

"It's perfectly decent," I say, "and I'll come back often. Your position here will be safer if there's no-one else to cook and manage the house."

Thursday 20 February 1902

"Spuds and boiled bacon," Lottie says, sniffing the moist air wafting up the passage from Mrs Pegg's quarters. She, Kathy and I haul ourselves up the two flights of stairs to our rooms, bone weary after a day in the sewing room and hugging the railings all the way home as we crept back through a sulphurous London fog.

"Friday tomorrow," Kathy says.

"That meant to cheer us up?" Lot says, coughing. "Me and Em are working Saturday, finishing that trousseau."

On Monday morning I carried my bag from home to Fenton's, then brought it here to the boarding house after work, but this week has been too busy to allow time to reflect on my new life – unless to be grateful that I haven't had to drag myself back to Stepney each night. The last few days have been like today, beginning with a grey, icy mist, which barely lifts by noon – and even then the daylight does not penetrate our sewing room – before returning in the mid-afternoon, yellower and dirtier than before, as the chimneys discharge their smoke into the still air.

Arthur Smythe makes no concession to our difficulties: we must complete our long day regardless of the weather. Lottie is working on the travelling clothes for a wealthy brewer's daughter whose wedding is the first day of March. Kathleen and I are sewing the lingerie, but she is excused from Saturday working as she has a cousin visiting from Ireland and had previously requested time off.

We wash the smuts from our hands and faces, tidy our hair and go down for supper. Three shop assistants from Dickens and Jones – Vera, Annie and Phyllis – also board here, plus Miss Dawkins, an older woman who takes in dress alterations, so we are eight with Mrs Pegg herself. The bacon and potatoes are served with boiled carrots and followed by a baked custard and tea. Our landlady is a competent plain cook and provides adequate rations, but I doubt she loves the work as Daisy does.

Conversation is encouraged at the table. Mrs Pegg rarely leaves the house except to visit the market at Covent Garden and expects her boarders to entertainer her with tales from the world outside and news of the latest fashions. As the girls forewarned me, there is one subject of which she does not approve. The disappearance of the faithless Mr Pegg makes her harbour a grudge against all the male sex and she frowns on any talk of young men, unless it is to show them being put in their place. Miss Dawkins, a spinster said to have been disappointed in love, shares her prejudice. If Lottie wishes to repeat what Jimmy whispered in her ear when he brought up the last delivery of lace, she knows she must wait until we retire to our rooms. We have a rota for helping to wash the dishes; otherwise, we sit downstairs for an hour or more after dinner and play some rounds of cards and sometimes Phyllis picks out a tune on Mrs Pegg's piano.

I remember William Baines' conviction that few women opt to work except out of necessity and I decide to question my companions.

"What made you choose shop work?" I ask Phyllis.

"My sisters are all in service back home in Kent," she says. "and I see the lives they lead, what little free time they have and how their mistresses drive them. Shop work's hard graft, but at the day's end my time's my own and I have money in my pocket."

"And if you were to marry, would you still work then?"

Miss Dawkins has retired to her room and Mrs Pegg is supervising Kathy and Annie in the scullery, otherwise this conversation would be censored.

"She wouldn't be kept on, more's the pity," Vera says. "But I suppose it's only sense, as most brides are in the family way within a year of marriage."

"There's some as know how to avoid it," Phyllis mutters.

"Who would turn out first thing on a February morning – as we must tomorrow – if she could rise at leisure?" Lottie asks. "I should like to work for myself. To have a little shop perhaps, with rooms over, so I needn't rush out in the morning, but stay in bed till eight – " she gives us a knowing smile – "with my Jimmy to keep me warm."

"Lottie!" cries Vera in shock. "He's not even proposed to you!"

Lottie gets up and goes to the fireplace where she inspects herself in the speckled mirror above the hearth. She tweaks a strand of her pale hair, brushed back from her brow in a high, rounded curve, to make sure the fabric which pads it is covered.

"Not yet," she admits, "but he will. If only this weather would change and we could walk in the park again, I'd see that he did!" Vera frowns disapprovingly, but Lottie goes on. "Jim's visiting his mother in Clapham this weekend and I think he means to tell her about me. Oh, but Sunday is going to be a dreary day – what will you do, Emmie?"

I haven't even thought. "I should go home," I say, "to check how my father and Daisy are managing."

"Oh, don't go, Em," Lottie begs. "Kathy will be at mass and I'll have no-one to talk to."

"Never mind her," says Kathleen, coming into the room, "but it's a poor idea to go back when you've only just left. It will look like weakness, so it will, and they'll be prevailing on you to stay."

"Your Pa made his bed when he took that fella into the house. He must learn to do without you," Lottie adds, resting her arm on my shoulder.

"I dare say you're right, but it's Daisy who concerns me most."

"She's older than you, Emmie, I remember you told us so. Chances are she'll be walking out with a young man herself."

"Daisy's thoughts still run too strongly on my brother for that."

I do not add that, except for the baker and milkman, old men both, Daisy has little male acquaintance outside the house. I'm afraid of sounding like one of the heartless mistresses Phyllis described. Even young Ernie, who frequents our kitchen, will soon be sent away to his grandmother when Elizabeth is confined. Then I remember that Daisy was lately reconciled with her eldest sister. Lottie and Kathy are right, it *is* unwise to go back too soon, but when I do I will encourage Daisy to visit that sister again.

I am glad I am not sharing my room here, otherwise it would be hard to keep up this journal. As it is, I tell Lot and Kathy I am too tired for talk, close my door and write until my candle burns low. I keep my book hidden at the bottom of my carpet bag: I do not think they will spy, but I would not want them to read the passages about seeing Aysha, lest they think my mind is unsound.

34
Aysha

February 2002

The Roman numerals of the massive black and gold clock read a quarter to six when Aysha gets back to York station. The illuminated Victorian arches glow in the dusk; there's a chill wind and she wraps her scarf closer: it's colder here than in London. Having treated herself to a coffee from the buffet, she walks with it along the platform, remembering the likely order of the carriages from the morning and wanting to avoid carrying her cup the length of a crowded train. Nobody claims the place next to hers, however, and she's able to spread herself, read, relax and, most of all, review an extraordinary day.

She'd woken to a bright sparkling sky, showered, dressed, packed and repacked her bag before seven-thirty. It was half-term week, so there was no compulsion for Karen to rise, but she had sat up suddenly saying, "God, you're going to York today – I meant to get up." She scrutinised Aysha's outfit – black trousers, blue shirt, bargain boots from the market and grey jacket – then reached into the drawer beside her bed and threw her a long cream scarf saying, "Text me, won't you?"

Janet had pushed a foil-wrapped parcel into her hand. "Just

a baguette," she'd said, "the prices on the train are ridiculous." Mike offered to drop her at Aldgate station. To make sure she wasn't late, he explained, but she knew they were all concerned she shouldn't bump into her family. "Good luck, princess," he called as she got out of the car, "look out for platform nine and three-quarters."

Their kindness overwhelmed her.

King's Cross Station was crowded, but she was carrying only a small bag and found it easy enough to weave in and out of the throng. Family groups stood guard around piles of luggage, young people shouldered massive rucksacks which covered each back like a colourful carapace and elderly women wearing gloves and hats trundled suitcases on wheels. Aysha bought an overpriced can of Coke, then ventured to ask a woman in railway uniform which was the platform for York. The woman gestured in the direction of the departure board, shrugged and walked on. A man with a briefcase observed her. "Platform's never shown till five minutes before it's due to leave," he told her, "then it's a right scrum."

Eventually she joined the dash for platform three, and found her reserved seat in coach B, opposite a middle-aged American couple who had already spread a slew of maps and guide books across the table. They introduced themselves as Bob and Martha from Philadelphia and asked where she was going. Martha said her great-grandmother came from York*shire* – that's how she said it. They were hiring a car in York and aimed to visit her birthplace, as well as Castle Howard, Ripon for the cathedral, Haworth and the Brontë country. Aysha could only shake her head when asked if she knew these places. The seat next to hers was taken by a boy of about ten, the overspill of a family seated across the aisle, who never raised his head from his computer game unless to accept snacks supplied by his mother.

All this mobility was a revelation. Beyond the steel and glass city, beyond the Victorian tenements, beyond even the long, lawned gardens of outer London, lay an England of meadows and rivers, through which people travelled with ease and regularity. Fields were dotted with sheep and lambs; a solitary horse in a coat grazed a paddock. Towns, villages and isolated houses swept by and stations passed too swiftly to yield their names. Life didn't have to be spent in one place. Sel wanted to start again on the other side of the world; she could choose to live in a different city in the UK. There were planes, trains, motorways that would take you there.

Now that the daylight has gone, the carriage window reveals only her own reflected image. It seems hardly possible the long-awaited visit is over and she's already heading south again. Aysha finishes her coffee and pulls a clutch of handouts from her bag – course outlines, guides to accommodation and the collegiate system – plus other printed matter she's picked up. She sifts through her trawl – bus timetables, leaflets from the information centre and postcards of the city walls and the Minster. The city she'd felt so drawn to has not disappointed. Both the old cobbled streets and the modern university buildings could become the wallpaper of a new life; equally, she might never see them again. The desire for acceptance burns so fiercely that she wonders how she can bear the suspense of waiting for the university's response.

The interviews had gone all right. She thinks she made a good case for opting for the joint degree and made sure the interviewers knew it was a positive choice on her part, not an inability to make up her mind. The summer school had been a turning point, she'd explained; the tutors there encouraged her to think she could aim for the best.

She'd bought lunch in the university library café and sat with a red–headed girl who was also there for interview. Miranda came from Leicestershire; she said she supposed she might live in hall for a bit, but her parents would probably buy one of the poky little houses you could snap up for next to nothing, so she could live there and rent out the other bedrooms. For the first time, Aysha worries how she'll manage for money: she can get a student loan, but will it cover all her expenses? York is a busy tourist destination with lots of shops and cafés, so perhaps she can get a part-time job. She does need Dad's help to claim exemption from the thousand pound fees that are charged. Somehow she will have to find a way to see him alone.

She sent a text to Karen before leaving York, but now her phone pings with a message from Derrick offering to meet her at King's Cross. He's really busy this week, fitting in extra supermarket shifts and starting driving lessons, so it's kind of him to do this, but it bothers her too. Ever since she got up this morning, people have put themselves out for her – yet she's planning to leave them. Sometimes she doesn't know herself, this young woman who is developing a hard nucleus of ambition that leads her to separate from friends and family, yet who feels such a rush of affection when she spots Derrick smiling and waving beyond the platform barrier.

~

It's a relief to return to college after the half-term break. Her class is close to completing the history syllabus, which means another step nearer to university. She's glad of the company too. Janet and Mike are at work all day, Derrick's been doing overtime and Karen spent last Thursday and Friday visiting her nan in Clacton, so she has been often left to range through the flat alone. The festival of Eid al Adha had fallen on Saturday and she couldn't help wondering what was happening at home. One thing was sure: there would have been no more visits from the Rahman family. She spares a thought for Jamil, presumably suffering retribution for deceiving his family, but she can't manage sympathy.

After the day of new sensations in York, with the heady knowledge that her interview might determine her future life, it's hard to accept there's nothing more she can do except get on with her studies. Already college feels different: the building smaller, the students younger, the lack of outside space more irksome after the expansiveness of a university campus. Her college years are three-quarters through; the time will pass only too quickly now.

Andy Carstairs is keen to know how she got on and what she thought of the place. A five minute update at the start of the lesson establishes that six of the history students have at least one provisional offer – herself, Karen and Derrick included – while others, like Wahida, are still waiting. The girl is back in college now, coughing frequently and looking sickly enough to be genuinely recovering from flu. She watches Aysha and Derrick with guarded eyes, as if trying to work out what's going on, and is so subdued that she doesn't even join the debate on a *Times* article about UK support for an American assault on Iraq.

Tutors must be used to this: seeing the students they've taught change and leave them behind. That's the nature of the job. Friends are different. After living with Karen for the past few weeks, Aysha can't imagine a day passing when they won't find time to talk, even if they're at opposite ends of the country. She'll miss the others, too: Billie, for instance – not a close friend, but someone whose irreverent behaviour and cheeky smile have helped form her experience of student life.

And then, Derrick. How will their friendship develop over the coming months? Theirs is a strong attachment, a caring relationship, but so far not a physically intimate one. Lack of opportunity when she was at home allowed many questions to go unasked, but life at Karen's is freer. Karen's parents are used to their daughter going out on dates, and if Aysha were to announce she was spending the evening with Derrick, no-one would object, though Janet might check how she was getting back. In fact, on Sunday she and Derrick *had* spent the day together. They'd caught the Docklands train to Greenwich and played at being tourists, wandering round the market, admiring the Cutty Sark and strolling by the river. She'd never experienced a day like that before – just spending time with a friend, answerable to no-one.

If she is accepted by York and Derrick gets the place he wants at Leeds, they won't be too far apart. Will they still see each other? In the last few weeks he has become even more determined and hard-working. He's saving for a car and takes on all the shifts the supermarket offers, getting up early to do his college work. After the Greenwich trip, when they'd kissed in the lift to Karen's flat, was it her imagination or was his kiss more insistent than usual?

She's had no more calls from Sel and there's been no further enquiry from her family. Jo confirms that no-one has contacted her since Mum's call.

"It *is* funny they haven't come looking for you, especially if

Wahida reports that you're at college," Karen comments as they reach Limehouse together. Aysha never walks home alone, but their precautions all seem needless: no-one lies in wait outside college, no-one is watching the flats. "You'd think they'd guess you're with me."

"I don't think Mo knows your address," Aysha says, considering. "It was your old house where he used to come and collect me."

"What about that photo – could you tell where it was taken?"

"You could see boats and water, but it wasn't obvious – not unless you knew the area well."

"Wahida knows," Karen says.

Perhaps they've forgotten about her, now they've heard Sel's revelation. But not Dad, surely, she thinks? What if he's ill, or if something else has happened to drive her disappearance from their minds?

"Phone the old couple," Karen suggests. "You said you had their number."

Of course! Maud and Bert don't miss much, sat in the window of the basement flat all day. If anything's wrong, they're sure to know.

"'Ello, love." Maud's rich tones instantly cheer her. "We've been wondering if you'd call. You should've left us your number, you know. Me and Bert wouldn't tell anyone."

"Sorry," Aysha says, "I didn't want to involve you in my problems. I'm fine, but I'm worried about my dad. Have you seen him at all?"

She hears Maud turn to the old man. "It's Aysha, Bert. Wants to know if we've seen 'er dad. No, Bert ain't seen 'im," she says, "but there's been no end of comings and goings. That big car was here, the one your brother went off to the airport in, and then the other one, with the woman and the little boys – isn't she your sister? Other folk too. And your brother that lives here had a face as black as thunder when I passed him in the square. Reckon you're well out of it, love."

"I'll give you my friend's number," Aysha says after a long pause. "I've got a mobile, but it's expensive for you to call. If you do see Dad, would you let me know?"

Janet is unpacking her shopping in the kitchen, so Aysha explains who Maud is, in case she calls sometime.

"I'm sure she'll keep you informed," Janet comments. "You've given her the perfect excuse to look through her curtains all day. But she's not told you anything new – your brother's news was bound to cause an upset. I know you miss your dad, love, but don't forget why you left in the first place."

Aysha nods but, although they don't support her plans for the future, she still misses and cares about her family. If the atmosphere is tense, it will be the quiet ones who suffer: Reshna, the children, Dad. But Janet's right: she left home to have freedom and peace to concentrate on her studies. All she can do is keep her head down, work hard and trust that Maud will phone her if there's a need.

35
Emily

Friday 28 February 1902

At last the wind and rain have arrived and chased the fog away: umbrellas turn inside out on every corner, hats take flight and in Regent Street a hansom cab is blown off course, colliding with one of the new motor cars. The trousseau we've been working on left the workshop on Monday, all folded in tissue and ready to be worn by the bride on her Paris honeymoon – though I don't envy her the Channel crossing this weekend.

We finish at six-thirty as it is Friday and clatter down the outside staircase to the yard below. Jimmy is waiting to speak to Lottie when we reach the street.

"Give us a minute, girls," she says, and they wander a little way off, talking earnestly as they shelter in a doorway, away from the wind-driven rain. Lot is expecting to meet his family on Sunday: I hope that she is right and they are arranging her visit. Kathleen has heard that the shop windows have been re-dressed today and wants to see if any of our work is displayed. We are walking towards the street corner and the front of the shop, when I notice my boot is unlaced and bend to fasten it, telling Kathy to go on. I gather my skirt about me to avoid dragging it in the wet and have just tied my knot when two black-booted feet stop in front of mine. Their sudden closeness makes me lose my balance. I put out an arm to steady myself when a gloved hand cups my elbow and helps me to rise and I find myself looking into the frowning face of William Baines.

"All alone, Emily, in this dark and rain?"

He carries a large black umbrella which he positions over our heads. I look round: Kathy has disappeared; Lottie and Jimmy are preoccupied in their doorway.

"Not at all," I say, with more confidence than I feel. "My friends are just around the corner. What brings you here, Mr Baines?"

"A visit to one of our – your father's – customers, a store we supply. I found myself nearby and wanted to see *you,* to be able to tell your father how you are." He lowers the umbrella to admit light from the gas lamp and peers closely into my face, "Good God, Emily, you look done in!"

"We have been busy, but it is the end of the week. I can rest."

There is no Saturday work tomorrow, now that the wedding order has been completed, and Lottie has promised to take me to the public baths where we can soak our aches and pains away.

"Come home," he says urgently, "for the weekend at least. Let your father spoil you and young Daisy wait on you. I'll come with you to your lodgings now, if you need to collect anything."

I smile to think of Mrs Pegg's likely reaction to William Baines at her door. "I'm sorry, but my landlady does not permit gentlemen callers. As I told my father, it is a respectable house."

"Some doss house near Covent Garden! Dammit, Emily, don't mock me!" He pulls me back from the kerb as a passing carriage sends a spray of dirty water over the pavement and shakes the drips from his umbrella.

"You can tell my father I am well and will visit him soon." I'm eager to get away, alarmed to think he may know where I live. "I'm accustomed to the journey now. When I choose to come, I can travel by myself."

"Fenton works you too hard; I knew he would. See here!" He catches my hand, which is still ungloved from retying my boot, and examines my pricked fingers and thumb, before seeking my face again. "And take heed you do not strain your eyes. *I* would take care of you!"

Sometimes I think he does love me, but that would not stop him bending me to his will. Even now, he blocks my way.

"Mr Baines," I say, "I left home because my own father was careless of my reputation and because *you* took advantage of your position in his house. I don't want to be taken care of. I am quite capable of looking after myself."

I want to show how I despise him, but he takes whatever I say as encouragement.

"Such spirit," he murmurs, as if reading my mind. "How do you know it would not be *me* who is tamed?"

Kathleen has come back around the corner and Lottie and Jimmy are watching us.

"My friends are here – I must go."

"At least take some shelter from the rain."

He puts the umbrella into my hands but I thrust it back at him, pull down my hat and turn up my coat collar. "No, thank you," I say, "for I do not know when I should be able to return it."

"Won't you even let me do this? I know I blotted my copy book with you, but can it never be wiped clean?"

"No," I say, seizing my chance, "it cannot."

"Take care you don't live to regret this," he says. "Your father's precious business depends on me. I'm offering security for you – and those you love."

"Security! You may choose not to remember, but I *know* how you treat women. Don't come again – if you want a wife, you must look elsewhere."

I see Jimmy straighten his shoulders and take a step forward. Baines' cheeks flush. He wipes the raindrops from his brow and grips the umbrella, holding it resolutely over his head, then turns on his heel and marches off. Lottie and Kathleen stand beside me, each taking an arm.

"You all right, miss?" Jimmy asks. "I've seen that bloke hanging around before – both here and near Ma Pegg's place – I didn't know it was you he was after."

"Is that him?" Lot asks. "The man who...?"

"William Baines," I nod.

"He's a well set-up fellow, though," Kathleen comments, "with that black hair an' all. I'd have taken him for a gentleman any day."

"Gentlemen are no better than the rest," Lottie says, shaking her head, "and that one's got the look of the wolf about him all right. You keep clear of him, Emmie. Jimmy'll make sure he doesn't follow us and let you know if he hangs round here again."

36
Aysha

March 2002

"Aysh," Karen says, putting her head on one side and generally assuming an air of entreaty, "come to Canary Wharf with me this morning. I need to get Mum's card and present for tomorrow."

The shop windows are filled with cards and gifts for Mother's Day. Her own mum could be quite dismissive of the hand-drawn missives and floppy daffodil stalks she and Sel used to bring home from primary school, commenting that good Bangladeshi children should honour their parents every day. If Abdul has made a card, she hopes it will meet a more gracious response. Saturday is Mum's day for shopping, but Canary Wharf is unlikely to be her destination.

"Sure. Perhaps I could get your mum something too, as a thank you. She likes chocolate, doesn't she?" She wishes she could buy something more – a book, perhaps, since Janet is a keen reader of a certain type of romantic fiction – but her budget won't stretch that far.

"I've never known her refuse," Karen laughs.

They leave home mid-morning and walk to Limehouse station. The little train trundles over the still waters beside West

India Quay and they alight beneath the triple arches of Canary Wharf Station for the shopping centre. Aysha soon chooses a small box of caramels, but when it comes to selecting toiletries for her mother, Karen does nothing by halves. Karen's dad Mike jokes that some people take less care buying a house than Karen does in choosing clothes and make-up.

The shops exhibit desirable objects on every side – coats and boots at sale prices now that spring has arrived, beautiful pens and stationery, exotic plants and flowers – but Aysha's not keen on window gazing when there's no hope of purchase.

"I think I'll go and look in the bookshop," she asks, remembering that there's a branch of Waterstones on a higher level. "I'll be okay," she adds, when Karen looks around them, cautiously.

"Fine. Let's meet back here." Karen indicates the coffee shop nearby. "I'll text you when I'm done."

Aysha takes the escalator up two flights to the shopping centre's highest level and wanders into the bookshop. A prominent display table holds piles of bright-covered paperbacks which form part of the store's special offer. They are mostly new to her: the A level syllabus doesn't leave time to keep up with recent books. Maybe some of these will be classics one day, but how do you choose? She picks them up one by one, reading the blurbs, before returning to a copy of Zadie Smith's *White Teeth*, which she remembers Jo mentioning. She finds a handy seat and reads a chapter before putting it back. Perhaps the college library will get it.

She crosses to the history section and examines a large format book on the Vikings, wishing she'd had time to visit the Jorvik Viking Museum in York, and is still browsing happily when a text arrives to say that Karen's on her way back. Aysha replaces the book on its pile and heads for the escalator. She spots her friend on the concourse two floors below and is about to call and wave when her attention is caught by a family group standing between the coffee shop and the entrance to the public toilets. The handles of their baby buggy are loaded with carrier bags containing shoe boxes from the sports shop nearby. The woman, who wears a black coat and headscarf over a long dark dress, lifts a baby girl from the buggy and sniffs at her tentatively; the man is carrying a small boy who appears to be trying to twist off his father's ears. His slight figure is dressed in a familiar blue anorak, brown trousers and worn trainers. From her escalator vantage point she sees that his hair is thinning on the crown. But Mo's not even thirty, she thinks.

It's too late to go back; there are people behind her and attempting to go up a down escalator is guaranteed to attract notice. She realises Karen has seen her and performs a desperate kind of sign language, finger to lips and head jerking urgently towards the family group. Mo bends to put Ibrahim down and at that moment Reshna looks up, over his shoulder. Her sister-in-law's eyes register confusion, joy and alarm in rapid succession, and then, to her surprise, a knowing complicity. In the space of the few seconds it takes for the escalator to descend, Aysha sees her despatch Mo with Ibrahim to the men's toilets, then, still carrying Safiya, manoeuvre the buggy into the ladies' room.

"You'd better go after her," Karen says, as Aysha steps off the staircase. "Your brother can't follow you there."

Without speaking, Reshna hands her daughter to Aysha while she spreads a cloth over the changing platform and extracts a nappy and wipes from her changing bag. Aysha inhales the sweet scent of Safiya's breath, the faint aroma of baby shampoo and then the sharp tang of ammonia.

"I don't think she's dirty," she says, passing the baby back.

Reshna kisses the child and lays her flat. "No, very wet." She removes the offending nappy and puts in it a bag, then, as Aysha pulls faces to distract the wriggling Safiya, expertly fastens the dry one and snaps the poppers on the pink babygro. Only when the child is dressed and safely strapped into her buggy, does she turn to face Aysha.

"Where did you go?" she asks, switching to a rapid Bangla. "My husband says you are a bad girl, not good Muslim, that you reject your family and run off with men. But you look the same, you don't look like a bad girl to me."

"It's not true!" Aysha whispers urgently. "It's just because I want to go to university and not get married!"

"You don't want children?" Reshna bends to take off Safiya's mittens and to place a bottle of milk in her hands.

"No – oh, I don't know, maybe one day. There are other things I want to do first. There's nothing wrong with being a mother – if you and Maryam are happy, that's good, but it doesn't mean I have to do the same."

"When I was little, I liked to paint pictures," Reshna says. She speaks slowly now and Aysha can see from her eyes that memories have carried her far away. "I even won a big competition for children back home. I used to think I could be an artist, but it was just a dream. My parents could not afford to send me to art school. It's different here; children have chances."

"But *you* could still go – to evening classes at least!" Aysha blurts out, amazed that her shy sister-in-law has been hiding thwarted talents all this time.

"Who will look after the children?" Reshna replies flatly. "If there is time and money when they are older, it is my husband who should improve himself. Become a doctor or chemist, not the man who pushes the trolleys. No, you go to your university, Aysha, while you have the chance."

"I miss you and the children," Aysha says, "and I worry about Dad." Then, when Safiya wriggles round in her buggy to see why she's going nowhere, "You won't...?"

"I not tell," Reshna says in English, the change of language seeming to signal the end of the conversation. "Husband think he know, but I not tell."

"If you talk to Dad on his own, you could tell *him*. Let him know you've seen me and I'm all right. You needn't say where."

Reshna nods. "Dad not happy. My husband argue him. And Selim not come home. Mum keep cry. Is good father know daughter okay." She gathers up the contents of her changing bag and gives Aysha a quick, light hug before disappearing through the wash room door. Still clutching her present for Janet, Aysha stands staring at her own reflection in the harsh light of the fluorescent strip above the washroom mirror. She puts a hand up to touch her cheek and realises she didn't ask about her mum.

A few minutes later Karen comes in. "They've gone. I watched until I saw them go up to the platform."

All Aysha wants is to leave the shopping centre, go back to the flat, go *home*; but Karen insists they need a cup of coffee. She sits Aysha down in a quiet corner of the café and makes her recount her conversation with Reshna.

"I'm sure Mum has figured out I'm with you, even if she doesn't have the address," she says. "After all, you're the only friend of mine she knows."

"Then why hasn't she come after you?"

"There could be a lot of reasons. She's probably not sure where to start. She knows I'm okay – Jo said as much when she phoned – but if she called your mum and I *wasn't* with you, she'd feel really awkward having to admit she didn't know where I was. And now Sel's not come back. If people ask, Mum can palm them off with an excuse about family business, but with both of us gone there are bound to be questions. She won't like that." She pushes her hair out of her face and drains the remainder of her coffee, avoiding Karen's gaze. "If she believes what Mo tells her, Mum may not want me back."

"Don't say that – she's your *mum*. She's probably waiting for you to go home with your tail between your legs," Karen takes Aysha's hand in hers. "But you won't, will you? When you go back it's got to be on your terms."

They sit in silence for a while and Aysha realises she's thinking about Emily. When she herself left home, the other girl was contemplating the same step. She wonders if she'll ever know what happened next. If Emily moved into lodgings, did her father pursue her, or did *he* expect his daughter to crawl home, unable to manage alone. And that William Baines sounded like a man obsessed, the type who would turn into a stalker today. She still hasn't talked to Grace about the journal, but Derrick has invited her to dinner next weekend. Perhaps there will be an opportunity then.

37
Emily

Sunday 16 March 1902

Somehow, I have lost the habit of writing my journal every day. At home, however tired I felt, I would sit and write before sleeping, but for the past two weeks I have gone to bed early, nursing a troublesome cough. Kathleen thinks I caught cold that day when Baines spoke to me and says I should never have refused his big umbrella!

The sales girls complained about being asked to clear up after supper and Mrs Pegg has – reluctantly – taken on a scullery maid to wash the dishes and scour the pans. She is called Mildred, a scrawny creature of fourteen who won't get fatter on our leavings, as we boarders rarely fail to clean our plates. The relationship between the seamstresses – Lottie, Kathleen and myself – and Phyllis, Annie and Vera, the sales girls who serve the customers in their store, is a delicate one. *They* hold themselves superior, because they're obliged to dress smartly and have dealings with ladies of fashion; *we* make sure they remember that our work involves the greater skill.

Most of our exchanges are good-natured, except when it comes to someone exhausting another's hot water ration.

There is a rota for the use of the hip bath in the scullery, half-filled from the copper pans which are heated on the range. The whole operation involves scalding your legs and feet while your shoulders and back sprout goosebumps. I manage as best I can but, after going with Lottie the other week, I can see why she sets such store by her visits to Endell Street and the luxury of plentiful hot water in the public baths.

Now that she has Matilda to skivvy, Mrs Pegg joins us for cards after supper and we all play cribbage or beggar my neighbour for an hour. I find it hard to write my journal later: we are not allowed to use the gas lamps in our bedrooms after ten and candles are rationed. I foolishly used up my share too quickly and am reluctant to spend the few pennies left to me each week on buying more. Besides, Lottie and Kathleen like to lie in bed and gossip late into the night and urge me to leave open the door to my room so that I can join in, although Lottie always whispers when she tells Kathleen about Jimmy. Then they both start to giggle and I can't understand a word they say! Lottie met Jim's mother two weeks ago and apparently passed inspection. Lot says we would never have known her, she was so proper and polite!

If the girls see me with pen in hand, they ask me to read my journal aloud to them and I cannot write freely with *that* prospect in mind. But today is Sunday: Kathleen has gone to mass and Lottie and Jimmy are walking in Regent's Park. I have washed my stockings and underthings, brushed my skirt and polished my boots, so am at liberty to write about yesterday.

Not being needed to work on Saturday, I set out for Stepney and the square. I felt uneasy about visiting so soon after encountering Mr Baines, but Dr Reynolds had written to say that Elizabeth's baby has arrived. Her little girl was born two weeks early, but strong and well. I intended to visit Elizabeth, but to call on Pa and Daisy only if Baines was away.

Last week, Mr Smythe allowed us all some remnants of ribbon and lace left over from the bridal trousseau – pieces too small to be of use in the workshop – and I got a small length of cream ribbon and a half-yard of lace. I wrapped the ribbon in a piece of tissue as a gift for the child, reserving the lace as a present for Daisy.

The Metropolitan Line train took me to Aldgate and I then walked east along the Commercial Road, stopping from time to time to shelter under shop awnings and dodge the showers. Shopkeepers hastened to protect their wares from the rain and mothers scolded children for spoiling their clothes with jumping in puddles. It seemed more than a month since I walked in the opposite direction, struggling to carry my carpet bag and stopping every few yards to switch hands.

When I called at the Blacks' house, the door was opened by Elizabeth's mother, a pretty, anxious-looking woman of about fifty, who seemed overjoyed that I'd come to occupy her daughter for a while. Elizabeth was propped up in bed, surrounded by magazines, bonbon wrappers, snippets of embroidery and empty tea cups.

"Oh, Emily, this is too bad! I'm sure I asked Mama to clear all these things and change my sheets –" she smoothed her nightgown beneath her – "but I feel like I'm lying in sugar. I thought we would send Ernie straight to his grandmother when the baby came – it would not have hurt him to miss school for a few weeks – but it seems Richard's mother cannot take him yet. And so *my* Mama spends all her time on Ernie while I lie here abandoned. I suppose you want to see little Sylvia," she added. "The crib is behind the screen, but don't wake her or we'll have no peace at all."

I tiptoed behind the lacquered screen to where a wicker basket held a perfect little being, eyes scrunched up in sleep, sweet mouth working as if suckling still. I had never seen a child so small before and longed to unfurl the tiny fingers and feel them wrap around my own.

"She's beautiful – you must be very happy."

"Yes," Elizabeth agreed, "she's a little doll when she's sleeping, but I tell you, Emily, you'll want to block your ears when she's hungry. And most of the clothes I've made are much too big yet. I cannot dress her as I wish."

I gave her the ribbon and she said she would use it on a bonnet she's knitting.

"When are you allowed up?" I asked.

"Humph! Dr Reynolds would have me on my feet now. He talks about Indian women who give birth in the fields, then go straight back to harvesting their rice – as if that was an example for a civilised Englishwoman to follow! Besides," she whispered, "if Mama thinks I am well enough, she will hurry back to Brighton. She doesn't trust her housekeeper to run the hotel alone."

I sat a little longer, admiring Elizabeth's knitting and reading her magazines, then asked if Ernie might run next door for me to see if Mr Baines was at home.

"Oh, I see, you've had a tiff," she laughed. "Richard said he put his foot in it by talking of your wedding. That Mr Baines is just too naughty, giving secrets away. I hope you make him suffer!"

"Elizabeth, whatever Mr Baines has said, there has never

been any understanding between us. I wish only to avoid meeting him."

"There, Emily, don't get agitated – see, you've woken Sylvia – any woman can change her mind. I'm sure Ernie will run your errand – he's always skulking off to that girl Daisy. Ask Mama to step up here a minute before you go."

Ernie reported that both Pa and Baines were at the warehouse, so I slipped down the entry steps and found Daisy ironing in the kitchen. I hurried forward to give her a hug, but she stiffened and turned aside to place her flat iron on the trivet.

"I thought I'd get some lighter clothes while I'm here – in case it turns warm," I said, hurt by her indifference.

"Everything's in your room, miss."

I waited, hoping she would stop work and talk to me, but she picked up the other iron, spat on it and carried on smashing the life out of the sheets.

"I'll get my things, then," I said.

I went up to my bedroom, my *old room* as I found myself already thinking of it, wondering when I would sleep there again. Nothing was out of place, but my skin prickled; something was wrong. *He had been here!* There was the slightest of scents on the air, but I knew it for the stuff he uses on his moustache. As I selected some clothes – a nightdress, some bodices and a grey cotton skirt that had been Ma's – I was convinced that *he* had handled them, that he'd fingered my garments as they hung in the wardrobe or searched through my drawers. If he had followed me from work, for sure he'd have spied on me here! I pulled back the rug to see if the loose floorboard had been disturbed, though of course my journal is here, at Mrs Pegg's. The boards looked reassuringly dusty, but I plucked a couple of long hairs from my head and trapped them in the crack between the boards before replacing the rug. Finally, I found an old drawstring bag from school and folded the clothes I was taking inside.

"I've made you tea." Daisy slid the tray across the table towards me but still didn't raise her eyes from the ironing. "You're all right then, are you?" she muttered. "Made friends with the other girls in that place?"

"Yes, I'm fine." I thought she must be jealous of Kathleen and Lottie and wanted to tell her that no-one could ever be what she has been to me. But her pursed lips discouraged me and I just said brightly, "What about you, Dais? I hope Pa's not working you too hard."

"I manage," she shrugged.

I considered inviting her to visit me on her half day. We could window-shop the stores or walk in the park; I could take her back to Mrs Pegg's for tea. But, even as I thought it, I imagined Daisy eyeing the laundry lines critically, tutting at the disorder in the scullery and finding fault with my landlady's baking; as for the girls, they would think her sadly lacking in knowledge of the world. I said nothing.

"Am I to tell him?" Daisy asked.

"What? Tell who?"

"Tell your Pa you've been."

"Well – yes, I suppose so," I replied. Elizabeth was bound to mention that I came. "I'm not trying to avoid him, just Mr Baines, but I imagine they'll both be back soon."

She raised her eyes and gave me a long look, then switched flat irons again, without stopping to test the heat. There was a sudden smell of burning and I saw a shield-shaped scorch mark on a white shirt, which I was sure belonged to Baines.

"I brought you this," I ventured, handing her the lace. "I've missed you, Dais."

This time she stood still and let me embrace her.

"Him and your pa'll be back soon," she said. "You'd better go."

As I write now, I can't help thinking it an unsatisfactory visit. I expect Elizabeth's spirits will improve when she feels stronger, but motherhood seems only to have made her more selfish. Perhaps *I've* changed, but her concerns seem trivial to me. I shan't hurry back. My time off is precious and I don't know how I can see Pa alone, if I can't tell when William Baines will be there. Daisy's attitude puzzles and disappoints me most though: we've been through so much and I thought we were friends.

Thursday 27 March 1902

Tomorrow being Good Friday, the store will be closed. The wages are sent up early and Arthur Smythe calls each of us individually to receive our envelopes. A few of the machinists are wanted Saturday, but most are not and, even though the extra money would be welcome, the prospect of an extended weekend puts us all in a holiday mood. Kathleen has been invited to spend Easter Day with an Irish family at the church she attends and Lottie's convinced there must be a young man somewhere in the case for her to be so keen. Kathy nods straight-faced, admitting that the O'Connors do have a son, Patrick – before telling us that he's only nine years old!

"I'm going home to see my mum on Sunday," Lottie says. "Thought I ought to put in an appearance at St Benet's so they'll know who I am when it comes to reading the banns."

Lottie's family home in Kentish Town is not so very far from

Oxford Street – no further than Stepney, I should say – and I have often wondered why she decided to live in lodgings. She tells me her mother is a widow and occupies rooms above a butcher's shop. There are two younger sisters – twins – living at home. "Mrs Pegg's might not have all the home comforts you were used to, Emmie," Lottie adds, "but it's luxury for me. No Lizzie or Pammy to borrow my clothes or to spy on Jimmy and me, and a meal on the table each evening!"

She's known Jimmy over a year, since they both started at Fenton's when the store opened last spring. They've only been walking out together these past few months, but that was because Lottie kept him waiting. He hasn't exactly proposed, but Lot says it's as if he's skipped that bit, since he's always referring to where they'll live when they're wed and the shop of their own they will open some day. Now, she gives me a quick, furtive glance as she wraps her shawl round her shoulders, then says in an off-hand way, "You can come if you like, Emily, but you must take us as you find us."

I'm not sure what to say. I should go to my father, but Baines is certain to be at home. A few days ago, Mr Fenton stopped to tell me that Pa had visited Mrs Fenton at the Watney Market shop and enquired after me. "I'm told you're a good worker, Emily, and I don't want to lose you," he said, "but I don't want to come between you and your father. If you decide not to carry on, I'll understand. I know this is not the life you were born to."

It's what the other girls expect; even though I do the same work as them and now share lodgings with Lottie and Kathleen, they don't forget that my pa is in business and Mr Fenton's daughter is my friend. I don't want Lottie to think I am too grand for her and look down on her home. Perhaps I did hold myself superior at first. I went home each night to a comfortable house, my meals cooked and my laundry done for me – I had choices the other girls did not. Pa was convinced work was a whim I'd grow tired of, and he might have been right were it not for William Baines. Life here *is* harder than I expected. But I *won't* go back for Baines to act as if he has rights over me, as if I'm some plaything for his amusement, not even for my father's sake. I'd willingly keep Daisy company this weekend, had she not treated me so coldly two weeks ago. I've wept to think she no longer loves me and I cannot bear to be rejected again. Perhaps Lottie is right: if she *has* found a new admirer, Daisy may not want to admit that she has forgotten my brother already. No, I must accept that my life has changed and look for friendship among my workmates here.

"Thank you," I tell Lottie. "I'd like to come, if you're sure your mother won't mind."

"You will?" Her pale face lights with pleasure. "We should find a sweetheart for *you*, Emmie, take your mind off that horrid Baines person. What d'you say I ask Jimmy if he knows of a nice boy?"

I shake my head vigorously. Perhaps I *am* still guilty of thinking myself above my fellows, but I cannot imagine walking out with a friend of Jimmy's or enjoying the sort of familiarity Lottie and some of the others allow their admirers. I know all men do not behave like William Baines, but I can't help seeing each compliment, every little intimacy, as a step on the road to one end. My own parents married young because my mother was pregnant; Ma even questioned Daisy how far her friendship with Charlie had gone. I was shocked at the time, but William Baines has driven both ignorance and innocence away. Lottie looks about to try to make me change my mind, but there is a sudden shout from the other end of the workroom. Doris is leaning over

Arthur Smythe's table and spitting out fury.

"Yer can't do this! Who told yer? I can still do my job – I don't even show – how am I s'posed to support meself now?"

Arthur brushes a thread from his lapel and looks distastefully at Doris through narrowed eyes.

"You should have thought of that before you got yourself in that state. It's company policy. Customers don't want the likes of you stitching their clothes. There's a half-crown extra in your envelope in lieu of notice and that's more than you deserve."

Doris snatches her wages angrily and pushes past us to the staircase. "What you lookin' at?" she hisses. Her pimpled face is a picture of misery, but no-one dares to offer comfort. Her friend Bella turns on Lily who has flattened herself against the wall. Kathleen crosses herself and looks down.

"It were you, weren't it?" Bella accuses Lily. "You told him Dorrie was knocked up."

"What if I did?" the other girl shrugs. "She's had it coming a long time. You can't tell me blokes buy her drinks for the pleasure of her conversation."

Bella reaches out and pulls Lily by the hair and for a moment I think they are actually going to fight, but Arthur Smythe interposes himself between them. He looks meaningfully at Lottie and gestures towards me and Kathy.

"Come on girls, we're no part of this," Lot says, pulling my arm, and I let myself be led trembling down the stairs. There is no sign of Doris in the street. I think of the women outside the music hall and wonder what will become of her.

38
Aysha

Sunday 17 March 2002

Derrick gets up to clear their dinner plates away. Aysha starts to rise too, but Grace rests a detaining hand on her arm, saying, "When I have cooked, it's my son's job to clear away."

"But I've done nothing to help," Aysha protests.

"You're a guest," Grace replies, "and what's more a guest who has something on her mind."

On this second visit to Derrick's home, dinner has been a spicy Caribbean fish stew with rice, and once more, the flavoursome food and the rainbow appearance of both the flat and Grace herself have contributed to a wonderful sense of occasion.

"What's Derrick said?" she asks, raising an eyebrow.

"Not me," he grins, learning round the door frame. "Mum always knows how people feel."

Grace pats her hand. "Don't be offended, sweetheart, it's written all over you. You're not worried about accepting this York offer, are you?"

Aysha shakes her head. The meal has been something of a celebration. Friday evening, Janet had handed her a long white envelope, delivered after she and Karen had left for college that morning. Aysha's hands had trembled as she ripped the seal and rapidly scanned the letter inside to find she had been offered a place on the York joint honours course, dependent on her achieving AAB at A Level. One last hurdle and she could be there! Karen and Janet clearly believed her gaining these grades was a foregone conclusion and even started planning the wardrobe of warm clothing they thought she would need *up north.* Aysha, realising the future now depended on her alone, panicked, convinced she wouldn't be good enough. A day's reflection has calmed her: as Jo and Andy have said, it's just a matter of staying on track.

"No, not that," she tells Grace. "When I was here before, you made a really strange comment about someone watching over me. A presence, you said. I've been waiting to ask you... I've been really wondering about that."

Grace looks uncharacteristically self-conscious. "Sometimes I get these feelings about people," she says, "but I didn't mean to disturb you."

Aysha pushes back her hair earnestly. "I wasn't disturbed. I wanted to tell you who I thought it might be."

Both of them glance around for Derrick, remembering that he had put an end to the conversation, but he just shrugs his acceptance. Aysha begins to tell Grace about finding the journal, about the new entries that have continued to appear, about Emily's life and how close she feels to the other girl. She's hesitant at first, but then the story takes over and Grace listens intently.

"I didn't want to leave it behind," she says, "but I thought that if I took the journal out of the room, Emily might never find it."

Derrick hovers at the kitchen door, then drifts back to

the table, tea towel in hand, shaking his head as if all these conundrums are too much for him.

"I think I understand the connection between you," Grace says. "It sounds like Emily was a remarkable young woman who was badly let down by her father. And you, like her, have lacked the family support you need."

Although this is true, Aysha finds it hard to admit her family's failings to outsiders, even to Grace, whom she really admires; or perhaps especially to Grace, who has such high standards of parenthood.

"Dad would support me, if he were stronger."

"No doubt. And Emily's troubles would not have happened if her mother hadn't died." Grace's gaze lights on the space above Aysha's shoulder. "To a child, a parent's death is the ultimate desertion. But tell me, Aysha, why does your father defer to your brother so much?"

"To Mo? Well, he acts like *he's* the older generation, more traditional than they are, or Dad is, anyway. It was his decision to marry a girl from back home."

"Your father kicked the traces, then, coming to the UK?"

"I don't really know much about his early life. He came here as a student and became an engineer. He's always been interested in education."

"Your brother turned his back on that?"

"Not exactly. He's educated too." She wonders what Grace intends by making her articulate the relationships in her family and think them through. "Dad's older than Mum, by about twelve years. He had a heart attack nine years ago and had to give up work. Sel and I were still at primary school and Mum was pregnant with Abdul. They'd spent most of their savings on my sister's wedding the year before. Mo wanted to study pharmacy – he was in the middle of his A levels when Dad nearly died. He passed chemistry, but he missed some exams for biology and maths. He could have taken them again the next year, but he started working at the hospital and somehow it never happened."

She's never fully understood why Mo persisted in his manual job when there was the chance of returning to school and qualifying for a profession, or why he elected to constrain himself further with marriage and a family. Somehow, the moral standing he gained by making this sacrifice had become more important to him than a career.

"Guilt and a sense of obligation are powerful motives," Grace says, "but it sounds like it was your brother's choice to continue on this path."

"Mo's a good father," she says. "It can't be easy watching me get the chances he missed."

"It's what parents do all the time."

Aysha is silent. Maybe Grace has other ambitions too.

"What's this to do with the journal?" Derrick asks.

"I imagine Emily's father felt guilt at the deaths of his wife and son and somehow let himself to fall under an obligation to an unscrupulous man," Grace explained. "Like Aysha, Emily suffered for it."

Aysha is uncomfortable that Grace puts Mo as on a par with William Baines, but she doesn't want to argue. "I wish I could show you her writing," she says. "It should've been Emily going to university. I'm sure her sewing was good too, but she deserved a proper education."

Derrick asks, "Have you tried to find out what happened to her?"

"The next census isn't released until 2011."

"You could try local churches," Grace says. "Look at parish records and graves."

"It will have to be after my exams; I don't have time just now. Would you come with me, Grace? I feel awkward walking into a church."

"Sure, darling," Grace replies, "I'll come if I'm able."

"This presence – whatever – can you still see it?"

Grace observes her steadily. "No," she says, "not at the moment. Perhaps you have enough live protectors now." She glances at her watch. "You'll have to excuse me for an hour or so. I've two old ladies to put to bed tonight. I'll drop you back at Limehouse, Aysha, after I've finished my calls."

She leaves the room for a few minutes, then reappears wearing a white overall over her purple top and with her hair tamed. "Be good, children," she smiles.

Aysha looks nervously at Derrick. For the first time they are together, indoors, totally alone.

Derrick up-ends the washing-up bowl and balances the last plate precariously on the drainer. Laughing, Aysha retrieves the tea-towel."That one's going to fall," she tells him. "I'll dry, you put them away." When the last utensil is safely stashed, Aysha picks up a cloth to wipe the bench. Derrick stands close behind, wrapping his arms around her and dropping a kiss on the top of her head. She turns and tilts her face towards him, then stands on tiptoe to reach up and stroke his cheek.

"I'm sure you grow overnight."

"I can't help it." He shrugs his shoulders in an exaggerated gesture. "Hang on," he adds, sweeping the spice jars on the kitchen worktop to one side. He places his broad hands on either side of her waist, then swings her up onto the worktop. "Now you're nearer my height."

Aysha smiles, but her feet dangle in mid-air like a puppet's and she's not used to their faces being on the same level. Derrick still has his hands around her middle and she's conscious of his thumbs resting between her ribs, just beneath the line of her bra. He leans in to kiss her and the thumbs move almost imperceptibly upwards. Her own body's responses take her by surprise: she feels hollow, needy. Derrick's left hand moves to support the back of her head as the kiss becomes more intense and the thumb on his right hand gently kneads her breast. She gives a little gasp, a sudden intake of breath, and feels him draw her bottom lip into his mouth. His tongue plays with hers, darting in and out of her parted lips, and she strains forward.

For a moment he doesn't exhale; his eyes widen but he stands motionless, as if she were a wild creature who dared to take food from his hand. Then his breathing quickens, he presses his lips firmly over hers and his right hand slips down beneath her bottom, lifting her towards him. As his hesitant, teasing tongue becomes an urgent probe, a sudden image comes into her head – of William Baines, thrusting Emily onto the bed and forcing his tongue down her throat as he struggles to pull up her skirts. She gags and pushes Derrick away, slipping awkwardly to the floor and scraping her back on the worktop edge.

"Careful, you'll hurt yourself," he protests.

"I can't do it."

"Do what?" Derrick asks. "We were only kissing. I thought you liked it, but you just had to say."

She crosses to the sink and draws a cup of water, trying to

steady herself.

"I did, at first. Then you scared me."

"Scared?" He sounds incredulous. "What do you think I am, Aysh? I wasn't going to hurt you. I can stop, you know."

She can't answer. She grasps the bench to stop the room spinning.

"It doesn't feel right, in your mum's kitchen, the moment she goes out."

"Well, we don't have much choice," he mumbles. "It's not like we can go to Karen's place."

"Del, I'm sorry. I didn't... I've never..."

"Yeah, well, it's probably my fault."

She reaches out to touch his hand, but he steps back. He looks crushed, but there's no way she can explain that she was thinking of Emily and Baines – she'd hate him to feel that the journal is coming between them. When his mum returns the two of them are sitting apart on the sofa, Aysha reading and Derrick watching football on TV. He jumps up to fetch her coat, but doesn't offer to go with them in the car when Grace drives her to Limehouse. She knows his mother will pick up the atmosphere, so, scared of being asked what's wrong, she packs the short journey with questions about the elderly clients Grace has just attended.

Karen and her dad Mike are also watching the match, although Karen does have a token business studies text book balanced on her knee. Janet is ironing at the other end of the room.

"Give me five," Karen says, looking up. "We're in extra time."

Aysha nods and goes to the bedroom. When Karen comes in a few minutes later, she has already undressed and is sitting on the camp bed, plaiting her hair.

"Not coming back through?" Karen asks.

She shakes her head dumbly.

"What's up?"

"I've spoilt everything."

Words spill from her – incoherently at first – but her friend gets the gist.

"So, you backed off. Del'll get over it."

Aysha's not sure.

"Kas – you and Paul – have you ever...?"

"Slept with him? No way. I'm gonna dump him before I go to uni. He's nice enough to go out with, but he thinks too much of himself."

"So, you've never...?"

Karen pulls a face and starts to pick at a chip on her pink varnished nails. "Remember year nine? When I really went off the rails?"

When they were fourteen, there had been a time – perhaps a term or so – when they'd drifted apart. Karen had discovered boys, and with her long blonde hair, laughing blue eyes and newly rounded figure, boys had discovered her.

"Josh Smedley," she says quietly. "We had sex in his bedroom when his mum was at work. He didn't know what he was doing and the condom split. Thank God I had the sense to tell mum and she took me to the doctor's for the morning after pill."

"I didn't know."

"I didn't want you to. I needed to be your friend again. I realised I'd never be as clever as you, but I knew I could be *something*, if I didn't mess up." Karen stretches out a hand, across the aisle between their beds and Aysha grasps it.

"Do you think Derrick...?"

Karen considers. "He hasn't been out with anyone else at college, but we didn't know him before. Still, think how close Del is to his mum. He's got no time for his father for abandoning her. Grace'll have taught him to respect women all right. Look, Aysh, it's never wrong to say no to something you're not comfortable with. I reckon Del was upset because you didn't trust him, not because you said no."

Aysha crawls into bed and pulls the duvet over head. She knows Karen means to make her feel better, but she feels hopelessly ignorant and ill-prepared to deal with the conflicting emotions and desires that this evening has aroused.

~

Classes end at midday and the students spill haphazardly across the pavement, discharged into the spring sunshine. Two weeks' holiday before their last term in college, and not much longer before exams begin! Aysha's rucksack is full to bursting, weighed down with books from the college library. She's not leaving anything to chance; she can't afford to slip up. She has given up two other offers in favour of York. Cardiff required similar grades, but the Southampton offer had been lower and would have been a safer bet. Karen has a place to read Business Studies at Kingston, while Derrick is holding two offers for Primary Education degrees – at Leeds and Roehampton. Neither university has called him for interview, but both have upcoming open days. Aysha worries that he has taken on too many other commitments. His driving test is scheduled for next Thursday, he still works three or four evenings in the supermarket each week, and he's started coaching football for a local boys' team.

They'd spoken of being able to spend some weekends together next year, if she is studying at York and he at Leeds, but now he seems to be hesitating over making up his mind. He says he wants to wait until the open days, but Aysha can't help wondering if doubts about their relationship are behind his uncertainty. Outside college, they see each other Wednesday evenings and Sundays, but since that evening in his flat, there's been an unspoken agreement not to spend too much time alone together, as if each is nervous of making any move that would unbalance a fragile status quo. He says he'll call her and gives her a quick peck on the cheek before heading off across the park.

There's nothing she can do; they both need a little time and space and with exam pressures looming, neither comes easily. Derrick isn't her only concern: somehow, she needs to speak to Dad about her fees. Since meeting Reshna, she's been tormented by the thought that *she* has caused the friction between him and Mo, but she needs to know if he will help.

She's thought of going to the square, waiting in the gardens and watching until Mo and Mum are out; she could slip into the basement and watch from the window of Maud and Bert's flat. Karen and Derrick were horrified when she mentioned the idea, sure that she'd be spotted and coerced into the house. Twice this week, she's phoned Maud and Bert but got no answer: not worrying in itself – Bert's notoriously deaf and plays the TV too loud and Maud can't always hear from the kitchen – but Aysha relies on the old couple being able to inform her of any changes at home.

That evening, she's debating whether to try the old couple's number again when the phone rings and Janet hands her the receiver. Derrick usually calls on her mobile; besides, he's working tonight. It must be Maud: who else knows she's here?

"Aysha, it's Grace, darling. Tell me, what is the number of your parents' house?"

Aysha answers *eleven* automatically, then adds, "Why?"

"And the couple in the basement, the ones you said you used to visit – they live at 11A?"

"Yes, but..."

"You understand what I am telling you is confidential, darling? Putting my job on the line, you could say."

"I don't understand."

"Just listen, sweetheart. The old man is my new client. He's had a spell in hospital after a fall and was discharged today with a care package. Which is where I come in – I've just come from putting him to bed."

"Is he okay? I've been trying to phone them." Maud was probably visiting him when she called. Aysha doesn't like to think of the old woman coming back late to the empty flat.

"No bones broken, just bruising, but none too steady on his feet. I've been trying to persuade his wife to move some of the furniture."

Aysha visualises the cramped basement flat with its small side tables loaded with photo frames and the numerous rugs and runners on top of the carpet: Grace will need all her powers of persuasion to make any changes there.

"I wish I could help," she says. "Did you tell them you knew me?"

"You know me, darling, I like to talk to my old folk. They asked if I had a family and I said I have a son at college. They said their son lives in Australia and that the only person they used to see was the young Asian girl who lived upstairs. She went to college too, but she'd left home some weeks ago because of family problems. It was only then I realised where I was – in the house where you lived."

Bert and Maud must feel she's abandoned them. "Give them my love please," she says.

"I can do better than that. I'm on the bedtime rota at the weekend so I can take you with me. It'll be getting dark by then and your folk won't see a thing."

It's more than six weeks since Aysha was in the square and she's still scared of being spotted, but Grace is right: there's little chance she'll be noticed. By eight o'clock, Mum will have the curtains closed and, if Mo is working the night shift, he'll already have left. She really wants to see how Bert and Maud are, but perhaps she can learn something of her family too. Mum and Maud do no more than nod to each other, but the old couple have little to do except look out of their window and Maud doesn't miss much. If there have been visitors, if the usual car has collected Dad for the day centre, she will know.

She wonders what Grace had meant by saying that telling Aysha about Bert was more than her job's worth. Presumably, she's not allowed to discuss clients with other people, which means she probably shouldn't be taking Aysha into Maud and Bert's home, even though they know her.

"Are you sure it's okay, Grace? I don't want to get you in trouble."

"You want to see them, don't you?" Grace replies. "Maybe hear about your father? We'll make it Sunday. I'll be at church in the morning for the Easter service, but come and eat later. I'll tell Derrick to collect you."

She and Derrick haven't arranged when they'll see each other next and Aysha feels awkward accepting the invitation without speaking to him first. But Grace is like an elemental force; she doesn't suffer resistance. Aysha gives in and says she'll come.

~

She wakes to the sound of rustling paper on Sunday. Karen hasn't outgrown an Easter egg and is tucking into chocolate soon after seven.

"Got to start early or I won't be ready for lunch at Nan's – she always cooks for the whole family at Easter." She tosses Aysha a caramel from the centre of her egg. "Sure you don't want to come? She won't mind."

But Derrick rang yesterday to ask her to go to Greenwich. They've wanted to go back ever since their visit at half-term: if it rains they can do the museums this time, he said. She asked if his mum mentioned taking her to the square.

"Yeah," he laughed. "She's really pleased with herself."

When he calls for Aysha at nine-thirty, Karen and her family are just leaving too.

"Not going by river bus, are you?" Karen asks, glancing at the dark clouds massing across a darkening sky.

"No, taking the train," Derrick says, then turns to Aysha. "If I pass my test, Mum's offered to match the money I've saved towards my car. It won't be anything flash, but we'll be able to go further afield after the exams."

Karen catches Aysha's eye. There you are, she seems to be saying, does that answer your question? If Derrick is planning summer jaunts, he must think they have a future.

Greenwich is a dream for the history lover and Aysha could

willingly spend more time in the Queen's House, the home built by the extravagant Charles I for his wife, but Derrick insists they need time for the Observatory.

"I remember coming here with school," he says, "and there's something I want to do."

They stand either side of the Greenwich meridian so that he can step across half the world to reach her.

Grace is enfolded in a large striped apron when they get home. The emerald jacket she has worn to church hangs on a chair, but her hair is still wrapped in the matching turban.

"Roast lamb, very traditional," she says, smiling at them, "but I've added a few extra spices."

They eat around five-thirty. Aysha expected to feel awkward, after her last time in the flat, but time goes quickly and she's surprised when Grace goes to change her clothes for her evening's work.

"Are you okay about this?" Derrick asks.

"Going back to the square? Yeah – sort of excited, but sad as well. Being so near my family and not seeing them."

"Well, don't be tempted to go knocking at their door, not till you know they've changed their minds. But, Aysh, there's something I've been meaning to tell you: I'm holding onto the Leeds offer."

She reaches out quickly and grasps his hand. They start to move towards each other then stop.

"I'm sorry about, you know, the other week," he says.

"No, I'm sorry. I overreacted."

"Ready, sweetheart?" Grace says, opening the door from the hallway. "Not interrupting anything, am I?" They blush and laugh and Aysha's still looking back when she picks up her jacket and follows Grace.

"Nice to see you both friends," Grace says, as they reach the main door of the block. She points her car key ahead of her and they make a dash for the little blue Fiesta. The rain that threatened all day has settled to a persistent steady stream. Traffic lights reflect fuzzily on the dark wet streets and the carriages of the Docklands trains light the sky as they stop and start overhead. Aysha finds herself counting the junctions; almost too soon, Grace pulls up in the middle of the high road, waiting for a gap in the traffic to make her turn.

They stop across the street from Aysha's house, parking beside the railings which surround the gardens at the heart of the square. Sel's red Peugeot is parked outside number eleven. For a moment she thinks he must be back, then realises that the car hasn't moved since he left.

"My brother's car," she says, "the one in Bangladesh."

"I wonder your elder brother doesn't use it," Grace comments.

But Mo has never taken his test.

The curtains to both ground and first floor windows are closed. Only her own top-floor window is uncovered, its unlit panes throwing back the glare of the street lamp. She feels a pang of guilt at her abandonment of the room and all the things contained there – Reshna's kameez, bangles from Maryam, drawings done by the boys. Emily's journal is there too, under her floorboards, perhaps with new entries waiting to be read.

"Shall I tell them you're here first or do you want to go straight in?" Grace asks.

Aysha shivers, suddenly unwilling to sit in the car alone. "I'll come. I don't think they'll mind."

"Good," Grace says. "You can talk to the old lady while I attend to Bert."

Maud peers out suspiciously on seeing two figures, then she opens the door wider to give light from the hall and her lines around her mouth draw together in a smile. Her face resembles a weather map on a particularly windy day.

"Aysha, love, you're a sight for tired old eyes. This lady said she knew you but I didn't think you'd come."

She looks worn out, Aysha thinks. Bert sits in his armchair, nodding cheerfully at them; the small side table holds the remains of his supper. A bruise over the old man's left eye is in the process of turning from brown to yellow.

"Anyone'd think I beat him up," Maud says, "but he slipped in the bathroom and hit his head on the sink."

"Daft old bugger, ain't I?" Bert laughs.

Grace moves the table to one side and places his walking frame in front of the chair. "Let's see you into the bathroom, Bert," she says, "then we'll get you ready for bed. Aysha, why don't you make Maud a cup of tea."

Aysha takes the hint, realising that Bert will be more comfortable without her looking on. It must be hard; the couple have always been fiercely independent. She picks up Bert's plate and follows Maud into the little kitchenette.

"She's a good one, that Grace," the old woman comments. "Some of them carers are in and out before you know they've been, but she's got time for you. How do you know her, love?"

"I'm friends with her son, at college."

Maud looks at her shrewdly. "Good friends, eh? Don't s'pose that goes down well with your mum and that brother of yourn. You going up to see them?"

Aysha shrugs then shakes her head. She thinks of Abdul, Ibrahim and Safiya in the house upstairs.

"Don't worry, we won't tell anyone you've been."

"Maud," Aysha says, anxiously, "you mustn't mention it to any of the other carers either. Grace could get into trouble for bringing me here when she's working."

"All right, enough said. Can't be helped if the pair of you comes to the door at the same time, can it?" The old woman hands her the teapot. "They wouldn't've let Bert home if we didn't have carers. We'd rather manage ourselves, but well, if that Grace can bring you to see us once in a while, it's an ill wind as they say."

Aysha wonders if Maud had called upstairs when Bert fell, but she hesitates to put the question, uncertain what help Mum or Reshna could have given.

"Have you seen anything of my dad?" she asks instead.

"Not much," Maud replies. Your sister came in her big car on Friday and it looked like she took him and your mum out for the day – them and the boy, your little brother, ain't he? Your other one," she adds, with the sniff Aysha knows she reserves for Mo, "keeps his head down. Doesn't give no-one the time of day. I don't doubt he's a good father, I see him taking his boy and the baby out in the pushchair, but I wouldn't be that little wife of his for all the tea in China. He only has to look at her and she jumps."

39
Emily

Saturday 12 April 1902

What sort of day is it, Emily?

You always wanted to know the weather, even in those last few months when you were too weak to leave your bed. Well, today the sky is crossed by swiftly moving clouds and the wind comes in great gusts – the sort of day that makes children run wild at playtime, sets the dogs in the square barking and sends Mabel and her grown kittens leaping up the nearest tree. Torn branches litter the ground and the wind tosses the daffodils beside the footpath, but the daisies peeping through the grass are unharmed and you sleep quietly two yards beneath my feet. I am here alone. My friends Lottie and Kathleen offered to come with me. They are nice girls, decent and hard-working, but I don't want to share you with anyone. Is it only a year since Daisy and I raced back from the market and learned from the doctor's sorrowing face that it was already too late? I was just a girl, not long out of school, but in twelve months I have seen Pa reduced to helpless grief, drowning his sorrow in spirits, unable to protect me or his business from an unscrupulous man's scheming. I can't blame him for needing you so much – I've missed your love and guidance every day – but you can't have wanted him to grieve like this. Perhaps you think me unfeeling, turning my back on him and on home? I know my present life is not the one you chose for me, but that path is no longer open. You will say I should have returned to my grandparents perhaps, but when I realised there was ill-feeling between them and my father, I feared to anger him more. I hoped I could help him to free himself of Baines, but I know now it is not within my power. All I can do is keep myself apart from that man. I have health, intelligence and some skills; it must be possible to make my own way. If only you could tell me you approve what I've done, but your grave is as inscrutable as ever, the headstone telling the barest facts of your life: Maria Jane Watts, beloved wife and mother, 1864-1901.

The stone urn on her grave is filled with heavy white lilies; Pa has already been here. I've brought a little pot of yellow pansies with me, but the wind threatens to blow them away. Ma always liked to plant pansies in our window boxes so she could see their cheerful faces from the house, brightening the cold spring days. I pick a large stone from the ground at my feet and start to scrape some earth away so that I can sink the pot into the soil, but it is slow work. After a while, I become aware that the sound of stone on earth has been joined by the crunching of feet on gravel and that something or someone is sheltering me from the worst of the wind. I look round in alarm, and then relief.

"Emily?"

"Dr Reynolds! Oh, I can't tell you how glad I am to see you."

The doctor produces a penknife and kneels by my side, helping to loosen the soil with his blade. For several minutes neither of us speaks, but we concentrate on the task at hand; then, when my pot is securely anchored, he makes another hole with the knife, takes a root of primrose from inside his overcoat and firms it in. I feel a large drop of rain fall on my head.

"I meant to bring water," Dr Reynolds says, getting up and surveying the darkening sky, "but I think the heavens will provide. Shall we go inside, Emily?"

The church interior is cool, dry and full of light from the high windows above the wide rounded arches. As we stand together beside the font, I realise that I don't mind sharing my memories with this good man. Dr Reynolds grasps both my hands in his and looks at me keenly.

"Forgive me, Emily," he says, letting me go at last, "but you are so like Maria and I need to know that you are well. Have you seen your father?"

"No," I say, shaking my head. "You will remember, Dr Reynolds, that before I left home a rumour was spread concerning a wedding. It was an untruth, intended to put pressure on me, to make me feel I had no other choice. That situation... has not changed. But I will be glad if you can give me news of Pa."

I watch as the many questions he does not ask describe their traces on his face; he bows his head and closes his eyes for some seconds before replying.

"I do not see him as frequently as before. Since your... since Maria died, he avoids all company except that of... his business partner. I'm not talking of formal invitations, no-one would expect that, but of everyday neighbourliness. He did have cause to call on me recently, though, being troubled by a persistent cough."

"Do you think..." I hesitate, not wishing to put my thoughts into words, "do you think he takes too much strong drink?"

"Not so much that he cannot work; I hear he keeps long

hours at the warehouse."

"Mr Baines encouraged the drinking. He means to take Pa's business for himself."

"A doctor may not discuss all he hears, but I fear you may be right," he says. "I never saw this coming. He appeared a decent enough young man, a bit brash no doubt, but hard-working and eager to please."

He seems unwilling to say more about Pa and I have no wish to debate William Baines' character.

"Talk to me about Ma," I beg. "You were one of her oldest friends, were you not?"

"Maria first came to see me before Charlie was born," he says, "when your father brought her to the square. Mr Watts senior, your great-grandfather, had recently passed away."

"Did you know then... about her first baby, the one who died so young?"

"Of course," he nods. "Your mother was frightened, afraid she would lose this baby too. I promised to do everything I could to make the pregnancy safe."

He turns away from me a moment and reaches into a pocket. I see him pull out a handkerchief and wipe his eye. "I had... great affection for your mother, Emily."

"She always valued your friendship," I say, but I know that's not what he means.

"I was nearing forty, well on the way to the crusty old bachelor you see now, when I met Maria and realised the only woman I would ever love was half my age, married to another man and expecting his child. Not only that, she and your father idolised each other."

I don't know what to say. Here is a man who cared for

my mother selflessly, offering friendship and support where he couldn't give love and knowing better than anyone that the disease which afflicted her was beyond his power to cure. How he must have suffered! I put my hand into his and we sit together in the back pew and watch as a sudden ray of sunshine lights up the altar. The shower is over.

"If you see my father *alone*, tell him I am well," I say.

"I will. And if you ever need help, Emily, do not forget you have a friend."

40
Aysha

May 2002

Amazingly, the first week of exams is over. Aysha has two more next week; the rest are after the half-term break. At first she'd felt a kind of suppressed elation at finally reaching the summation of nearly two years' work, but A levels are a drawn-out tournament, not a one-day event, and sustaining motivation is hard.

Both Karen and Janet insist she takes time to relax: Janet, because she's read an article about helping teenagers organise their revision; Karen, because she says Aysha will make her feel nervous if she doesn't let up.

Derrick is working hard too; he's still got his supermarket job, so has precious little spare time. All in a good cause, he says; he passed his driving test and hopes to buy a car before starting uni. He drove the Fiesta to Limehouse and took both Karen and Aysha out soon after passing, but Grace needs her car for work most evenings and he wants to be able to afford his own.

Aysha has visited Maud and Bert three times in all, but Bert's care plan was a consequence of his hospital discharge and now that he has recovered some mobility, carer visits are no longer funded. Grace has offered to drop her at the flat while she makes her other bedtime calls, but the evenings are lighter, curtains stay open later and Aysha's not confident of remaining unseen. Being in the basement, has been both comforting and frustrating, knowing that family life is going on as normal, upstairs. At nine months, Safiya is probably crawling; Ibrahim is nearly three and due to start nursery soon. She'd asked Maud if she'd seen Reshna and the children.

"What? The little mother?" Maud had said. "Yes, I see her and the kiddies going in and out, but your mum or your brother's with her as a rule. Don't she know anyone her own age, now you've gone?"

There's a crèche at the college. Reshna could go to classes to improve her English and take the children there: she'd make friends that way. Aysha mentioned it to Mo once, but he'd just looked puzzled. There was no need, he'd said, he or Mum could speak for her. Aysha wonders if he's afraid of letting her go.

Maud could give her no news of Dad. Those old men in hats had visited, she said, but there'd been no ambulances, no doctor's car; nothing to worry about.

"Looks like they've washed their hands of you, love," she said. "I don't like to say it, but I reckon you're better off where you are."

At one o'clock, the history students linger outside college, still picking over the bones of their exam paper, reluctant to let each other go. Billie even quizzes Wahida about which questions she chose and what answers she gave.

"Well, that's me done for," Billie says after Wahida elaborately reconstructs an essay she has just written. "I didn't put any of that."

Aysha won't be drawn. She'll admit to what questions she

chose, but nothing more; she's quietly confident, having done all she can; there's nothing more to be said.

"Fancy coming Pizza Hut?" Billie asks. "We can get the lunchtime deal if we hurry."

Derrick can't make it – he's starts work at three and needs to go home first to change – but he persuades Aysha to go, and she, Karen, Billie and a couple of others set out. Pizza Hut is crowded with local office staff all busy thanking God it's Friday – it seems to be somebody's birthday – and apparently determined to consume their money's worth. Billie and Karen immediately decide to take them on, piling everyone's plate with more salad and pizza slices than they can possibly eat. An elderly couple sharing a platter by the window throw both groups disapproving looks, but the staff don't seem to care. Aysha feels as if just for a moment she has stepped out of time, poised precisely between the exams completed and those still to come, between the past, known life and the unwritten future. At last they pool resources and call for the bill.

Karen texts Janet to tell her they won't want dinner tonight, but Aysha has no reason to look at her phone until ten o'clock, when Derrick sends a good night message after finishing his shift. Her screen shows several missed calls from the afternoon and the number is Maud and Bert's. Aysha is in an anguish of indecision.

"Is it too late to ring?" she asks Karen. "Something must be wrong for them to keep calling. Why didn't I hear it?"

"I'm not surprised with the noise in that place," Karen says, "but if you're going to phone, do it now. They're probably expecting you to ring back."

"No, love, we're not in bed," Maud reassures her, "just watching the news and 'aving our cocoa."

"Bert's all right then?" she asks.

"As right as 'e'll ever be. It's not us, love, it's your dad. They've taken 'im to the 'ospital."

One question trips over another, but Aysha is forced to slow down and allow Maud to tell the story at her own pace. In the morning she'd seen the woman with the big car – Maryam, Aysha supposes – come and take her mother out. Later, when she and Bert were sharing a can of tomato soup, there was such a knocking at the door she'd nearly had a fit, and there she was, the little mother, with the baby grizzling in her arms and the toddler clinging round her leg.

"Please. You make phone, talk hospital?" Reshna had said. "Husband father ill."

Then she had banged her fist on her heart, Maud explained, and made it go boom, boom, boom. "With your mum and your brother both out, she didn't know what to do, poor thing. She couldn't talk sense on the phone, anyway."

"My dad... did you see him?"

"I saw the ambulance men wheel 'im out in a chair. He was conscious, love, don't worry. I didn't want to alarm you, but Bert said we'd promised. The doctors'll sort 'im out – they'll 'ave taken 'im to the Chest Hospital, I'll be bound."

It takes some time for the hospital switchboard to answer and then to confirm that Dad has indeed been admitted; longer still before Aysha's call is transferred to the correct ward and a somewhat disgruntled nurse asks what relation she is to the patient. Phrases like *resting, comfortable* and *as well as can be expected* wash over her: she cannot fathom what they mean.

"When can I see him?"

"Visiting's from three o'clock," the nurse tells her, "unless the doctors decide to operate."

"Can I give him a message?" she asks.

"He's resting. I'll tell him you called in the morning."

Aysha's own night is neither restful nor comfortable; she reflects that she herself is but as well as can be expected in the circumstances.

~

"Tell her she shouldn't go alone, Mum," Karen appeals to Janet. She and her parents are going to a cousin's wedding.

"What about your young man?" Janet asks. "Can't he go with you?"

Aysha doesn't think that's a good idea. She'll be fine, she says: after all, it's a hospital, a public place; if her mother and brother are there, they will hardly make a scene when her father's so ill.

"Text me," Karen says. "I'll keep my phone on silent in the church."

She dresses carefully in jeans and a long-sleeved cotton top: perfectly decent, though probably not sufficiently enveloping for Mo's tastes. She unpicks her plaits, brushes her long hair over her shoulders and wraps a long scarf loosely around her head. She's not out to offend but doesn't mean to appear something she's not.

Janet drops her at the bus stop and she arrives at the hospital over an hour before visiting time. Outside, there is the redbrick symmetry of Victorian architecture; inside, the building has been transformed. Large ceiling light panels illuminate pastel walls, pale woodwork and brightly painted doors. It still smells like a hospital, though: faintly antiseptic overlaid with an indeterminate vegetable odour. She watches as two orderlies manoeuvre a patient's bed into a lift: that's what Mo does, she thinks. The ward manager directs her attention to the visiting hours, but on impulse Aysha risks spinning a tale about studying away from home and having to go back that same afternoon. The woman observes her keenly, then nods and points in the direction of Bay Two.

Dad's bed is one of four and in the far corner, by a window. He appears to be sleeping and looks smaller, shrunken, swaddled in a blue hospital nightgown and encased in the high, white, functional bed. A clear plastic tube spirals from a suspended bag of fluid, ending in a small syringe or catheter taped to the back of his hand. Aysha watches for the rise and fall of his chest, relieved to see that he's breathing unaided, though the breaths seem shallow, but she's shocked at the colour of his skin: grey, as if his blood has taken fright. She reaches out to touch his fingers and he stirs, opens his eyes and claps her hand in his.

"Daughter," he says. His eyelids close again, but she can tell from the pressure of his grasp that he's not asleep.

"Does it hurt?" She points to the catheter and winces.

"Nuisance, mostly," he says, patting her arm.

A doctor clutching a clip board approaches the bed. Aysha asks if she needs to leave.

"Not unless the patient wants it," the man says. He turns to Dad. "The diet and exercise regime we gave you is either not working or you find it difficult to keep it up." Fully awake now, Dad catches her eye with a guilty glance as the doctor continues. "A bypass operation would be the best solution, but it's your decision, of course."

"Is that dangerous?" Aysha asks.

"Heart surgery – all major surgery – carries a risk. But," he turns to Dad, "so does continuing as you are. Another heart attack might be fatal; an operation could give you a new lease of life."

"When would it be done?" she asks.

"As soon as possible. I'll make some enquiries and come back to let you both know. Give it some thought, Mr Ali, talk it over with your family."

"What will you do, Dad?" she asks when they are alone.

"What the doctor said. Think about it. But now I want to look at you, Aysha. Why did you run away?"

"Mo was going to send me to Maryam's. I knew that if I went there, I'd never be able to finish college. I've worked so hard, Dad, and I'm doing my exams."

"But I thought you wanted to go to your sister's, to forget about that silly young man with his dentist in Birmingham. Your mother said..."

She shakes her head. "No Dad, that wasn't true. Mum..." Her hand moves involuntarily to touch the cheek her mother slapped.

"Your mother wants you to be happy, but she doesn't understand you. I blame myself for that. You are my daughter." He looks at her sharply, wheezing with each intake of breath. "You didn't run off with some boy?"

She doesn't even consider not telling the truth."I've been with Karen's parents. They've been really kind."

"You're doing your A levels?"

"I had some exams last week; there are more to come."

"And you have a university place?"

"Yes, Dad, to read English and history at York. If I do well enough."

"You will do it, I know." He rests back on his pillow and squeezes her hand.

A nurse comes to check his fluids and take his pulse. Dad sighs, but puts up with the disturbance without complaint. The nurse writes on his notes, then leaves.

"York?" He turns back to Aysha as if there had been no interruption.

"It's a good course and I like the city. I've been for an interview and been accepted. I want to be able to give it my best, Dad."

"No wedding then?"

"No, Dad, not now. Maybe one day, but it's got to be my choice, not Mum's or Mo's."

"Or even your father's?" he chuckles. "Don't think I don't understand, Aysha; you are like me. I always said I wouldn't speak about the past to my children, but I was wrong. It's time you knew your father's history."

"Dad, don't tire yourself..."

"I am stabilised, they say. I need to tell you."

She rearranges his pillows and helps him sit up. His voice is low and breathy, the words frequently punctuated by the need to clear his throat. Sometimes his eyes droop and she thinks he's fallen asleep, but then the lids flicker and he continues his narrative at exactly the point he left off.

He had come to England in 1964 as a young engineer on a Commonwealth scholarship: a village lad from what was then East Pakistan, in the middle of swinging London.

"And boy did I have fun. There was cricket at Lords, rock and roll, fish and chips – and girls! Students with mini skirts and long blonde hair, who were happy to dance with the brown man from the Engineering Department. I thought there was nothing I couldn't do."

"Did you have a girlfriend, Dad?"

She sees a shooting star of memory flash across his clouded eyes. His expression is a curious blend of sheepishness and pride.

"Marianne. Same name as Rolling Stones man's girlfriend. Me and Mick, I used to say, we both have our Mariannes." He gestures towards the water jug on his locker; Aysha tops up his glass and holds it to his lips.

"What happened?"

"She invited me home. Big house. Lincolnshire."

"Her family wouldn't accept you?"

"No, not at all. They were liberals – I was the proof of their tolerance. For Marianne, I was the means of seeing how far she could push them. Huh! The problem was mine, not theirs. I thought *they* thought I should be grateful, because all the time I knew *my* parents would object. We started to argue and drifted apart."

He sinks back on the pillows and Aysha fears the effort of speech has been too much.

"Why are you telling me now, Dad?"

"I want you to understand your mother. After Marianne, I threw myself into my studies. No more girls. I went home and asked my family to find me a wife. Your mother was very young; I thought we could make our own lives. I didn't know how fixed her opinions were."

His eyes evade hers, fix themselves on the brick wall visible beyond the window next to his bed. Across the room, the man in the bed opposite fiddles with his headphones, then lies back tapping his fingers on the bedspread. The bed next to Dad's is vacant; screens are drawn around the fourth.

"Did you regret getting married, Dad?" she asks.

"How could I regret five wonderful children? I regret working away from home so much and leaving my wife to bring up our eldest children alone."

Yes, there is a difference, and not just of age: Maryam and Mo are products of her mother's upbringing. Maryam has inherited her acquisitiveness, her concern for reputation, Mo her rigidity, her certainty of being right. A chronicle of guilt has been transmitted down the years, leading to ground subtly yielded, battles never fought. He's never loved Mum, she thinks. Five children and over thirty years of marriage – how does it feel to know that?

Maud and Bert are devoted after a lifetime together; Janet and Mike clearly fancy each other still. But arranged marriages can work: anyone can see that Maryam and Hass are well-suited and happy.

There is a small commotion at the entrance to the bay, where Mum, laden with several plastic shopping bags, is struggling to free one which has caught its handle on the corner of a trolley. A Tupperware bowl tips out, rolling across the linoleum, and the man with the headphones says – probably more loudly than he realises – "there goes dinner!" Mum looks flustered. She clutches at her long robe with one hand, while reaching beneath a chair for the wayward container with the other. Mo, who is close behind, clicks his tongue. They don't notice Aysha at first – the screens round the adjacent bed shield her from view – but then her brother steps forward and stops.

"Why is she here?"

"To visit her father?" Dad suggests mildly.

Mum drops her bags and hurries across the floor. She grabs Aysha's wrist roughly and tugs at her daughter's scarf, trying to cover her hair; yet Aysha is sure she glimpses relief in her eyes.

"Take Aysha home, Mum," Mo says quietly.

"No!" Dad raises the hand with the catheter and the connecting plastic tube sways wildly across the bed. "Aysha will leave when I say and go back to where she is staying until she finishes her exams."

Mo and Mum exchange a startled glance. Mo walks to the window, biting his lip, while Mum covers her confusion by unpacking her bags and piling food boxes, towels and striped lungis onto the locker.

"What's all this, woman?" Dad teases. "I told you they feed you, they give pyjamas. Why make yourself work?"

Aysha stays at his bedside, not looking up, but feeling Mo's eyes burning like lasers into her head. There's a quiet cough and they all turn to see the doctor waiting to speak.

"I've had a word with the surgeon and checked theatre. We can schedule the bypass for Tuesday morning."

"Tuesday!" Aysha echoes.

"Problem?" the doctor asks.

"No, it's just that I have exams that day..."

"Well, young lady," he says drily, "we weren't thinking of asking you to operate."

Mo turns directly to her for the first time, face charged with bitter irony. "See, sister, now you know how it feels."

He's tired, she thinks. Probably he worked the night shift and has only had a few hours' sleep. She holds his gaze; she's not frightened anymore. The doctor seems to pick up the atmosphere; he takes in the clutter on the locker, eyes Mum, Mo and Aysha and beckons to a passing nurse.

"I'm afraid only two visitors at a time are allowed," she says.

"Son work hospital," Mum protests, indicating Mo.

"Then he knows the rules," the nurse says evenly.

"I'm going," Aysha says. "I got here early. Dad, how will I know what you decide?"

"Oh, I think I will trust in Allah and put myself in the hands of the good doctors." She bends to kiss him and he adds, "Do well, Aysha, and don't worry. Call the hospital after your exams on Tuesday and when I am better, you can come home. Now I need to talk to my wife and son."

41
Emily

Monday 19 May 1902

In the weeks since Doris was turned away, there have been changes in the workroom. Two new girls have been taken on but neither is as good a machinist as Doris, and if we hand-stitchers run out of work, Arthur Smythe sometimes sets me working on the machines. Last week, Mr Fenton himself came into the workroom and spent several minutes in conversation with Arthur. Once or twice, they looked in my direction and I was sure they spoke about me, though I took care to keep my head down. I can't help worrying that I will be taken off the fancy stitching and embroidery, which, though taxing, give me a sense of achievement, and put to operating a machine all day. I find the work less engaging, but also it means leaving Lottie's and Kathy's table and working beside Bella, who has always resented me.

At ten-thirty today, Arthur calls me up.

"Finish the piece you're sewing, Emily, and go down to the first floor. Mr Fenton wants to see you in the ladies' fitting suite."

I complete the collar I'm working on, straighten my hair in front of the basin mirror and splash my hands and face. Surely Arthur would tell me himself if my job is to change? Mr Fenton leaves such decisions to him. I wonder if Sally is in town and wants to see me.

The fitting room is a large luxurious area, newly furnished with couches, side tables and full-length mirrors, plus screens for the ladies being fitted. Tea cups and a cake stand are set on an elaborately carved buffet, together with dishes of grapes and bonbons. A great number of fabric samples are spread across one table – rich plummy velvets, jewel-like satins which reflect the electric beams of the wall-lights, soft pale wools which I know will drape beautifully. There are books of drawings too, designs for ladies' gowns and walking costumes.

At first I think I am alone, but then I hear voices coming from a screened alcove by the window: one is Sally's, the other sounds as if it belongs to a much older woman. I wait awkwardly, not knowing if I should speak. Then a door I haven't noticed because, like the walls, it is papered with a pattern of peacocks in fig trees, swings open and Mr Fenton steps out from what looks like a small office.

"Emily, I hope you don't mind me interrupting your work?"

The loss is his, since he pays my wages, but he has always remained kind and courteous to me, so I shake my head and say no.

"Am I here to see Sally?" I ask.

"In a while," he says. "She's with my mother at present. Firstly, I want to make you an apology."

"I don't understand."

"I was wrong to keep you working upstairs so long. Arthur told me about the scene you witnessed with that trollop we sacked. You shouldn't have been exposed to that. I'd never have engaged her had she not been a good machinist."

"But it's my job, sir!" I cry, fearful that he has decided not to employ me any longer. "Plenty of other girls were there too."

"Not girls whose families I know socially. Not friends of my daughter. I've had too much to occupy me lately, but now I mean to make changes. Sit down, Emily. Let me explain."

He tells me he has always intended a different role for me, but needed me to learn the basics of garment construction first and wanted to see if I had the determination to stay. I have the potential to be a first class seamstress, he says, but other girls can do that too. Mr Fenton hopes to launch a new service for ladies who cannot afford a couturier but wish to buy made-to-measure evening gowns. His mother's French dressmaker, Madame Martine, has been hired to supervise the venture, but he needs someone who can help with fittings and alterations, who can assist these ladies in selecting suitable styles and fabrics and generally engage them in polite conversation.

"That's what all this is about," he says, sweeping his arm around the well-appointed room. "I want my customers to feel pampered. I want them to *enjoy* buying clothes at Fenton's and tell their friends."

I don't know what to say; just a minute or two ago I feared losing my job and can now hardly believe that Mr Fenton has been making plans for me this all the time.

"Well, Emily, will you do it? There'll be a raise for you and a dress allowance as well."

It concerns me that this new job will set me apart from the girls in the workroom, but it's an opportunity I cannot refuse if I mean to continue to support myself. I hope Lottie and Kathy will still count me a friend.

"If you think I can do it," I reply, "then I will. Thank you."

Mr Fenton smiles broadly and grasps my hand. "I know your

father disapproves of girls working, but even he will see that this is a job with prospects. Stores like mine are the future – stores for the twentieth century!" He jumps up and pulls on a bell cord, then moves to the screened area on the other side of the room. "Sal! Come and talk to your friend. I'll get some tea sent up."

The screen folds back, revealing Sally and a very upright elderly woman, formally costumed in lilac and black.

"Emmie!" my friend cries, leaping up.

"Deportment, Sally," the old woman says in a low, warning tone.

Sally pulls a face and glides towards me with exaggerated style. "My *grandmama*," she mouths.

I think of my own grandparents at Harlow: of Granny rolling pastry in her kitchen, pushing back her wiry grey hair with floury hands, or darning socks in the evening while keeping an eye on Grandpa George. Sally's grandmother is nothing like that and I begin to understand why she has always been in awe of her.

"So this is the young woman who left her home and father," the old woman says. She looks me up and down critically and I feel myself straightening my back. "I hope you're not one of these suffrage types?"

"This is Emily Watts, Mother, who went to school with Sally," Mr Fenton says. "Emily, this is Sally's grandmama, Mrs Rachel Fenton. She has a financial interest in the store." He takes the woman by the arm and leads her to the office hidden behind the papered door. "I want to go through costings with you, Mother – we can take our tea in here," he says, winking at Sally and me behind Mrs Fenton's back.

A waitress in a lace apron and cap comes in with a tea tray and a selection of fancy cakes which she places on a side table.

She serves Sally and me, then takes the tray into the office.

"Thank goodness," Sally cries, when all the doors are closed, "now we can talk in peace! It's *months* since I saw you, Emmie. I called at the square two Sundays ago and was told you no longer live at home."

"It's true," I say. "I board with some of the other seamstresses in a lodging house."

Sally pouts as she smooths the folds of her red and grey striped skirt. "I wish I'd known – I so wanted to talk to you. That man of your father's said I should persuade you to go home."

"He is the reason I do not."

For a moment I am tempted to tell Sally everything. Her eyes sparkle with interest and I can see she's hoping for some piece of juicy gossip; perhaps those rumours of an engagement reached her ears too. I quickly change my mind.

"I don't believe he has used Pa fairly – in business, I mean. But Sally, what were you so eager to tell me?"

"My grandmother is taking me to Paris in September. She is planning a big party next winter for me – when I am seventeen. I am to be launched, Emmie, like a ship!"

"Paris! How wonderful – will you see Notre-Dame and the Louvre?"

"Oh, I expect so, but we go for the fashion. I thought it would be a real spending spree, but I am only allowed a few things. Dad wants to copy them, you see. He says if I'm to get my name in the society pages, it must be wearing a gown from this store."

I realise we both have a role to play in Mr Fenton's ambitious plans. A thought strikes me. "But, Sally, you say you're going in September – what about your teaching?"

"There, I knew you would ask," she says, wrinkling her nose.

"I feel bad giving up when I know it's something you always wanted. But now you're going to be the one with the career after all. They have such assistants in Paris, Dad says: *vendeuses* they call them, and that's what you will be.

"Now, you must promise to keep it secret, but there's another matter I came to tell you. Joshua and I will be announcing our engagement at my birthday. Grandmama says I won't want for offers once I'm known as Dad's heir, but I don't want to be courted for a store. Besides I've given him my word. It's lucky he's her favourite grandson."

"What about *your* mother, Sally? Doesn't she have a say in it all?"

"Mum?" Sally laughs. "Oh, Mum's happy enough for me, but she has no money of her own, so what she says doesn't count."

I remember what Pa said about Sally when I wanted to go back to school: he was right not to believe she would ever become a teacher. But *I* wouldn't have given up. Mr Fenton's offer is a generous one and I am grateful, but if I had the freedom to choose, I'd rather use my brain for something more worthwhile than coaxing money from a rich woman's purse.

42
Aysha

May 2002

"History candidates, you have five minutes."

Aysha is still furiously writing the answer to her last question. With points to make and no time to elaborate, she remembers her tutors' advice, pushes back her hair and starts making notes to summarise her remaining facts and arguments. When Andy Carstairs, who is invigilating, eventually tells them to stop writing she puts down her pen and slumps in satisfied exhaustion. This has been her second exam today. The morning's psychology paper went better than she'd expected – she'd mostly revised the subject alone as her tutor, Magda, was on maternity leave and there'd been a series of replacements. But history was different: she, Karen and Derrick had spent Sunday working together: this was Derrick's idea, he wanted to stop her from dwelling on her father's operation.

"It sounds like he's on your side," he'd said, "maybe this bypass will make him stronger and things will change."

She wants to think so. Karen and her parents couldn't be kinder, but she misses home and her own room: she wants to go back to Emily's journal; she wants to be reconciled with Mum.

Across the room Derrick is testing the confines of his too

small desk by stretching out a long languorous arm and Karen has slumped theatrically, head on answer booklet; in the next aisle, Billie is stifling a yawn: she'd stopped writing twenty minutes ago. Aysha's right wrist and knuckles have stiffened up and there's a painful crick in her back; she tries flexing her fingers and rotating her shoulder. At last, when all the scripts have been collected, they are allowed to leave. No-one is meant to speak until outside the room, but Andy raises a quizzical eyebrow and gives her a quick thumbs up. Only two more papers to do, and those not until after half-term, so she can relax for a bit. She retrieves her bag from a pile by the door and waves to Karen, who is already waiting in the corridor. But before she can join her, Jo Massey steps forward and places a hand on her arm.

"Aysha, could I have a moment? I think you'd better come into the office." Jo glances around and her eyes find Karen. "Perhaps you wouldn't mind waiting for your friend?"

"Is some...?"

She hears Karen start to speak, but Jo has already drawn her into the small cubicle and closed the door. The room is hot and airless and smells of stale coffee. Aysha's stomach plummets like a lift in free fall as she scrabbles in her bag to find her phone: no missed calls or texts are shown, but she knows with absolute certainty that something is horribly wrong.

"It's Dad, isn't it?" she whispers, ashen-faced. "The hospital's rung you."

Jo waits until they are seated before answering. "It's bad news, I'm afraid."

"The operation? But the doctor said he'd be fine." She could be standing naked in bitter weather, she's shaking so violently. Then she whispers, "What happened?"

"The planned operation didn't take place," Jo says gently. "Your father had a massive heart attack late last night. I'm so sorry, Aysha, but the doctors were unable to save him. Your brother phoned this morning. I hope you'll forgive me. He wanted to speak to you but I said I'd tell you once you'd finished today's exams."

Mo phoned college? Aysha sits dumbly, unable to comprehend. But what does it matter? What does anything matter if Dad, who has always loved her, is dead? Dad, who shared his past with her just days ago and gave her his blessing? The heart the doctors never got the chance to mend must have stopped beating while she was still asleep. How could she not have known? Jo slides a box of tissues towards her; she hasn't realised she's crying.

"Your brother said..." Jo begins. "If I understand correctly, the funeral took place this afternoon."

Aysha nods slowly, then blows her nose. "Muslims bury people without delay," she says, "and women don't go to funerals. Don't worry. I wouldn't have been allowed to attend. But I must go home. I need to see Mum, my little brother..." She breaks off, staring ahead as if at an unseen videotape scrolling before her eyes. Abdul will be heart-broken. What about Sel – does Mum have a phone number to contact him?

"Aysha," Jo says hesitantly, "I know now's not the time, but don't throw everything away. If there are problems with your remaining exams, I'll write to the boards and to your universities." She fills a plastic beaker with water for Aysha, then steps outside. A moment later, Karen edges uncertainly around the door.

"Oh, Aysh!" she says, and wraps her in her arms.

~

Karen is still asleep when Aysha comes from the shower. She dresses carefully in a long-sleeved shirt and black trousers, covers her hair with a grey headscarf, securing it with grips, then places a note she's already written on her pillow. Both Karen and Derrick have tried to dissuade her, but she has to go. She fills a glass with water from the tap, drinks half and rinses it out. She imagines her friends' anxious eyes following her as she walks down the hall and lets herself out of the flat.

Two elderly men in prayer caps enter the square ahead of her and stop at her house. Hass's blue Volvo is parked by the railings and a small, thin woman wearing a long black coat and niqab is climbing the steps to her front door. She waits until they've gone inside. Perhaps she should knock at Maud and Bert's flat first, to let them know she's here, but what could they do if she needed help? She still has her house key to let herself in.

The kitchen door is ajar, revealing a room full of women. Maryam has her arm around Mum, Reshna is at the cooker and there are five or six others of her mother's generation. The thin woman she saw on the street looks up at her sharply and she's convinced this is Monwara Begum, Wahida's mother. Mum's face shows pain, resignation and just a trace of self-importance: she is the bereaved, the widow; she has a role. One of the visitors is cuddling Safiya. Deprived of their electronic toys, Maryam's two boys sit on the floor beside Ibrahim, scribbling with crayons in a Star Wars colouring book.

"What you want?" Mum says.

"I'm here for Dad," she says. Then, looking around, "Where's Abdul?"

Reshna looks anxious. "Husband make stay with men."

She returns to the hall and opens the door to the lounge. Whatever conversation has been taking place stops instantly. Five elderly men are compressed onto the long sofa. Hass perches on the arm, looking uncomfortable. Mo occupies a stool normally used as a side table and Abdul is in the centre of it all, seated on the pouffe, his face a picture of misery. His shoulders twitch as he struggles to stop shaking. The last thing Dad would have wanted is his youngest son put through this.

"Go to the kitchen, Aysha," Mo says. "You shouldn't be in here."

The old men stare into their teacups. Hass inspects his fingernails. Anger steels her and she swallows hard. "Nor should Abdul," she says quietly. "Come here, Ab."

She reaches out her arm and the boy leaps to her side. "I'm taking him to his room," she says.

She'd hoped for a few minutes alone, but Emily's journal will have to wait for another day. She can't leave the boy. At first he just clings to her, sobbing violently, burying his stubbly head in her side; later, when the sobs become more sporadic, he starts to speak. He hasn't been naughty he says; he hasn't hurt Ibrahim or touched Sel's things. She's shocked to realise he thinks everything's his fault. But it's she who should feel guilty; she and Sel who've put stress on Dad and broken the family apart.

"You know Dad had been ill a very long time," she tells him, "even before you were born. I bet he'd have loved to be able to run around and play football with you."

There's a tap at the door. She jumps, expecting Mo come to berate her; instead, she's surprised to find Maryam at the door.

"We need to talk," her sister says. She points across the

landing. "In your room."

Aysha gives Abdul's shoulder a squeeze. "It's okay for you to stay here, Ab. I'll bring you a drink in a bit."

She opens the door to her room. It looks just as she left it, though perhaps a little dusty. Her eyes dart instantly to the rug which covers her floorboard cache: there's no sign of disturbance. The journal lies beneath their feet, but for now it's out of reach. She sits on the bed, giving Maryam the only chair.

"I owe you an apology," Maryam says stiffly, "for taking Jamil at his mother's word."

At least she has admitted being at fault; Aysha feels ridiculously grateful.

"What's happened to him?"

"Found a job in Walsall, I've heard. His parents will come round eventually. Find reasons to be proud." Maryam looks away, out of the window, and takes a deep breath. "Mum says you saw Dad in hospital – that you spoke to him alone?"

Aysha nods.

"What did he tell you?"

"It was private," she murmurs. "About before he was married. I can't speak of it now."

Whatever Dad did in his early life, he had over thirty years of marriage.

Maryam laughs bitterly. "You think you know something we don't? You think he told you everything?" The voice sounds unnaturally hard.

"He talked about when he first came to England. About an English girl he broke up with before he got married. Did Mum find out about her? Is that what you mean?"

"You're a woman now, Aysha. Have you never wondered why

there's such a gap between me and Mo and then Sel? Why it suited our father to work away?"

What does she mean? She's talking of a time before Aysha was born. Families come in all shapes and sizes: why should she wonder about that?

"You didn't grow up with the rows, the lies, the pleading for forgiveness. The weekends when he didn't come home. Broke up! Oh, they did that more than once, and got together again. Mum thought everything was okay when Selim and then you were born. He took a job near home. He learned to be a father. Then came the phone call – he'd had a heart attack. Only later when we found her at his bedside, Mum learned it had happened in that woman's flat."

Aysha cannot speak. The floor falls away and she plunges into the darkest place. It can't be true! All the time that Dad came home to tell her stories of his working life, could he have been cheating on them all? The educated, liberal father she felt so proud of – had he really, knowing his life was at risk, chosen to tell her less than the truth? Yet it all makes sense: Maryam's coolness towards Dad; the assumption of moral superiority with which her brother took over his role; his rejection of all Dad stood for. A groan breaks from deep in her chest.

"How do you think Mum feels seeing you and Sel going his way? Or Mo, after everything he's done to reinstate this family?" Aysha's amazed at the bitterness in her sister's voice. "These things get around. Mum needed help after I was married. Our brother went home for a wife because no decent local family wanted their daughter to join ours."

"You still shouldn't speak ill of him. Not today. He loved us all – I know he did."

"Yes! *I* was his princess once and he gave me a name as near to *hers* as he could." Maryam takes a tissue from her sleeve and sniffs violently. "It doesn't get any better, knowing I was never enough to keep him home. Go away, Aysha. Mum doesn't want to see you now. Go to your uni, but don't you dare to criticise us."

Maryam opens the bedroom door and pushes Aysha towards the stairs; she's being thrown out.

"I promised Abdul..." she protests.

"The boys can come up. They're kids, they'll be all right."

She just keeps walking when she leaves the house: through the playing fields to Stepney Green, across busy junctions, losing her way down countless back streets, only stopping when she gets to Victoria Park. She needs space to breathe. It had taken all her courage to go to the house, to confront Mum, rescue Abdul from a room full of men, but she'd done it for Dad. *You're like me*, he'd said; she'd said it herself. But who is she now? Her whole life – her valuation of Mum, her brothers and sister, her very idea of self – has been based on a lie. She sits for hours until the air starts to cool, then slowly makes her along the canal to Limehouse.

It's eight o'clock when Aysha finally rings the bell to Karen's flat; she's been gone all day. Janet flings opens the door, calling out *she's here!* and Karen and Derrick rush from the lounge.

"I thought they'd locked you up," Karen cries, relief flooding her face. "Del's been frantic – why didn't you call?"

She shakes her head.

"I must have phoned twenty times," Derrick protests. "Where have you been?"

Her eyes roll; she barely shrugs. "Park. Canal."

"Alone?" Karen looks anxious.

Again she shrugs. The green waters hadn't tempted her, but she could have gladly chugged away into deepest England on one of the narrow boats she'd seen.

"Something must've been wrong," Karen says, "for you not to pick up your phone."

"My dad died. It doesn't happen every day. What more d'you want?"

She's hurting them, she knows, with her flat indifference and cynical words. But she's hurting too, more than she knows how to say. She feels foolish, resentful, angry; ashamed of making an idol of a father whose failings she'd never seen. He'd let them all down, but they had looked after him, prioritised his welfare, allowed him to maintain his status in the community and the home.

"Well as long as you're back now," Derrick says, resting his hand on her shoulder.

Aysha stiffens. They'd planned to drive to the coast at half-term, to take their minds off exams for a day, but she can't face the cheerful intimacy that such a trip implies. She has an English and a psychology paper still to come, but at the moment she'd gladly take all her notes and sink them in Limehouse Basin.

Janet sends out for fish and chips for them all. Aysha's eaten nothing all day, but can only pick at the food, hating herself for seeming ungrateful. Karen's dad buries himself in his paper while Janet talks office gossip to Karen in hard, bright tones.

Days pass and her mood doesn't change: she barely eats or speaks, never opens a book. Janet and Karen tiptoe round her. Derrick comes each day with a look of renewed hope that quickly turns to one of frustration. At last, he takes out his phone.

"What you doing?" Karen asks.

"We need help," he says. "I'm calling Mum."

43
Emily

Saturday 9 August 1902

Coronation Day! It should have been six weeks ago, but the king was dangerously ill with appendicitis in June and there is all the more cause for celebration now. So many ladies wanted new outfits for this day that we've been working at full stretch. Every customer wants her dress to be unique and I am responsible for recording individual orders and ensuring that all our made-to-measure garments are different. We've none of us had Saturday free for several weeks, but today is a holiday and we are at liberty.

I am afraid that it's almost four months since I was in Stepney and longer still since I visited the square. Sunday is truly my only day of rest and now that summer's here I like to spend it in the park or walking along the embankment with the girls. My freedom is precious. I do feel guilty about neglecting my father and have written to tell him of my promotion. I want him to be proud of me but, though he replies hoping I am well, he neither congratulates me nor urges my return. He always thought I would tire of working and go home, so perhaps my news is not entirely welcome.

My new job has been much more enjoyable than I expected.

Mr Fenton's venture is a great success and I like to think that Ma would have enjoyed shopping there, and to imagine what she might have chosen. Not all the customers are spoilt rich women. Many are wives and daughters of prosperous tradesmen; some even earn a living in their own right – nurses, teachers and typewriter operators – and have saved to buy a special outfit for today. Everyone's money has the same value, Mr Fenton says, and whereas Madame Martine can offend them by her condescension, it is my job to put these customers at ease. Girls, brought to town by their mothers, are glad of a friendly face and rely on Miss Watts to persuade their mamas to accept more modern styles.

The salesgirls at Mrs Pegg's are more jealous of my promotion than my own workmates have been. Vera and Phyllis wonder that Mr Fenton did not choose someone with more experience of the shop floor, but Lottie and Kathy are proud that such an important new appointment – as they see it – has been made from their ranks. I can't afford to be a spendthrift, but now that I have a dress allowance and need not use all my wages for stockings, I allow myself a supply of candles to read and write by at night and sometimes treat the three of us to iced cakes. Any spare money goes into my post office account.

I've been back to Harlow just once. Grandpa's speech has improved a little and he manages a few steps now, with the use of two canes. I know that Granny could use more help, but am almost glad I've had no time to visit. I feel so guilty when I have to leave.

Kathleen and Lottie have gone with Jimmy to watch the procession to the Abbey, but I cannot face the idea of joining them. It's summer now, the war is over and the coronation is a joyful occasion, but the crowded streets and all the troops and carriages remind me too forcefully of that February day when Ma and I watched the old queen's last journey: the day that changed our lives for ever.

My idea is to go back to Stepney and see Daisy. The last time I saw her she was strangely cold, but I'm sure she'll be glad to celebrate today. There may be a party in the square, but if not we can make a picnic with Elizabeth, Ernie and baby Sylvia. I have brought a bag of cherries and Daisy is bound to have baked goods in her larder. I'll take my chances of meeting Pa and Mr Baines; indeed, I'd like them to see that I am making a success of work. Already, I've saved nineteen shillings in the Post Office through putting a little aside each week. My store will soon grow and I will have proved that I can survive.

Travelling eastwards is easy today as everyone is heading in the opposite direction. The omnibus conductor looks at me curiously – I fear he suspects me of being unpatriotic. At the entrance to the square, I stop to admire the flags fluttering from every window and the red, white and blue bunting which loops from the iron railings. A large crown chalked by children on the pavement, with the letters E and R either side, has been allowed to remain, but otherwise all the paths are swept, every doorstep has been washed, every brass letterbox and knocker gleams.

As I hoped, Elizabeth is at home with Sylvia: bored and a little resentful, I think, because Richard has taken Ernie to watch the parade. I watch her privately appraising my new green skirt and blouse, but she is genuinely glad to see me – eager for me to notice Sylvia's progress and keen to quiz me about the latest styles in the store. One of her magazines contains an advertisement for our service – *a personal dressmaker for every lady,* it reads – and Elizabeth is amazed and not a little impressed to learn that the *confidential adviser and fitter* is me!

I am bursting to tell her my latest news, but will wait until I can tell Daisy too. I am to go to France with Sally and her grandmother next month! Mr Fenton wants us to visit the Paris stores as well as the fashion shows, so that I can learn how customers are treated there – no doubt he will advertise the confidential adviser and fitter as *Paris-trained* when I get back! I have hopes that Mrs Fenton senior will agree to some sightseeing and that I may yet see Notre Dame and go boating on the Seine.

At first Elizabeth agrees to my idea of a picnic in the square, but when I mention inviting Daisy, she prevaricates.

"It looks a little like rain now, Emily. The grass in the square will be wet. My poor Sylvia is teething and I don't want her to take a chill."

The baby is kicking contentedly on the rug and looks well enough to me.

"I saw your father and Mr Baines go out," Elizabeth adds. "You may wait for them here if you want, Emily; I have already eaten lunch but if you watch Sylvia for me I dare say I can make you some tea."

"Thank you, but I want to see Daisy before they return. It's easier to talk with her when no-one else is there."

When I get up to take my leave, Elizabeth looks as if she would say something, then appears to alter her mind. Knowing that Pa and Baines are out, I slip down our entry steps and lift the latch to the basement kitchen rather than go up to the front door. I see Daisy straight away; she has her back to me and is scrubbing the big pine table. The kitchen looks strangely bare.

"Dais," I say, "It's me! Emily."

Slowly she turns. I see the familiar plump, pink cheeks, the cornflower blue eyes, the wispy blonde curls escaping from her cap. And then I see the unfamiliar curve of her belly beneath her apron, the straining seams of her bodice and the awkwardness of her gait.

"Dais, you're not..."

"Pregnant?" she finishes for me.

"Who...?" But she cries so bitterly that I cease questioning and put my arm around her.

"Why me? Did he set out t'ruin me? That's what I want t'know."

"Who, Daisy? Who?"

"That devil man, that Baines."

I stare at her, stunned. Outside, on the street, some children run by, waving their Union Jacks and singing a boisterous *Rule Britannia.*

"Mr Baines forced you? Have you told Pa? He must report him to the police."

"What – five and 'alf months later? What good would that do now? 'E's got your pa in 'is pocket. D'you think, when 'e didn't listen to you, 'e'll take my word? Besides..."

My mind is whirring. "Daisy – when I came back in March, had this already happened?" I thought her jealous and resentful, but perhaps her coldness was due to shame or fear.

She blows her nose and nods.

"I didn't tell you because what 'appened was all my fault."

"I don't believe that, Daisy! Surely you wouldn't – not knowing what you knew about him."

She sinks down heavily, massaging her back with her hand. I remember how poorly Elizabeth had been when first pregnant and think of Daisy cooking, scrubbing, and hauling clothes from the boiler all these months without help. When she speaks, her voice is harsh and broken with misery. Ma taught Daisy to talk nicely, but that's all forgotten now.

"I cooked dinner for 'em, 'im and your pa. They were celebratin' making a deal with some West End store and wanted roast beef and claret. I 'ad the leavings of it. I know I shouldn'ta drunk the claret – there was a good glassful left in the second bottle when they went on to the port. I'd bin sittin' an' thinking about Charlie, an' readin' 'is letter, imagining what it would've been like, if he'd come back and we'd bin wed – when *'e* come down. 'E puts his arm around me and takes me cap off and starts playin' wiv me 'ands like, and says 'e knows 'ow I feel but I'm a pretty girl and Charlie wouldn't've wanted me to waste me talents, and 'e don't mean the cookin' neither. Then before I know it, 'e's kissin' me and 'is 'ands are ev'rywhere... and... and I'm kissin' 'im back." She sobs violently, bringing up her apron to wipe her face. "Me mind was tellin' me no, but I 'ad such feelin's I didn't say it at first and then when I did 'e wouldn't stop. I never meant it. It was missin' Charlie, wantin' 'im so much, that and the wine. I bin so lonely 'ere, what wiv Charlie, and yer ma and then you all gone. Oh, miss, what'm I gonna do?"

I can't speak; my throat is dry; my tongue is glued to my mouth. How could I have thought it was only me who was in danger? When I find my voice, it's a whisper.

"Did he hurt you?"

"The second time was worse. When 'e found out you'd bin 'ere, that last time, I could tell 'e was wild. I'd already gone to bed that night –" she points to the alcove where she sleeps, under the stairs – "and 'e came down late, saying 'e was still 'ungry, and started taking cold pie and stuff out of me larder. Then 'e asked if I'd told you what e'd done. I said I 'adn't but 'e didn't believe me. 'E said I'd ruined 'is chances and slapped me and called me names, filthy names I can't repeat. Then 'e grabbed me and did it again, only this time there weren't no kisses or playing with 'ands, 'e jus' wanted to 'urt me."

"And does he know – Mr Baines – about the child?"

"Oh 'e knows all right. But 'e told your pa I'd bin 'angin' round the docks on me 'alf day, that I'm a loose woman and should be turned away. I've got till Friday, 'e says and then I've got to be gone. It's 'is kid, but I wouldn't marry that Baines if 'e asked me, even in the condition I'm in."

"Pa is not a cruel man. Surely, he'll let you stay?"

"How can 'e, miss? Not with a kid; not when I've bin livin' 'ere in the 'ouse wiv 'im and the other one. People might say it's yer pa's child. That Elizabeth don't give me the time o' day no more – even stopped young Ernie from comin' round for 'is slice of pie. An' she's right, ain't she, 'cos I must be a bad woman, lettin' another man do that when it's Charlie I loved."

"No," I grip her shoulders and stare into her tear-swollen blue eyes, "it's not you who's bad. He knew what he was doing, taking advantage of you when you were so low. It's my fault, too. I've stayed away too long. I've looked after myself without thinking that you were at risk. I thought he only wanted me because of the business, but he can't be trusted where any woman is concerned."

Was that the only reason? Was he one of those men who routinely prey on women, taking advantage of them simply because they can? Or did he get pleasure in knowing he'd taken the girl Charlie loved, just as he has taken Charlie's place with Pa? Perhaps he even planned to rob me of my one friend in this house.

"But where will you to go? Can your sister take you in?"

"Ethel won't even speak to me. None of them 'ave room anyway."

"Then we'll go to Dr Reynolds. Surely he will help."

"I've 'eard e's away, visitin' 'is sister in Wales what's poorly. Another man's bin doin' 'is rounds. Besides, the doctor's a single man an' respectable – I ain't imposing on 'im. I'll ask around. I'll walk a bit and ask around. There's 'ostels, ain't there? Not the workhouse – I ain't goin' there – but Sally Army ones? There must be places for women like me... though I never thought I'd end up somewhere like that."

Only two weeks ago Kathleen and I came upon Doris begging outside Lancaster Gate Station when we came back from Hyde Park. She didn't seem pregnant, though whether she'd given birth or lost the child I don't know, but she looked dirty and ill-used and Kathleen said I was foolish to give her my sixpence. Surely Daisy can't mean to walk the streets in her condition, with no fixed refuge in mind? She's two years my senior – how can she be so naïve? She was the youngest of eight and grew up in an overcrowded slum: she knows the facts of life and death. Yet, when I consider, Ma took her in aged twelve, and after that she led as sheltered a life as I did; her only sweetheart was Charlie, six months younger than herself. These last months at the boarding house have opened my eyes; Daisy hasn't had a Lottie to teach her, or the dubious advantage of supper-time conversation at Mrs Pegg's. If anyone shelters her, I fear it will be the likes of the two women at the music hall, who knew Baines only too well.

"I don't s'pose I could come with you?" Daisy mumbles.

I have to help, but I can't take her with me to Mrs Pegg's. Our landlady guards the reputation of her house too zealously to admit a girl in her condition and, although my wages have increased, they are not sufficient to provide for us both and a child. Mr Fenton turned Doris away without a second thought; I doubt he'd let me near his customers if he thought I was living with a poor ruined girl. But Daisy was Ma's special protégée; she took her in when Daisy's own mother died and her older sisters would have left her to the workhouse. I can't let her walk the streets.

And then I have an idea. "I can't take you to my lodgings, but you're not going to any hostel either," I say. "I'll take you to my grandparents. Granny needs help to run the house and won't turn you away if we tell her the truth. If I tell her what Baines did to me nearly a year ago, she'll have to believe you."

I wish I felt sure. My grandparents looked after Ma when little Edward was born, but she was their own daughter and married, even if against their wishes. However deserving Daisy may be, they are more likely to see a pregnant girl as a burden than a help.

"I ain't gonna be much good just now," she says, resting a hand on her belly, "and they won't want me there with a kid. What use'd I be?"

"They will take you if I stay too."

I didn't know I was going to say this, but I can't think of any other way. I've always known I could go to Granny's if times were hard, but I wanted to prove I could survive on my own. "You can still cook, can't you?" I ask her. "I'll do the heavy work and take over for a bit when the baby's born."

"But what about your job, miss, and your friends? Look at you – smart new clothes and shoes – you must be doing really well."

"It can't be helped. I'll talk to Mr Fenton."

I swallow hard, not liking the prospect. I can give Grandpa's illness as my reason for leaving, but he will still think me ungrateful and Sally will be angry. I'll have to use my savings to pay Mrs Pegg in lieu of notice; perhaps return my new clothes too. As for Paris... But this has all been my fault. *I* told Baines to find another wife; instead he took his revenge on Daisy.

"There are things I must do first," I tell her, "but I'll come back on Monday, when Pa and Baines are at work. You must pack your things, but tell nobody. You and me, we're both going to Harlow. We'll raise your child there and teach him everything."

Daisy's lip trembles. "I'm scared. What if I can't love that man's child? What if it's wicked too?"

"He won't be. Not if we teach him right." Somehow I feel sure her child is a boy. "As for... that man, I'll make sure he never finds out where you've gone. The child will never hear his name. It was Charlie you loved: we'll bring the baby up as we would Charlie's child."

Her eyes still drown in quivering pools of tears but I see the beginnings of hope in her exhausted face. I talk about the house in Harlow: about the dusky currant and gooseberry bushes, the apples that even now will be starting to turn rosy in the orchard and the soft mutterings of the hens as they turn over the soil beneath the trees. It will be a good place to bring up a child.

I realise that when I collect her on Monday, I'll be leaving this house for good – the place where I was born and where once we were happy. I suppose I always thought I would come back to my home. While Daisy boils water for tea, I go to Pa's study and take the birth certificates from their pigeon hole in his desk once more: mine, Charlie's and that first baby boy's, together with the baby's death certificate. It occurs to me that it was baby Edward who was recorded as dying at the Cape – that awful War

Office letter referred to *your son, Edward Charles* – even though I hold the true record in my hand. Somewhere in South Africa, poor Charlie is buried under his brother's name; no-one recorded *Charles Robert's* death. Who will know the truth in years to come? Who will know when he died, that he and Daisy weren't engaged or that he did not father her child? When I return to the kitchen, the kettle is singing and she is busy scouring all the baking tins.

"What on earth are you doing, Dais?" I ask.

She raises her chin defiantly. "People will say what they like, but they can't say I left your ma's house in a mess. I'll fix the scullery tomorrow."

I cannot persuade her that her efforts are unnecessary. She has been working day and night to make sure she leaves the house in good order.

"Go up an' see your room, miss," she urges, "I've cleaned and polished ev'rything, an' I thought you might need your summer clothes – they're all clean and mended."

I nod and go up to my old top-floor room. I don't think my old clothes will fit me now, but I'll take them to please her. Despite all the problems we must face and the regrets I can't help feel, I am strangely content that we are friends once more.

It is many months since I thought about Aysha, but somehow the moment I rest my hand on the doorknob, I know what I will find. She sits reading at the open window of the room, a neat pile of letters and volumes and a suitcase at her feet, but I would recognise the book in her hand anywhere. It is small and bound in green leather. It is my journal.

I wish I could talk to you, Emily. You lost your mother – my father died too. You had to leave this house once, just like me. I wonder if you came back? What happened to you Emily? What did you do with your life? I know you could see me sometimes – why can't I see you?

I edge cautiously towards her, but she doesn't fade or waver in the air as she's done before. The room looks different, smaller somehow. Where is my old bedstead with the ironwork roses, where is the chrysanthemum wallpaper and my wash stand with its ink-stained marble top? But it is I who have become insubstantial. I have lost my boundaries and I flow through and around her like a gentle current of air.

"Aysha!" I say, and my voice is a mere breath on the breeze from a window that opens onto another world.

But she starts and looks around her. I am sure she hears me; perhaps she sees nothing, but she leans into the space where I am. She puts out a hand and I reach for it. I see the translucence of *my* hands as they wrap around hers, my wrists showing just the palest suggestion of veins.

Emily? she gasps.

The warmth of her touch courses through me.

Tears cover my hands; I don't know if they are hers or mine. I want so much to stay with her, but I'm becoming afraid. I must leave her and claim my own reality, or I will be trapped like a ghost in that room forever.

"Tea's ready, miss!" Daisy calls from below.

The room spins and our hands slip apart. Aysha's figure is veiled in mist; only her voice remains.

Emily, she says, *don't go! How will I find you again? How will I know what happens to you?*

"I can't tell you the ending," I whisper, "but you shall have the story up to now."

I know now what I must do. Tonight, at Mrs Pegg's, I will write in this journal one more time. On Monday, before we leave my father's house, I will lift the floorboard in my room and slide my book as far back in the cavity as I can and trust that one day a girl called Aysha will find it. Then Daisy and I will take a last look at her spotless kitchen and close the basement door behind us. I'll hold her arm as we cross the square and we'll not look back to see Elizabeth's curtain twitch.

44
Aysha

August 2002

"So she did come back!"

Aysha tugs a stem of ivy aside and traces the words on the weathered marble with her fingertips.

"How do you know?" Grace asks.

"Look," she says, pointing to the inscription beneath the dates of Maria Watts' life, "someone had to arrange for that to be done." Together they read: *Edward Watts, 1863-1913, husband of the above. Also in memory of a beloved son and brother, Charles Robert Watts, killed in the South Africa War.* "It could only have been Emily."

"Ah, I see that now of course," Grace sighs, "but that's why you're the historian and I'm not."

Now that Aysha has overcome her initial qualms about traipsing across a Christian churchyard she's both fascinated and moved by the stories these old stones tell. She's struck that Emily's father's name has not been prefaced by some loving epithet. His daughter did her duty by him, but Aysha doubts they were reconciled.

"Emily's not here, though," she says.

"We haven't checked those headstones over there."

"I don't have to. I'd know if she was here."

Grace rests an arm gently on her companion's shoulder. Aysha has recently shared parts of Emily's journal with her. "Yes," she says, nodding slowly, "yes, I think you would."

"I'm glad she's not. Of course I know she must have died years ago, but I *heard* her, just two weeks ago. I'm sure of it, Grace. And I *felt* her – she was *there*!"

She'd like to find the house that Emily and Daisy fled to, but Grace says a new town was built in Harlow in the sixties: Emily's grandparents' cottage has probably disappeared beneath some shopping centre or car park.

"I haven't much time to search," she says. "I'm working full-time at the bookshop for three weeks and I have to be in York by the end of September."

"You do indeed, sweetheart," Grace agrees, "and I hope that family of yours appreciates your achievement – two As and a C, after all you've been through!"

None of this would have happened without this woman, Aysha thinks, and grasps her hand in grateful acknowledgement. It was Grace who had saved her, wading in fearlessly where the others had held back.

"Is this the girl who wanted to test how far she could go?" she'd asked. The floodgates had opened and Aysha's tears flowed freely. Grace had stayed with her, held her, made her talk in the way only she could accomplish, until she'd seen that loving her father was nothing to be ashamed of, yet she could also honour her mother; that life was messy and complicated; that a good man could be caught between conflicting worlds, but love for a child transcended morality. As for the remaining exams, Aysha had been preparing for weeks, Grace said: she'd just have to do what she could.

The last few days have passed in a flurry of correspondence and a whirlwind of emotion, which started with the arrival of her A level results. She still can't believe that the university has accepted her. It was Grace who phoned the college and got Jo both to contact York and extract promises from Mum and Mo. Her brother had eventually agreed to provide the financial information needed for her fees to be waived, reluctantly admitting that supporting Aysha had been one of his father's last requests. He's been helpful, even courteous, but it feels like he's fulfilling a duty, not acting through love.

"A penny for those thoughts of yours," Grace smiles, brushing grass cuttings from her yellow print skirt.

"Sorry – I was miles away," Aysha says. "I guess we're finished here – it was good of you to come. I'm glad we found Emily's parents."

"My pleasure, darling, but you'll have to get used to this when you're doing that medieval history course of yours."

Back at Grace's flat, Aysha reads aloud the last few pages of Emily's journal and closes the book. Grace exhales with a long, theatrical sigh.

"Describe what you felt again. Go slowly this time."

They are sitting among the window box geraniums and the fragrant tomatoes on Grace's balcony, waiting for Derrick to return from work. Since Grace persuaded her to visit her family again, she'd been regularly checking Emily's journal, making excuses to slip up to the room where she no longer slept. Each time, the last entry had been the same: February 1902 – when Emily had left home.

"I was just sitting with the book in my hand. It felt like the door had opened, but I knew it hadn't. There was a sudden draught and the whole room was charged with emotion. It was like how I feel watching a play, like when Jo took us to see Hamlet. I felt her pride, fear, regret, but, most of all – does this sound strange? – love. I heard her call my name and – just for an instant – I thought I saw... something. Just the faintest outline. The whole experience didn't last long, but it was overwhelming. I'm convinced she was there. I put the book back under the floor. I knew I had to."

"And then?"

"When I went home last Thursday, with my results, all the new stuff was there. But you've seen what she wrote, Grace: she left the journal for me to find. I can take it now; there won't be any more."

September 2002

Aysha arrives in the square on a rainy morning to find Mo sitting at the kitchen table with Mum, reading a letter aloud to her.

"Selim coming!" Mum says excitedly.

"Sel? When?" she asks. "What about his wife?"

"Not until Ramadan, November," Mo says. "It's just a visit. But it seems we have reason to thank our new sister-in-law."

Aysha frowns, puzzled.

"She was in a position to know what went on in our uncle's house and he hadn't been straight with us. Dad's land *was* sold, but another plot in town was bought and that land is now wanted for building and worth good money. Uncle has agreed to sell it and Sel will bring our family's share."

I wish Dad had known, Aysha thinks; and about his resourceful new daughter-in-law.

"It's not a fortune, but there should be something for us all."

"Sel always good boy," Mum says. "Not book clever, but smart. Reshna know wife Shilpi family."

Mo draws his eyes close together and she sees a shadow of irritation flickers across his face. Suddenly, there's a new world order. No sooner has he become the man of the house than the dynamics threaten to change. Sel will return a hero and who knows what an alliance between Reshna and Shilpi may mean.

When she goes to sort through the remaining clothes in her bedroom, Mum follows and dumps a cardboard box outside her door. It contains odd socks, bangles, an old pair of sandals missing a buckle and a clutch of brown envelopes – mostly rubbish; the things she intends to take to uni have already been stashed at Karen's house. The mail consists of the usual unsolicited circulars sent out by stores and banks, but then she spots a cream envelope nestling amongst the rest.

"When did this one come, Mum?"

The post mark is unclear.

Mum shrugs. "Some day. Junk letters – come all the time."

"But this is handwritten, it could be important."

For days, they've been tiptoeing round each other. Aysha would gladly tell her mother about York – she tried to show her the pictures in the tourist guides – but Mum gave just a cursory glance then looked away. It doesn't matter: they have years yet to learn to be friends.

"Huh!" Mum taps her nose and manages to look both scornful and triumphant. "Is what business do. Computer writing. Make you think from real person."

But this *is* handwritten, Aysha thinks, taking it back to her room. The envelope is long and thick, a heavy textured paper, the address written in blue-black ink: all except her surname, which has been added by a different pen. There is something about the fluid, looping style of the main handwriting that makes her catch her breath. Carefully, she slits the top to extract several matching sheets covered with the same, familiar script. The letter is headed April 1970.

My dear Aysha (she reads)

I trust I may call you that, as we have known each other such a very long time. I know now we will never meet, but I hope you will be glad to hear of me.

I have lived into my eighty-sixth year and seen many terrible and wonderful things. Why only last year I watched on my television set while men walked on the moon! Yet I have never forgotten seeing you, all those years ago, in my room in the square. But perhaps I should say your room, because if you have received this letter I must have been right in believing you to live there, in my future.

I once thought you might be related to me – a granddaughter, great-granddaughter even – but my only child married a French woman and they too had just one boy who hasn't married. Lately, I have seen people from all parts of the old Empire arriving in England, coming to try their fortunes on these shores, and among them are people from India, the lands which were once the British Raj. Your family will come, I'm sure, and settle in the East End of London, as the Jews and Huguenots did before.

I used to tell my grandson stories of seeing you. Perhaps he humours me, but he has always professed to believe them true and recently we have formed a plan. Every year he will check the voting register for the house where I grew up, looking for the name 'Aysha'. Young people can now vote from eighteen, I understand, which means you will be listed from the year before your eighteenth birthday. I have every hope that one day he will find you.

You have read my journals and know that the time after my mother's death was sad and difficult for me, but the years when both Charlie and I were at school were good ones and I treasure them still.

What happened in our room? The strange connection between you and me was, I think, conjured out of my unhappiness and perhaps out of some of your own. In my darkest hours, feeling your presence was a comfort. I have long outlived those years, but you may still be struggling. I wish I could hold your hand!

I named my son Robert, which was my brother's middle name, and his son is Edward, after my father. When you get this letter, Edward will have included details of where he lives (we cannot tell how long it will take to find you so his current address may have changed). Please go to see him. I have left some mementos for you and my grandson is a good man who will give help if needed.

Ah, Aysha, you are a scholar, do you know Hamlet? 'There are more things in heaven and earth than are dreamt of in your philosophy' – we know the truth of that, you and I. My life is nearly ended, but it has been mine, Aysha. I've made my own choices – make sure you do the same!

Your very old and loving friend

Emily Parsons (nee Watts)

Tears slip down Aysha's cheeks as freely as raindrops on a window pane: not sadness, but simple overflow of emotion. It is too sudden, too much. Another, thinner sheet of paper slides from the envelope and flutters to the floor – the grandson's letter? She dries her eyes on her sleeve and picks it up.

Dear Miss Khatun

If you have read my grandmother's letter and understand its meaning, then my search is over. If her words mean nothing, then I can only apologise for troubling you. But I hope that I am right and have at last found 'Aysha', the young person I have heard of for most of my life. I imagine the time scale is different for you, but if, as Emily was convinced, you have found her journals, perhaps you can accept what I say.

Writing of Emily's journals reminds me that there is another slim volume, written some seventeen years later, which she particularly wanted you to have, together with a trinket or two. Please telephone and arrange to visit me at the address below.

If I do not hear from you within three months, I will assume I am mistaken, or that you do not wish to hear more.

Sincerely,

Edward Parsons

The letter is dated 29 June, which Aysha quickly calculates as nearly eleven weeks ago. She panics, then sees Edward Parsons' address is in Harlow, Essex. Not too far, not too late! She grabs her jacket and slips the letter and her mobile phone into her pocket, ignoring her mother's queries as she leaves the house and heads for the gardens in the square. A light rain is falling but the lime trees' foliage is dense enough to provide shelter. She looks back at the house, up at her bedroom window, the window through which Emily had looked out onto the same square, and scents the coming autumn in the cool moist air. Double-checking each digit, she dials the number and a man's voice answers: a light, friendly tone.

"Mr Parsons? It's Aysha," she says.

~

The man who introduces himself as Edward Parsons looks to be in his early sixties. He has serious brown eyes and an unruly shock of curly grey hair.

"I hope you don't mind," says Aysha, indicating Derrick,

"I've brought my friend."

She'd relied on Derrick to get her there, braving the M11 in the small blue hatchback he's recently bought.

The man steers them into a square hall with a door either side. The traditional cottage exterior is deceptive: a central spiral staircase of glass and steel rises to the first floor and a glazed panel in the roof above floods the house with light. Along one wall, a collection of black and white and sepia photographs has been arranged in simple modern frames.

Aysha sees a wedding portrait with the bride in austere, wartime dress and the groom in RAF uniform; a different young man, light-eyed, with fair curls, arms folded across his chest; another wedding portrait, earlier, Edwardian perhaps. She's drawn to the photograph of a slight, pretty woman with two children: the boy, about fourteen or fifteen, is bold-faced and grinning; the girl, slightly younger, thick hair curling on her shoulders, has a clear, honest, intelligent gaze. Aysha feels the hairs on her arms and neck rise as Edward Parsons points towards the family group.

"My great-grandmother Maria, my great-uncle Charlie, and Emily, my grandmother. But I think you guessed that."

When Derrick steps forward and puts his arm round her, Edward opens one of the side doors. "I'll make some tea. Come through when you're ready."

Aysha traces the outline of Emily's face with her finger.

"I can't believe it was all so long ago."

"Do you have her journal?" Edward asks.

They are seated in a monochrome lounge which houses a large cream sofa and grand piano. Derrick looks round uneasily for a safe surface for his tea.

"I do. I found it beneath a floorboard in my bedroom. In my family's house in Stepney, the house she grew up in."

"May I see?"

"There are parts which may be difficult to believe. About me, I mean."

"You're forgetting that she left me the task of finding you. My grandmother was convinced – and convincing. You're the proof that she was right."

"Do you really believe she saw me?" she asks. "It was so weird, reading it. What was I to her – a sort of ghost?"

"She didn't know who you were at first. She thought you might be her descendant," he says. "I was an only child and when I was little, my grandmother would tell me that, if ever I had a daughter, I should name her Aysha. But," he smiles gracefully, "then she realised I wasn't the marrying kind and started to look for another explanation. You've read her letter."

"Why did you leave it till June?" asked Derrick. "Aysha's been on the electoral roll since the beginning of the year."

"I used to check it regularly," Edward Parsons says thoughtfully. "For thirty years I hadn't missed. But last winter, I was preoccupied with other things – someone I was very close to was dying. I'm so glad the letter reached you in time."

They follow his gaze to the piano, where there is a photograph of Edward and another, younger, man. Aysha puts down her cup and leans towards him.

"When I was leaving home, last spring, it seemed that she was leaving too and I thought I'd lost her. What happened when she went to Harlow with Daisy? Did she ever go back to her job or to her father's house?"

"Not to Fenton's, and not to Stepney for several years. She

and Daisy wanted to conceal the existence of Daisy's son from his true father. You saw Charlie Potts's photo in the hall, the laughing young man with the golden curls?"

"From William Baines? So the child – Charlie – never knew him?"

"No. They made certain of that. With my great-great-grandmother's help, they connived at a small deception. When Charlie was born, he was registered under Daisy's name, illegitimate, as he had to be, but the old lady gave out that Emily's brother was the father and that he and Daisy had been engaged before he left for the Cape. It was hard in those days to have a child outside marriage, but a romantic story and a dead hero helped. Luckily the local butcher's lad took a shine to Daisy and when they married he adopted her son. I believe she had a comfortable enough life. Young Charlie emigrated to Canada. But tell me about yourself," he adds.

"Well," Aysha takes a deep breath, "my family is from Bangladesh, but I was born in London. We moved to the house when I was sixteen. The basement's a separate flat now, but my family has the rest."

"And your bedroom...?"

"... was Emily's, I think. I'm going to York next week, to read English and History. I sort of had to run away for a while too, because I was under pressure to get married. I suppose that's why I identify with her so much."

No-one speaks for a while. Both Edward and Aysha need time to assimilate what they've heard.

"So what did happen to Emily in Harlow?" Derrick asks at last. "Is this her grandparents' house?"

"Much altered, but yes," Edward says. "I'm afraid I can't

live with Victorian clutter, hence the changes. Emily nursed her grandfather until his death and helped raise little Charlie before Daisy married in 1907. Then she worked as a dressmaker for several years. Her work was sought after locally – but it was never satisfying enough for her."

"Hadn't she wanted to be a teacher, like her friend Sally?" Aysha asks.

"I believe so; but the experience of caring for her grandparents changed that and much later she trained as a nurse. She was a VAD in the First World War – that was how she met my grandfather, a doctor. He was sent out to France, but she stayed in London to nurse the men being sent back from the trenches."

"She felt she was paying a debt," Aysha says, "caring for the wounded in that war when she couldn't help Charlie and his comrades."

Edward looks at her curiously and Derrick opens his mouth to speak, but closes it again.

"I can't explain; I just know," Aysha says. "But I'm glad she met your grandfather, I'm glad she was happy. I suppose I should give you the journal," she adds, looking at Edward, "since you're family."

"I'd like to read it, yes. She told me the stories, but that was years later. I've an idea it will be different reading the events as they happened."

Aysha takes the green leather book from her bag and hands it to Edward.

"I know it's hard for you to give it up," he says, "but I will return it. In the meantime, I have a trade for you. Nineteen eighteen was another troubling year for Emily and she took to writing again. There's one last journal, which she would want you to have. It will explain more than I can. Don't read it now, take it away." He goes to a bookshelf and picks up a maroon notebook plus a small packet wrapped in brown paper and tied with white string. "This is also for you – again, for opening later. Valuable, I believe, so take care. Come and see me at Christmas, when you're home from university. Both of you if you can."

45
Emily

December 1918

Sixteen years have passed since I left my journal beneath my bedroom floor in Stepney, but recent events recall those early chapters of my life and demand to be written down.

In 1914 I came as a VAD – a Voluntary Aid Detachment – to the hospital in Whitechapel. I felt some trepidation, returning to an area where I might turn a street corner and find myself face to face with William Baines, although I no longer had reason to fear him. I was not wealthy, but I had funds enough to be independent. My grandparents left me the Harlow house and I had money saved from the dressmaking business I had there. No, I was not concerned for myself, but I could not forget that Daisy and I had conspired to conceal young Charlie's parentage. What if I met Baines and he asked if I knew what had become of her child? I didn't know if I could maintain the lie.

The chance meeting I feared never happened; I had no time to re-visit the streets around my childhood home. Wounded men flooded back from the base hospitals in France. Some had lost limbs, some had lost eyes; all had invisible wounds even more difficult to heal. Then, two years ago, I was sent to work at another hospital and met David Parsons, an orthopaedic surgeon who had returned from the front to follow up his patients' treatment. We had little time for courtship, but we both knew we had found the person we wanted to spend our lives with. Worries about William Baines seemed a world away. Then, in June this year, David was recalled to France and I went back to Whitechapel.

Soldiers continued to arrive with the usual injuries, having been crowded in camp hospitals, corralled onto troop trains and stacked side by side on ships crossing the channel. We had few cases of influenza at first. Soldiers had been cautioned against spreading tales, although there were rumours of outbreaks in America and of the illness sweeping through the lines in France. In neutral Spain, news was not censored and, when the disease multiplied there, the world knew.

Civilians were affected too. It was known that crowds helped to spread the disease but, when the Armistice was signed, thousands poured onto the streets. After four years of suffering, the government could not prevent the celebrations. Parties continued all week, with singing, dancing and bonfires in every public place. On Friday night, when I finished my duties, the public houses were full and drunken soldiers called, *Nurse, nurse, come and have a drink with us*, as I made my way to my quarters. Music and laughter spilled from doors and windows and, tired as I was, I found it hard to sleep.

"There's a new one in the end bed," the ward sister told me next morning, "collapsed outside the Blind Beggar. Constable thought he was just sleeping it off – to be fair there's whisky enough in him – but one of our porters was drinking there and noticed his colour."

"Blue?" A discolouration of the skin was one of the

symptoms of this epidemic.

"Like deadly nightshade. Looks a strong chap, well set-up, but they're often the first to go. Mind you keep your face mask on."

Sister directed me to sponge the patients, administer aspirin and encourage them to drink. I worked methodically down the ward until I reached the last bed.

Whatever meeting I had feared, it was not this. William Baines tossed on the narrow bed, his black hair damp, his skin slick with fever and a bloody froth discharging from his nose. His breath came harsh, broken by intermittent coughs. The basin of water I was carrying slipped from my fingers and its metallic clank echoed down the ward.

"Nurse Watts!" Sister hurried to rebuke me, then stopped when she saw my face. "Do you know this man?"

I stooped to pick up the basin. "I once believed him my worst enemy."

She looked at me keenly. "And does this prevent you from nursing him? Would you wish this illness on anyone?"

I looked down at the man on the bed and thought how all his scheming had come to this.

"No, Sister."

"Then fetch a mop, dry the floor, and attend to your patient."

I cleaned the spume from his face and sponged him down; the discolouration of the skin had spread to his neck and chest. His eyes twitched and fluttered open and I saw confusion register as they darted around the ward, before settling on my starched bib with its red cross.

"You're in the London Hospital," I said. "You were taken ill last night."

A kind of tremor ran through him as he heard my voice and his hand jerked upward to grip my arm. I detached myself easily and poured a beaker of water.

"You have influenza, Mr Baines. You need to take aspirin and fluids."

"Is it... *Emily?*"

"Nurse Watts," I said firmly. "Drink, please."

I raised his head and held the cup to his lips, steeling myself as his hands wrapped around mine. He fell back on the pillow and I emptied my basin and returned to the nurses' station. The Ward Sister looked up from the papers she was reading.

"How well do you know that man, Watts? He was admitted without identification – does he have family?"

"His name is William Baines," I said. "He used to live in Stepney. To the best of my knowledge he has no relations." Then I remembered. "Wait, there was a cousin, Fred – but I don't know his surname."

"Try to find out if there is anyone we should notify – while he's still conscious."

I took tea around the ward and stopped at his bedside.

"Sister wants to know if we should contact anyone," I said. "Your cousin or a friend perhaps?"

A trace of the old amusement contorted his mouth into a smile. "Why, when fate has sent you to look after me?"

The speech took its toll: he struggled to breathe and froth spilled from his mouth. I saw panic rise in his eyes.

"Some people wish to put their affairs in order. Just in case."

He was silent for a good half minute, digesting this. I couldn't remember ever seeing him ill before; he had always seemed the picture of flamboyant vigour and health. If *I* found it difficult to believe he could be dying, did he understand the danger he faced?

"The lawyer," he gasped at last. "Your father's man."

I'd last seen the lawyer, Matthewson, in 1913 when Dr Reynolds wrote to say that my father was dying from a lung disease and had asked to see me. I hoped for a reconciliation, but Pa only sought to blame. *All of you were headstrong,* he said. *Maria, Charlie, you, Emily. You never thought how your actions affected me.* Then he told me not to expect any inheritance as the Stepney house was no longer his to bequeath. Matthewson confirmed that everything belonged to Baines. I never saw the man himself: he had taken himself away and did not return until after Pa's funeral.

I gave Sister the lawyer's name and she arranged for a note to be sent. When I returned to his bedside, Baines was more restless: his head thrashed from side to side and his back arched.

"We've sent for the lawyer," I said.

"How long... you been... a nurse?"

"Four years. I'm a VAD."

"Here... all this time?" He looked almost reproachful.

"Mostly. Did you really expect me to call?"

He closed his eyes and shook his head. The burden of life seemed too much for him.

A note came back to say that the lawyer regretted he could not attend the hospital, but if the patient cared to send his instructions he would do what he could. But by the afternoon, the patient was delirious. He asked for my fountain pen and drew it across the piece of linen I'd used to dry his face.

"There... made it... right. House... yours."

I didn't correct him. If he really believed he had written a will and paid his debt, let him take that illusion to his grave. Speech was difficult for him and I leaned forward to catch his words.

"Always... wanted... only you... Emily," he sighed. "Should have been patient."

He attempted a laugh but only succeeded in retching up more blood and spume. "Self made man but... nothing... no-one... to show for it."

His face was more black than blue now; a bloody tear issued from his right eye and I could hear the mucus choking his lungs. I put my gauze-covered lips as near to his ear as I dared and whispered,

"Daisy had a child, Bill. You have a son, almost sixteen. He's a fine boy, called Charlie."

The words would not have passed my lips if I had not known him to be dying, but to this day, I can't say if they were a comfort or a torment. I thought of my father, betrayed into drunkenness and debt; of Daisy, brutally used and cast away. I drew nearer still and whispered, "I swear he will never hear your name from me."

His hands seized mine in a rigid, painful grip and an awful gurgling filled his throat. His grasp loosened, his arms fell slack across the bed and the impression of his fingernails slowly faded from my palms.

I cannot say how long I stood there. My whole body shook: I trembled from my starched white cap to my sensible shoes. Eventually, Sister noticed, took my arm and led me away.

"I don't know what came over me," I said, between sips of water. "I've seen men die before and I had good reason to hate this one."

"It is the strength of your feelings, not their nature, that affects you."

I realised she was right. Fear of William Baines had burned into my brain more than half my lifetime ago: I could not believe he was dead. This was the man who flattered my young self with his conversation, while repelling me with his attitudes; who idealised marriage, while indulging his lusts on the streets; who began as his employer's right-hand man and ended as his destroyer; a handsome, affable man with the power to make my skin crawl. How could I ever comprehend such contradictions?

Mr Matthewson put in an appearance soon enough when he realised there was an estate to settle.

"Nurse Watts thought that the patient wished to make or amend a will. It was why I sent word to you," Sister told him.

The lawyer ignored her implied criticism. "I'm not aware of any pre-existing will. If he left it too late and there is no family, the Crown will inherit."

"There was a cousin called Fred," I said, "the son of his late aunt. He served in South Africa."

Matthewson brightened, perhaps at the prospect of a fee, asserting that his man would find the beneficiary easily enough. I asked to meet the cousin if they managed to trace him and he promised to put forward my request. I felt the need to understand how Baines had become the man he was, if only to reassure myself that young Charlie was not destined to follow his father's path.

~

After three weeks, the lawyer's spies unearthed Sergeant Fred Donaldson, recuperating from a shrapnel wound in a Lambeth hospital. Matthewson delivered the news of his inheritance and my request. At first the sergeant was reluctant to see me. He had been told of my connection with the house in the square and probably feared I intended to dispute his claim. I sent word that I just wanted to talk and paid him a visit.

The sergeant was a slight, wiry man of about forty, with thinning sandy hair and a bushy moustache tinged with red. He bore no resemblance to Baines, except perhaps in the pale blue eyes, which, in the sergeant's case were narrow and keen. I recognised the impatience of a man ready for discharge and, though he softened noticeably when he saw my uniform, his first words were a challenge.

"Well, miss, what do you want from me?"

"Just to ask you some questions," I said. "I am sorry for the loss of your cousin."

"That's more than I am," he snapped. "I never wanted to hear his name again, unless to learn he was dead."

"Then I was misinformed," I frowned, "for he often spoke fondly of you and your mother."

Sergeant Donaldson's lip curled scornfully, elevating the brush-like moustache. "If that was the only thing he deceived you in, you were in luck. I heard he did well for himself and I'm sorry if it was at your family's expense, but that's none of my fault, or my poor mother's. He was what he was."

"Do you mean to say he was a devious child? At what age did he come to you?"

The sergeant folded his arms and blew out his cheeks.

"His mother and mine were sisters, both poor enough, but while Mum married respectably, Ida was a bad lot. One day she'd turn up at our house flaunting a new dress, another time she'd be covered in bruises and desperate for a bite of bread. I doubt she knew who Bill's father was. I suppose she loved him in her own way. They had a room in Wapping and she never let him out of her sight while she lived. She took her customers home, so God knows what he saw, if you know what I mean."

"How did she die?"

"Washed up off Wapping Steps. Knocked about a bit, I should think. Bill was found in their room, hiding under the table. He'd been alone there a few days, living off bits of bacon rind and apple cores. My dad didn't want to take him in – thought he had bad blood, you know – but there was no way Mum'd leave her sister's nine-year-old to starve." He broke off to take a drink of water and looked at me, "Surely you don't really want to know all this, miss?"

I told him I had my reasons and hoped he would humour me: had Bill proved his father right?

"Well, not at first," the sergeant said, gnawing his lip. "Oh, he was clever, was Bill. He knew how to please when it suited his interests. My dad said he learned that at the whore's tit, saving your presence, miss. He'd run errands, fold up the sheets Mum took in to wash, and mind me and Lizzie while she carried them back to their owners."

"Lizzie?"

"My little sister. Not the brightest spark in the hearth, but a sweet, trusting child. She followed Bill around like a love-sick puppy. He showed her card tricks, taught her riddles, magicked pennies from her ears. She had no use for me once Bill came."

I saw the hurt this had caused and intended to turn the subject.

"He once told me his eyesight was damaged by the measles," I said. "Was that the truth?"

"There was a winter epidemic, back in '87. I caught it first, then Bill and Lizzie. He was a strapping lad of thirteen by then, already sprouting whiskers and built more like a man than a boy. I was a year or two younger and Lizzie was nearly ten. I'd gone back to school, but there'd been complications in Bill's case which affected his eyes and Lizzie hadn't shaken off her cough. Dad worked on a stall down the market all day, so Mum would leave them while she collected the washing.

"I dare say I was jealous, but I always held my tongue while Bill was good to Lizzie and she was happy. And sometimes I was glad of the peace, because she used to pester him instead of me."

The sergeant hesitated and looked at me again. I held his gaze and slowly nodded to him. I suspected that what he was about to tell me would be dreadful, but we had gone too far to stop now. He waited until a passing nurse was out of hearing then swallowed hard and went on.

"So when he told her he knew a secret new game, there would have been no containing her. I remember once she sang out to me *you don't know what I know*, and Bill put his finger to her lips. She was off school all the next week too, with Bill meant to be minding her. But at the end of that week, it rained so hard that the market packed up early and Dad came home to find Lizzie in Bill's lap. *Ladies and gentlemen*, he'd called it, but the games he'd been teaching her were the tricks of his mother's trade. My dad thrashed him raw and turned him out that very night."

The sergeant slumped back exhausted. I guessed he had never spoken of this before.

"Your sister, Sergeant Donaldson – is she living still?"

"If you can call it that. She wept and screamed after her cousin, demanding to have her *little gentleman*. The tantrums grew worse, lasting for days on end. My innocent sister swore, scratched and bit my father and had to be locked away from company for fear of what she'd say or do. It broke Mum's heart. For the last twenty years, Lizzie's been in the asylum. If Bill Baines lived in your house, count yourself lucky he didn't harm you."

I asked him if he thought of taking care of Lizzie himself, now that he had a house to bring her to, but he shook his head: he had the wife and young'uns to mind and he didn't think it would suit. He hoped he hadn't offended me by his history; he would never have told me had I not been a nurse.

I felt badly in need of counsel, of some wise head to help me make sense of it all. Eventually, I went to see Dr Reynolds and asked him to share the burden of my discoveries.

"He was so much worse than I knew, but so were the wrongs done to him as a child," I said. "All those stories of letters from his cousin in South Africa, they were just fictions. As if he wanted to be part of a family still."

Dr Reynolds laid his hand on my arm.

"Listen to me, Emily. Pity the child if you will, but not the man. Perhaps he did want a wife and family of his own, but he did nothing to deserve them. He was a clever enough fellow, he knew right from wrong. David will be coming home soon. You have the love of a fine man: it's time you put this all behind you and thought of your wedding."

I have taken his advice. I have waited a long time for marriage. I turned down offers from two good men in Harlow, a schoolmaster and a farmer, because the idea of intimacy with either disturbed me too much to risk their happiness or mine. I used to fear that Baines had spoiled that aspect of life for me forever, though Daisy always said I'd yet to find the right man. Finally, I am satisfied that Mr Baines' character was the product of his childhood and that young Charlie, who has known only love and security, is in no danger of repeating his father's crimes. Tomorrow, David will board a ship for England and, God willing, in two weeks' time, on New Year's Day, we will be wed.

46
Aysha

Aysha and Derrick stroll along a deserted towpath beside the River Stort near Harlow. After leaving Edward's cottage, Derrick had driven until he found a secluded parking space; neither of them had been ready to talk about the visit. Instead, he'd taken himself off for a walk, leaving her to read Emily's words in private. Now, the light is fading; they both have to get home.

"Are you sure you'll be okay?" he asks, when they're back in the car.

She's not sure if he's referring to the day's events or to spending her last days before uni at her family's house. At some point she'll share Emily's last chapter; not yet.

"I still feel a bit like an uninvited guest there, but it'll be fine."

She turns the maroon notebook over and over in her hand, desperate to read it again, to reassure herself of the happiness which had come to Emily after so many years, but unwilling to lose time with Derrick when they've only a few short days left.

"I'm gonna miss you," he murmurs.

"Yeah, me too. But we'll both be home for Karen's birthday. And Leeds isn't far from York – you could drive over some weekends. I've read the regulations – we're allowed friends to stay in our rooms for a night or two –" she raises her eyes to meet his – "if you want to, that is."

She looks down quickly, taking up the packet Edward Parsons had given her and picking at the string, but Derrick takes both journal and packet from her and places them gently on the back seat, before beginning a long and satisfying kiss.

Acknowledgements

Many of the ideas for *The Tissue Veil* were incubating during the years I worked in Tower Hamlets, but it took a move to Frome, Somerset, to bring them to life. Thanks to my Wednesday morning writing buddies – Gill Harry, Mary Macarthur, Liz Hutchinson, Sue Watts and Debs Dowling – for their unfailing support and encouragement, to Laura Wilkinson for her invaluable editorial advice and to Silver Crow (the book brand of Frome Writers' Collective) for embracing *The Tissue Veil* as one of its first titles. I am also indebted to photographer, Darren Higgs, and my granddaughter, Jasra Uddin, for providing the cover image.

silvercrowbooks.co.uk
individually inspired - collectively published